THE LAND OF RUMBELOW

By the same author:

Novels

A FRIEND IN POWER
THE LAND OF RUMBELOW

Poetry

A YEAR AND A DAY

Criticism

SHELLEY'S MAJOR POETRY
HEMINGWAY: THE WRITER AS ARTIST

THE
LAND OF
RUMBELOW

A Fable in the Form of a Novel

by **CARLOS BAKER**

Charles Scribner's Sons *New York*

LEGAL NOTE

This is a work of the imagination. Persons and places are wholly fictitious. Except for recognizable names here and there, no persons who ever lived in Arizona or elsewhere during the action of the novel are here depicted or represented, even in disguise.

The mind is its own place, and in itself

Can make a Heav'n of Hell, a Hell of Heav'n.

Paradise Lost

꙳.   ꙳.   ꙳.

IMAGYNACYON:

What, brother, welcome, by this precyous body!
I am gladde that I you see;
That ye were hanged hyt was told me.
But out of what countree come ye?

HYCKE-SCORNER:

Sir, I have ben in many a countree;
As in Fraunce, Irlonde, and in Spayne,
Portyngale, Sevyll, also in Almayne . . .
I have ben in Gene and in Cowe,
Also in the londe of Rumbelowe
Three myle out of hell.

Old Play

CONTENTS

This book is for
ELIZABETH AMES
who had time to give
and gave it

PROLOGUE

IN THE stark gray-black of the desert night, the hashhouse lights gleamed like passing train-windows. Only one old car, he saw, was parked on the gravel by the door. Okay. He began to bear down on the brake pedal. Five hundred yards west he eased the green Olds gingerly onto the road shoulder. Dowanna get stuck in no gravel. But it crunched firmly and hard-baked under the right-hand wheels, and he pulled off far enough to hear the sage-brush whip and thump against the whole side of the car.

An eastbound truck, plastered with lights like a beer-joint, barreled past doing seventy or eighty. He watched it recede in the rear-view mirror. It was going too fast to stop at the hash-house, but he watched and waited until the bright image had flashed out of sight and the roar was dead. Then he cut the engine and his own lights, except for the dim green glow that came from inside the dash-panel.

All he could hear now was the wind in the sage, and another much fainter sound which was the girl's breathing. He glanced over. Her legs in the tight checked pedal-pushers were curled under her and her head was cramped back into the corner made by the back of the seat and the door. When he cut the engine she did not wake up, but only stirred slightly, hugging her folded arms across the bulging front of the pink sweater. Pooped out, he thought. Plenty workouts the last couple days. In the dim green light he grinned, letting his bulk sink back into the stained upholstery. While his right hand probed the pocket of the green windbreaker for a cigarette, his left reached down beside his leg for the bottle. Held up against the light, it showed a quarter full. He unscrewed the cap and took a good slug, wiping his mouth with the back of his hand. Only when he had lighted the fresh butt and exhaled the cloud of smoke did she start to wake.

For maybe a minute he sat waiting. The rye glowed hot and raw inside him. The car-heater, beginning to cool, tinked one time the way they do, and the wind brushed the sage against the side of the Olds. He glanced over again. The almost shoulder-length hair, smelling of french fries, in which he had buried his nose the last two nights and twice more in the days, spread like pale straw against the plastic seat-back behind the slightly too long column of her neck. The arms, bare to the elbow except for the down of hair, looked thin as a kid's in the green light. But the checked fabric of the pedal-pushers stretched tight over the curve of her left hip. Her mouth closed and she mumbled something he could not get. Then the pale, blue eyes flashed open and she sat up.

"Stopped," she said. "Why you stopped, Buddy? I'm cold here. Where are we, Buddy?"

He did not answer. She straightened her legs into the well of the front seat, and stretched the thin arms, one fist beside each ear. "Wow," she said. "Where is this, the North Pole? Buddy, it's cold."

Without moving anything but his arms, he groped again

for the bottle and carelessly held it out to her. "Take a finger," he said. "Furnace-water. Warm you up good."

She fended it off with the back of her hand. "No," she said, grouchily. "I had enough that rotgut. You tryna make me a souse or something? I want to eat. I'm hungry, Buddy. Hungry and cold. I want a nice cup of coffee."

Hunched at the wheel, still without moving anything but his arms, he lowered the bottle to the floor. "Okay," he said. "Okay, okay. So you're hungry. Place back there is open. Nice cup of coffee warm you up good."

She glanced quickly back over her shoulder. "What place? You kiddn? Where are we, anyway? It's dark. What you want to stop here for?"

"It's a eatn place back there," he said. "Just come past it. Still open. Lights on so it's still open. You just go on back there get you a nice cup of coffee."

She did not look back again but peered across in the dim light to see his eyes. "All right," she said, with maybe a hint of suspicion in her tone. "You take me back there, Buddy. We'll get us a nice meal, a nice hot cup of coffee."

"Listen, Charlene," he said. "You go on back there, little ways back. You can see the lights from here. I ain't hungry. You get yourself a good meal, feel better."

This time she did glance back momentarily. "I don't see no lights," she said. Her voice was sharper now, and he watched a nervous swallow tighten in the column of her throat. "You say it's open, you just turn around and take me back there."

"Not me," he said. "You think I'm nuts? Now you ease out and get on back."

She sat frozen, except for the hands with the ten-cent rings working in her lap. When she spoke again her voice had gone thin and small. "Okay," she said. "You scared to go here, other places up the road some place. I'll go in one of them, bring you something out to the car."

"Listen," he said, again. "Places up ahead ain't going to be open. Getting too late in the night. You go on in here while it's still open. All cow-country up ahead."

The girl shuddered involuntarily while the hands still worked thinly in her lap. "Owoo," she moaned. "You going to skip me, Buddy. You going to just wait 'til I get out of this car, down the road, then you'll skip me."

He did not say anything.

She tried firmness. "Now you just start the car, we'll go up ahead see if an all-night place is open. They got them for the trucks. Never close." She squeezed back into the corner and folded the thin arms across the bulging sweater-front.

He felt it rising in him, but he stopped it and held it steady while he said, "State line up ahead. Ain't carrying nobody across no state line. *Now get along.*" He spoke the last words as to a dog, and out of the corner of his eye he could see her flinch.

"*Are* going to skip me," she cried, her voice rising. "Are, are, *are*. After all I done for you, Buddy. Now you just listen to me. I'm not gettn out. Gonna stay right here. Ain't gonna budge. You not skippn me."

For a few seconds he did not speak, staring straight ahead while the green dashlight glinted on the surface of his eyes. He felt it rising again, like bile after a binge, thin in the back of the throat. But he set his lips and held it back and thought he spoke quietly. "Now, Charlene, I'm tellen you. You haul ayus."

Her right hand fumbled in the gloom for the inside door-handle until she found and gripped it. But she did not open the door. "No," she said. "No. I'm staying right here."

Before she was finished speaking he reached over suddenly past her body and wrenched the handle backwards. The door swung ajar and the black desert wind swept through. She tried to shut the door, but he swung his booted foot off the floor and against her hip, pushing her halfway out. She kept her thin grip on the door-handle and fought to pull back in. But the pressure of the boot held her suspended. Now she was beginning to scream.

He felt it rushing up inside him but still he held it in check. She lost her grip on the door-handle and fell out knees-first onto the desert gravel. He slid across the warmth of the car seat where she had been and stood above her and lifted her up under the arms and gave her a push through the sage-brush in the direction of the lights. She had hurt her knees on the desert gravel and she was screaming louder. "See them lights," he said. "You get along back there."

Now that they were out away from the green glimmer in the front seat, the strange desert light, moonless, clear-star-studded, came glooming down over them and over the empty miles of whipping sage-brush and the low hunkering shapes of mountains at the far edge of the desert. In that light he could see her turn like a terrier and raise her fists, her screams lifting and caterwauling above the stream-sound of the wind as she began to hammer blows against his chest. He caught her thin wrists and held them while she wrenched and tore to get free. Immobilized above, she began to kick with all her strength with one dirty white pump against his shinbone, screaming all the while in high, desperate bursts like racing a truck-motor.

"Shut up," he said. "Shut up your goddam noise." He worked his left hand until it gripped both her slender wrists and slapped his right hand hard over her open mouth. But she sank her teeth into the heel of his hand, biting strongly. As he yanked back, she managed to get one of her wrists free of his grip, and he felt her nails rake down his cheek like a rusty razor blade.

Now he did not bother to contain it any more. "Shut up," he yelled, and with a single pull away dropped her wrist and hit her full in the face. She was crying now and her screams were thickening in the cave of her throat. Ignoring the thin, punching hands, he felt his own long fingers close round the narrow column of her neck. "Shut up," he said again. They could probably hear her as far as the hashhouse. "Shut that fuggen noise."

He did not know how much pressure he was bringing to bear with his hands until he felt her lurch and stiffen. The screaming stopped suddenly like the stuck car-horn that some-body finally gets to. Boots wide apart, heavy shoulders hunched, arm-muscles cording under the green windbreaker, he held her almost suspended until he thought she had—would—quit screaming. Then he let her go. "There now," he said. "You quit that goddam noise."

She fell heavily among the bushes of the sage and lay on the harsh desert gravel without moving. Up the road where the lights were burning, he saw no sign of any action. After the screaming it all seemed quiet. Though he prodded her with one boot-toe, she did not stir. He went back to the car, crunch-ing and slipping on the gravel, and reached for the bottle. By the green dashlight he saw that his bitten hand was covered with blood, and he stopped to wrap it in the dirty bandanna from his hip pocket. He was sweating and thirsty. He drank from the bottle and carried it back to where she still lay unmoving. He lifted her head and dripped whiskey into the partly open mouth. In the strange desert light, like darkness you could see by, the mouth was a smear of lipstick and of black blood from her nose and his bitten hand.

"Charlene," he said. The whiskey ran out of the side of her mouth and she did not move. "Charlene," he said again, more loudly but not loud. He removed his cupped left hand from behind the head, which flopped back deadly against the desert floor. Kneeling lower, he held his head against the pink sweater and listened for the heart-beat. But the wind was still blowing and he could hear nothing. He stood up again and peered in the direction of the lights. Still no sound, no one coming. He lifted the head again and slapped the wet cheek twice, almost gently. Nothing.

Now he unzipped the green windbreaker, loosened the wide belt, tucked in his shirt back and front, tightened the belt, adjusted the strap of the shoulder-holster, and zipped up the windbreaker. Then he moved off a few feet and urinated. She still lay motionless when he came back. A low sedan, doing at least eighty, roared past along the road. He ducked down quickly, though at that speed the driver could have seen nothing but the Olds parked along the highway shoulder. Maybe not even that.

In the quiet after the roar he knelt to listen to the chest again. Still nothing. The wind burned like ice against his sweating forehead. Leave her out here, she'll freeze before morning. Cold in the desert. Cover her up some, she'll be warmer. He reached out to the nearest clump of sage-brush and yanked. He had to spread his legs before it pulled loose.

Six or eight of those give her some warmth. Man from the hashhouse find her in the morning. Feed her up, rest her up. Send her back where she come from the next truck heading east. He moved now fast, yanking the tough sage up by the roots, stacking it around and over the girl. He could smell the sharp, clean smell of the sage on his hands and clothes.

When she was well covered he went to the Olds without looking back and slid in on the driver's side. The ignition key glinted under the green dashlight. The blackjack in his right boot had worked down and was galling his ankle. He fingered it up higher and started the motor. No cars in sight either way. The tires crunched over the gravel and smoothly onto the black-top of the highway heading west. He did not know what time it was, but back down the road the lights of the hashhouse were no longer burning.

PART ONE

THE ROAD

CHAPTER ONE

THREE MILES west of Show Low, where the road took a long gradual curve to the left, Dan saw the figure standing and beckoning among the green shadows of the scrub pine grove.

Afterwards, he was never able to remember exactly why he chose to stop. Perhaps it was somehow connected with this sun-splashed morning after the nine long days of gray and black weather all the way across the nation. He could close his eyes at any time and still see the windshield wiper describing its captive arc back and forth, back and forth, like that descending knife in the story of the pit and the pendulum.

For days he had assured himself that things would be different once he had reached and crossed the Great Divide. In a way they had been. From Denver south, at least, the weather had cleared and the land had dried out. But even in this gross sunlight, he could not shed the pit-feeling. The cold and the rain and the low-lying gray clouds, to say nothing of the two-legged rats, hung dripping in his memory. Now, though, in the brightness of the early morning, almost without thinking except to wonder momentarily why the dusty green Oldsmobile was parked so far off the road, deep in among the scattered winking beer-cans and strewn paper of the rabble-ruined grove, he braked down and stopped abreast of the stranger.

The curious fact was that he needn't have been on that road at all. Twenty minutes earlier, as Dan paid for bed and breakfast, the elderly motel man had gone over the possible choices. He looked like a merger of Walt Whitman in Camden and Blake's Ancient of Days with the wind-whipped eyebrows striking the first circle of the uncreated earth. He had the over-bright intense blue eyes of a life-long asthmatic, and he talked loudly between wheezes with a kind of hearty desperation.

"Mr. Sherwood, sir, been right nice haven you with us. Now I certainly hope you in-joyed a good night's rest."

Dan chose to lie. "I doubt if I moved an inch after I hit that beauty-rest," he said.

"You hit it right," the old man heartily wheezed. "Just like we use to say back there in At-lannic City, beauty-rest the playground of the nation. Huh-huh-huh. I s'pose a young feller like you seen the beauty-queen contest."

"No," said Dan. "Afraid not."

"Or read about it in the papers," said the old man, wisely grinning.

"I don't read the papers much," Dan said, beginning to move towards the door. "Hardly ever."

"Well, it don't matter," the old man said. "Point is, they got that salt air back there, and all them beauty queens in them tight bathing-togs, but I'm tellen you like I tell them all, it ain't no comparison with this mountain air. We pride ourselves on it and rightly so. Long life and good di-gestion. I certainly hope now, sir, that you in-joyed your breakfast."

Dan groped in the gloom for a heartiness to match the old

man's. He could not find it. "First-rate," he said automatically.

"Speaken of At-lannic City," the proprietor said, "I see you got Jersey plates. You are sure enough a long ways from home."

"Nine days," said Dan. Nine days, he thought, that were supposed to change your point of view. Nine therapeutic days. And nothing is changed. The escapist who couldn't escape. The nine-days unwonder. The nine-days fool, running in guilt from the bright vision of your best friend's wife.

"Now you took nine days to come out to a spot that is worth looken at," said the old man. "What we call God's front yard. Mr. Sherwood, might I in-quire where you headen?"

"Nowhere special," Dan said. "That is—" He stopped the sentence, watching the old man's eyebrows lifting. Let's not go into it with Walt Whitman, he thought. He's got that glaze-eyed look of one who talks but will not listen. I can see his lips already forming the next syllable. The clock on the pine-paneled wall behind the old man's head showed seven-thirty-five. Let us skip the background, Dan thought. "I was thinking of Phoenix," he said.

"Now, Phoenix," said the proprietor. "There's a fine city, beautiful city, a city we rightly take pride in. One hundred some odd thousand people in that city today. Plenty money in that city and they don't mind spenden it. Now, for Phoenix right out of here, there is two ways to go." He cupped his hand under Dan's elbow, leading him onto the office porch. "Two ways to go," he said again. "Long way up around north, all high country, fine country. Shorter way down here, snaken down to the desert."

"What if I stay on Sixty?"

"Now, sir, you stick to Route Sixty she'll bring you down

to Globe, ninety mile we call it from here or such a matter. Easy run from here to Phoenix on Sixty. Get there this forenoon if you was to go right along." He paused for breath, the sound of his wheezing like a tea-kettle on the boil. "Go right along, I mean, without no stoppen to feast your eyes on the scenery. Down there through the Salt River country. Mighty pretty down that way, but you better drive slow. You seen the Salt River Canyon?"

"This is my first time this far west," said Dan.

"Now you head down that way you're gonna see some real country. Feller come through here last week all the ways from the coast. Come snaken up the gorge from Florence Junction. 'Why don't they tell us about the Salt River Canyon?' he says. 'Why,' he says, 'it's the poor man's Grand Canyon,' he says. 'It don't stagger a man quite so much.' "

Dan bent to pick up the suitcase again. "Sounds good," he said. "Just stay on Sixty, right?"

"Straight ahead on Sixty," the old man said. "But don't count on finden her straight. Huh-huh-huh. She's got more curves than a At-lannic City beauty queen. Just foller your nose is all."

Dan shook the old man's hand and swung the suitcase into the car beside the portable typewriter and the laundry bag now bulging with nine days' wash. On the seat in the rear was the Carstairs whiskey carton from the liquor store off Harvard Square, tightly bound with a length of clothesline, and crammed from bottom to top with the Keats typescript and the hundreds of pages of handwritten notes.

And the Kemp stuff? Dan bent to peer into the dark space under the driver's seat. Still there, he thought. Still there in the dark where he's always preferred to stay. Cheek by jowl with the dried and crinkled chamois, the spare fan belt, and the handle of the bumper-jack. And what a place for this best of the novelists— This one, out of the whole modern crew, who for years had been your favorite among the living. The one you put aside in deference to Mr. John Keats, five feet tall, with the towering imagination. Dan brushed his hands together, and slid in behind the wheel. Another book waiting to be born after we knock off the Keats. One dead writer, one still living. And Mr. Nicholas Kemp, Kemp Agonistes. My pal, he thought, who would understand all about this flight to nowhere. My spiritual godfather, if the term's not too fancy. The dead one in the back seat, the living under the front. And the living will be the one who has to wait.

Walt Whitman was still standing at the top of the porch steps, gazing down benignly. Dan started the motor, waved to the old man, and moved off in the morning light.

Straight ahead on Sixty, clanking past a cattle-guard where the fences marched back on either side of the road into the deep shadows of the pine woods, sniffing the cool, resinous air like wine under the dome of that lucid and enormous sky, he came to the long leftward curve, the raddled and beer-canned grove, and the beckoning stranger. He wore, Dan noticed, a dark green windbreaker, and a pair of greasy levis thrust into dust-caked engineer's boots. He leaned forward grinning to peer through the car window, both hands possessively on the window-ledge. Around the right hand was bound an experienced bandanna, and the grin was framed in a two-day stubble.

"Little car-trouble, Mac," he said. He opened the door quickly and stepped in. The shoulders were those of a heavyweight, and the smell was that of a bull-moose in rutting season. "Foller your nose," the clean old man had said. Well, okay. We'll drop this nose-filling character off at the next garage—the very next garage—and then pause for fumigation. Touch of brimstone. Clear cautery of fire.

"Serious trouble?"

The stranger grinned, three-quarter-face, showing all his stub teeth. "She don't go."

"The road-map shows a town down this way," Dan said. "They probably have a garage."

"Could be," said the stranger. He did not seem much interested. He turned to look over the contents of the back seat and then faced front again, the big hands with the black-nailed fingers lying loosely in his lap.

"You live around here?" Dan asked.

"Nah," said the stranger. "I been here, times past."

He volunteered nothing more. Laconic type, Dan thought. Olfactorily speaking, the barnyard type. Even at fifty miles an hour in this fresh mountain air, and with both car windows open, the bull-moose stench hung steamlike in the front seat.

"Nice morning," Dan said.

Slumped lazily against the back-cushion where all the preceding hitchhikers had sat, the stranger grinned again—the full, wide, lazy grin, showing the stub teeth, stretching the whiskered flesh around the loose lips. By God, Dan thought, somebody told this worthy once that he grins like Burt Lancaster. He glanced quickly across the space that mercifully divided them and then back at the twisting road. One major difference between the star and this clod would be those visible gums. They came far down, and the teeth were short and blunt like those of a depraved child.

Route Sixty curved again, this time into the outskirts of a

settlement of sorts—a few scattered cabins among the pines, a taut washline where denim shirts flapped idly.

"This must be the town," Dan said. "Should be a garage here."

The stranger with the bull-moose smell glanced right, then ahead. "No fuggen sense stoppen here," he said flatly. "Ain't a good enough of a place. Wouldn't have no spare parts." He shifted slightly in the seat, bringing one heavy boot to rest against the hump in the floor. With his left hand, almost carelessly, he partly unzipped the green windbreaker.

Dan braked to thirty as the paltry town developed. Three store fronts. Post Office with a small weathered sign proclaiming the town's name and elevation, a clutch of shabby houses, a restaurant off by itself with one lonesome gas tank for the local trade. No garage. Obviously no mechanics.

"Guess you're right," said Dan, reluctantly. He pressed the accelerator and the car gathered speed. The town fell away and the pines closed in once more. Still snakelike, serpentine, glinting as with scales in the flicker of the sun, the road slanted gradually southwest. High on the right you could begin to see a few beetling rocks, the color of umber slashed with red, shouldering up against the intense blue of the sky, and seeming to enlarge and deepen, like an echo in a tunnel, the roar of the car's engine. Then, very suddenly, the swarming pines were gone. The car roared hollowly through a cut full of final shadows and at once burst out into a flood of light.

Dan looked and caught his breath. They had emerged upon a high shelf, blasted from solid rock, along the edge of an enormous chasm. It might, he thought, have been a landscape on the moon. The vast gulf, stretching beyond eyeshot, was filled with dusty haze. Out of it, at irregular intervals, rose huge peristyles and pilasters of eroded rock, like the remains of a titanic temple, an earthly pandemonium long since skeletalized, and ranging for mile on mile across the sunken floor.

On the first straight stretch of the road Dan glanced at his companion. But the other's eyes were narrowed to slits, perhaps because he was dozing, more likely because of the blaring sunlight. It was only when Dan swerved sharply at the next bend to clear a rusty truckload of broken stone laboring up the grade that the stranger moved and grunted.

"Wanna watch that, Mac," he said.

Dan said nothing, snaking the car around the outer edge of a hairpin turn, hearing the tires crunch and slip in the loose gravel. The road angled down and down, full of sharp twists and brief straightaways, towards the bridge, toy-sized from this height, deep in the bottom of the cleft.

"Looks like something in Spain," Dan said.

"Salt River," said the moose. "Go allaway down there you gotta climb up again." With one filthy hand he pointed towards the cliffs beyond the bridge where the road they must travel rose up and up towards the high blaze of the morning sky.

Dan said nothing more until the car leveled out for the bridge crossing. The moose sat slumped in silence, the bandaged hand thrust inside the unzipped windbreaker as if it were a sling.

"Hurt your hand?" said Dan.

The eyes opened lazily, red-rimmed in the fiery light. "Scratched is all."

"Garages are scarce," Dan said. "It's a long way back to your car from here."

The moose seemed not to have heard. For a full minute he said nothing. Then, deliberately: "No use goen back there. All bust to hell anyhow leave her there for junk."

So, Dan thought. So we have picked up a roadside burdock that aims to stick with us. But he did not speak, concentrating instead on the succession of dizzy curves that were lifting the car by degrees up the sheer wall of the canyon. Far faster than the car, his mind was racing into what lay ahead. "All bust to hell anyhow leave her there for junk." Even if we find a mechanic, it will be no use, he thought. We are stuck with this character until he chooses to leave.

—Are you fond of this car?

—Not especially.

—But you would like to keep it.

—Yes. I would like to keep it. I need it to get where I'm going, wherever the hell that is.

—You don't seem to know.

—I don't seem to care.

—Do you care enough about the car to fight for it?

—Don't be romantic. Who said anything about a fight?

—But you would fight to keep it?

—If I had to. Especially what's in it.

—The clothes and the typewriter? The dirty linen?

—No, the irreplaceables. The Keats in the carton. The Kemp notes under the seat.

—So you would fight for these. What with? Your fists, as in the palmy days at Amherst?

—If necessary. If I could get the son of a bitch out of the car.

—Suppose that's a gun in a shoulder-holster inside his stinking jacket. What would you do?

—Bash him with something. That old flashlight in the glove compartment.

—Don't be silly. What about the handle to the bumper jack? Can you reach that?

—With luck. It's down there with the Kemp notes.

—How do you know he has a gun?

—I don't. I could always find out.

—All right. Find out.

The road was running straighter now through a domain of high pines with broad savannahs of parched grass. Dan waited until the red-rimmed eyes had closed again before he took one hand from the wheel and groped in his shirt pocket for the cigarettes. The stranger stirred and straightened, then relaxed as he saw the pack.

"Smoke?" said Dan, and reached the pack quickly across, bumping his knuckles into the nearer armpit. Under the greasy cloth he felt it plainly: the hard hummock of leather with the yet harder bulge of metal inside.

The rider slid towards his corner. "Doan use them," he said curtly.

End of round, Dan thought. If it was a round. And now we know where his strength lies. It is in his left armpit, black and metallic, holstered up in sweat-stained leather. And his weakness? This we don't know, unless it is his stupidity. On that we know nothing except that it is not guaranteed.

The dusty road-sign said "Globe, 5m." Dan drove slowly past a stone-crushing outfit with a huge dusty shed and a truck loading at the chute. Dust hung in thick clouds across the road. Around the next curve a loose cluster of convicts worked in the dirty sunlight. They were handling picks and shovels under the eye of a paunchy guard with a sawed-off shotgun. He sat suspiciously on a boulder, wearing sun-glasses and a hat like Truman's. Dan slowed, peering at the guard.

"Get goen," said the moose, nervously. "Doan try nothing funny."

Dan ignored the order, still moving slowly. The convicts glanced unseeingly at the dirt-streaked car. Their faces were powdered with the dust. The car moved past them through the descending gorge.

"Globe is where I stop," said Dan.

The stranger straightened. "Oh, yeah?" he said. "Why you stoppen?"

"Little business," Dan lied.

"How long you take?"

"All day," said Dan. "Stay in Globe tonight. Head back tomorrow."

"Back where?" said the moose.

"Back east," Dan said. He guided the car slowly down the main street, scanning the corners and the dusty sidewalks. There was no one in uniform. Three or four women were moving along, peering into store windows. Two men in sweat-stained Truman hats were talking, leaning on a traffic sign.

"Just lemme off down ahead," the moose said, surprisingly. "Down where the town stops."

Dan's heart leaped. He speeded past a long, blank-faced warehouse where the shadows of the telephone poles were heavily etched at intervals along the wall of cinder-block. Beyond it the town suddenly ended. A hundred yards to the west lay an open gravel pit with a wide entrance. He swerved onto the road-shoulder and braked down.

"How's this?" he said, and turned to see the hand whipping out of the windbreaker, the boot coming to brace against the floor-hump—and, without surprise, the gun-snout black in the bandanna-ed hand.

The smile was back but the voice was a low growl. "So keep goen, shorty," the moose said. "Get the hell back on the road."

Dan jammed the brakes and reached for the ignition key. The moose clubbed the gun, whacking viciously at Dan's extended fingers. Dan brought his elbow up sharply under the leaning chin and heard the infantile teeth click together. But the heavy body was sliding across the seat, crowding him against the door. He brought his left fist around and connected, but too lightly, with the nose. The thick boot thudded down on his own shoe, pushing the accelerator to the floor. Dan yanked the car out of gear and the engine raced. The moose reached for the gear, breathing heavily. The gears clashed and meshed and the car began to gather speed.

A low yellow sedan covered with dust came down past the warehouse, and its driver hit his horn in a long angry wail as his car slid past no more than a yard from Dan's front fender. Dan kicked free of the boot that held his foot on the pedal, but the moose jabbed the gun-snout hard into his ribs.

"Son-uh-bitch," the moose panted. "Steer down the road."

"Get away and I'll steer," said Dan. The car swerved dangerously across the center line towards the ditch beyond.

"Steer right," the moose roared. "You wanna kill us?"

Dan jabbed his right elbow into the moose's side. "Move over," he yelled back. "Give me room."

The moose slid away a few inches.

"Get that gun away," Dan said. "We hit a bump and it goes off, the last thing I do is steer for the gully."

The moose slid over a few inches more and lowered the gun to his lap. "Drive," was all he said, still breathing hard.

They were coming to the desert now and the heat was intense. Dan felt the sweat-drops running down his back. Now where are you? he thought. He can shoot you any time, dump out the kicking remains, and drive off. He felt, momentarily, the old flood of despair. But he pushed back at it, his mind still racing ahead.

The jack-handle, he thought. It's too cramped to swing it here. But if I could get him out of the car. Yes, and the gun. There is something wrong with his gun-hand in that filthy bandanna. Can you twist the gun loose and throw it out? Say you have got him out of the car and he is without the gun. Can you take him with the jack-handle? With those long arms he has the reach on you. With those bull-shoulders he has you by fifty, maybe sixty, pounds. And he is at least five inches taller. But say you can get at the jack-handle. It is jointed in the middle and you could flail it like a whip.

—Listen, Samson. Give him the car. He will drive it until it runs out of gas and then leave it as he left the green Olds in that pine-grove. Sometime you will get it back. And you will be rid of him. And his stink and the gun.

—And the car. No, by God. They get away with too much as it is. The cheap hoodlums and the bandits and the greasy trigger-boys. No.

They were in the flat desert now, with the dried-looking low bushes and the occasional cactus like green fingers. The moose waved the gun menacingly. "Pull over there and stop," he said.

Dan held the car steady on the road, ignoring the order. Fight him for everything, he thought. Make the son of a bitch work.

"Come on, pull over," the moose growled. He held the gun-snout against Dan's neck. Dan raised his arm suddenly and hit the gun-hand as hard as he could. He heard the muffled curse and the sound of the gun bumping the car roof, but the bandaged hand held on, whipping down again and jabbing hard into his side. All his right ribs were bruised and sore. "Stop the goddam car or I blow you out the side of it," yelled the moose.

Dan held the car steady on the road. "You go to hell," he said.

Without warning the moose's long arm snaked out, ripped the key from the ignition, and flung it to the floor of the car. As the motor coughed and died, the moose crowded Dan against the door, steering for the roadside with his left hand, the gun-snout still in place. Before the car had stopped, he kicked open his door, leaned to scoop up the fallen keys, and backed out with the gun still pointing at Dan.

His face, Dan saw, was lathered with sweat and dust, but the old Lancaster smile was back. "Wise guy, huh? Come on, now, shorty, stop playing. Get the hell out. You've had it."

The car was stopped dead, with one front wheel in the shallow ditch. Dan slumped forward over the wheel, head on his left hand, right hand hanging limply, knuckles on the floor. If the jack-handle was where he had seen it that morning, one end of it would be no more than three inches from his fingers. He edged his hand back slowly, felt the flat metal inside the old towel, took a firm grip.

Then he sat up suddenly, made a face of horror, and pointed with his left hand over the moose's shoulder.

"Look out, moose," he yelled.

The moose glanced backwards. Dan swiveled fast, fumbled the jack-handle momentarily, then swung it hard in a single

arc down into the moose's wrist. It was no more than a glanc-
ing blow, but he heard with delight the moose's howl, saw the
gun drop away out of sight, and hurled himself feet first
through the door, raising the jack-handle for another swing.
But the moose was already diving for the gun. The handle
whistled in the air above his head, and Dan spun to kick
the gun under the car in a spurt of gravel. The moose's
head banged against the side of the car but he managed to
lurch forward, his face a mask of dirt and sweat, to grab Dan
around the knees. Dan aimed the handle at his head, swinging
it with both hands, but the moose lunged in with surprising
speed, and as Dan fell backwards, brought one knee up hard
between his legs. The paralyzing pain spread through all his
lower body as he felt the jack-handle ripped from his grasp,
dimly saw it lifted between his eyes and the burning sky, and
knew that it was slashing down as surely as he knew that he
was powerless to stop it.

CHAPTER TWO

ACROSS THE smoothest of turf, spangled with flowers red and white, small star-shapes turning toward the light, and without fallen leaves or branches or any underbrush; and at the edges of that rectangular plot tall trees like towers, like turrets, where sun filtered through, diffused and softened as in the late afternoon; and no sound but birdsong, twitter and chirr, notes gentle as rain; and the fruit-bearing trees, apple, plum, and pear, reaching towards you with hand-like branches, gesture of offering, to where you moved, without consciousness of any effort, across the deep-piled plush of the turf.

A place like a park, an interior garden, where you looked for satyrs and nymphs, or for Ovidian goats and lambs and milk-white heifers, clean and glossy of flank and withers, chewing somnolently in the chequered shade. Yet they were not there. Nothing moved there except for the slow rock and sway of branches high in the turreted trees. And high up, too, the coursing clouds across the oblong of sky, blue and gold and white, edged and framed in the perfect symmetry of the surrounding branches.

Gliding now into the green tunnel at the northern edge, the path descending steeply among jagged rocks, the pines closing in, the path twisting through thick underbrush where the smell of rotting vegetation, dank and mouldy, the heavy swamp-smell, rasped in the laboring lungs. Somewhere now the distant ugly yammer was beginning and the line coursed through his head, *They yolleden, as feendes do in Helle*. A sound like yelling, far-off, continuous, and ugly.

You have been here before, he thought. How many times? But he found, with the huge and rhythmic beating in his head, that he could not even arrive at the idea of number. Instead he seemed to see, as from somewhere else in the room, a figure that could only be himself. Himself, long ago, a thin schoolboy in pajamas and bathrobe, wrapped in a blanket on the old mission couch, and with the waves of pain, intense as lightning, rising and rising to that great crescendo and the sudden, plosive cracking relief which had made him start up on one elbow to cry out loudly—LOUDLY, "It broke, Abby, it broke," turning then to look with astonishment at the blob of pus and blood on the turkish towel beside his ruptured ear as she came—his already aging aunt, with that old-fashioned dust-cap, dropping the broom in her desperate haste, across the threadbare old green rug to his side.

Ugly and persistent as pain now rose that other sound, not of hammering from inside but of yammering from outside. Ugly, fiend-like and unending. He turned on the axis of his mind to run, through the park and the garden to the edge of the rocks, while above and around his head the yammering rose and rose. Backing away, he tripped and fell, his head cracking like a melon hurled against a boulder. "It broke, Abby, it broke," he seemed to himself to be shouting and shouting. Then the sound stopped as suddenly as it had begun and he lay still, gazing up into the bland oblong of the sky.

Voices had come like mice to nibble the edges of silence.

"His eyes is open and you said I was to tell you."

"Good. Let's see where he is."

He felt the hand spread gently on his cheek and jaw.

"Hey, old boy. Can you hear me?"

—Yes, I can hear you.

But he heard no sound and knew that the words had been spoken only inside his head.

"Speech center may be involved," said the voice. "Listen to me, old boy. If you hear me, just blink one time. Can you do that?"

He closed his eyes and opened them again.

"Good," said the voice, quick and snappy. "We're getting through, Agnes. Check again. Can you close your eyes again and open them?"

He closed them again.

"Fine," said the head with the voice. "Now, Agnes, you stick around him. I don't mean every minute, but keep checking. The goose-egg's normal enough. But look at those black eyes. Some whack. We have to assume petechial hemorrhage. Retain the flat position and absolutely no motion."

"Suppose he starts thrashing around?"

"If we have to, we'll strap him down. But you keep an eye on him, right?"

"What about feeding?"

"Nothing by mouth until he's fully conscious and co-operating. You can get that needle out of his arm. That's enough for now."

*   *   *   *   *

Flat on his back facing the single burning oblong of the window with the steady yammer in his ears, Dan watched a creamy cloud change shape as it coursed majestically across his line of vision. The Florentine sky, he thought. Not that ancient Italian one where the shades of the fierce religious ascetics and the mild, absorbed sculptors brooded over the soup-green Arno, but a new Florence, set down in a plot of desert gravel. If there were shades here, they belonged to Wyatt Earp and Billy the Kid and the James boys—not to be confused with another brace of James boys, who had been walking the shady and orderly streets of Cambridge about the time this American Florence was being established.

He searched his mind for ideas of order. It felt, still, like the black swamp. But it was beginning to firm up towards the middle and only at the edges now were the rotten trees, the bland deceptive quicksands where in a minute you could sink out of sight among festooned creepers filled with flat-headed snakes. He could remember things far back, and even up through the summer. But from his leaving Enfield he could not remember anything until the last two days in the hospital of Florence, Arizona.

"Fifteen beds," Agnes had said, yesterday. Or was it yesterday? "And Dr. Nash and me and the night nurse. And Mamie." Mamie was the Mexican woman who handled the kitchen. "And we hope they're never filled." Agnes twisted her mouth in the grotesque way she had, signifying wry humor. You were supposed to laugh or at least smile when she paused and drew her mouth down at one corner, casting up her prominent eyes behind their glasses, and standing perfectly straight and still, awaiting your response. Tall and rawboned and jib-nosed, with a big breast like a pouter pigeon and sturdy, shapeless legs ending in the white nurse's shoes, she was easily, Dan thought, the homeliest woman in the world. One of the homeliest, anyway. And one of the kindest.

"Somebody loves you," she had said loudly, bringing in Sandy's night-letter, which she insisted on reading aloud. "There, you see? He's found out where you are and all. And he's going to telephone you Sunday. Lucky you. Dr. Nash use to have this room for his office and the telephone plug is still here. I'll bring in the phone and plug it in and you can lay right there and talk like a millionaire."

Yes, he thought. Lucky you. But he only lay without speaking.

"So you just sit tight," said Agnes. "They're looking for your car all over."

"What do you bet they find it?"

"Just you wait," Agnes said. "They're used to this. Sometimes you take them, they'll head across into Mexico and then they get them at the border. Or Vegas, up there with the bright lights and the girls." She twisted her mouth and rolled her eyes. "I s'pose you got a girl?"

Dan ignored the question. "How did they find out about the car? I mean when the policeman was here I couldn't remember a thing."

"Your wallet," said Agnes. "Registration and all. Lucky you. Alvin keeps his on the sun-visor. I tell him to keep it in your jeans, Alvin. Just keep it in your jeans and stay out of trouble."

"Who's Alvin, your husband?"

"Well, ain't you the observant one?" Agnes said, with simulated scorn. "You din even notice my sparkler." She held out her left hand, large, efficient, corded with thick blue veins. The small diamond shone briskly. "We would of been married by now, and then what happens?" She paused and drew down the corner of her mouth. "Alvin falls off a tractor. He's laying in a bed down the hall here right now with a busted leg. Dr. Nash got it in traction. You hear that raddio?"

Dan nodded slightly before he thought, and felt the stab of pain through the back of his skull. For days now—or was it days?—the persistent yammer of the announcer's voice had been boring in like a dentist's drill.

"Alvin's listening to the Series. He's crazy for baseball. Only thing is he's got this brother in Brooklyn, and he figures he's got to be for Brooklyn."

"How is Brooklyn doing?"

"Brooklyn is not doing so good," said Agnes, rolling her eyes. "New York is leading after three games and they're ahead in the fourth game. Alvin is sunk. He says it's all over. He don't give Brooklyn a prayer tomorrow. You want to listen tomorrow? I've got a raddio in my room."

"Thanks," Dan said. "I guess not now. I mean I'll let you know. Maybe tomorrow."

"Does that noise bother you? I'll get Alvin to turn it down."

Now on the Sunday as the sun dipped westward, Alvin's radio was blaring again, and the Yankees seemed to be wrapping things up for another year. Dan groped for Sandy's telegram on his bedside table and unfolded it to read again. It had come from New York where the athletes in the baseball suits and the cleats were capering around the ball-park and the customers were sitting like shirt sleeved monarchs with their hot dogs and their beer, marking the frames in the programs in their laps.

MUCH DISTURBED NEWS ATTACK IN PAPERS HAD STATE
POLICE CHECK YOUR LOCATION CALLED WEBB AT EN-

FIELD WILL TELEPHONE SUNDAY NINTH WISH QUICK RE-
COVERY WILL FLY OUT IF YOU SAY THE WORD LETTER
FOLLOWS JESS SENDS LOVE ALL BEST   SANDY

Alexander Stone, called Sandy, had a head for law, a head
for investments, the brains to keep the Stone fortune intact
and growing, and for a short time—too short a time—he
had been Dan's brother-in-law. The rambling, comfortable,
slightly shabby old house on the Sound was in good repair
without loss of income because Sandy went shares with Arch
Acorn, the neighboring Yankee farmer who supervised the
raising of pigs in scientifically sanitary pens, fattened them
and the white Leghorn chickens with scientifically raised
corn, pruned and sprayed the acres of apple trees, picked and
marketed the fruit, and watched over the Connecticut house
in the winter season when the Stones moved back to their
New York apartment.

The books stayed in New York. In gleaming rows on the
shelves the collections grew and grew. First alone, and then
with Jessica after they were married, Sandy sniffed around the
better bookmarts like a persistent bloodhound. Thoreau was
right, he always said, with the rich man's slight obtuseness. To
earn your bread and butter didn't require more than few
hours each day of intensive application. The rest of the time
you could spend on more important matters. For Sandy, besides the charity drives and the hospital boards, this meant
books.

He was one of the first to collect Nicholas Kemp. "There's
a man to work on," he had told Dan. "Never mind your an-
cients. Get the new ones while they're hot, or at least still

warm. Why wait until they've been dead a hundred years, Dan?"

The allusion was to Keats. But Dan was already too deep in his doctoral dissertation on Keats and the graphic arts. For years he had read and reread all the works of Kemp. Now it was Keats who filled his days and nights. Even after Sandy's mysterious phone-call.

"Something I'm thinking of buying," Sandy had said. "Can you come into the city tomorrow, Dan? I need your advice."

Next day in the decorous office on the thirty-second floor overlooking Wall Street, Dan sat watching Sandy's well-groomed head across the polished desk.

"Call to mind the first short story you ever wrote," Sandy said. "I mean in college. You said it was a frank imitation."

"Of Nicholas Kemp, yes."

Sandy slapped the desk softly. "Yes, Kemp. Now what would you say if I told you that there is in existence a whole diary, in Kemp's handwriting, that he kept right up to the time he lost his arm at Belleau Wood?"

"All his life?"

"No. It starts in March and runs into June, 1918." Sandy opened the drawer of his desk and brought out a flat, brown-paper package. It had been sealed with red wax and the seals had been carefully broken. Inside was a red-leather folder which Sandy opened reverently to reveal a worn note-book, like a French schoolboy's *cahier*. "Almost perfect condition. Perfectly authentic. The soldier's diary of Nicholas Kemp. It begins in the training area and runs to June 9, the day Kemp was hit. Absolutely priceless, but for a price I can have it. Quite a price, too." Behind his clean glasses, Sandy's eyes flickered with enthusiasm. "Here, Dan, have a look at it."

He came around the desk to lean over Dan's shoulder and turn the pages. "Almost perfect," he said. "And here we run into a little mystery. Four pages have been cut out." He turned rapidly to the back of the diary. "See there? The stubs are still there, but the pages are missing. Obviously sliced out with a razor-blade. See here? See that cut where they pressed down a little too hard? Now of course that justs adds salt to the popcorn, you might say. If you should ever want to do a life of Kemp—and it's high time somebody did—I'll photostat it for you and keep the whole thing secret until you're ready to publish."

"Do you care how long it takes?"

Sandy waved his long white hand. "How long *would* it take? Two years? Three? You're the writer in this family. Now, Dan, what do you say?"

"I say you ought to be damned sure it's authentic before you meet this man's price. Can you trust him? Who's your secret spy?"

Sandy went back around the desk. "I can't tell you, Dan. But I can tell you he's one of the best in the business. Absolutely honest. I'm perfectly satisfied that this is the real McCoy." He sat looking across the desk, hovering over the question like a mild hawk. Behind his head, the great man-made peristyles of steel and stone soared up from the canyons of Wall Street.

"How about it, Dan?" he said.

"I'd rather you'd keep it until I'm ready to use it," Dan said. "I'm superstitious about photostats."

So the Kemp project had lain fallow all these intervening months. For which thank God. If the pages of the Keats manuscript even now were blowing around the bloody desert, at least the Kemp diary had survived intact, locked up in a vault in New York, unreproduced, unphotostatted—a unique object.

Through the blather of Alvin Kane's radio came the silver burring of a bell. He could hear Agnes's voice down the hall. In a moment she hurried in.

"It's a Mr. Stone," she said with excitement. "Is that your Sandy? He's calling from New York, person to person. Here, now, you lay still. You just lay still and don't move a muscle while I plug in this telephone."

CHAPTER THREE

THE FAMILIAR voice, though distant, was clear enough.

"Dan, how are you?"

"Hello, Sandy. In good hands here. Coming along. Thanks for the telegram. I still don't know how you located me."

"Hell, boy, you were splashed all over the morning papers. Did you get my letter? With the clippings?"

"Probably tomorrow."

"They call you the Enfield prof. Said the Arizona Highway Patrol picked you out of a ditch near Globe, out like a light. What a thing! Have they found your car?"

"Working on it, but no luck yet. They say they are hopeful. Half the stolen cars in the nation end up out here somewhere."

"But you're out of danger yourself?"

"Sure. Almost out of bed. What did you think of the Series?"

"Bye-bye Brooklyn," said Sandy. "How long before they let you out of the hospital?"

"That depends, the doctor says. He's noncommittal but cheerful."

"Well, don't worry. I called Webb at Enfield. He thinks

your Blue Cross coverage is good out there. He's finding out. I also called John. At least I tried."

"John who?"

"John Sherwood, your uncle. They say he's out of the country."

"The last I heard he was inspecting installations in the Pacific."

"Well, here's your rule of life," said Sandy. *"Don't worry and don't hurry.* Are you staying there until they find your car?"

"If they find it. Yes. I guess so. Plans are vague."

"You sure as hell surprised us," Sandy said. "Jess and I have been poring over road maps ever since last Wednesday. How'd you ever get way out there? I was thinking of you sitting in the Enfield Library, beating out another paragraph on Keats, and then I pick up the morning *Trib* and here's the story datelined from Arizona. We just couldn't believe it. Webb thought you were going to stop in New Mexico. Mentioned Albuquerque and Taos. And now Arizona. Where were you going—out to the coast?"

"I still can't remember. What they call a mild amnesia. Nash says it will straighten out pretty soon."

"Nash? Who's Nash?"

"The doctor. Thaddeus Nash. There's the three-minute signal."

"Yes. Never mind. Look, Dan, be frank now. Are you getting tired of talking?"

"No. I was thinking of the phone bill."

"Never mind that. I've got news for you, Dan. Listen to this. You remember the Kemp diary?"

"The war-time diary, yes."

"All right, *now hear this.* That place where you are is called Florence, right?"

"That's right."

"It's near Tucson. Quite close on the map. Now my agent, the man who sold me that diary, got that Kemp diary in Tucson. *That's where he picked it up!* What do you think of that?"

"I'd call it curious. What was the diary doing out here? Kemp lives five or six hundred miles up north."

"That's all I know yet. But I've got one lead for you, Dan. Dan?"

"I'm on. I'm listening."

"I say there is one lead that you might be able to follow up when you get out. My man was visiting Brooks Nagle out there. You know Brooks Nagle, the columnist? He has a big house in Tucson. Lives there all the time now. Telephones his columns to a Chicago syndicate or something."

"And *some* columns!"

"Never mind Nagle's politics. They don't have anything to do with the case, Dan. My man paid him a visit in the winter of 1948. That's all I know, except that Tucson is where the diary was picked up."

"Would Nagle know about it?"

"Maybe, maybe not. But you could probably sound him out. If you talk to Nagle, mention Bill Baxter's name."

"Baxter? Who is Baxter?"

"Nobody is supposed to know it, Dan, so keep it strictly under your hat. Baxter is the man who sold me the diary. Now what do you say?"

"I say it's a small world. And coincidence has a long arm. And you are running up a hell of a big phone-bill."

"All right, Dan, I'll ring off. But you see what I'm getting at: why don't you go to Tucson when they let you out of that hospital? I hear it's a good place. There's a university there with a good library. The climate is warm and dry—good for the old bronchial tubes. And think of the good sport, running down the source of the Kemp diary. Maybe Kemp's aged mother lives there in penury. Think of that."

"No, Sandy. His mother died long ago. Anyway, there's still the Keats book."

"Keats died long ago, too. Why fool with antiquity? Catch 'em alive. Bring 'em back alive. That's my motto. Dan, now please keep in touch. You should have told me where you were going. Now the least you can do is tell me what you decide to do. How about money?"

"It's all right. I've got travelers' cheques. They stole the rest of the stuff, and the Keats and the Kemp. Otherwise I was not robbed."

"You mean they didn't take your pants."

"Pants ripped. Otherwise intact."

"Well, Dan, get somebody to sew them up and go on down there to Tucson."

"I'll think about it, Sandy. What was that agent's name?"

"Bill Baxter. And he was visiting the columnist, Brooks Nagle, at the time in question."

"All right, Sandy. I'll write them down. Thanks for the call."

"You bet," Sandy said. "Take care, old boy."

After he had replaced the receiver in its cradle and scribbled the names of Baxter and Nagle on the back of Sandy's telegram, he sank back into the pillow, his head beating steadily. The room was growing darker. He still doesn't know, he thought. She hasn't told him, and why should she? I hope to God she never does. He saw her face, ruddy in the wind, smiling down from the ladder in the apple tree, and the same patrician face, flushed with the pleasure of her passion, smiling up from the rug before the fire. But it only blackened his despair because beyond it, like a wraith, he could see that other face, his wife's face, putty-colored in the roil of surf, absolutely and finally and irrevocably dead. When the mousy night nurse came in to take his evening temperature, he could not even speak.

* * * * *

By the seventh day he had reconstructed most of it. The start at Enfield that rainy morning a million years ago. The long roar of the westrunning turnpike. The cities and the plains. The mountains capped with snow like clouds. And Show Low. Yes, Show Low, where the curtain of blank gray shut down like an August fogbank rolling in off Long Island Sound.

Sitting in the chair beside the window in his room, at first dizzily but now more and more with the consciousness of returning self-command, gazing out at the huge clumps of paloverde trees still in full golden leaf, he searched his memory for all the points of bearing.

"What you need is maps," said Agnes. "I got a set. Now you just wait a coupla minutes and we'll see."

She brought the set of road maps from her car. She had sent away for them last summer, she said sardonically, pulling down the corner of her mouth. "I call 'em my just-in-case maps."

In case of what? Dan asked. In case, she said, that Alvin

decided to take her on a wedding trip back east. "Now it don't look like no trip till next summer," she said. "If then."

She spread the brightly colored maps on the low table before him, running her finger along the thick red lines of the suggested routes, laid on with a water-color pencil by some geographical genius at happy-motoring headquarters in New York.

But he scarcely saw the maps. Only the remembered faces. The pale face of that baker's apprentice at the stoplight in Independence. The blue lips murmuring thanks as he stepped from the car ten minutes later into the rain-swept center of Tonganoxie, walking away down the street with his head sunk into his chest, his ragged jacket flapping in the merciless wind like a damned soul out of Dante.

Dark, he thought. They all go into the dark. All the furtive faces with eyes that slink or scuttle away like snakes or scorpions. Faces like what you would see if you peered into a tub of rancid pork. The ape-face that seems secretly wise until you catch the glimpse inside, the curtains swishing back from the windows—haha—of the soul. And what do you see? Nothing. Complete psychic unemployment. Or if there is something, it is sly. It is self-indulgent, superstitious, sentimental, avaricious, cruel. It says things like "all-righty" or "be right with you." But it is never all right nor is it ever with you. It holds out the promise of something for nothing which turns out to be nothing for something.

Oh, come off it, he thought. There is a sourness that is tart and healthy and another that blackens the soul. There is a scorn which is needful and another that is proud and self-centered and truly cancerous.

Still, it had not been a joyous journey. Two thousand miles

of leather pie and anemic coffee, while the juke-boxes in a hundred roadside bar-and-grills wailed the song that bade Irene goodnight, over and over, and the slattern waitresses mopped the tables. Two thousand miles of intermittent rain, while the roadsigns issued their silent and peremptory commands, and the Chicago-bound steers bellowed all night long at the railroad siding you had not noticed when you paid in advance for the sleazy bed with the suspiciously stained blankets at the Apache Courtel and Traveler's Rest.

Agnes finished making his bed and came to stand beside his chair. "How you doing, Mr. Sherwood?" she asked.

"Most of it's come back now, Agnes. Down to Show Low, anyway. There was an old man in Show Low like Santa Claus with a sun-tan. He told me about the Salt River Gorge, and it was somewhere down there that I picked up this—"

His voice trailed off to silence and he sat gazing out at the paloverde trees, shimmering in the sun. Out of the black interior void the face was taking form, framed in its growth of dirty stubble, leaning to peer through the car window, with the red bandanna on the right hand, and the baby-like short teeth in the pink gums. Behind it, among the jetsam of the ruined grove, the green Oldsmobile was parked in the shadows.

"Agnes," he said thickly, "I can tell them now what he looked like."

"Who?" said Agnes.

"The one—the son of a—Agnes, the slug that stole the car."

*　*　*　*

The lieutenant from the Highway Patrol was a tall, beak-nosed, yellow-haired ex-Texas Ranger who said in his deliberate drawl that the car was still missing. But they had sent out all the information on teletype, and the prognosis was good. Nodding crisply, he wrote down Dan's description of the assailant. It wasn't, he said, until they had searched Dan's effects and found the car registration that they suspected he had been robbed of the vehicle and contents. Lieutenant Casper called it "vee-hickle," going on to say that a woman by the name of Sawyer, driving west from Globe to Yuma, had seen Dan lying in the ditch. She was too scared to stop until she got to the next filling-station where she phoned the Highway Patrol.

Dr. Sherwood's description was good. Now if all the descriptions were that good, the Highway Patrol would be much better off. People just didn't keep their eyes open. With all these details, though, they would have a staff artist draw a picture of the criminal based on this account. Dr. Sherwood could rest assured. The case was getting their full attention and the prognosis was good.

* * * * *

Agnes said that Tucson was a very nice town, if the tourists would stop spoiling it with their money and their big cars. She got down there usually about once a month. She had a married sister living in a little stucco house just off the Speedway. Name of Notofrancesco. Her husband was a deputy sheriff. Everybody called him Mr. Noto for short, like that Jap detective in the *Saturday Evening Post:* Mr. Moto. Her sister's husband was a good detective, too.

"And don't think Mr. Noto don't have his work cut out for him," Agnes said. With all that money floating around Tucson, the town was full of stick-ups. You'd lay in bed at her sister's house and hear the sy-reen when a police car went racing ninety miles an hour out to the latest robbery. And in the next room you'd hear Bruno pulling on his pants and stomping into his boots, often in the middle of the night.

"I wouldn't care for that," said Agnes. "I want my man home in bed. My sister can't never count on a good night's sleep." And then there was the noise from the Speedway, always increasing as the city grew.

"What is that?"

"What is what?"

"The Speedway. What is it, a race-track?"

"Oh, no," said Agnes. They had a race-track out near the veterans' hospital where she had worked during the war. They raced jalopies and stockcars, and ran the rodeo there in winter. But the Speedway was a long street leading out from the older part of town. It was growing up with big stores like El Rancho where Agnes often bought kites for her nephew, Bruno Junior, nicknamed Pruney because that was what he had called himself when he first began to speak.

Pruney was crazy for kites, but the ones she bought him were always nose-diving and getting hung up on telephone wires. When that happened, Pruney would blame his Aunt Agnes. He had some handcuffs his father had given him, and he would lock them on her wrists and then pretend that he had lost the key. Pruney looked like his father, short and compact, with brown Italian eyes and olive skin. "I tell my sister I think he's got Indian blood in him," said Agnes.

Did she think it would be a good place to spend the winter? Oh, yes, he would like it. And the university was nice, with a lot of olive trees around the campus. "And I hear," said Agnes, with dignity, folding her arms across the prominent pigeon-breast, "that they give a very good education there."

If Dan wanted to go look around, he could stay with the Notofrancescos until he found a place. She would drive him down next Wednesday if he was well enough. No trouble. She wanted to see her sister anyway. She would telephone today. She pulled down the corner of her mouth and said that the Notos would be pleased to have an honest-to-God English professor staying at their place a few days.

"Only I'll tell her she better watch her grammar," said Agnes, and went off down the hall to rub Alvin Kane's enormous back.

PART TWO

THE DESERT

CHAPTER FOUR

THE NAME that Mrs. Noto gave him was Mandeville Lee. "He buys and sells real estate," she said. "Maybe he might rent some. I'll call him, Mr. Sherwood. He don't live far from here."

She came back from the telephone, still in her breakfast apron, and said that Lee would see him right away. Dan walked half a mile along an unpaved road called East Rachel Street, turning in at a low stucco ranch-house with a red sports car parked in the driveway.

The door opened immediately to his knock. Music blared from the interior of the house. Lee turned out to be six feet tall. In certain lights and from certain angles, he was handsome as a movie star. His skin looked clean and was deeply tanned, and his hair, which was the color of molasses taffy or walnut meats, was bleached unevenly by the desert sun. That morning he was wearing pink jodhpurs and English riding boots, an expensive green-and-gray shirt with an open collar, and a reddish paisley scarf. You had to look closely to see that under the shirt-front his belly was beginning to bulge softly against his two-toned green belt.

He did not shake hands. He surveyed Dan coolly, nodded

curtly and professionally, disappeared into the kitchen, and came back with a key. Leaving the music blaring, he beckoned Dan outside and into the bucket seat of the red sports car. He gunned the motor forensically, made a quick turn in the street, and drove some three hundred yards, pulling up before another low stucco house slightly smaller than his own. The patch of brown grass which served as a lawn was diversified with mock orange trees whose leaves and fruit were covered with dust. A brick path led to the front door.

Mandeville Lee said that he would not ordinarily have a house available, but a couple of bastards from Baltimore who had signed up to take this one, beginning on the first of November, had just written him that they wouldn't be able to come to Tucson this winter after all. They asked for the deposit they had made. Mandeville Lee said that they damned well could kiss their deposit good-bye, and that when they wrote him they had been too cheap to even use an air-mail stamp, just sent the letter along by surface mail, and here he was holding the bag on a house he could have rented three or four times over.

He showed Dan through the place, which was sparsely furnished with worn modernistic furniture. The tables were covered with a fine film of dust, and when Mandeville Lee leaned down to punch one of the twin beds, to show that it was comfortable, a thin cloud of dust rose up in the shaft of sunlight and settled softly onto the composition floor. Carelessly, over his shoulder, Lee said that if Dan wanted the place, he had a woman who would come and clean it again. It had just been cleaned recently but in the meantime some strong winds had been blowing, and out in this part of the town where they had not yet got around to paving the streets, that always meant that dust would get into the house through various crevices and crannies.

When Dan asked him how much the rent was, Mandeville Lee answered that he usually got one-fifty a month if you signed a year's lease, or a little more if you didn't. But he was not out to rook anybody; all he wanted was a decent return on his investment. Besides, he had a little head start on this house with the deposit from the Baltimore couple, so what would Dan think of one-twenty a month, with a thirty-day notice of intent to vacate in case his plans changed? Dan said that this was about twice what he had thought of paying and he guessed that he would have to look around the town.

Mandeville Lee looked down at Dan from his six-foot, taffy-topped eminence and the trader's glint flickered in his wide-set brown eyes. He said that all he was trying to do, after all, was to clear the taxes on this particular place, and he could probably let it go for seventy-five a month cash. If Dan paid by check, the price would have to be ninety-five. He put his hands carelessly into the pockets of the jodhpurs and explained that he was already paying enough income tax to support four senators and a couple of representatives, keeping them with limousines and chauffeurs in Washington, and he was not going to pay Uncle Sammy a nickel more than those bastards with the money-bags could prove he owed them. So if Dan wanted to come through with the rent in cash, he would knock the price of the house down to seventy-two-fifty, cash on the barrel-head.

He said that they ought to be paying him instead of his paying them because he had gone in there on D-Day plus one and fought their goddam war for them until he met up with a piece of shrapnel that put him in the hospital for nineteen

months, four of them partly paralyzed. He said that he was
only getting a fifty-percent disability pension out of them in
spite of the silver plate in his skull, and if they thought he
owed them something instead of the other way round, they
could go collect it from the ghost of Adolf Hitler. In the end,
Dan rented the house.

When he moved in it was still dusty and there were no
sheets for the bed, but the next afternoon a Mexican girl
named Chita knocked on the door and said she had come to
clean the place. She had very white teeth and very dark eyes.
When she found that the vacuum cleaner in the kitchen
closet was broken, she went over to Mandeville Lee's house
to borrow his. She said she worked for Lee—"very nice man"
—and he would not only lend the vacuum cleaner but would
also supply some sheets and towels. Chita was gone on this
errand for some time, and when she came back, it was in the
red sports car. Mandeville Lee sat behind the wheel while
Chita unloaded a vacuum cleaner and an orange dust-mop,
and then drove away while she came up the front walk with
an armful of sheets and towels. Chita had trouble opening the
door with her arms full and when Dan opened it for her he
noticed a strong sweet smell of gin.

In cleaning the house Chita missed many of the places
where the dust lay thickly, and as the gin wore off she often
yawned widely, showing her strong white teeth and tapping
her lips politely with the back of her hand. She said on leaving that this cleaning job was for free, but she asked Dan if
he would like her to come in once a week during the winter.
Dan said thanks, but he thought he could take care of it himself. Chita yawned again and left.

A couple of days later he noticed that during his absence

the broken vacuum cleaner had been taken from the kitchen closet. The next day it was back again in working order. After supper at one of the places on the Speedway he walked over to Mandeville Lee's house to thank him for having it fixed and for Chita's cleaning job. Chita answered the door and opened it just far enough to say that Mr. Lee was not there, he had gone out; but when Dan had left the message and turned to walk home, he saw that Mandeville Lee's red sports car was parked in the narrow driveway behind the house.

*   *   *   *   *

In the long paneled room the sunlight lay in warm squares and oblongs on the well-scuffed floor. Dan turned slowly away from the circulation desk, blowing on the wet ink of the card which gave him guest privileges at the library.

"We're used to this," the young attendant had said, briskly. He was pale and slender with what looked like prematurely gray hair. A company of automatic pencils protruded from his breast pocket. "You'd be surprised how many visiting firemen we have in the course of a year."

Dan said that he thought it was rather odd, Tucson seemed to him a very remote region. The young man said that, to coin a phrase, appearances were deceptive. As a matter of fact, Tucson could be called the Hub of the Southwest. Sooner or later everyone seemd to fly in and fly out. One kept running into people on the street that one had formerly known. He thought that this would happen to Dan, as it happened to everyone else. "Have you met anyone here?" he asked.

"My landlord," Dan said. "Mandeville Lee. And a family named Notofrancesco. Mr. Noto is a deputy sheriff."

The young man said that he didn't know them. "Just give yourself time," he said, wisely. "How long have you been in Tucson?"

"Ten days."

"That's hardly long enough," the attendant said. "I'll ask you, though, how you like the Southwest."

"It's very nice," Dan lied. "How do you ever get any work done with all that sunlight outside?"

"We ignore it. Now I hope you will feel free to use the library. If you should need any inter-library loans, we can arrange it. Are you working on something or just reading?"

"Just reading, now," Dan said. There would be time enough to work if they could find that damned car, he thought, and if the head-aches would stop. If I had the Keats materials. Or the notes on Nicholas Kemp. But he said nothing of this as he thanked the brisk librarian and turned away, blowing on the fresh ink to dry it.

Halfway down the long room, he seemed to hear his name. He turned to see a tall, stooped man, with a huge, wedge-shaped head set low between very wide shoulders. The face was red and the weight of shaggy hair made the whole head look enormous. The hair had once been reddish-blond but now, streaked with gray, it made you think of a mixture of mustard, mud, and milk.

"Forgive me," the man said. "Are you called Sherwood?"

"Yes, I'm Sherwood."

"Forgive me," the man said again, bending the great head down towards Dan. "Are you the Sherwood I read about some weeks ago in the papers? From Enfield, I believe?"

"Yes. You mean the episode of the hitch-hiker?"

"Frightful business," the man said grimacing. "Put me in

mind of what used to happen to respectable citizens on the English high-roads in the eighteenth century. I hope you've recovered."

"Pretty well," said Dan. "I'm about ready to get to work now. Just got my library card."

"Yes," the man said. His voice was rich and orotund, his manner formal. "I'm afraid I was eavesdropping a moment ago. I was near the desk as you were giving the information to Henry there. I ought to intrduce myself. My name is O'Keefe."

"O'Keefe," Dan said. "Not the Pope O'Keefe?"

"The same," the big man said. His glasses and Phi Bete key glinted in the light. The wild eyebrows, also mustard-gray, stood out from his forehead like the tufts on the ears of a wildcat, and each of his enormous ears, where the sun hit them, sported a frosty flower of hair. He was smiling with pleasure at having been recognized.

"I had no idea you were out here," Dan said.

"My wife and I are old settlers," O'Keefe said. "Are you teaching at Enfield?"

"I have been," Dan said. "Now I'm on leave to write a book. I brought two typescripts along in the car. They're still missing."

"Frightful," O'Keefe said again. "I must hear about them and your plans. Could you spare time for some coffee? There's a place just down the street. I'm hungry for a whiff of the eastern seaboard. The busy hum of men."

When Dan nodded, O'Keefe seemed delighted. He led the way down the stairs. "You know, in a way, we're prisoners out here."

"To people on the eastern seaboard this looks like freedom," Dan said. "Sun and wide open spaces. All bright and glittering in the smokeless air."

"Ah, Wordsworth," O'Keefe said, happily. He led the way across the squared-off campus to the street, his great head swinging, his near-sighted eyes watching where he walked. "We are smogless, it's true. But Tucson is a city of prisoners, full of people who can't live anywhere else. I mean literally, and I include myself."

"You don't act like a prisoner," said Dan.

"Ah, possibly not, but when I feel the call to roam, and to get out of this everlasting sunlight into a New England sea-coast fog, or one of those good, slow gray Connecticut drizzles —then I know the prison feeling. Because, sir, if I go and stand in that Connecticut drizzle, I will be tied up in the most excruciating knots within a week. This is a very strange place. Many a man—and many a woman—imprison themselves here, like your friend Wordsworth in that other sonnet, in order to be free."

O'Keefe led the way grandly through the door to the coffee-shop, and signaled the Mexican waitress. He stirred the coffee she brought, sitting back like an ancient king. "The willed sacrifice of freedom," he said. "I see that you have raised your eyebrows in the inevitable question. But what I mean is that this strange city is crawling with people who formerly lived somewhere else—Boston or New York or Washington. Most of them suffered some awful physical afflic-tion like arthritis or asthma or infected sinuses or tuberculosis. You know the list. So they heard about this desert Côte d'Azur and came to try it out."

"I've met one or two," Dan said. "My mailman is a former

asthmatic from Hoboken. A great admirer of *Arizona Highways* magazine."

"Ah, just so," O'Keefe said. His voice went with the red face and the shaggy hair. It sounded, Dan thought, like thunder mixed with honey. "He belongs to the tribe of exiles. Your mailman walks miles every day through this dust. Yet at home, in Hoboken or Albany, he would be at best bedridden, and at worst dead."

Dan sipped the coffee, nodding.

"The first time we saw this place," O'Keefe went on, "the first time we gazed around us at this tree-less plain with those damnable pseudo-phalluses they call saguaros, this waste land with its prickly pears, the dirt-colored mountains, the vulgarian raw frontier either just under or erupting into the surface of nominal civilization, we both heaved a sigh and said no. Ah, no. My wife said it aloud; I said it silently. I believe I meant it more. We breathed in a lungfull of the dry dust and we said, 'Surely this is the land of Nod. The authors of Genesis had it wrong, for Nod lay east of Eden, and this hell-hole lies *west* of that New England Eden beside the Atlantic. Yet Nod it must be,' we said, 'for clearly this is the place of exiles. Only exiles would come here.' I'm sure Cain, and probably Cain's children as they were pupped, looked round him and told himself that Nod was the most Godforsaken hole on the face of the earth. When you ask people around here—now, Mr. Sherwood, you test this out—you will see the pattern. Like the pattern in a Navajo blanket—trustworthily recurrent. They will all tell you that at that stage they used the adjective *Godforsaken*."

"It occurred to me," Dan said.

"Ah, *did* it?" O'Keefe crowed. "If it hadn't, I'm bound to say, I should have been surprised. And I've no doubt, not the slightest, that your Hoboken mailman said it to his wife as soon as they had arrived. They told each other that they couldn't stand *this* any longer. They were lonesome and they wept, and they said they must pack up and go back to Hoboken. Which they subsequently did, at great trouble and expense. Then we have the predictable series of events."

"They came back," Dan said.

"Yes, they came back. For they had, at home in Hoboken, the most frightful attack of whatever it was that had driven them out here in the first place. If they weren't bedded immediately, the attack made them so miserable that they had no choice. They packed up, again at great trouble and expense, and rejoined the tribe of Cain."

"Are you sketching from personal experience?" Dan asked.

"Precisely," O'Keefe said. "New London and environs was my damp shroud when we returned from the Land of Nod. New London, it soon appeared, could well have been my tomb. So my poor wife and I followed the many others. Now, of course, after something like three years, neither of us would live anywhere else on the face of the earth. Here I can live—in exile, indubitably—but live I can."

"Still," Dan said, "the people I see look healthy enough."

"Then, sir," said O'Keefe pontifically, "you simply have not looked closely." He emphasized the words with his finger on the table. "Look into the bedrooms of the houses, as of course one can't, but if it were possible, you would see dozens, scores, hundreds no doubt, who are far-gone or going. On the streets you see those still capable of locomotion. *Look behind the walls, Mr. Sherburn.*"

"Sherwood," said Dan, gently.

"Forgive me, Sher*wood*," said O'Keefe, unabashed. "I named my rival in the fields of Pope. No doubt a Freudian slip."

"I'm honored," Dan said. "But you make this sound like a regular city of Castorps: a magic mountain flattened out on the desert floor."

"Possibly I exaggerate," O'Keefe said. "It is a city of exiles, but we have to admit that all of them are not here by requirement. Some are doubtless voluntary. Not only the lame, the halt, and the—er—tubercular, but also a certain infusion of artists, composers, and writers of various shades. Then there are the retired people, among whom I count myself. The very rich and the very poor. To say nothing of what Henry called you—the visiting firemen."

"And the goods and services people," Dan said. "Including the landlords and landladies. Do you know a man called Mandeville Lee?"

O'Keefe pulled at one of his prominent eyebrows. "Lee? Lee. Is that the man who runs the race-track?"

"Maybe," Dan said. "I hadn't heard about that."

"Drives about in a small red car with a very loud motor," said O'Keefe. "A sporting man, by all accounts."

"That's Lee," Dan said. "He's also in real estate. What you would have called in Pope's time a man of parts. He's my landlord."

"I think," said O'Keefe deliberately, "that some friends of ours had dealings with him several years ago. They were not, as I remember, deeply impressed with Mr. Lee's character. What do you think of the gentleman?"

"*Comme çi comme ça,*" Dan said.

O'Keefe did not reply. Since the conversation had turned to Mandeville Lee, he had been showing signs of polite impatience. Now he lowered the great particolored head to peer at his watch. "Sherwood, I'm afraid I must go. You must come to see us. Let me have your address."

He paid for the coffee and stood for a moment outside the café, chatting with Dan and fingering his Phi Bete key. Then he moved off down the baking sidewalk, waving once, his shoulders enormous, his wedge-shaped head sunk forward between them.

Dan watched his receding figure and then turned back into the campus. The sun shone hot on his back. He felt aimless. Now that he had the library card, he did not feel like using it. He sat down on one of the benches in the shade of a dusty orange-tree. Where was that damned car, anyhow? Where were the voluminous Keats manuscript and the notes on Kemp? Drying to tatters in a desert gulch, blowing in yellow leaves from here to Mexico? You could not tell. There was no way of knowing. But in the meantime, until you found out, there was no sense in staying idle.

Well, then, why not Kemp? Why the hell not Kemp? You wouldn't need all that scholarly paraphernalia for a book on Kemp. There were dozens of Keats books, but not one on Kemp. And Kemp, after all, was a demigod of yours long before you ever thought of working on Keats. The good bitter Kemp, like a draught of wormwood. You could begin to-morrow. You could even start today.

And then there was the matter of Kemp's war-time diary. Picked up here, in Tucson, in this very city, under conditions of secrecy, by a rare-book dealer who flatly refused to reveal his source of supply. Maybe you could find out something. If not, if it turned out to be a dead-end street, there were always the printed books to work on, the novels and short stories of Nicholas Kemp.

He found that he had left the bench and come to a halt under the shadowy portico of the library. The steps led to the reading-room. He began to ascend.

CHAPTER FIVE

IT TOOK him a solid two weeks of reading and note-taking to work his way once more through the novels of Nicholas Kemp, to recapture Kemp's tragic vision and his own sense of continuing spiritual rapport with that remarkable ten-inch self of dark and bloody fiction by which Kemp had established and consolidated an international reputation in the short space of fifteen years.

Luckily, the books were few: a half-dozen, all told. The four major novels; the collected short stories; and the unauthorized edition of those early sketches, carefully gathered and pedantically edited by the hapless Bellmyer just before the war, and then withdrawn from circulation by court order when Kemp, enraged at their exhumation, brought suit to return them to the obscurity they probably deserved.

The novels were altogether a different matter. "With *The Hinges of Hell*," wrote a reviewer in the *New Republic* in 1924, "the American novel of the Great War at last comes into its own." It was so. Nothing else until Hemingway's *Farewell* in 1929 combined so effectively the themes of love and war. Nothing in print, in or out of fiction, provided a more harrowing account of the American Marines in action at the battle of Belleau Wood. "A smashing good yarn in the naturalistic vein," said the reviewer in the *Times*. But it was much more than that. Neither the contemporary reviewers nor any critic since had seen what Kemp was really doing, working out from the Biblical story of David and Bathsheba and the betrayed Uriah, elevating the whole story into a universal fable of crime and punishment, guilt and expiation, which even now, a quarter-century later, made all but the best fiction seem anemic by comparison.

Four years later came *The Kingdoms of the North*, that brutal story of the lumber industry in the Pacific Northwest. In spite of the presidential elections, Kemp was on every tongue. The book raised cries of protest from the Canadian government, was banned in dozens of cities for alleged immorality and anti-Christianity, and enjoyed a clandestine circulation for upwards of a year before the famous court decision set it free to climb the best-seller lists and make Kemp a small fortune just when so many others were losing theirs.

The critics were split half and half. The most balanced of the lot was Tate in *The Bookman*, who argued that the portrait of the Christian minister should not be construed as an attack on religion in general. Tate alluded with enthusiasm to the power of the prose and called the Indian massacre "the most hair-raising single episode in twentieth-century fiction."

Again, though no one had recognized it, the book was almost literally a jeremiad against modern civilization. For Kemp had returned to the Old Testament, borrowing ideas and even disguised quotations from the prophet Jeremiah, using them in a subtle kind of counterpointing unknown to American fiction since the time of Hawthorne and Melville.

Nor had anyone suspected that under the surface-horrors of

The Straits of Magellan in 1930, Kemp had been working with the Biblical story of Jonah. What made the reading-public flock to buy this narrative of an ill-starred voyage around Cape Horn was its shocking revelation of homosexuality among the crew. But there were other rewards: the shipwreck in the stormy waters off Tierra del Fuego, and the idyllic rehabilitation of the young hero at the hands of an Indian girl in those far latitudes. Some few critics held that the closing incidents made a rift of sunlight in Kemp's gloom-filled vision of life. For a time, partly for this reason, the novel was a leading candidate for the Pulitzer Prize. In the end it was passed over in favor of LaFarge's *Laughing Boy,* as if the western world, deep in the clutches of the Great Depression, had known enough of gloom and fear and longed instead for the gaiety that LaFarge's title seemed, at any rate, to promise.

The proponents of the rift-of-sunlight theory found little support for their views in the evidently autobiographical stories of his Idaho boyhood which Kemp collected in *Pieces of Eight.* The theme of remorse ran through them so darkly that the Freudians had a field day when the book appeared in 1934. But it was generally held that the collection was a mistake. Kemp's genius did not show to best advantage in shorter fiction. The critics began to say that Kemp was slipping. He had shot his bolt in the three novels. It was doubtful if he would write any more.

If Kemp was aware of the doom-criers, he gave no outward sign. Instead, five years later, he countered with a huge three-generation novel called *The Sleep of the Fathers.* The locale was Idaho ranch-country and the opposed forces were cattle-men and sheep-herders. In several ways it was a new departure, though in *The Hinges of Hell* and *The Kingdoms of the*

North Kemp had proved his skill in the handling of large forces locked in mortal opposition. In fact, all the earlier works had concentrated on single sweeps of time, working with mounting emotional intensity towards climactic events. In *The Sleep of the Fathers,* Kemp abandoned this principle, risked the obvious dangers of the three-generation novel, and built slowly to a bloodless denouement in which most of the moral issues were movingly resolved.

Once more, though Dan was the only one who knew it, Kemp had used a disguised and remotivated Biblical story as the ground-plan of his novel. This was the little-known tale of Zimri, the traitor in the First Book of Kings. Zimri, Omri, and then the curious character of Ahab, Omri's son. Since the publication date was September, 1939, the reviewers of ten years ago had hinted broadly that Omri was a portrait of Hitler. This line of interpretation had befuddled the reception of the novel. If you recognized the Biblical analogue, Kemp's whole meaning came clear. He was preoccupied, as always, with the aftermath of sinful action stretching down the generations. If Hitler had been in the picture at all, it was only as one in a long line of powermongers—a line that went far back into the earliest mists of Hebraic antiquity.

And Bellmyer, the hapless collector of Kemp's early sketches, who got out his book with Anson and Son in Chicago and sat back to reap the rewards of his critical perspicacity. Until all hell broke loose. Kemp brought suit against Bellmyer and his publisher and compelled the withdrawal of the whole edition. The dozen or so review-copies that slipped through the legal screen were now bringing close to two hundred apiece in the rare-book market. But Bellmyer was crushed. He left the teaching profession, enlisted in the Navy hoping (they said) to get shot, and instead sat out the war typing pamphlets at one of the desks in Church Street. He was last seen selling Pontiacs in Manchester, New Hampshire, around 1946 or 1947. No doubt he had been a simpleton to go as far as he had gone without clearance from Kemp, though it was doubtless Kemp's reputation for irascibility which had made him desist from asking in the first place. Kemp had been harsh and ruthless in the prosecution of the case. As soon as you read the early sketches, you understood why. They were the kind of mannered razzmatazz that any man would want to bury and forget.

Dan dropped the 5 x 8 card back into the black box. If the great Kemp chose to go on suing critics, they—or we—would all be selling Pontiacs. But for a full nine years now he had been strangely silent, holed up like a hibernating bear in his northern wilderness, drinking whatever wormwood it was which had made him the Dostoievsky of his age, and earned him a wide company of fanatical admirers. Including, Dan thought, myself.

*   *   *   *   *

In one of the booths at the coffee-shop, Axel O'Keefe was reading a newspaper, his glasses shining in the light from the window. When he saw Dan he waved and beckoned.

"Ah, Sherwood," he boomed. "Hoping to see you. How are you getting on?"

Dan said that he was now working every day at the library or at home. Last night he had stayed up too late drinking beer with Mandeville Lee.

"Oh, yes, Lee. The sporting gent in English boots. Your landlord. Drives a red car with the top down. And have they found your car? Have they caught the bandit?"

They were working on it, Dan said, so far without result. He began to tell O'Keefe about the Western Academy of Arts and Crafts. "When Lee found out that I was once a writer of pulp fiction, he offered me a place on his staff. Pulp fiction is one of the arts he wants to push."

O'Keefe grinned broadly and said that he had never heard of Dan's career in pulp fiction. What sort, detective, Martian, or western? Dan said that they had all been westerns, with an occasional touch of detecting, when the hero had to discover the hidden grazing-land to which the rustlers had driven the cattle.

"Tell me more," cried O'Keefe. "No synopses, please. I demand particulars, and the more particular the better. You remember Blake's views. To generalize was idiocy, he said. To particularize—ah, Sherwood—Blake was right. To particularize is the alone distinction of merit."

"Well, then," Dan said. "The first particular would be Mr. Demarest Palley, who looked like a Methodist minister but made enormous amounts of money in publishing. He was the father of one of my classmates, a tall, gangly kid named Pal Palley, and he came driving up there one week-end in a luxurious sand-colored Cadillac."

"Driving up where?"

"Amherst," said Dan. "It was in the winter of my sophomore year. Pal had told his father that I was a natural-born writer because he had seen a story I did in our literary journal."

"What journal?" O'Keefe asked, grinning, the tufts on his eyebrows wagging. "Remember Blake."

"It was called the *Lord Jeffrey Spectator*," Dan said. "It was printed on newsprint, and it ran for three issues. The story Pal had admired so much was a third-rate imitation of one by

Nicholas Kemp—the one in *Pieces of Eight* about the finding of the drowned man. Pal didn't know that."

"Didn't know what?"

"I mean that it was an imitation of Kemp. Rather slavish, though not a plagiarism. Pal never read much beyond his assignments. Trying to keep up with those threw him into a terrible sweat."

O'Keefe grimaced, showing his stained old teeth. "Are they still with us?" he asked, with a trace of bitterness. "The non-readers and the loafers and the fast talkers who generalize to conceal their ignorance?"

"They're perennials," Dan said. "Pal had been raised on pulp fiction, and he avidly read whatever his father sent him, with his feet on top of the fraternity radio, which he had turned up full blast. Eating chocolate bars and throwing the wrappers vaguely towards the fireplace."

O'Keefe extracted an immaculate handkerchief from his breast pocket and began to polish his glasses. "I weep for all such," he said, grandiloquently, "but most for Polyhymnia, the ruptured muse."

"Demarest Palley, the father in the Cadillac, owned an outfit called the Golden West Library. He took us to dinner at the Inn, and spent most of the time, egged on by his son, in trying to persuade me to write a western. It was flattering for a sophomore who had never been west of Schenectady."

"So you became a hack in his stable?"

"In a nutshell, yes I did. Or maybe nuthouse is the better word. The Golden West Library must have been a nuthouse to take what I sent in. My twenty thousand words had been blown up to thirty thousand, and the book I had sent in under the title of *The Buffalo Drum* came out a few months later as

The Lonesome Belle of Pecos. I hardly recognized it. The opening was different, the conclusion was completely changed, and the whole interior had been, you might say, redecorated. Jazzed up. That was the first I heard of Squirrel Burrell."

"Particulars," said Axel O'Keefe.

"Squirrel was Demarest Palley's rewrite man. The true begetter of the Golden West Library. The Squirrel not only rewrote; he invented in the spirit of the story, made huge block interpolations, added whole chapters. He called it *sharpening*. Mr. Palley thought of him as a plot-builder. If any author in the stable was poor at design but could spin a cobweb when you gave him a suitable framework, then the Squirrel got to work."

"Details," said O'Keefe.

"The details of the plots came from a library of genuine classics," Dan said. "All along one wall of his office were copies of Loeb Library translations, cheap editions of Shakespeare and Cervantes, Dickens and Thackeray. The Decameron. The Arabian Nights. The whole range from Homer to Sherlock Holmes. Whenever the Squirrel wasn't sweating at his typewriter rewriting someone else, he would go poking and peering among his own books, looking for plots. When he found a good possibility, he would sum it up in a few paragraphs, invent a new setting, rename the chief characters, and file the page in an old, orange-colored cabinet. Then when Mr. Palley had corralled a new writer, the Squirrel could feed him from this silage-bin."

"Hence the Squirrel," O'Keefe said, with his histrionic laugh. "The hollow tree filled with the nuts and fruits of industry."

"I'm not sure," Dan said. "It was possibly that, or possibly a feature of his dentition. His incisors were long and narrow. Not exactly squirrel teeth, but enough like them so that he had gnawed his way through all the Confessions from St. Augustine to Cellini and on up to Rousseau. The Squirrel's specialty was the insertion of lascivious passages—"

"All publishers must employ him," O'Keefe said.

"He's dead now. Him and his head for business, which he frankly called monkey-business. You'd see him in his cubicle, lined with books to the ceiling, smoking away at a corncob. Said it was made from the corncob in Faulkner's *Sanctuary*. Once he set his lap afire. He was working on a story about a detective who had cornered a beautiful murderess in a Las Vegas motel."

"Had her dead to rights," said O'Keefe, laughing.

"Dead is right," Dan said. "He is sitting in a chair, holding a revolver he has just wrested from her. Outside there is a red and blue neon light, flashing through the window. I could quote it once—all pure Squirrel Burrell. 'In the perfumed darkness she made a few rustling motions. When she turned toward him, the colored lights threw their magic over her perfect and pear-shaped breasts as with a gesture of abandon she moved—' "

"St. Agnes Eve in Las Vegas," roared O'Keefe, wiping his eyes.

"That was it," Dan said. "Then the detective holds the revolver in both hands and shoots her between the third and fourth ribs."

"Virtue won," said O'Keefe with disappointment.

"House rule for the Golden West Library," Dan said. "Burrell invented a term for the other force. The Chthonic Undercurrent."

"And what is that?"

"It's a subterranean river of dirt and scum—the stream of sewage that flows through men's minds from generation to generation. The Squirrel had a rhyme he had found blowing around the streets of New York. He said it was Exhibit X of the Chthonic Undercurrent. Here, lend me the margin of your newspaper. I have to reconstruct it. The first word in each line has to be just right."

Dan worked quickly with his pencil. "This is roughly it," he said, after a minute or two:

> "When you and I are far apart,
> Can sorrow mend my broken heart?
> I love you, darling, yes I do.
> Sleep is sweet when I think of you.
> All you are is a blooming rose.
> Night is here so I must close.
> With care read the first word of every line.
> You will there a question find."

O'Keefe scanned the scribbled lines. "Ah, God," he said. "But what's the Chthonic Undercurrent?"

"This is part of it," Dan said. "It fascinated the Squirrel. How many parents find this sort of thing under their teen-aged daughters' pillows? The Squirrel said that such verses used to be passed around in Fifth Century Athens—from old men to boys. Others like it were carved on the walls of Pompeii. It was more than the puppy-doggerel of the juvenile experimentalist, he said. It was the Chthonic Undercurrent, Tenth Grade level, subhistorical, without beginning or end."

"Well," said O'Keefe, "your man was either crazy or correct. From one point of view it's harmless enough. But on second glance it leads us into the dope-dens and the bawdy houses; the Black Massers and the Klansmen. Even the barracks of Buchenwald. Is this remarkable firm still in business?"

"Oh, yes. The Golden West Library marches on."

"How many of these did you write?"

"Ground out, you mean?" said Dan. "Five in all, under the name of Standish Miles. I wrote them clean, the Squirrel jazzed them up. They got around, too. Mandeville Lee read one of them on the transport going to France."

The light from the window glistened on the gold tooth of the Mexican waitress. Soundlessly, in the rope-soled shoes, she had come to stand beside O'Keefe. He was wanted on the telephone. He returned in an obvious fluster. His horn-like eyebrows quivered.

"Forgive me, Sherwood," he said. "Let's talk another day. My wife has just reminded me that we are already late for someone's lunch." He moved off in his determined way, waving once over his shoulder.

Dan held up the rumpled newspaper. "You forgot this."

"Through with it," O'Keefe said, pausing among the white-topped tables. "You keep it, Sherwood. Read all about the Veep and his bride."

Dan ordered another coffee and read about the marriage of Alben Barkley to the handsome widow in St. Louis. Truman was pleased. The Democrats and the Republicans were pleased. Bipartisan sweetness and light pervaded the paper. He turned the page, skimming the lesser headlines inside. One of them caught his eye.

WOMAN FOUND SLAIN

QUEMADO, N.M., Nov. 19 (AP)—The thinly clad body of a young woman was found near here in the New Mexico desert late yesterday afternoon a few rods off Highway 60. According to I. F. Craney, medical examiner, the woman had been murdered, probably by strangling, four to six weeks ago. The victim wore a pink sweater, brown check slacks, and white pumps. Uprooted sagebrush had been used to partly conceal the corpse, and it is thought the intent may have been to dispose of the body by burning. No marks of a struggle were visible. "She may have been killed someplace else and her body dumped in this spot," Dr. Craney was quoted as saying. The region is lonesome and desolate.

Discovery was made by E. K. Slattery, a truck-driver for a Kansas City concern. Mr. Slattery had stepped into the sagebrush to relieve himself when his eye caught sight of the woman's clothing. He reported his find to Bert Foscolo, who operates the Desert Rest Bar and Grill a half mile east of the spot. Mr. Foscolo was questioned and released. A check of missing persons is taking place.

CHAPTER SIX

IN THE packet labeled BIOGRAPHY he read through the first card, the product of his early weeks of fact-finding. It was already dog-eared from multiple re-readings. It said that Nicholas (Young) Kemp had been born 10 August, 1897, at Boise, Idaho. His father, Harold Kemp, had come from a dot on the Idaho map called New Meadows. Born 1867; in business as butcher-storekeeper in Boise from 1892 until his death in 1916. Nicholas's mother, Josephine Murdock Kemp, was born in Ogden, Utah, 19 October, 1870, of Mormon ancestry. Around Boise she had had some local fame as a writer of tolerable "western" verse. Unlike her husband, she had been to college, class of 1891 at the University. She married Harold Kemp on 6 October, 1896, in the First Presbyterian Church of Boise. And why had she done it? You did not know. It was merely a fact. She had died at last in the same town, aged fifty-six, in 1926. From 1920 until her death she had worked in the Public Library. She had done a noble job in acquiring and arranging the books. Her death was signalized by a three-inch obituary notice in the Boise paper.

Dan flipped the card over, reading on. The Kemps had issue, besides son Nicholas, of one daughter Mellissa, born 12

November, 1899. Educated, like Nicholas, in the public schools of Boise. Married in 1919 to one Winship Moore, dentist, trained God knows where, but in practice in Salt Lake City, Utah, since 1919. By whom no children.

And what if I write to you, Mellissa? thought Dan. With your name like honey and your dentist husband and your thirty childless years in Salt Lake City. Will you tell me about your famous brother and your growing-up in Boise? Will you give me access to the letters Nickie wrote home from France? Probably not. Do letters exist, or were they lost when you got married and left Boise? Perhaps Nickie did not write home after all. And what would you say of your father's drinking? What about that barrel in the back yard, and your father's beating of poor Nickie with the razor-strop? Mellissa, with your name like honey and your tooth-drilling spouse, I will bet you won't reply to my intrusive queries.

He withdrew the next card from the black filing-box. NICH-OLAS KEMP, it was headed. BIRTH AND PARENTAGE: RUMORS.

Character of Harold Kemp (Source: photostat of typed letter to Alexander Stone, Esq., from Mr. Seymour Hassett of the law firm of Iseman, Hassett, and Parker, 47 Wall Street, New York City.) "Dear Sandy: Yours of the 11th to hand. I send you this reply for what it may be worth. My family used to buy meats and groceries at Harold Kemp's store in Boise during most of my boyhood. Sometime around 1912-1913 (I can't be sure of the date) I recall my mother's saying to father that she was not going to trade with Harold Kemp any more because he was overcharging her and sending poor quality meat. There was also a persistent rumor that Harold was hitting the bottle. I judge the rumor was not wrong. I can testify, again for what it's worth, on the basis of one personal experience. I had a red bicycle, from which I used to deliver morning papers around our neighborhood. This must have been about 1914 or so, and

I saw a man lying on the grass in the front yard of the Kemp house, which was a small, brown-shingled bungalow on one of the side streets in the eastern end of town. When I got up closer, I saw that he had vomited on the lawn and on his clothes and I think he must have passed out there sometime in the night. I rang the front door-bell and his wife, who used to write poetry, I believe, came to the door in an old bathrobe and curlers on her hair. She didn't know he was out there, but she went right out in her bare feet and shook him by the shoulder. He groaned but didn't come to, so I had to help her drag Mr. Kemp to the front porch. It was early in the morning and she gave me 25¢ not to tell anyone."

Harold, thought Dan. Harold Kemp. Was it whiskey or wormwood you drank, and why? A night out with the boys, or some silent snorts in the back room of the store whose sign said *H. W. KEMP   FRESH MEATS AND GROCERIES*? Or did you run with a fancy lady, Harold Wormwood Kemp, while your poetess wife sat in her curlers and bathrobe, dropping tears on the five-cent scratch-pad where her latest lyric was taking whatever form it was to attain? And why? Did you start hitting that bottle about the time your son Nicholas ran away to Canada? The times seem to check, at any rate, for here is this article by Robert M. Rose (*Cosmopolitan,* December, 1929) which dates the runaway in the summer of 1914 when Nicholas was 17 and had just finished high school in Boise.

Dan took down the big bound volume from the shelf of his carrel and turned to the article, which was partly a review of *The Kingdoms of the North.* Mr. R. M. Rose, it was clear, had lately encountered some of the writings of Dr. Freud. The gimmick, rather speculatively established, was the Oedipus complex, and Mr. Rose was out to trace the murder-drives in

Kemp's novel to an early father-son conflict. He described a
large barrel or hogshead, held in place on its side by pipes
driven into the ground, and equipped with straps like a
pillory, where the Kemp neighbors used to watch furtively
as his father bound Nicholas down before flogging him un-
mercifully with a razor-strop. Mr. Rose told a story by one of
the neighbors, who insisted on remaining anonymous, to the
effect that the boy smashed this barrel, dousing it liberally
with kerosene and then making a bonfire of the pieces sometime in July, 1914, before he ran off to the woods. Nick of
the Woods, thought Dan. How do you establish the truth of
this story? And who the hell is Robert M. Rose?

The facts about Kemp's education were sparse but probably
right. Beside certain other large patches of time you could
only write the marginal comment, TERRITORY UNKNOWN. Nicholas attended the public schools of Boise from 1901–1911. He
entered high school with the Class of 1914. Was it then or
later that he took the girl named Waterhouse to the movies?
Dan reached for the old bound volume of the *Literary Digest*.
On 6 April, 1926, they printed an article by Miss or Mrs.
Cecilia Waterhouse called "I Knew Him When." She said that
Nicholas was a college boy that night they went to the picture
show and stopped for a soda on the way home. Much of what
she said was gush. She had once had a date with the author
of *The Hinges of Hell* and she would like history to record
the fact. She thought *The Hinges of Hell* was a great book.
She "hazarded the guess" that Nicholas inherited his literary
talents from his mother, Gertrude Kemp, the well-known
Nebraska poetess. Ah, Miss Waterhouse, we have you there.
She was neither named Gertrude nor was she from Nebraska.

The first interlude in Nicholas's education came in the

summer of 1914, when he ran off to Canada, working as a lumberjack in British Columbia, in the region of Kamloops and Stump Lake, and later in the Douglas fir forests in the Willamette region of Oregon. After thirteen or so months of this, having absorbed the background later to be used in *The Kingdoms of the North*, he turned up in St. Paul, a long stone's throw from the University of Minnesota to which he wangled admission, Class of 1919. Straight C record, complete through sophomore year.

Interlude the second was longer and rougher. Withdrawing from Minnesota in good standing, he enlisted in the Marine Corps, finished his overseas training at Quantico, and went off, though he did not know it yet, to lose that left arm in the battle of Belleau Wood. Here the material became suddenly voluminous. The novel, of course. Sandy Stone's secret diary. And for the military background, Catlin's book, *With The Help of God and a Few Marines*.

The third of the educational interludes was also rough. But here you ran into problems. All that was absolutely established was that in August, 1919, Kemp made a voyage aboard a tramp steamer from some part of the Gulf Coast, with various ports of call on both the Atlantic and Pacific coasts of South America, and a stormy rounding of Cape Horn. In mid-September he had suddenly appeared in San Francisco. And that was what you really knew. Of course again there was a novel. But how much of *The Straits of Magellan* was fact, as, for example, a great part of *The Hinges of Hell* was demonstrable fact? How did the one-armed veteran Kemp get a job on a tramp steamer? Did he jump ship at San Francisco, or was that the final port of call?

One thing was clear. Kemp really wanted a formal education to go along with the informal instruction in soldiering,
sailoring, and lumber-jacking. He transferred credits from
Minnesota and entered the University of California at Berkeley with some kind of advanced sophomore standing, Class of
1923. He took all the English courses in the catalogue, it
seemed, including one (Dan had underscored the fact in red
pencil) in the Bible as literature. His most devoted teacher
there was Beryl Curtis, later his first wife. Already thirty years
old, Beryl was a native of New York City and had come out to
Berkeley with a Columbia M.A. about 1915.

I could make up a good picture there, Dan thought. The
thirty-year-old schoolmarm, in white collar and cuffs and New
York accent, probably dark-haired and with skirts the length
they wore them then, smelling ever so faintly of chalkdust and
eau de cologne. And the tough, rumple-haired young ex-
Marine, left arm gone at the shoulder, hard-bitten and sun-
tanned from the long sea voyage. He sits in the classroom,
looking too big for the chair, and takes notes. He winks at
Beryl Curtis. He is twenty-three. She blushes and stumbles in
the lecture she is making. Soon she is in love with him.

All right, he thought. So much for Fancy. And what about
Truth, that lady in the speckled veil? How do you get at the
truth about Kemp, about his father and mother, his girls and
his money, his books and his wounds? By facts and dates and
visual statistics, yes. These are the tiny trail of star-shaped
blood-drops he leaves behind him as he goes. It is so with him
as with the rest of us. The spoor. The footprints slowly dis-
solving in the drizzle of time, the beaten grass where the
struggle was, the telltale vomit on the morning lawn, the

patches of fur where we took our pleasure, scratching our backs against the rough bark of trees. The conquerors and the criminals; the obscure butchers and the genteel writers of lyrics. Yes, the writers.

And you, why are you so reluctant to probe into the biography of this writer named Kemp? You know that sooner or later you must find out the facts, work out the chronologies and the itineraries, uncover the hidden motivations, the cowardly acts, the cruelties done or endured. Yet you veer off. Why?

Could it be, he thought, a simple act of self-defence? Aren't you projecting yourself into Kemp's position? Aren't there facts—whole sequences of action—in your own life as in his, that you do not want to reveal or to have revealed by someone else: something to hide, something to keep hidden? Like the fact of Jessica Stone, the wife of your best friend? To take a recent example. A recent and significant example. Is it this that explains your reluctance to explore the pits as well as the peaks in Kemp's career?

He found that he did not wish to answer the question. Once more the fingers of gloom began to pick and pluck at the corners of his memory. He stretched the thick elastic band around the biographical cards, as if around the gathered bones of Nicholas Kemp, dropping the bundle into the coffin-like black filing-box. Sometime soon it would have to be done. But not now, he told himself. Not necessarily now.

*　*　*　*　*

Coming round the corner into the bright reading-room, Dan nearly collided with Henry, slender and efficient with the row of pencils in his breast pocket.

"Just coming to find you," Henry said, puffing slightly. "There's a phone call for you. Long distance. You can take it in my office."

The Phoenix operator was waiting. "Here's your party," she said. It was a man with a voice like pebbles in a bucket.

"Dr. Daniel Sherwood? Right. I'm calling for Lieutenant Casper. I believe you talked to him earlier. Arizona Highway Patrol."

"Right," said Dan.

"And you are the owner of the 1947 Ford sedan with the Jersey plates LO-373?"

"That's correct. Or I was the owner once."

"Dr. Sherwood, we have located your car in the town of Hope."

"Hope? Where is Hope?"

"Actually the car was found near Vicksburg, three miles from Hope."

"So he took it back east?"

"I beg pardon?"

"I say he took it back east?"

"I don't get you. The car was found with two flat tires late yesterday afternoon up around Hope on the road to Blythe. Close to Vicksburg, Arizona."

"Hope. Blythe. Phoenix."

"I beg pardon?"

"Excuse me. I meant I was very glad you've found the car. What shape is it in?"

"I said it has two flat tires. Dusty and dirty. Not more than a spoonful of gas in the tank. But when we gassed her up she ran."

"What about the contents of the car?"

"She was pretty well cleaned out. Now, let's see. I have a list of stuff you gave us. Suitcase and typewriter in the back seat. Another suitcase and raincoat in the trunk. No sign of these."

"And a big cardboard carton," Dan said. "Wasn't that on the list?"

"Cardboard carton," the pebble-voiced man said. "Yes."

"Did you find that?"

"No, I meant it was on your list. No sign of the carton. Pretty well cleaned out, like I said."

"And that's all? Did you happen to check under the front seat?"

"Front seat? I don't know. Hold on, I will check. Hey, Eddie. Eddie, did you check under the front seat of that Ford?"

Dan could hear Eddie's voice in the background. Then Pebbles: "He thinks so, yes. The car was checked out completely. It was empty. The criminal either threw the stuff away or pawned it or sold it. We have men checking the likely places in Phoenix, but chances are he just heaved the stuff out somewhere. He left his signature, though."

"Signature?"

"Prints. Finger-prints. This guy remembers to wipe off most places on the car, but he forgets the chrome buttons on the radio. Now we know who he is. We don't know *where* he is, but we know *who* he is. Feller by the name of Harry Sachs. Some calls him Buddy. One of these bush-league bruisers. He is wanted for a filling-station stick-up in Amarillo. Armed robbery. Pistol-whipped the old man at the filling-station when he started arguing. Then we may have a murder rap. Little girl from Clovis. Carhop girl name of Flagg, found her dead out in the desert. Her ma is a waitress herself down in the town. The girl wanted to go to Hollywood, get a job there. Girl had threatened to go off. She was seen with a guy that resembles Harry Sachs. So we may have three to hang on him. Now about your car—"

"Excuse me, has this Sax—how do you spell his name?"

"Sachs. S-A-C-H-S—Sachs."

"Does he have any previous record?"

"Oh, yes. Like they all do. Stolen cars, atrocious assault, all like that. He may be an army deserter. We alerted the Army, CI Branch. Might be they got something on him, too. Though, like I say, this boy is still at large."

"He was no boy," said Dan.

"Just a term we use, Dr. Sherwood. Now, about your car. We got a man coming down your way the next couple of days. How about we get the flats fixed, have them bill you down there, and our man can drop off the car wherever you say?"

"That's great," Dan said. "I certainly owe you men a lot."

"Think nothing of it," the pebble-voiced man said. "Glad to be of service. Now where should he drop off the car?"

"What about the Pioneer Hotel?"

"Pioneer, right. I got it down here. He'll give you a call when he leaves. If you ain't there he'll leave the message. He meets you in the lobby of the Pioneer Hotel, right?"

"Right," said Dan. "And thanks."

He replaced the receiver, conscious at once of gain and loss. Car returnable but empty. Keats and Kemp gone, cleaned out, dumped or burned. And Sachs still at large—shoulder-holster, dirty bandanna, baby-teeth, and stench. He had come like a toad up out of the sewer that is under us everywhere. Under our feet when we walk the floors, under the grass. Under the world, thought Dan, while his spirits sank lower and he sat staring at the telephone and the curling smoke from his forgotten cigarette in the ashtray on Henry's desk.

CHAPTER SEVEN

MANDEVILLE LEE raced the motor of the red car, pulled on his gauntlet gloves, and said that Dan ought to change his mind about joining the faculty of the Western Academy of Arts and Crafts. With Dan there, and a little organization, plus the recruitment of local talent, they would soon be running a cultural goldmine.

Out around the ragged edges of Tucson you could pick up painters and ceramics people at a dime a dozen. Most of them were half-starved anyway, and though they professed to be rebels against middle-class habits there was one middle-class habit they would all go for if they had the chance and that was three squares a day. Lee said that Chita had a Mexican Indian cousin who worked in some damn sweatshop over in Phoenix making Indian silver jewelry for a cigar-smoking sheeney from New York, and this brave would like nothing better than the chance to join the craft-faculty and to give lessons in jewelry-making.

He swished the car around the corners fast but never dangerously and went on to say that he could get himself any number of those old Papago squaws, who were mostly stupid but could make rugs with their eyes shut. He would set them up some looms and frames and dye-pots or whatever the hell it was they needed, and the Academy could offer courses in weaving and rugmaking. Getting a student body would be about as much trouble as spitting into the Grand Canyon of the Colorado, what with all the winter visitors that were flock- to Arizona these days. This would include all the sun-struck dudes at the new swimming-pool ranches, and the middle-aged wives on a reducing holiday while their husbands slaved back east, and all the old biddies who wanted to learn how to mold some goddam ashtrays and glaze them and stick them in the ceramic furnaces as Christmas presents for their long-suffering in-laws in Ohio or Michigan or Florida, to say nothing of the malcontented change-of-life women who had got tired of run- ning the Ladies' Aid and the Garden Clubs of Buffalo or Rochester or Mamaroneck and dreamed of having a romance with a sun-bronzed cowpoke who could wrassle yearling calves. And then there were the juicier dames, recent divorcées living off the fat of alimony settlements, diddling around out here with plenty of time on their wicked little bejewelled hands and Adventure with a capital A in their doggy little brains. Mandeville Lee said that there was no question in his mind but what the Western Academy of Arts and Crafts could be rolling in dough within six months' time.

The tires of the red sports car crunched on the gravel drive- way. A broken neon sign at the entrance said that this was— or had been—the El Dorado Motor Court, recommended by Duncan Hines. The adobe buildings looked shabby in the fading purple light. Several dry date-palms rustled in the air- stream that was beginning to move across the desert off the northern mountains now that the sun had set. In the gloam- ing Dan could see that a battered pick-up truck and a white

motor scooter were parked side by side at the bottom of the
U the buildings made. From one of the units came a muffled
sound of hammering.

Mandeville Lee said that this was the Academy, or would
be. He had a carpenter working nights now, after his regular
job was over, ripping out some of the bathrooms to make
more studio space.

"That's his pick-up truck but who the hell owns the
scooter?" said Lee. "He'd better not be jellyrolling on my
time." He swung his long legs out of the car and disappeared
quickly in the direction of the hammering.

Dan sat still in the bucket seat of the car. The Academy did
not much resemble an educational institution. He raised his
eyes beyond the rusty buildings to the fiery sunset and the
black silhouettes of the dry peaks far off to the west. Just as
he looked down again, Lee's tall figure reappeared, accom-
panied now by a girl in gray slacks and gray sweater. She
stood facing Lee, a yard or so away, looking small and compact beside his rangy height. Lee talked with some animation,
pointing around the court. Presently the girl started the
motor scooter and rode it across the courtyard. She did not
look at Dan as she passed. He had a fleeting impression of
neatness, compactness, smooth dusky hair, and lipstick.

Lee went inside again. The evening wind raised small
whirlpools in the dust. The sound of hammering did not
resume. Dan swung out of the car and sauntered in the gathering darkness under the shallow colonnade. He had com-
pleted two circuits when Lee reappeared, walking quickly
toward the car. This damned carpenter was not moving fast
enough, he said. Get a crew in there and fix the place up and
you could have the Academy rolling by the first of the year.

A lot of people came out after Christmas, spoiling for amusement and instruction. The pickings should be good. Very, very good. He raced the motor of the car and pulled on his gauntlets.

"Did you see that girl?" he said. "Smart girl. She can do me some real good. Writes for the papers. Cultural features."

"What's a cultural feature?"

"She wants to do a piece on the Academy," Lee said. "I told her to hold off awhile. Couple of months, maybe less, we can use some publicity." He swung the nose of the car around the corner into the Speedway. For the next few minutes he drove silently, threading through the traffic. The hashhouses and the gaudier drive-ins were thick with cars. A policeman with an electric torch was beckoning a line of cars into the entrance of an outdoor movie. The huge oblong of its screen bulked darkly against the southern sky.

"I think we have got ourselves a good little idea there," Lee said musingly.

"What's the idea?"

"The girl," Lee said. "Public relations job. Plug the Academy in all the papers, coast to coast. Did you see that cute little rump of hers, Danny?"

"She was sitting on it when she went past me."

"Well, take my word for it, Dan, this girl is built. Fore and aft. Traveling around, placing publicity hand-outs, that is going to do no harm. Absolutely no harm."

"You talk as if she's already yours."

Lee glanced over at Dan, closing his nearer eye in an elaborate wink. "It won't be long," he said complacently. "How about some beer, Danny? Wet the old desert whistle. Chew the fat awhile."

Dan hesitated, already sick of this tall glamour-boy with his gauntlet gloves and the riding-boots, his smug self-confidence, and that flaunted sexuality, like a male peacock on parade. He was going to demur, say that he had to work, but Lee was already turning off the Speedway into the arc-lighted parking-lot of the Purple Heart Bar and Grill.

"This guy says he's a war veteran," Lee said. "I'll patronize any war veteran that took his screwing along with the rest of us as long as he don't serve poison." He led the way through a green fog of neon lights, jerking a careless thumb at a placard in the front window:

TUESDAY NITE IS POULTRY NITE
Bring your girl around for a
FREE GOOSE

"Some joker," said Mandeville Lee. He slid into one side of a booth and imperiously summoned the nearest waitress. "Couple of beers," he said. When she brought them, Lee gulped half of his quickly. "Happy days," he said.

A short jug-eared man with a nose like an inverted spoon came along the row of booths. Thin strands of hair were raked across the top of his head, and large pouches supported his small dark eyes. "Everything gall right?" he asked. When they nodded he smiled paternally and moved along to the next booth, leaving in his wake the acrid smell of his cheroot.

Lee waited until he had disappeared. "If that guy won the Purple Heart," he said, "I am Princess Elizabeth. Can you see that character lined up at a reception center?"

"We had a lot like him," Dan said.

"That character learned his gunnery in a back room in

Cicero," Lee said. "But it was no worse than the place where I learned gunnery."

He began to tell Dan about the hot, flat reception center where they had dumped him down in the summer of forty-two. The first week was like Saturday night in a Turkish bath. Half the time they had you stripped to the buff and lined up for some stupid reason or other, and if those flat-chested sway-backs were soldiers it was a wonder the army could fight its way out of an orange-crate. He said they didn't give a damn how they stuck you with needles, and it was a big laugh how they separated the men from the flits. He imitated the bored medic asking the boys if they liked girls, and slammed his palm down on the table of the booth to show how they rubber-stamped your papers to prove that you were a red-blooded, recoil-operated, All-American, ball-bearing mechanism worthy of a spot in the army.

Dan had been in the army four or five months when the news of Pearl Harbor came through. That Sunday, with a cold wind blowing through the late sunlight, his company was swarmed all over one of those hip-roofed barracks, washing windows on a disciplinary detail. The captain lined them up and spoke quietly. Now they would settle down to the busi-ness they had come for. Soon they would be moving out. They would work hard to get in shape for whatever lay ahead.

Mandeville Lee said that this was the usual horse-shit and if he had known ahead of time what lay ahead when they marched onto that lousy transport, he would have gone AWOL in thirty seconds flat. He described the jerry-built bunks in the hold where they crammed you so you couldn't turn over without scraping against the bed above. He had slipped one of his cell-mates a five-spot to get a top bunk where you were out of range of the All-American puke-artists who plastered the decks all the way across.

He ordered two more beers, waving Dan's money aside munificently, and told about the convoy's arrival at the French port. The boys were kept hanging around half a day aboard that stinking tub, and just to show you what bastards they were, he told how they had played the trick on the French sea-gulls. They took these chunks of doughy bread, wrapped them around old safety razor blades, and threw them into the harbor. The boys would laugh to beat hell when the gulls swallowed the bread and cut their throats from the inside.

By the middle of the third beer, Dan found himself telling Lee the story about Irsch. His job then had been Civil Affairs Officer. He remembered the return to Europe after O.C.S., with the fresh-cut orders in his 201 file, the rough and gloomy winter crossing in the blacked-out convoy, and the gray rain of February all through France. With Otto driving they had come at last to the line of Kraut fortifications along the Moselle and the Saar. The days now were steadily cold, the spirits low, and he remembered sharply all the hacking coughs each time the boys lined up for chow. When they had put up a bridge that the tanks could cross, rumbling heavily and consolingly over the planks, close above the black water flecked with ice-fragments, they took the town of Irsch.

"What's this civil affairs business?" asked Lee.

"We rounded up the civilians," Dan said. "Then we'd pack them into four or five houses in the middle of the village where we could lock them up and set a guard. Our job was to help the companies that had taken the town, counting noncombatants, slapping a curfew on them, and combing out deserters from the Wehrmacht."

"So what happened in Irsch?"

"I was asleep in that house we had," Dan said. "Otto woke me. He said two G.I.s wanted to see me. Had to check something with the lieutenant. I went out into the musty-smelling front hall and they were standing there in the lantern-light. They said they were guarding the civilians. There was an old woman in one of the houses that was sick and moaning all the time and raising hell so the others were milling around and couldn't sleep. They wanted to shoot her."

"Why the hell not?" said Mandeville Lee.

Dan felt his anger rising. "Why not? You should have seen this pair. One had a raw face like a side of beef and the other one looked like a rat. The beef was thick and stupid. The rat stood behind him, moving his thin eyebrows up and down. I told them to get the hell back there and guard the prisoners. I told them to leave the old woman alone."

"So they went back and shot her?"

"I don't know," Dan said sullenly. "It was the worst—"

"Listen, Danny, you ever see a tank flattening a dead G.I.? Or one of our noble group grinding a bayonet in a dying Kraut's belly? That's what they taught us, boy."

"We didn't teach them to shoot sick old women in the towns we took in winter," Dan said, his voice rising.

Lee sat with the empty beer-glass before him on the table. He did not say anything.

"We're never far from it, anyway," Dan said. "The beef-face and the rat-face. It keeps bleeding up out of the throats of those French sea-gulls. It opens up under us like earthquake cracks in the ground. Like toads out of the drains. It stinks to hell, like that front hall in Irsch."

"You got it bad, Dan," Lee said quietly. "How about another beer?"

CHAPTER EIGHT

OUT OF the midst of one nightmare he awoke into another. Two thousand miles away and ago—and how many years? Lying restive and taut, he counted them out with his fingers on the moonlit surface of the blanket. Three years, six months, and some odd days. Call it an even three and a half years, and it was still as sharp in his memory as the musty hall in Irsch.

The worst of it was the sand in the sockets of her eyes.

Yet that day had begun like any other, except that it dawned so darkly. A cold shower of rain, moving up from Long Island, obscured the rising sun. It pock-marked as with acid the flat, metallic waters of the Sound before it came to beat in flurries on the weathered shingles of Sandy's great gray house where it stood in the park-like acreage of green lawns, with the view from the wide front windows down to the sullen lapping waters at the edge of the tide.

Far out, the Sound billowed massively, but there were neither high waves nor heavy wind: only the majestic, north-westward movement of the rain-clouds; the roaring five-min-ute showers; the rush and gurgle of the water in the eaves-troughs, the clipped grass turning the color of emeralds in that strange half-light. And afterwards the slow drip of moisture from the shrubs and trees.

When he awakened to the roar of the rain, she had already left his side, soundlessly as always. Where was there ever so quiet a girl? he thought. And saw again in his mind's eye the large bedroom with the wide spool-bed and the Italian armoire by the windows where now the rain was beating. While sleep cleared from his head, he lay staring at the inadvertent design the cracks made in the ceiling, like the map of a newly discovered country drawn from hearsay by an indifferent cartographer. Then he rolled out of the wide bed, glanced from the rain-freckled window across the now-puddled green lawn, brushed his teeth and shaved quickly at the small sink in the corner behind the Chinese screen, pulled on the green sweater and trousers, and went down to breakfast.

She had eaten already, already disappeared somewhere, leaving the neatly folded morning paper beside his place. Though he cocked an ear, he could not hear her voice anywhere in the house. Drinking the orange juice, he strolled to the French windows that gave upon the Sound. Through the gray haze of the rain, he saw the boat, sails neatly furled, riding at anchor thirty yards offshore. In spite of the rain, she might have been out there, in slicker and sou'wester, throwing sticks for Sandy's old black Labrador retriever. But she was nowhere in sight, and he turned back to the coffee, set out on the sideboard with a candle under it. He was just buttering a slice of toast when Sandy came down, neat as always, his black hair crisp and wet from combing, his spectacles clean and shining, his eyes still puffy from sleep.

"Dan," he said, with the familiar rising inflection, "how goes it? This shower will be good for the grass."

"The paper says more rain and possibly some wind. Storm warnings out from Block Island to Cape Hatteras. They may know, or they may not."

"Then it will be a good day to spend in the city," Sandy said. "Where's my darling sister?"

"Nowhere in sight," Dan said. "She was up when the rain woke me, and she's had breakfast already. She has glanced at the paper, folded it neatly, and made herself scarce. What a girl! Was she always so neat?"

Sandy carried his orange juice to the window and glanced out. "We're too neat," he said. "An old family fetich. We were both raised to leave everything just as we found it. Nothing ever—ever—to be displaced. Never—ever—a loose end, whether it was a hangnail or a torn coatsleeve or a hole in the bottom of the skiff. That's where Cindy is right now, I will bet a dollar. Gone to see if she can get Arch to fix that skiff today. Sometimes I used to feel an adolescent urge to destroy. Dismantle something, wreak havoc. But it never worked. Right now I find myself sliding the ashtray on my office desk four inches eastward or westward, whatever the case may be, back to precisely the spot where it stood in my father's time. Cindy's the same way. Like a couple of old maids, the both of us."

Dan refilled his coffee cup at the sideboard and brought it back to the table. "I take exception to that," he said.

"Exception to what?"

"The old maid. I have done my best to see that Cindy will never be an old maid. Although of course she was never in any danger of that from the time—from the time she was born."

"Oh, you don't see her defects yet," said Sandy, owlishly. "You haven't been married long enough. A year from now you will stage a revolt from all that neatness. You'll dump pipe ashes or nice big fat cigar ashes on the rug in that Enfield apartment. You'll burn a black hole in the sofa. You'll scatter the Sunday papers all over the room, and dump cracker crumbs from your lap, and roar at Cindy when she shows up with the carpet sweeper."

"Not me," said Dan, grinning. "There's enough havoc. There'll always be more because there always is. But not caused by me or by Lucinda. Not that girl."

Mrs. Munch appeared soundlessly from the kitchen, nodded to their greetings, set Sandy's boiled eggs before him, and soundlessly disappeared.

"Even Mrs. Munch has the habit," Sandy said. "Two four-minute eggs for me every morning. Shells left in the kitchen to avoid debris. And if you go out there, no mess at all. Just the shining chrome and everything exactly where it belongs. Not for nothing has Mrs. Munch been with us these twenty years. My mother caught her young. Imbued her with the family fetich." He finished the eggs and folded his napkin neatly, smoothing it on the table with his hand. "Of course you can't tell what Mrs. Munch does at her daughter's place," he said. "With those three kids, all in diapers, the place could easily be a pigsty. Maybe it's Mrs. Munch's escape valve. Maybe she goes there to revel in disorder."

"I'm supposed to drop her off there this morning," Dan said. "What time is your train?"

"Nine forty-two," Sandy said. "Are you sure you don't mind taking me to the station? I could call a cab. I don't want to hold up the budding scholar."

"It's no holdup," Dan said. "I can be in New Haven in an hour."

"With me and Mrs. Munch gone, you'll be very snug to-night," Sandy said. "Ideal bride and groom situation."

"When are you going to propose to that beautiful blonde?" asked Dan.

The rain was stopping, and a thin ray of sunlight came through the wide front windows. Ignoring Dan's question, Sandy went once more to gaze out over the Sound. "You'd better tell your beautiful brunette to bail that sailboat," he said. "Look, the sun is coming out. The weather prophets once again confounded. Brightness falls from the air."

"You're a poet," Dan said.

"I'm quoting a poet," said Sandy, slowly. "But I can't for the life of me remember who. *Brightness falls from the air.* And what comes after that? And who wrote it? Do me a favor, Dan. Look it up in the library while you're there today. It's in Bartlett's. I'm sure it's in Bartlett's. And I'm sure to forget to look it up myself."

"You'll forget it because you'll be taking your beautiful blonde to dinner," said Dan.

He carried his cup and saucer to the kitchen. Mrs. Munch was hurriedly wiping the counters with a sponge. She did not know where Lucinda had gone. She did not even offer a speculation.

Dan's wife was still nowhere in sight by nine-fifteen when he backed the station-wagon out of the garage and drove it around to the narrow porte-cochere. Mrs. Munch was already waiting with a red net satchel. Sandy came down the steps carrying a brief-case. Dan went back into the house to write Cindy a note, saying that he would be home by six at the latest.

Mrs. Munch explained that she had left their dinner in the

refrigerator. She was still repeating the directions when she got out of the car at her daughter's house. The bungalow was set back from the street under dripping maples. In the small yard the grass was worn by children's feet.

Even with the occasional shreds of sunlight, it did not look like a promising day. The clouds lowered darkly and you could see that they were being pushed by a strong wind high up. Dan said that he could just as well drop Sandy at the New Haven station. Sandy searched his billfold for a time-table without finding one. He was sure the nine forty-two out of here was the better train. At the rural station the locomotive was just pulling a string of coaches into position beside the platform. When Dan stopped the car, a heavy shower suddenly began.

"You'll have to run for it."

"Don't forget my quotation," said Sandy.

"What was it again?"

"Brightness falls from the air. Sure to be in Bartlett's."

"It's sure as hell not in Connecticut today," said Dan. But Sandy was already dashing for the train, holding the brief-case over his head like an umbrella.

* * * * *

All that dark morning in the Yale Library Dan worked on Old English. The war-time training in German made it easier, and he had already finished the *Anglo-Saxon Chronicle,* the voyages of Ohtere and Wulfstan, Gregory's preface to the *Pastoral Care,* and some of the prose of Alfred the Great. The *Beowulf* was tougher going. You could always bone up on the paradigms, and Grimm's Law was at least theoretically rational. But Dan had found no way to handle the *Beowulf* except word by word and line by line. The pages of the glossary at the back of the book were darkening daily from continuing contact with his searching fingers. Still it was worth it. Webb had explained that incoming graduate students at Enfield could attempt—*attempt* was the official word—an examination in Old English at entrance. It was an experimental arrangement, designed for veterans like Dan who were good at languages and who had some time on their hands between coming out of the armed services and entering the graduate school.

"Strictly an experiment," Webb had explained during the interview. "Most of you veterans are a little older than average. If you can get the Old English out of the way in September, it will earn you some credits and save you time in getting the doctorate." Webb had handed him a typed list of books to be read in preparation. For the past month, he had been working his way through it.

When he looked up again towards noon, the rain was still falling intermittently and the wind appeared to be freshening. Cold drops splattered on the library panes, and he pictured all the small-boat owners from Block Island to Cape Hatteras battening down the hatches. It was clearly no day for Arch to repair the hole in the bottom of the skiff unless he and Cindy had hitched Arch's jeep to the painter and hauled it into the cave of the old-fashioned garage to be worked on out of the weather. I wonder where she had got to this morning, he thought. She certainly disappeared fast, that neat quiet girl with the arching black eyebrows and the pensive mouth. She might have gone over to Laird's as she sometimes did to get the pick of the day's vegetables. Or taken one of her solitary walks along the shore. He left the window and went back to the long table where he had spread his dry books.

We could have met in plenty of other places, he thought. It might have been at an Amherst houseparty, or that time when the bunch of us went up to crash the Dartmouth Winter Carnival and slept—when we slept at all—in the frigid attic room of the C. & G. house, with the snow coming through the north window onto the nearest of the cots. Cindy would have made a good Carnival queen, in parka and ski-boots, and the dark hair drawn smoothly over her ears. Or we could have met at one of those pop concerts on the Charles River Esplanade, with the traffic roaring past and all the people sitting on blankets or in aluminum deck-chairs facing the lighted shell where the trombones glittered and the fiddlers sawed mightily in unison, and the tympanist waited as they all must do until his moment came for the roll of drums, the clash of cymbals, or that one triumphant *ting* on the triangle.

But it was not in any of those places. It was the evening of a winter's day not long before Roosevelt's fourth inaugural in front of a luggage locker in the Union Station in Washington. It was the evening also of the day Dan left O.C.S. with the newly cut orders and the second lieutenant's insignia, and the right to ten days' delay en route before he had to report to the staging area for the return to Europe. He could have used the time to go back to Lenox, but with the two aunts dead and the house closed up and the water turned off until either he or John could get clear enough of the war to go up there and settle affairs finally, a visit to Lenox did not make much sense.

So he knelt gingerly before the only available locker in that long row near the entrance, trying to force the over-stuffed duffle-bag and the valise with his kit into the too-small locker. Although it was chilly in the war-time winter station, he was sweating from the effort when he saw the neat small shoes near his elbow, and raised his eyes quickly up the neat small figure and kept looking upward until, for the first time in his life, he saw her beautiful face.

Back home in Lenox he had gone around with some fine girls. During the first few months of his freshman year at Amherst he had even corresponded with one of them three or four times a week. But she chose to pick a quarrel with him when he came home for Christmas vacation. Later he had met some girls from Smith and Mount Holyoke and Skidmore at the Amherst houseparties, but by this time he was in training more often than not. The dances they asked him to at Smith or Wellesley had a way of coinciding with scheduled boxing-matches or ball-games in which he wanted to play. At the Winter Carnival there was one girl. He had liked her immediately and they laughed and talked for an hour in a corner of the dance-floor at the C. &. G. house while the brethren whirled and dipped to the band-music. But even with low heels she was four or five inches taller than he was.

So when he stood up from the crouch in front of the luggage locker in the Washington station and found that the strange girl's dark brown eyes were exactly at the level of his own, something had turned over inside him. She had set down her suitcase on the pavement. Now she began to explain with that wonderful unself-conscious directness of hers that she was waiting at his heels because she thought he was taking the duffle-bag out instead of putting it in. There was not another empty locker in the station.

Dan said that his duffle-bag would not fit. She could have the locker. For an answer she put one of her small shoes against the end of the duffle-bag and kicked it astonishingly into place. They both laughed at that and Lucinda said that all she wanted anyhow was a place to stow the bag while she ate and telephoned her brother. Dan settled the problem by carrying her suitcase to the station restaurant.

Lucinda's brown eyes flashed and her even white teeth smiled as she explained that she had come down to see her brother Sandy. He was a colonel in the Pentagon and so busy now that he had warned her he might not be able to meet her train. She was supposed to call him at the office. But this was much more fun and the call could wait.

Whether it was the sudden release from the final drive of O.C.S., or the prospect of the ten-day leave, or this meeting, Dan had never felt better. Nor ever in his life had he met anyone like this clean and shining girl who sat across the restaurant table talking as if she had known him since childhood.

Sandy's obligations kept him so busy during Lucinda's stay that Dan had her almost entirely to himself. She had come down for a week but she called her Civilian Defense boss in New York to ask for an extra three days, and they explored the war-time city. She said afterwards that they had seen three great presidents, Jefferson and Lincoln and Roosevelt, because on the last day in town she had caught a glimpse of FDR moving fast in a closed car along one of the avenues. Lucinda thought his face looked dangerously gray for a man who was about to take his fourth oath of office. But Dan could not tell: he had been looking at Lucinda.

The day Dan's time was up she repacked the heavy suitcase and they rode together in a crowded coach as far as Trenton. He gave her his APO number and she promised to write him as soon as she got back to New York. She walked with him to the end of the coach carrying his valise while he bumped the duffle-bag along with his legs. He kissed her goodbye so deliberately that the train was moving again before he managed to sling the duffle-bag to the station platform and leaped after it, running.

*   *   *   *   *

Unferth smugly finished and sat down, leaving the way clear for another long oration by Beowulf. Dan closed the well-smudged book with a snap. Enough was enough. It was already after five o'clock. He would have to hurry to get home by six. Coming out of the library he found that the high-flowing wind of the morning had now lowered to the land. Trees waved and dipped their month-old leaves and the rain made a small river in every gutter. A large dead branch had fallen across the hood of the station-wagon. His pants legs were soaked and his bare head dripped with water by the time he had disposed of the branch and unlocked the car door, but he had kept the books dry under his jacket. The car, he found disgustedly, would not start. Moisture had condensed around the sparkplugs and he had to wipe them dry with a rag before the engine would respond.

Downtown the traffic was heavier than he had expected. The storm had hastened the darkness. Lights from the cars and the stores gleamed yellow and red on the slick pavements. At every crowded corner there was impatient jostling for positions and much blowing of horns. It was already six when he got clear of the suburbs, and though he drove fast on the straight stretches, it was after seven when he nosed the station-wagon through the gates and under the narrow porte-cochere.

As he bounded up the front steps he could feel the wind whipping his sodden trouser-cuffs against the backs of his legs. The front door stood ajar, and lights were on in the dining-room. Two places had been set. His own gleamed emptily, but broken bread lay on the edge of her plate, and he saw quickly that she had already eaten. The coffee in her cup was already cold, the surface cream skinned over like a wound.

In the kitchen the light shone silently on the chrome and stainless steel. She had been there, obviously. But not now. He went quickly to the foot of the stairs to call her name. When she did not answer he took the steps three at a time. Their bedroom was dark and silent. He switched on the light and was leaning down to untie his wet shoes when the three ideas came together: the wind, the boat, the open front door.

He was running now—down the sea-dank hall stairs and the front steps and across the sloping turf while the rain pelted heavily in his face and he began to hear the chopping sound the sea was making at the bottom of the lawn. In that strange light, dark and yet not dark, he could see the white tops of the waves.

A dozen yards downshore he could make out the sailboat, lying on its side, half in and half out of the water. Every breaker smashed against it with a hollow sound, but she was not there. Where? Gone to get Arch to help beach the boat? As good a guess as any.

He was turning away towards the farm-house when he seemed to see something dark in the waves. "Cindy," he yelled and vaulted the low wall into the waist-deep slosh and suck of the breakers. Now he had lost sight of whatever it was, and he began to wade desperately forward, groping with his arms under the tossing surface. He had half-walked, half-swum almost down to the boat when he saw the arm in the water.

He lunged for it, missed, and lunged again before he had it —had *her*, lifting the lolling head clear of the sea, gathering her into his straining arms, finding that she was fully dressed except for her shoes. Come to save the boat as the anchor tore loose. Come into that icy water just after she had eaten. Come warm to that cold where a cramp or even a sudden failure of the heart had felled her, pulled her under, left her to toss— how long?—in the roil of the breakers.

He got her clear of the sea, over the wall, and face down on the sodden grass. In the tumult he waved and gestured when he saw Arch's car-lights moving slowly down the lawn and felt the big-bodied rush of the black retriever come to see what was happening. Arch stopped the jeep where its headlights would shine on the place where her small figure lay. Her skin was the color of mustard. They put Dan's rolled-up jacket under her head and Arch spread his coat for warmth over her limp shoulders. It was when Dan reached to free her tongue that he saw her eyes for the first time.

He thought it was the worst thing he had ever seen—in Germany or before. In her open eyes was the sand—all in and around her open eyes and the froth-covered lips.

*   *   *   *   *

He accepted it. For days afterwards he told himself that he accepted it as he moved drily through the necessary arrangements. When it was over he drove down to Enfield to cancel the apartment they had taken after his acceptance at the graduate school. Three weeks later he moved alone into the room on Madison Street where he lived during graduate work and after he began to teach. It was only later, it must have been in the fall or winter of that first year at Enfield, that he came on the poem of Nashe's with the line about brightness falling from the air. With three or four other graduate students, he was reading at the long table. His eyes leaped ahead to the lines that followed: *"Brightness falls from the air, Queens have died young and fair, Dust has closed Helen's eye."*

But there was nothing to be done about it and he went on reading.

CHAPTER NINE

ALL THROUGH the month of November, the novels of Nicholas Kemp filled Dan's waking hours. As if, he thought sometimes, you were a renegade priest, reading and rereading a black satanic breviary, seeking between the lines the hints and clues that would admit you, finally, into the Unholy of Unholies, the huge caverns underground, linked each to each with echoing subterranean corridors where, turning any breathless corner, you would come upon the nameless and ultimate horror. Or like a hermit of that fanatical breed which stops only to feed and sleep, resolved to determine the actual dimensions of Hell: its length, its breadth, its far-spreading area, and above all its depth. For here, again and again, under the always moving though often melodramatic surface of the prose, lay the evidence of a human soul so tortured that you needed to torture your own in order to comprehend it.

So much in the fiction itself awaited finding out that he continued to neglect the biography. Yet on three separate occasions that month it was as if the maimed and mysterious figure of Kemp himself emerged from the shadows, drew near, stood scowling down for the briefest of intervals, and then stalked silently away.

Three incidents, he thought, and three totally separate agents. Two of the three had come uncalled for and unasked, like windfalls. And the first of the agents was of all the most unlikely: Harry Walker, the mailman from Hoboken.

He stood in the doorway in his dusty shoes handing Dan the day's batch of mail, piece by piece. Harry Walker was small in stature, thin to the point of cadaverousness, and this was one of the days he had not shaved. Except for the eyes, his face was like the skull beneath it. But his eyes were merry and hazel-colored as he stood searching the mail-pouch for the copy of *Time,* with his uniform cap on the back of his head and beads of sweat running down the bony dome of his forehead.

"Lots of stuff today," he said.

"It looks heavy," said Dan.

"Tell you the truth," said Walker, grinning, "my back is damn near broke. After I get rid of this I am going to have me six beers. Line them up on the bar and drink them one right after the other." He winked and grinned again, running his tongue along his thin lips.

"I've got those magazines you lent me," Dan said. "Would you feel like picking them up today?"

"Let's have them, sure," the mailman said. "How you like *Arizona Highways?*"

Dan said that it was a beautiful magazine, all right, and asked him to step in out of the sun while he went to gather up the half-dozen back numbers. The mailman accepted them happily and began to leaf through the pages.

"Some pictures," he said, admiringly. "I never see anything like these pictures. You notice this spread on Sabino Canyon? Comes close to home. Sabino Canyon ain't but twelve or fif-teen miles out east of here." He held up for Dan's admiration

a full-page kodachrome print of some yellow trees beside a
brook. The caption read: "Clothed in Autumn's Gold."

Dan said that he had been working and had not done much
exploring.

"I *see* you're working," Walker said. "Looks like you're
writing something." He pointed to the papers on Dan's work-
table.

Dan said that he was trying to write a book.

"A book huh?" the mailman said. "You come to the right
place. Plenny authors out here. Ever hear of John Dewey,
quite an old man? I carry his mail for him. Used to carry for
Brooks Nagle, man writes the columns. What book you
writing?"

"I didn't know John Dewey lived out here."

"Oh, sure. Got a wife and son. Little kid. Very nice woman.
Mind telling me what you're writing?"

"It's a book about Nicholas Kemp," Dan said. "Ever hear
of Nicholas Kemp?"

"Writes stories, don't he?" the mailman said, quickly. "Sure.
I know him. I mean to say I heard of him. He was down
around here not too long ago. Not in the city I don't mean but
up above here somewheres. They was looking for this cat up
in the mountains."

"Cat?"

"Catamount. Mountain lion. Raising hell, killing calves.
Seems this Kemp heard about it and come down to check."
Harry Walker sat on the edge of a chair, fingering the batch of
magazines. "But no cat. I mean they didn't catch it, shoot it.
It was in the papers. And no pictures. Seems this Kemp don't
let no one take his picture."

My God, Dan thought. "How about some coffee, Mr.
Walker?"

The mailman consulted his pocket watch. "Awright I will,"
he said firmly. "Don't mind if I do. I don't have but three-
four blocks left. I guess Uncle Sam won't holler if I have a
cup of coffee." He put his uniform cap on the floor beside his
chair and slid back comfortably. When Dan returned with the
coffee he was leafing through the pile of magazines in his lap.
But he put them carefully down when he took the cup.

"Just looking through here trying to see where that article
was," he said.

"You mean the one about the mountain lion?"

Harry Walker blew on his coffee. "Oh, no. I shoulda said.
This was another article. Lion article was in the papers. This
one was about a place they call Walnut Canyon way up north
here, northern part of the state. Cliffdwellers' place. Kemp
come poking around down there. After he left, some woman
tipped off the park ranger that it was Kemp. Seems she rec-
kernized him. Very inneresting. So this park ranger wrote it
up. They had this big spread on Walnut Canyon. Indians use
to live there. Way back this was. You remember seeing the
story in any of these magazines?"

Dan shook his head.

"Must be in one I didn't bring," Walker said. "I'll look it
up. Being it's about Kemp you might like to see it."

"You bet," said Dan. "How long ago were these Indians
there?"

"This would be way back. Before Columbus. Fourteen and
ninety-two." He finished the coffee and stood up. "I'll look it
up, bring it around. Right now I better shove. Uncle Sam

sure as hell be breathing down my neck if I don't get this mail delivered."

After he had gone Dan rinsed the cups in the sink. So Kemp was still on the Indian trail. Canadian Indians in *The Kingdoms of the North,* South American Indians in *The Straits of Magellan,* and one North American Indian, a Marine corporal, in *The Hinges of Hell.* And now these extinct Indians of Walnut Canyon. What do you suppose the old boy is up to? It is about time he wrote something. It is over ten years since *The Sleep of the Fathers.* Maybe he took the hint from his title and has been sleeping out his time up in that island fortress of his in the state of Washington, with the roving police dogs to keep off the curious.

Or has he? Here in one ten-minute conversation with the Tucson mailman you learn that Kemp has left his island at least twice. Once to explore Walnut Canyon incommunicado. Once to come way down here to hunt a mountain lion.

Dan stood gazing at the cards and papers on his work-table for a full minute before the idea clicked inside his head. Mountain lion, hell. Kemp came down here to sell that diary. He must have known what a price it could command. He has published exactly nothing since before the war. He needed the money. He wrote the rare book dealer. Whatshisname? Baxter. He wrote Baxter, and Baxter arranged a secret meeting at the house of Mr. Brooks Nagle, columnist, whose mail Mr. Harry Walker used to deliver. So what do we do? We telephone Nagle.

He found the number and called it. The distant bell burred for several minutes without response and he was just about to hang up the receiver when a voice answered. It was a woman's voice and she sounded out of breath and somewhat angry.

Mr. Nagle was out of town and was there a message? Dan identified himself and asked when Nagle was expected back. The woman said that she had no idea. Mr. Nagle was in Europe. Dan said he would try again later. The woman said all right and the line went dead.

*　　*　　*　　*　　*

Three incidents, he thought, and three totally separate agents. The second of Kemp's emergences took you far back, back to the month of June, 1918. And the figure which stepped forward, stood briefly still, and then vanished once more into the shadows was that of Lieutenant Nicholas Kemp, USMC, stumbling through the trampled wheat of that field just west of Belleau Wood, sickly holding the shattered remnants of what once upon a time—not ten minutes ago—had been a whole and healthy arm.

> 889 Arlington Ave.
> Silver Spring, Md.
> November 20, 1949

Dear Dan:

Before I get to the matter at hand, I would just like to compliment you, both as your admiring uncle and as a long-time follower of this stupid trade of war, on your decision to keep up your reserve commission. Those reserve drills don't take much time but whatever time they take is probably worth it. You and the regulars are the ones that keep the fences repaired between wars, and don't let them tell you there are not going to be any more wars.

In some ways the human race is quite bright, or so they tell us. But in one way we are as dumb as all hell because every generation or so some bastard gets the notion he is unbeatable. Then we have to go out and beat him. It costs him plenty to find out he is beatable and it costs us plenty to beat him. By the time he is beaten he is usually dead, like Adolf or Benito or the others, but the rest of us have to pay the bills and clean up the mess and bury the poor buggers on both sides. Then, pretty soon, somebody else gets the notion he is Mars and we have to go do it all over again. Which has nothing to do with what follows except I am glad you decided to keep up with the drills out there, even if it does take some time away from your other work.

Now about Kemp. I have done some checking, both in the records and with another old guy named Freddy Udall. My check indicates that Kemp was in the Sixth Regiment which was combined with the Fifth as a brigade under Doyen. Most of one company in the Sixth came from the University of Minnesota. Many Swedes, I would judge, and a few great athletes. Bastien, for example, was All-American end. There was a track star named Overton from Yale, later KIA, and a few fire-eaters from Princeton—Moore, Murphy and Bill Eddy. Eddy was active in this last war, too. So it was partly a college outfit, though run by old-timers.

Last week I called Freddy and yesterday we got together over at the Club. Freddy is a good deal of a poop and a great rummy. But he is the only character I have run into who was actually at the Bois de Belleau in Kemp's outfit.

Freddy remembers Kemp as a fairly unpleasant lad. He ran his platoon well enough, but it got around that he would not volunteer for anything—and in a regiment of eager beavers who would volunteer for anything, and did. Freddy has read some of Kemp's books and expressed the idea to me that with a little hindsight you might conclude that Kemp was trying to keep Kemp safe to write the great American war novel, as I guess he did. Of course the job is to keep alive and keep going if you can. But there are different ways of going about this, and Fred says Kemp used to lean pretty heavily on one man in particular, another second lieutenant named Joe Collier. Fred recalls one time when volunteers were needed, and he thinks Joe spoke up quickly so Kemp wouldn't have to. It was Joe who brought Kemp back after he was hit, but I am getting ahead of the story.

The notes I took on Freddy's conversation describe Joe as the Dan Boone type: rangy, slender, slope-shouldered, with a long horse face. Kemp was shorter, stockier, maybe five-ten or eleven. Round head, it says here. Thin eyebrows and very pale eyes. Used to irritate Freddy by fiddling with a big ring on his left hand. Freddy played poker with him once in the rest-billet. Says he liked him less and less as the evening wore on. Arrogant and cruel. This was in May, 1918.

When the Krauts got through to the Marne with their big offensive late in the month, the brigade moved up. It was the morning of June 2 that they got their first sight of Belleau. They were dug in on the slopes above the forest. It was farm-land: green wheat and poppies in the wheat. Good weather, sunny and not too warm. So they sat there and looked at the Bois, which was a thick woods about two kilometers long part way down the slope. It was crawling with machine-guns and mortars and something like a thousand Krauts.

The Marines kicked off the afternoon of the sixth of June, crossed the field, reached the edge of the woods, and fell back at dark. They spent the next three days rooting out emplace-ments. By the tenth, when they fell back to the western edge of the woods to give the artillery a chance to lay in a barrage, the enemy had begun to give up in groups, but there were still nests in among the rocks and tree-trunk emplacements which had to be rooted out. On his fourth highball, Freddy said to tell you the best short summary of Belleau Wood: take a stick and poke it into a hornet's nest.

Kemp went in with the Sixth under Sibley. A machine-gun burst caught him in the left arm and damned near tore it off.

Freddy saw him being pulled back by Joe Collier, both of them trying to hold Kemp's arm on. Freddy says he thinks Joe stayed with the battalion until he picked up a bad dose of gas over beyond Château-Thierry on the river during the big offensive launched by us about the third week in June.

That mustard gas was bad stuff, Dan. The masks were so damned uncomfortable that the men would get careless with them, especially in warm weather. There are still some men around in the various veterans' hospitals that got a good whiff of that stuff over thirty years ago. Not many, though. Most of them died long since.

So that is what I know about Kemp in May and June, 1918. I am sorry it is not more, and I wish I could report that Freddy thinks he was a great man. Joe Collier, apparently, was very well-liked, and Freddy is puzzled that Joe was able to get along with Kemp, who was so surly a character.

Good luck with your book. Jane and the girls send their love.

As ever,

John

Major General John Sherwood, USMC

*   *   *   *   *

Kemp's third emergence came, uncalled-for and unexpectedly, at Axel O'Keefe's Thanksgiving dinner. When Dan stopped the car by the curb, he saw that it was a square stucco house whose forbidding face was softened by rows of dusty oleanders. Axel met him at the door, shaking his hand warmly and leading him into the study. Mrs. O'Keefe was named Moira. She was a young ash-blonde in a pale green dress, nervous in manner, and she went immediately to fetch Dan a drink. When she handed it to him he saw that the flesh of her cheeks had a hollow look, as if from nervous strain. It occurred to him that Moira was worrying about her duties as hostess.

Five minutes later another couple arrived. Axel introduced them as the Wileys, formerly of New York. Wiley was slender and dark. His hair was so thin that it looked to have been painted on his head. With the high forehead and the ascetically aquiline nose, he had almost the face of an Italian cardinal. Mrs. Wiley was a tall red-head who jangled when she moved. A dozen necklaces surrounded her plump neck, and her wrists and hands blazed with bracelets and rings. She had a habit of punctuating her talk with sweeping gestures, and she had no sooner come in than she summoned Dan to sit beside her on the couch.

"Axel's been telling us about you, Mr. Sherwood. He says you're from one of the greenest parts of the Garden State. How long have you been at Enfield? My husband went to Enfield many years ago but he never goes back for the reunions. Of course they don't make so much of reunions at Enfield as they do at Princeton with those marching bands and the silly costumes and all. I don't think Harcomb has been back since he graduated, in spite of all that time we lived in New York, not thirty miles away. Isn't that true, Harcomb? He doesn't hear me, he's deep in some philosophical discussion with Axel. Harcomb! (*Clank*). Mr. Sherwood is from Enfield."

"Yes, my dear," said Wiley, blandly. "How is the old place, Sherwood?"

"It's still in business," Dan said. "What was your class?"

"In the dark ages," Wiley said, pursing his thin lips. "The medieval period. What we now refer to as the Sweatshirt Era. It was shortly succeeded by the Era of Bathtub Alcohol, when everyone drank his way to the good old B.A."

"B.A.," said Mrs. Wiley. "That's one of Harcomb's jokes.

It stands for Bathtub Alcohol. I hope you don't mind my saying so, Mr. Sherwood, but Harcomb abominates Enfield. He would much rather have gone to Princeton. He could hardly wait to get out of Enfield and into publishing, could you, Harcomb? Harcomb was for many years in publishing in New York City. No thank you, Moira, I must not. I simply must not. I stepped on the bathroom scales this morning and almost fainted. You don't have to worry about weight, Mr. Sherwood."

"I'd rather not be thought of as a lightweight," Dan said, grinning.

"Oh, you mean intellectually," said Mrs. Wiley. "Moira, stop passing those delicious-looking things and sit down. We're talking about weight. *You'll* never have to worry about weight, that's one thing sure. You and Harcomb could eat and eat until the cows come home and never gain an ounce. I must take up smoking."

Moira tamped out her cigarette and sat down nervously on the edge of the couch, holding the small plate of biscuits. "I wish I could *give* up smoking," she said. "Axel has never smoked in his life and he wants me to stop. Have you finished your drinks? Are you hungry?"

"I'm starved," said Mrs. Wiley promptly. "After I stepped on those scales this morning, I solemnly swore not to eat all day. Harcomb, I leave it to you if I've eaten since breakfast."

Harcomb Wiley looked ecclesiastically quizzical and said that as far as he knew no single morsel had passed her pretty lips since morning. He said that eating had nothing to do with it, anyway: it was a matter of metabolism. He named a lady author the size of a young chickadee who used to come in from Nyack every couple of weeks for a publisher's lunch. Three cocktails, followed by a thick soup, salad with mayonnaise, an entree with two vegetables, and for dessert a pudding with whipped cream. Year in and year out, the lady authoress continued to weigh ninety-seven pounds. Her fiction, of course, weighed far less than that. But it was very popular, and richly repaid the firm of Macmillan for what it cost to feed this little chickadee.

Moira O'Keefe presided tautly over the dinner, a Mexican casserole and a salad with pre-buttered slices of Italian bread. Ceremoniously pouring out the glasses of claret, Axel said boomingly that he had chosen the wine as a special tribute to Dan Sherwood's special author, John Keats, and Mrs. Wiley remarked clankingly that she wished all poets were as simple as Keats. These modern ones just simply made no sense.

"I should have thought Keats had his complicated moments," said Axel.

"Yes, of course, but nothing like Yeats," Mrs. Wiley said. "You know Macmillan brought out Yeats, and I used to do some of the proofreading. *Byzantium!* Did you ever read *Byzantium,* Axel?"

"You know, Sherwood," Axel said, "that both the Wileys used to work at Macmillan's."

"We *met* there," Mrs. Wiley said. "I was working there when Harcomb came over from Littlefield's in 1920."

"Nineteen-nineteen, my dear," Harcomb Wiley said. "July, 1919, just after Kemp had come and gone."

"Kemp?" said Dan. "Who was Kemp?"

"Nicholas Kemp, the novelist," said Wiley.

"At Littlefield's?"

"Briefly at Littlefield's," Wiley said. "He worked there for a month or six weeks in the summer of 1919. Then he left for parts unknown."

Moira said that they would have coffee in the study. She would ask them to excuse Axel, who always brewed the coffee. She and Eunice would join them in a few minutes. There were cigarettes on the study table. Dan followed Wiley into the next room.

"You know Littlefield's are Kemp's publishers," he said. "I never heard he worked for them."

"Not for long," Wiley said. "There was a rumor at the time that he had been keeping or living with a woman in Paris. They said he wanted to break it off. The job at Littlefield's was his first step. Promised to bring her over as soon as he got established. I don't remember exactly. But he threw the whole thing up and took off."

"Did you know Kemp?" Dan asked.

"Slightly," said Wiley. "We were in different departments but I would see him now and again. You know he lost his arm in the war. Something of a hero, I believe."

"He was with the Marines in Belleau Wood," Dan said. "What sort of a man was he?"

"Oh, medium height," Wiley said. "Soft-spoken. Rather quiet. I remember the empty sleeve. I forget which it was, right or left."

"Left," Dan said.

"Do you know him?"

"I'm writing a book about him."

Wiley had only time to raise his Italianate eyebrows in what seemed surprise and to open his mouth as if to reply when his wife returned, jangling her bracelets like a Siamese dancer. Once more she began the bewildering flood of interrogatives and declaratives. Was Dan enjoying Tucson? Wasn't it a remarkable city, way out here, and really unexpectedly civilized? Many people came for their health. Tucson was filled with people who had medical histories. Of course sometimes it worked in reverse. When she had first come, perfectly healthy as far as she knew, she had developed a terrible affliction called desert fever. What was Dan's trouble?

Under her relentless questioning he admitted to the persistent cough of last winter and the pneumonia of the past summer.

"There you are," Eunice Wiley said, clanking triumphantly. "Harcomb was obliged to retire from Macmillan's because of the smog in the city. He used to call New York *the enemy,* didn't you, Harcomb?"

"Axel O'Keefe, too," said Dan.

"What about Axel O'Keefe?"

"Wasn't it arthritis? He said he left Connecticut because of his arthritis."

Harcomb Wiley's eyebrows ascended once more. He had opened his mouth to make some reply when his wife placed three bejeweled fingers against his lips and firmly changed the subject.

She was still talking breathlessly and without a pause when Axel and Moira came in with the coffee. Her subject was some people whom she called the "Penney-tennies." They were half-Christian Indians who beat themselves with whips and scourges as a religious penance. It took Dan several minutes to recognize that the word was spelled *Penitentes.*

Moira, handing the coffee around, said that it was a very interesting sect. It had been written up in the Tucson paper not long ago.

"Ah, yes," Axel said, stirring his coffee. "The work of a young lady reporter. She writes feature articles."

"She interviewed Axel," Moira said, with her taut giggle. "She's going to do something about his Pope book."

"Very smart little girl," Axel said, wagging his great parti-colored head. "You men can expect a visit from her shortly."

"Oh, not Harcomb," Eunice said. "Harcomb's not a cultural feature, are you, Harcomb?"

"Indeed he is," Axel said. "The girl seemed much interested when I told her he had been so long in New York publishing. And then, Dan Sherwood. We talked about that business of the Golden West Library."

"Oh, God," Dan said. "I think I've seen her. What does she look like, Axel?"

"Small," Axel said. "Neat and compact. Ably lipsticked. Rather a nice sort. Constance Haybright her name is. Where did you see her, Dan?"

Dan told them about the visit to Lee's Academy. Moira seemed to be greatly interested in what Lee was proposing to offer, and he described it for her in some detail. Eunice Wiley said that it was obviously a tourist trap. She and Harcomb knew Mandeville Lee very well indeed. Far too well. When they first moved to Arizona after the war, Lee had tried to sell them a house for a ridiculously high price. They had taken their housing problems elsewhere. (*Clank*).

Wiley said they must forgive him for changing the subject. He had just now learned of Sherwood's interest in Nicholas Kemp the novelist.

"Eunice, do you remember that tall, schoolmarmish girl at Macmillan's?"

"They were all schoolmarmish," said Eunice gaily. "That's why you noticed me."

"This one affected the colors of red and black," Wiley said. "We called her Madame Stendhal."

"For the novel, yes," Eunice said. "Now what was her name?"

"She wore red and black thingumbobs on her head," Wiley said, making vague gestures over the top of his skull, "—velvet ribbons and such."

"I'll have her name in a minute," Eunice said.

"The title rather pleased her," said Wiley. "Madame Stendhal. Later she went over to *Vogue* magazine."

"Cissie," cried Mrs. Wiley, snapping her jeweled fingers. "Her name was Cissie Waterhouse. She was vaccinated with marriage but it didn't take. It's her maiden name. She's in Paris now with *Vogue*."

"Cecilia Waterhouse," Wiley said. "Now, Sherwood, you must drop her a note. She used to talk about Kemp when his first book came out. That one about the war in France."

"*The Hinges of Hell,*" Dan said. "I've seen a piece she did in one of the magazines."

"Write her," said Wiley. "And give her our best regards. Eunice and Harcomb Wiley."

"She'll remember me as Eunice Dudley," Mrs. Wiley said.

Dan said that he would drop a note to Cissie Waterhouse. Once more the figure of Nicholas Kemp had emerged from the shadows, stood scowling silently, and then stalked back into wherever it was he had been.

CHAPTER TEN

THE GIRL'S voice at the other end of the line was quiet and faintly musical. Professor O'Keefe had given her Mr. Sherwood's name. She was writing feature articles for the paper, and her subject was famous literary people in the Tucson area. Could she come and talk?

"I'm not a famous literary person," Dan said.

"Oh, you are," the girl said. "All those western stories. And Professor O'Keefe said you'd never been west of Chicago when you wrote them."

"Schenectady," Dan said.

"What about Schenectady?"

"It was Schenectady I'd never been west of when I wrote those books."

The girl laughed with a sound like silver and said that made it all the more curious. Her curiosity was really piqued now. Wouldn't he let her come and talk?

"It won't make much of a cultural feature," Dan said. "Have you tried Harcomb Wiley?"

"Not yet," she said. "I'd much rather do you first. Please?"

"Well," Dan said, "I'm going down to the university library around two. Maybe we could meet there."

The girl agreed at once. She would be there at two.

"What do you look like?" Dan asked.

The girl said that she would be wearing a yellow dress and a white belt. She would be carrying a stenographer's notebook. Her hair was darkish brown and her eyes were blue. She would be there in the reading room near the door at two.

All the rest of the morning he wrote letters, including one to Cecilia Waterhouse. He was still at the typewriter around noon when Lee's girl Chita rang the doorbell. She was wearing a white off-shoulder blouse and a very pointed brassière, and she stood there in the tight green skirt, talking about Mandeville Lee.

"I go to his house," she said. "Is locked. You know where that man is gone?"

Dan said that he had not seen Lee for several days.

"He is secret man," Chita said, scowling. "You know what this means—secret man?"

"Maybe he took a trip," Dan said. "He spoke of getting some people for his Academy. He's got a lot of irons in the fire. Maybe he's keeping them hot."

"Hot is right," Chita said, her black eyes flashing. "He keep them hot is right." She glanced quickly around the room. "What you do here?" she asked.

Dan said that he was writing most of the time.

"What you write? You write for magazine?"

Dan said he was trying to write a book.

"You have to smoke all that when you write a book?" Chita said. "You stink up the house." She walked over to the dusty table where the papers were strewn and picked up the overflowing ashtray. Bending forward with difficulty in the tight skirt, she emptied the ashes into the brimming wastebasket.

"Is a mess," she said. "Why doan you clean this place some-times?"

Dan said that he had forgotten to do it.

Chita flashed her white teeth and said look, she had come to clean Lee's house, but it was locked. She would clean Dan's house instead, all right?

"Thanks, Chita," Dan said. "I'll do it later."

Chita said look, what was he worrying about? It would not cost him anything. She could clean it in a short time, sweep the floor little bit, dust little bit. Okay? She carried the waste-basket into the kitchen and emptied it into the cardboard carton under the sink.

"My God," she cried. "You never wash your plates. I wash your plates for you, all right?"

"Never mind, Chita," Dan said. He stood uncertainly in the middle of the living-room. When she came back with the wastebasket, she brushed against him and he got a strong whiff of her perfume. She put down the wastebasket and turned towards him, smiling. Her perfume was all around him.

"How about?" Chita said. "No charge. Okay?"

Dan looked away from her and around the room. "I guess it needs it," he said.

"You bet your ass it needs it," Chita said. She went to the windows and began to open them. "I do the plates." She grinned at him broadly and went into the kitchen.

Dan sat at the table before the rented typewriter. A light current of warm air was beginning to flow through the room. After a time she left the kitchen and her heels clicked across the living-room floor. When he turned from the typewriter she was close beside him. She was drying her hands on a towel.

"Look," she said. "How about some food?"

Dan said he was not hungry. He had to go downtown soon and he would get something to eat on the way.

Chita said it would not take long to fix some food. He would write better if he had some food. He would get sick in his stomach smoking all day without food. A breeze from the window had blown one of the pages from the dusty table and Chita bent to pick it up. When she laid it on the table he saw that the blouse was loose around her neck and shoulders. Her perfume was warm and heady.

"Look," Chita said, softly. "You got some gin? I make you nice Mexican drink you got little gin."

Dan swallowed quickly, dry-throated, before he smiled at her. There was no gin in the house and almost no food. He was due downtown soon, in fact almost immediately, and he would eat down there. He thanked her for washing the dishes.

Chita had moved away. Now she shrugged her brown shoulders in the loose white blouse and said the dishes were nothing. She just hated to see a man with dirty dishes and no woman around to wash them. What time was it, anyway? She would have to be going. Dan thanked her again and she left, banging the front door behind her.

After she had gone he found that he was somewhat shaken. He shaved rapidly and took a shower. On the way to the library he stopped for a sandwich and coffee at one of the hashhouses along the Speedway. Only when he finished eating did he remember that he had no money.

The proprietor, a Greek with oily black hair, worked the

toothpick over to one side of his mouth and said what the hell, Dan could pay him the next time he was in. He got Dan to sign the chit and grandly waved him to the door.

* * * * *

It was already two o'clock when he parked the car under the olive trees and walked across to the library. They were flooding the quadrangle of lawn in the middle of the campus. The grass was laid out in sunken squares. Pipes buried in the ground conducted water to the inside of the squares and each week the spigots were turned on for long enough to submerge the sun-burned lawn. When the spigots were turned off, the water sank rapidly into the ground and for a short time afterwards the wet grass turned faintly green. By the time of the next flooding, it had always faded again to the color of old hay.

The girl was in the reading room, facing the doorway, dressed in sunny yellow. She stood up as Dan came towards her and he saw that her hair was indeed a very dark brown and that her blue eyes were on a level with his own.

"I'm Sherwood."

She smiled. "I don't know what I thought you'd look like," she said in the silvery voice, "but you're different."

"Did I sound like an ogre?"

"Professor O'Keefe did, both on and off the phone," said the girl. "You sounded quiet. You sounded eastern."

"I am eastern," Dan said. From where he stood beside the girl he could see Henry gesturing in his direction. He had waved back before he realized that Henry was beckoning to him. He went over to the circulation desk.

"Sorry," said Henry in a hushed voice. "No talking in the reading-room."

"This girl wants to have an interview," Dan said. "We'll go somewhere else, Henry."

"Use my office," said Henry, hospitably. "I'm going to be working out here."

Dan went back to the girl, who nodded quickly and brightly and followed him into Henry's office. It was on the side away from the sun. After the reading-room it seemed dim and cool.

Before she sat down the girl gave him her hand. It was small and strong. "I'm Connie Haybright," she said. She moved to the visitor's chair and opened the dictation book.

"Will there be enough light?"

"Oh, plenty," Connie said. "I even have the first word of the interview."

Dan sat down facing her. "What's the word: *ogre?*"

"*Schenectady,*" she said, laughing. "The town you hadn't been west of." With the bright merriment still in her eyes, she looked at him across the desktop and launched directly into the questions she had to ask.

"Before we begin," Dan said, "who are the others?"

"Others?"

"The other people you've been interviewing. Do you have many?"

"Not many," the girl said, thoughtfully. "Professor O'Keefe. And now you. And I'm going to do Hart Mackenzie."

"Hart Mackenzie?"

"A painter," Connie said. "A wonderful old man with

white hair. He studied in Italy once. You ought to hear him talk about Florence. Have you ever been to Florence?"

"Once, briefly, after the war. Where does he live now?"

"He lives out of town," Connie said. "Have you heard of Sabino Canyon?"

"I've seen pictures of it," said Dan. "It didn't look inhabited."

"He doesn't live in the canyon itself," said Connie. "He has a kind of cabin and studio just before you go into the canyon. He's doing a mural. So there are just you three; and then I'm going to try Mr. Wiley, four, and John Dewey, if he's well enough, and Brooks Nagle. Do you know him?"

"The columnist? He's in Europe, isn't he?"

Her blue eyes widened. "Is he? I didn't know. I haven't called him or Mr. Wiley or Mr. Dewey. Well, never mind. They can wait. You can't wait. Please tell me about those western stories."

Dan leaned back in Henry's chair and began to tell her about Demarest Palley and the Golden West Library. Her head was bent to the dictation book. He looked at the clean parting in her dark hair and watched her brisk fingers filling the first column.

"You write fast," he said, during one of the pauses.

"Shorthand," she said. "My own version. Not quite verbatim, but close enough."

"Close enough for this, anyhow," Dan said.

"Oh, this is good," said Connie, flushing. After that, whenever she glanced up at him, he watched the delicate rose-color coming and fading in her cheeks just where the bones were nearest the surface. "Tell me some more about this Squirrel Burrell," she said.

Dan described the Squirrel's dark office and the orange filing-case. At her urging, he told what Burrell had done to the stories he mailed in. Once or twice she chuckled so heartily and pleasurably that he began to invent anecdotes in order to hear the chuckle again.

"So those are the five novels," she said, after half an hour. "Were they the first you had done?"

"Novels, yes. If novels is the word for them. A few short stories."

"But not novels?"

"Unless you count one novelette," said Dan slowly. He had not thought of it for years. It had come from his boyhood fascination with a book called *The Wonder of War in the Air*. "Ever hear of it?" he said. "By Francis Rolt-Wheeler?"

Connie shook her head. "Was he English?"

"He must have been English," said Dan. "My hero was English—an aviator. Very dashing. Daring. Flew most of the Allied planes that you found in Rolt-Wheeler's book."

"A war story, then?"

It was about love and war, Dan said. In the story there was an extremely beautiful and completely sexless heroine who used to steal out every night and fly with her lover on secret missions over the German lines. She and the hero both wore long scarves in their helmets. These streamed out behind the plane as they flew bravely along.

"Doubtless very Freudian," said Dan, "except that I had never heard of Freud at the time."

Connie was writing busily, her neat head bent to the dictation book. "How did it all come out?" she asked.

"I've forgotten now. It was a long time back."

"Have you really forgotten?"

"I guess not really," he said. "I remember there were two versions. Or rather two conclusions. In the first they lived happily ever after. But that seemed too easy. In the second they crashed in flames. Into the Channel or the North Sea, I forget which. Usual romantic holocaust. But not before they shot down the Baron."

"The Baron? Who was the Baron?"

"Prussian Colonel," said Dan. "Also wore a long scarf in his helmet. His was black, ornamented with skull and bones. He may have been a Yale man."

"Which did you choose?"

"Which what?"

"Excuse me. I meant which version?"

"Oh, the second," said Dan. "At that time it struck me as very romantic to have them both incinerated *and* drowned."

"Oh, but it was," said Connie, still scribbling rapidly.

"It was not," Dan said, more flatly than he intended. "It was junk. Complete, unadulterated, romantic junk. Like the junk I did for Demarest Palley."

The girl had looked up now, the pencil poised in her alert fingers. "Aren't you in favor of romance?" she said. "I thought—"

"Maybe I was then."

"And now you're a—what? A classicist? No. A skeptic?"

"No," he said tonelessly. "Just not a romantic."

The girl's smile was no longer visible. "No scarf in your helmet?"

"No helmet," Dan said uncomfortably.

Her eyes had fallen again to the writing-pad. "Wherever did you lose it?" she asked quietly.

Dan's voice sounded too loud in the small room. "I'm not

being serious," he said. "Armor gets rusty. Helmets wear out."

Her face was without expression. "Couldn't you have found another?"

"None of them would fit," Dan said. Even in his ears his voice sounded harsh. How did we ever get onto this anyway, he thought.

He saw with a pang that the girl was closing her notebook.

"You've been very kind," she said. He thought her face looked pale in the dim light. "I hope this didn't take too much of your time."

"Not if it didn't waste yours," he said.

"Not wasted," she said shortly. Her handshake felt small and firm, but also distant. She thanked him again and went out.

He had risen with her. Now he sank back into Henry's chair and sat unmoving. The room seemed empty and the air stale. He crossed to open the window. Outside was a clump of the sour orange trees, the fruit a dusty green.

The talk had begun well enough, even gaily. In the end it had fallen to pieces, as if a wall had cut the room in half. As soon as she saw it, sensed it, she had closed the book and gone. It's you, he thought, with your stupid gloom. It was the same this morning with the girl Chita. She saw it there, too, whatever it was. But she was ready to push it aside. She was angry at Lee for going away. She would have made you that gin drink, cooked your food—even stepped clear of that green skirt, shed that white blouse. All that was needed were the right words. Right words? Instead you spoke the others. *Noli me tangere. Retro me.* And Chita left, slamming the door, insulted. And this afternoon it was the same again.

No, he thought, not the same. Between Chita and this girl the gulf is—huge. You brushed off the first one, you and your Puritan soul. The second one you froze out. The nice girl. Why?

But he knew that he knew the answer. Jessica, he thought. Jessica Stone. Another nice girl. And we will forget about Jessica, starting now.

CHAPTER ELEVEN

HE REMEMBERED the afternoon and the evening and the night much too well to forget about them. For the thousandth time they came back to run through his mind like a reel of color film. Jessica Ranger, he thought, the girl with the beautiful name, to say nothing of her beautiful face, who became Jessica Ranger Stone one winter afternoon in that dark old cathedral in New York.

She took the vows in a voice as firm as Sandy's, and turned with a smile, her hand on Sandy's black sleeve, to make the long recessional to the church door, to gather up her train where the protective canopy ended, and to climb into the waiting limousine while the snow fell soundlessly, and the tires of passing cars sizzled on the avenue, and the late Christmas shoppers stopped to stare at the smiling bride in cream-color and white, in the pearls and the lace, with the veiled tiara high on her head and her great beauty like a queen's.

Because Cindy's death was little more than six months past, they had kept both the wedding and the reception relatively small. Small, but in the high style of the Rangers and the Stones and the Axtons. Caterers moved in on Sandy's apartment with a fortune in food and flowers and another in champagne. The place was already filled to overflowing by the time Dan arrived. As he moved through the long hall, shuffling slowly with the other guests, he saw that Jessica's mother, Mrs. Axton, was making the introductions. When his turn came, he murmured his name so quietly that she presented him as Mr. Seward.

"*Sherwood,* mother," Jessica said. "This is Dan Sherwood, Cindy's husband." And then, as if she were conscious of the ghost at the feast, or of the possibility that Dan might be bothered by the memory, or even because she feared that in his private view this wedding had come too soon in the wake of Cindy's funeral, she leaned forward, flushing, to take his face between both her hands and to kiss him firmly on the lips. "How are you, Dan?" she said, kindly, in the short interval before Mrs. Axton introduced the following couple. "Are you working hard?"

He made some diffident, almost wordless reply, before he moved on to shake hands with Sandy, who beamed on the throng like a benign lighthouse. Afterwards, in the melange of people, champagne, sandwiches, and small talk, he found himself in the company of Jessica's own father—who looked like the country squire that he actually was—and then, minutes later, of her stepfather, Axton, who resembled a British brigadier and referred to the champagne as "the bubbly," but was in fact a semi-retired Philadelphia lawyer.

With each of them Dan felt a suspicion of constraint. They must have known him as a creature from another world than theirs. They might also have remembered how recently Cindy had drowned. He could not escape the conviction that he was out of place. As soon as the cake had been cut with Axton's old cavalry saber, he found his hat and coat and took the train back to Enfield.

He did not see them again for four or five months. Sandy sent him a postcard from the Bahamas, and there was a honeymoon picture on the *Times* society page. They were posed in shorts against a tropical background, and Sandy was grinning beneficently at the camera. Jessica's eyes were fixed on some object far outside the picture, perhaps a sailboat in the blue-green waters of the bay, and she wore the half-smile, half-frown which was one of her characteristic expressions.

That spring Dan went in for dinner at the apartment. When he rang, it was Jessica who came to let him in. She was wearing a black dinner dress, very modish and unobtrusively expensive. With her bright hair and flawless bare arms and those green eyes, she might have stepped queen-like—with some such name as Maeve or Deirdre—out of the earlier pages of W. B. Yeats. Again she met him warmly, with the slender cool hands on either side of his head and the firm kiss squarely and unabashedly on the mouth.

In the study Sandy was engrossed in the manufacture of martinis. "Dan," he cried. "It's about time you came in here. How's it going? You look fagged."

"March was a long month," Dan said, grinning.

"March was a real stinker," Sandy said, heartily. "Doesn't he look fagged, Jess? Here, now, wait a minute, and I'll have these potions ready."

During the considerable time it took him to measure out the gin and to drip the vermouth scientifically down a long silver spoon, Dan was conscious of Jessica's eyes upon him; and all through the excellent dinner, as he talked, chiefly to

Sandy, he felt Jessica's attentive stare almost palpably against the side of his face. Whenever he turned and spoke directly to her, she neither looked away nor even momentarily shifted the full, frank gaze with which her eyes met his own. In the enormous chair in the study, while Sandy dramatically displayed his newly acquired first editions of Yeats and A. E., she sat on the broad chair-arm, looking down over his shoulder at the books and exuding a perfumed warmth which would have stirred him if he had allowed himself to think about it.

Whether for that reason or some other, that was the last time he saw either of them for almost two years. When Sandy telephoned in September, asking him to spend a week at the house in Connecticut, he begged off on grounds of the coming opening of the fall term at Enfield. Through the winter and spring he was so preoccupied that he barely remembered to wish them bon voyage by wire when they sailed for Europe. They were gone for a year. The occasional postcards and letters, mostly from Sandy, let him follow their route in a rough way. But it was not until someone handed him a clipping which said that the Stones had been fishing at Bimini that he even thought to be surprised that they had come back from Europe and gone off again without letting him know.

He was pushing the thesis on Keats as hard as possible that day in the winter of 1948 when Sandy's mysterious phone-call summoned him to New York for the conference on Nicholas Kemp's war-time diary. Jessica was not in town then. She had gone to Philadelphia for a visit with the Axtons. She had sent him her love, Sandy said. But there was something in his tone which made Dan wonder, at least momentarily, whether the marriage was still as firm as it had seemed to be two years before.

Dan did not think of notifying Sandy when he got the Ph.D. In fact, he felt no special elation. He had been running a low temperature for weeks. "If you'll take my advice," said John Webb, "which you probably won't because you haven't yet, you'll go to bed and stay there until you shake that damned cough." Seven weeks later, driving him home from the hospital, Webb was magnanimous enough not to remind him that he had been duly and repeatedly warned.

"You get on out of here, Dan," he said. "This pneumonia is rough stuff. You get away. Can't you go up to Connecticut and lie on that beach?"

Dan said that he was out of touch with the Stones now. He was not even sure they were at the house on the Sound.

"Well, then," Webb said, "why don't you really get away? Take a year off. I'll hold your job. Find yourself a dry climate. Florida or New Mexico or Southern California. Remember how it gets here in November? You'll be hacking your head off by Christmas. That is, you will if you're still alive."

Dan said that he would think about it. But while the summer waned in sluggish heat he did not feel like moving. From his bookshelf the Keats typescript glared accusingly, awaiting the revisions and extensions that would make it, with luck, a publishable book.

When at last he took it down and got to work, he found almost immediately that he would need another trip to Cambridge and another long look at the Harvard materials on Keats before the job could be finished. Late in August he drove up and rented a room just off the square. He spent the days in the hush of the library, walking out at nightfall through the Yard where the summer school students strolled hand in hand among the institutional shadows or sat on the steps of Widener eating bananas or cherries out of paper sacks. In two weeks he had assembled what he needed. He packed it up in a Carstairs whiskey-carton and prepared to go home. Lying on the bed in his rented room he looked at the carton and told himself that now he could finish the book by Christmas. Then maybe he would go off somewhere. Maybe Bimini, he thought drowsily. Maybe the Dry Tortugas.

*   *   *   *   *

The next day was clear and bright. An early frost had tipped the swamp-maples with red, but the noonday sun glinted warmly and he drove with both windows wide open, past Worcester and past Hartford, until hunger stopped him for lunch at one of the diners near the beginning of the parkway. An hour later, as the car approached the familiar turn-off, he thought of the house beside the Sound, drenched in sunlight and salt air, surrounded by green lawns and clipped shrubbery as in a park, and drowsy with the fiddling of insects in the fields nearby. They would still be there, most likely. They would be reluctant to close the house in this golden weather, reluctant to shed the worn summer sneakers and comfortable loose clothes. They would be telling themselves that while such weather lasted New York would have to wait. The apartment would be there when they chose to come back to it. But not yet awhile. Not when the sun stayed warm all day and the breeze whipped whitecaps in the blue water.

Just before it would have been too late, Dan turned the wheel on an impulse and began to follow the familiar road. Even in three years it had not greatly changed. A few vegetable stands had sprung up, with old men or young girls waiting to sell you late corn or the rubicund tomatoes. Some of the houses had decayed visibly and yet others seemed to have been spruced up with fresh paint. He glanced into the yard where Mrs. Munch's grandchildren were playing. They would doubtless have grown in the meantime, but he went past too quickly to see. At the gates to Sandy's domain, he slowed only momentarily. Gravel crunched pleasantly under the tires and he stopped beside the wide-mouthed old barn. When he turned off the motor, the sea was softly audible, laving the shore at the foot of the lawn on the far side of the house.

After the roar of the road, the place seemed peaceful. A light breeze out of the west carried the smell of ripe apples from the orchard behind the barn. Far out in the blue and heaving Sound a few white sails were moving. He saw by his watch that it was after two. The air smelt green. He was nearly to the narrow porte-cochere when Jessica ran down the steps and came towards him. She was wearing a light brown sweater and a green tweed skirt and he saw, as she approached, that in her flat-heeled shoes she was only slightly taller than he.

"Dan," she was calling. "Oh, Dan, how nice of you to come." She ran the last few steps and put her arms lightly around his neck, kissing his cheek hastily and then drawing back, holding both his hands, to look into his face. "I saw the car from the upstairs window," she said happily. "But I didn't know it was you until you got out to stretch. How *are* you? You look so much better than I thought you would, but thin, Dan. Did you lose a lot of weight?" With one finger she traced very lightly the hollow under his cheek-bone.

"All right, now," he said quickly. "You look wonderful, Jessica. Where's Sandy?"

She made a small grimace with the perfect and patrician

mouth. "Oh, Dan, Dan. He had to go to Cincinnati. He flew from La Guardia day before yesterday for a meeting of a foundation out there. He's one of the directors, something to do with the Taft family, and they're having a week of meetings. He hated to leave, absolutely hated it. It's been perfect here for days and days. How he'll hate not seeing you after all this time. And it's hot out there, Dan. He called me last night and it's away up in the nineties."

Dan felt the muscles sagging in his cheeks. "I wish I'd known he was away. I might have come later."

"But you're here now," Jessica said. "After all this time you're here." She gently released his hand to smooth her burnished hair. "Have you had lunch?"

He said he had eaten below Hartford and refused her further offer of a drink. He stood uncertainly on the well-raked gravel of the driveway. "How's Mrs. Munch?" he asked, at last.

"She's tending her grandchildren," said Jessica. "They moved last year so that her daughter could be nearer to her husband's job. Even now he has to drive forty miles a day, twenty each way. There's another grandchild coming, and Mrs. Munch takes two days off each week now, just to help out."

"Give her my best," Dan said, turning back towards the car. "Those sillabubs will have to wait. Where's old Arch?"

"I don't know where Arch is," said Jessica slowly. "I know he was up at dawn to pick apples. We still sell them on shares. I saw his jeep some time ago, filled with loaded baskets. Or loaded with filled baskets. I don't know where he went."

"Remember me to him, too, Jessica." Dan took a step toward the car.

"You don't have to go *yet*," said Jessica. "Not when you

just came. Come sit down. It's nice on the porch now, with that western breeze."

They went together up the sun-warmed stone steps and she pushed him gently towards the longest chair, settling into another, crossing her slender legs and leaning her bright hair against the padded back. For five minutes she spoke animatedly of their new sailboat, gazing off across the apple orchard with the familiar look of distance in her green eyes. Then suddenly, as if struck by some realization, she changed the subject and began to question Dan about his work. He spoke of Cambridge, and the room off Harvard Square, and the notes and photostats in the whiskey-carton in the car. He mentioned the approaching leave of absence, saying that he would probably stay in Enfield now until the Keats book was done. After that he might go south or west for a while."

"Why don't you come here?" she said, sitting up straight and arching out her breasts under the light brown sweater. "We'll be back in town by the end of the month. You could have the place all to yourself. Couldn't you work here, Dan?"

He explained that he needed a library under his nose for this kind of writing. There were always a dozen items that needed checking before you could go on to the next paragraph."

"Oh, books," she said, with the merest shade of petulance. "Sandy would absolutely die without them. It's the only trouble with this house in the summer. There are books all over the place, but never the right ones. He gets lonesome for his collection in New York." The look of distance had come back into her eyes. "Sometimes I think," she said, smiling, and now with no shade of petulance, "that if Sandy had to choose between me and his books, he'd take books."

Dan grinned back. "Don't be silly, Jessica. Sandy's so proud of you he'd dump them all in a minute. You're the prize in his collection."

"That's just it," said Jessica, still with the distant smile. "I'm an item. I'm the chief item, but still an item. Where are you going, Dan?"

He had swung his legs over the side of the long chair. "It's getting on," he said, consulting his watch. "It's after three. There's a lot of traffic to wrestle with between here and home."

"Oh, you mustn't go yet," said Jessica quickly. "If you go now you'll hit the five o'clock traffic in the city. Wait awhile. Look at this day, Dan, it's much too good to lose. Come help me pick apples."

He turned from the staring sun to look down at her, still sitting like an enthroned queen in the padded chair. "Apples?" he said. "Do you have golden apples?"

"Just red ones," she said. She was looking him full in the eyes, her arms braced expectantly on the aluminum tubes of the chair. "I promised to pick some for Mrs. Munch. She's never content unless she can make us quarts of apple jelly. She's very good at it. Right now, today, she's making some at her daughter's house, and she'll be back bright and early tomorrow morning with her paring knives and paraffin wax and her steam kettle. I can see her face now if the apples aren't ready in the back entry. Come on, Dan. Can't you stay and help me?"

He looked at the sky and the park-like trees and said he would do it. He threw off his jacket and left it in the front seat of the car. While he carried the light aluminum ladders from the barn into the orchard, Jessica assembled a nest of bushel-baskets and a pair of wide-mouthed canvas bags, Arch's invention, equipped with sewn-in hooks to hang to the upper rungs of the ladders. All the rest of the afternoon they worked side by side in adjoining trees, twisting the green stems and carefully lowering the ripened fruit unbruised into the hungry mouths of the canvas bags. The work was absorbing and they spoke little as they moved the ladders from tree to tree or knelt to transfer the apples into the baskets on the grass. Several times Dan reached upwards to lower her filled bag to the ground, seeing from below her beautiful face, framed among green leaves against the glowing sky, smiling down like a Gaelic queen's.

The sun was nearly down when Jessica said they had done more than enough. Her arches ached from the ladder rungs and her shoulder muscles were sore from all that lofty reaching. "Look," she said, "we've done a lot. She'll be so pleased. Have you ever seen Mrs. Munch's apple-jelly look? It's almost predatory, as if she could hardly wait to get her instruments into action."

Dan went to the barn to return the ladders and bring the wheelbarrow. They found that with the sides removed it would carry two bushels at a time. When the baskets stood ranged under the long sink in the back entry, Dan was sweating liberally. While Jessica was upstairs, he stripped off his shirt in the kitchen and washed under the tap, drying with some paper towels. He was just drinking his second glass of water when she reappeared in the doorway. He saw that she had brushed her bright hair and renewed her lipstick, and that she was carrying something.

"My, you *are* thin," she said. She crossed the room and put her cool hands on his shoulders. "Here," she said. "Here's one of Sandy's shirts. You've lost so much weight that it won't fit, but you'd better wear it until yours dries out. It gets cold here after sunset. Where's your jacket?"

He said that he had left it in the car and she went out to retrieve it for him. He found that Sandy's shirt fitted reasonably well and when she came back he had finished putting it on and was drinking another glass of water.

"Poor Dan," said Jessica. "You were really thirsty. Are you as hungry as I am, or did you eat too many apples?"

"How hungry are you?" he said, grinning.

"Just this side of ravenous. You're so thin I'll have to feed you anyway. Mrs. Munch always leaves the ice-box full. She doesn't trust my cooking." Jessica opened the door of the refrigerator and bent in the green skirt to look at the shelves. "Um," she said. "Here's a whole platter of fried chicken. Do you like fried chicken?"

When he said yes, she went humming into the dining-room, returning with a large tray on which she had laid out dinner plates and silver. "I'll fix the plates out here and we can eat in the study," she said. "There's a driftwood fire all laid and ready, and we can sit on Axton's trophy."

"Axton's trophy?"

"Oh, you haven't seen Axton's trophy. My stepfather was once a great white hunter. Do you know him? Did you ever meet him? They live in an apartment in Philadelphia now and there's no room there for his heads and hides. He insisted we take his Bengali tiger. It's a huge thing, with the head left on and great grinning teeth. Mrs. Munch hates it. She says it's a dust-catcher but I think she's secretly afraid of it. Are you still thirsty, Dan? Wouldn't you like a martini? The materials are in that chest in the study. I'll bring ice."

He mixed gin and vermouth, thinking of Sandy's mathematical measurements. The fierce cat's eyes glared up from the floor as he bent to light the fire, and he saw that the room, since he had last been in it, had been completely redecorated, the dark woodwork painted in a lighter shade, the chairs freshly slip-covered. New green draperies were drawn across the bay-window on the seaward side, and Sandy's lesser books were ranged on shelves in every available part of the room.

When she brought the ice and the loaded tray, the sea-dank room was already warming and the air was filled with the pleasant odor of burning driftwood. Jessica put down the tray, handed him the ice-cubes, silently accepted the glass he poured for her, and sat down cross-legged on the tiger-pelt, watching the dance of the flames. "There's probably a poet who has written about this," she said. "Tell me one, Dr. Sherwood. Name me a name."

"A hundred poets," said Dan, from his seat on the couch. "Probably a thousand. Omar the Tentmaker didn't hit it. He skips the fried chicken and the driftwood fire. That's Omar's loss."

"Name me another."

"Well, Keats. John Keats. He's got it all somewhere, even if he never assembled the parts in just this way. His sister-in-law probably learned to cook fried chicken over here, but I doubt if she sent him any. It would have been gamey by the time it got to England."

"What was her name?"

"Georgiana. And her husband's name was George. It was a Georgey time in England then."

"Kissed the girls and made them cry."

"Keats would have liked to."

"We had George Washington," Jessica said. "I can't imagine our George kissing anybody but Martha. Tell me some more about John Keats."

"He would like this room. Right now he would revel in it. In one of his letters he says that sensations are better than thoughts."

"How does he say it?"

"O for a life of sensations rather than thoughts. Something like that."

Jessica drained her glass and stood up, smoothing the green skirt over her slender hips. She put the glass on the tray and wordlessly handed Dan a paper napkin and a full plate. "Here's another martini," she said, "for the thirsty apple-picker." She emptied the shaker into Dan's glass. "It's probably ice-water," she said. "Wouldn't you like another before you eat?"

"No, Jess. Time for chow."

She sat down again before the fire. "You're supposed to eat the chicken by hand," she said. "There are plenty of paper napkins if we get too greasy."

After they had eaten she gathered the plates and glasses and took them away. Dan leaned back somnolently, watching the fire. His face felt windburned from the afternoon in the orchard. It was now so warm in the room that the jacket was uncomfortable and he hung it on the back of one of the chairs. Even Sandy's woolen shirt seemed too heavy and he thought of finding his own where he had left it to dry in the kitchen. He had just entered the dank-smelling front hall on the way when he saw her coming down the stairs.

"Where are you going, Dan?" she said softly. "Come back and sit down." She took his hand and led him back to the fire. "You haven't tried Axton's trophy," she said. "It's really com-

fortable. Try Axton's special." She lay back with her head between the tiger's ears and stretched her legs towards the fire.
From his place beside her he saw that she had now exchanged
the low-heeled shoes for some slippers of dark green velvet.

"Where'd you get the slippers?"

"Aren't they nice? I got them in Florence on the Ponte
Vecchio. Sandy was somewhere buying books and I went bar-
gaining all alone. Got my bottom pinched twice that day."

"The old Italian custom?"

"With the young American customer. But they make beautiful slippers. I bargained for them, Dan."

"Was it fun?"

"Oh, great fun. They seemed to expect you to bargain, and
I found I was a very good bargainer."

"You don't look like one," Dan said. "You look like an
Irish queen and Irish queens never deigned to bargain. They
just took what they wanted."

"I was very good," Jessica said. "He argued and resisted and
argued some more. But in the end he came down to my price."

"He should have known better," Dan said, laughing.

Jessica turned her head and looked at him with so full and
frank a gaze in her green eyes that he felt his laughter drained
away to settle in savage constriction in the muscles of his
throat.

"He *should* really have known better," said Jessica. "Oh,
Dan. Lonely old Dan. He ought to have known he would
have to come down."

* * * * *

When they came out of the back door, unspeaking, a little
apart, Dan saw that the sky was filled with frosty stars. The

wind had shifted out of the west and into the northeast and you could smell the kelp-and-salt smell from the ocean. It was very much colder now, and he felt her shivering as the air flowed around them.

"You'd better go in, Jess," he said. "After the fire, it's much too cold out here. Will you be all right?"

"I'll be fine," she said. "I'll sleep like a top. Drive carefully, Dan. How do you feel?"

"Take how you feel and multiply by a thousand," Dan said. "Sleep well, Jess."

When she had gone back into the house and closed the door behind her, he started the car and drove without lights under the star-filled sky until he was through Sandy's gate. Then he switched on the high beams and drove fast along the empty roads until he reached the parkway ramp. Distantly, as from another country, he could feel in his arches the persistent pressure of the ladder rungs. But he was enveloped in a sensation of singing warmth and in the car, with the windows closed against the cold night air, he was conscious of the faint lingering of her perfume.

A long time later he skirted the enormous sleeping city and crossed the soaring bridge. The cold had begun to seep now into the corners of the car and he leaned forward to switch on the heater. After a moment it started to buzz unhappily, hurling waves of dry hot air upwards into his burning face. He endured it for five minutes before he leaned again to switch it off. He had come down from the heights and the car was roaring hollowly through the dark flatlands. In the dim light from the dashboard his watch showed half-past one. Only then did he begin to realize fully the enormity of what he had done.

CHAPTER TWELVE

THE ARROW on the roadsign pointed towards Sabino Canyon. He could not think why the name was familiar until he remembered the mailman's sheaf of magazines and the kodachrome prints. "Clothed in Autumn's Gold," the caption had said. Or something of the sort. The picture showed yellow cottonwoods bordering a watercourse among gray and brown ledges of rock. Beyond the clear pool in the foreground were dry saw-toothed peaks, sharply outlined against massed cumulus clouds in an afternoon sky. Dan turned the nose of the car in that direction.

The road led past the North Corral Bar and Grill where a beer-truck was disgorging barrels, and past a roughly fenced riding-ring where a white pony with a small boy on its back was single-footing dustily around and around the closed circle. Beyond the nearer huddle of buildings and barns stood the range of mountains. They rose harshly above the desert floor and above the lesser foothills into the glaring northern sky. Now, close to noon, they were the color of dirt, with piles of detritus at the foot of the slopes and the square white shapes of suburban ranch houses, small as postage stamps among the candelabras of the saguaro cactuses. But the mountains, he knew, showed as many colors as the winter or the summer sea. At night, black as ink. Roseate gold at sunrise. Dirty drab by noon. In the late afternoon, Pogany blues and chocolate browns. Blazing bloody crimsons at the setting of the sun. And with the onset of dusk, the incredible purples and magentas that seemed to pour into the enormous hollows until the western light had wholly gone. Then gray, then black as ink once more, unless there was a moon to turn them silver.

But now, with the sun straight overhead like the eye of a madman, you could see all the strange configurations, that tumbled profusion of inanimate forms, the tipping planes and lop-sided angles, like something hacked out of ironwood with a dull axe by a crazed Titan. The road angled slowly towards the range, and you were always expecting the ascent to begin. It did not, and when you looked again, the mountains were as far off—and as near—as before. From the spine of a low ridge, Dan glanced down into a small valley. It held a decrepit ranch house, a few clumps of trees, and the unbelievable arsenic green of an alfalfa field. Then the road left the ridge and the walls of the canyon began to shoulder inwards. Just where they narrowed he rounded a curve and saw a weathered cabin on a rocky height. It faced southwest, towards the alfalfa field. A wide-roofed porch stretched all across its front.

A tall old man with white hair was climbing the steep dirt track towards the cabin, carrying a tin pail in each hand. At the sound of the car he turned half around and seemed to glance in Dan's direction. Then the tires screeched around another curve and the old man was out of sight.

Inside the canyon the pavement ended and the land sloped away down to the watercourse and the straggling line of trees and low bushes that gained their sustenance there. Only a small rivulet dripped down the stony ledges and the leaves had fallen from the trees. No shade here, he thought. No soothing rush of water. He followed the gravel road deeper into the canyon.

It angled gradually along the right-hand side. Dust-clouds rose behind the laboring tires. On the rocky slopes a few gray-green saguaros lifted spiny arms like headless scarecrows in a posture of worship. Broken slabs of rock lay baking in the merciless sun. The bed of the stream was now far below him and he could look down into the tops of bare trees.

At last the roadway petered out, opening into what might once have been a gravel pit, a level gouge in the mountain-side, circular in shape, the size of a small playing field. Others, he saw, had been there before him. The place was littered with human debris: paper cups that had once held coffee or orangeade, crumpled paper bags and sandwich wrappings, green shards of broken bottles. Heaped near the center of the open space was a jumble of beer cans. The signature of American occupancy, he thought. On a field sable, a beer-can couchant.

He set the brake and got out, stretching. His shirt was stuck to his back, and he felt it drying quickly in the movement of air down the canyon. Why do we ruin everything? he thought. Not that this dry hole among the mountains was much to begin with, but we have made it worse. In Europe they think—or at least some of them think—that we are the King Midases of modern times. They still dream like the old Spaniards of streets paved with gold and coffers of coins heaped up in every closet. But we are the Unmidases, by God. Whatever we touch turns to dross.

The sun beat down into the hollow. Dan skirted a pile of excrement and strolled across the pit towards a battered trashbarrel. It was full to overflowing. Flies droned there busily, settled and crawled on thread-like legs, took off again in three-inch flights. He jumped slightly at a sudden movement beyond the barrel. But it was only a newspaper, yellowed pages flipping in the hot breeze from up the canyon. Near it lay the desiccated evidence of lovemaking, pitched with poor or indifferent aim from a parked car. Eros tyrannos, he thought. Cakes and ale.

He turned his back and stood gazing down the slope. A worn path zigzagged down. He pocketed the car keys, picked up the book and his sandwich, and began the steep descent. There was nothing at the bottom but a shallow ditch half-filled with dry sand. He sat with his back against one of the trees and mopped his forehead. At this level no breeze was stirring, but he found that his sweat dried quickly in the sparse shade of the leafless bole. The sandwich made a lump in his pocket. He unwrapped and ate it, chewing slowly, wishing he had remembered to bring some water.

From the tree-root beside him, Kemp's title met his eye. *The Sleep of the Fathers.* The gold-leaf on the front cover was barely legible. Like an old tombstone, he thought. Like that slab of lichened marble in the Massachusetts cemetery where my father sleeps, if sleep is the word. The late Mr. Prentiss Sherwood, Harvard '18, married Deborah Perkins June, 1920, sired Daniel Jackson Sherwood born March, 1921, died with his wife in a shower of Scotch whiskey when the speeding rum-runner's truck hit them broadside at that country crossroads 18 December, 1926. That's what put him to sleep, if sleep is the word. Those are the facts. And if you are not making it up, there is that hearse on runners, cutting deep into the snow in the street, snow mushy with the midwinter thaw and yellow with the stale of passing horses, the black oblong moving swiftly out of sight under the gray and leafless elms.

Maybe I made that one up, he thought, because the winter picture I have of my father also involves a sled. Only this time I am sitting on it, and my father is pulling me along the snow on the sidewalk. It is night, and as we pass the streetlights great flakes are falling lazily, adding another layer to the older snow. It must be a Sunday night because there is a great far clangor in the sky of many churchbells, partly muffled by the falling snow. My father is smoking a cigar, and the smoke drifts back to where I sit on the sled, and I can never smell a cigar in the fresh night air of a New England winter without that scene's coming into my mind.

The other scene is in sunlight, probably in late spring or summer because the street I follow is dappled in maple-shade. No one saw me leave the house and I am walking to meet him, carrying a stick of some kind, hitting the boles of the trees as I pass. Perhaps I am singing or humming. Then I see him far down the street. I cannot see his face but I know it is my father from his gait. He is wearing a white shirt and a straw hat, and he carries his jacket over one shoulder. I wave and shout but just at that moment there is a great crash behind me and I turn, startled, to see Con Horigan's grocery cart and the horse tossing its head and somewhere between a canter and a gallop, running away. He is pulling the heavy cart behind him and Con Horigan is not on the seat. The cart lurches crazily because it has only three wheels. One has been knocked off against the maple tree at the corner when the horse turned too sharply. I watch the cart careening down the street, and my father is running out in front of it. He has dropped his hat and jacket and I yell because he is too close. But he grabs the horse's cheek-strap and stops the rig expertly. And the reel flickers out like an old movie.

He opened Kemp's book and began to read, underlining words and paragraphs, scribbling marginal notes. Like the Old Testament story on which it was based, this one was stark, filled with old hatreds and festering cruelties. Sons revolted against their fathers, kicking free in irrational violence. Fathers grew to hate their sons, set up walls to keep them out, turned their faces resolutely away. The fault here, as in so much of Kemp's work, was the unrelieved darkness of his vision, like that view of the pit in Blake's poem where the bland-faced angel,—or was it the devil?—stood on the edge of an enormous precipice, pointing fearsomely down towards the hellbroth where leviathans writhed like Loch Ness monsters. Later Blake showed you that it was all a fantasy: what was really there was a musician in the moonlight. But for Kemp there was no music and the moonlight was the color of blood.

He would recognize that gravel pit up there, though. That is what one of the rooms in hell looks like, and Kemp has been to hell. He has been to hell plenty of times. Inside the Bois de Belleau, for one. On that tramp steamer off Cape Horn for another. Or in the green gloom of the Canadian woods where the howling lumberjacks buried their axe-heads in the felled and twitching bodies of the Indians.

Déjà vu, he thought. When we get to hell we will not be much surprised at what we see. We will have met it before in bits and pieces. In the wards for the incontinents in the state insane hospitals. In the streets of Camden where the amiable war veteran suddenly runs amok. The blue-eyed rat-face and the rump-steak face in the musty German hall. The strangled corpse sage-hidden. The grinning pirate with the jack-handle who knees you first and beans you after, hulking darkly between you and the sun.

The great Kemp, he thought. And what is this greatness? It is the badge we issue to those who have tackled some of the more profound problems of behavior or belief. The red badge of greatness. The purple heart all bloodied over with the cast of contemplation. For this is how we judge greatness, no matter what the estheticians say: no matter what even the moralists say. How widely and deeply did we range? What harpoons festered in our flesh? What stones from what slings have dented our skulls and disfigured our skeletons? Our books show it—not mine, but his.

And what do they show? The clear and present signs, the indubitable stigmata, of those who have been to hell and back. Yes, greatness. Books like Kemp's are scars healed over: the traceable record of all the wounds, asked-for or accidental, self-inflicted or God-inflicted, that Kemp sustained in his time. Relief-maps of his scar tissue. The fever-charts, he thought, of St. Sebastian Kemp.

The book lay open in his lap where he sat against the roots of the tree. Dan began to read once more, but he found that he could not concentrate. The print swam before his eyes and one of his legs had gone to sleep. This extramural study was not working. It might work for some: the Enfield students basking on army blankets on shaven turf under the shade trees on the peaceful slopes of the campus. It was not working here.

He climbed the hill laboriously on the zig-zag path. The interior of the car was like an oven. He looked sourly around the dry gulch. The pile of beer cans baked in the gross sunlight. He started the car and drove down the canyon, pursued by whirling clouds of dust. When he passed the old man's cabin, he leaned momentarily across the seat and peered up the glaring slope. But the old man was nowhere in sight.

PART THREE

THE WHEEL

CHAPTER THIRTEEN

ONE FOOT braced against the peeled cedar post, the other on the hard-baked earthen floor, he sat in the old horsehide chair, drank the beer, and let his eyes rove across that strange landscape. Satan's kitchen, he thought. Assaulting the eyes like acetylene flame, the raw cinnamon-colored ground shimmered in the afternoon heat, like something burned over long ago in a chemical holocaust.

From where he sat on Hart's porch he could look down into the valley with the battered ranch house and the acid green alfalfa patch. Over the flank of the rock-strewn hill an access road had been cut, like a scar in the flesh of an old Apache. There was neither wind nor any cloud, and the landscape lay quiet as a sealed room except for the country wagon, pulled by a black mule, which was moving like a beetle along the dusty road. Hunched on the wagon seat, holding reins fine as spider webs, was a single human figure. Even at that distance, in the enormous silence, you could hear the cricket-creak of an ungreased wheel, turning and returning and turning.

Dan sniffed the air. That odorless air so different from the pungency of Berkshire autumns when you tramped the woods

after rain and clear drops hung like emerald or topaz at the
end of every twig. Not the faint green aroma of drying
ground in spring, either, with the snow gone, thin sun streaming in, and in the deeper glades the delicate spice-smell of
partridge berries, the same that Aunt Abby used inside glass
globes as table ornaments. Black earth at the bottom, green
moss gouged up with a knife-blade, and finally the complex
design, much poked and fiddled with, of ground-fern and
red berries, gently uprooted and replanted in the earth and
the moss. "Better than ships in bottles," she would say. "Smell
that woodsy smell." She would hold the jar under his nose
while he sniffed with real or pretended appreciation.

But out here the dry neutrality, unless you were inside a
corral. Even there, twenty feet off, the sweet-sour horse-smell
had faded, baked out of the dust by the staring golden eye,
relentless and unquenchable, in the sky's Italian blue.

"How you making out, Dan?" said Hart's voice from inside
the cabin.

"All right, Hart."

"How's that?"

"Peaceful like New Year's, lazy like summer."

"Take it easy there, boy," Hart said. "It's a long year
ahead."

Dan made no answer. The creaking wagon was just disappearing beyond the flank of the low hill, with the inevitable dust cloud moiling up from where the wheels had passed.
You were unaware, unless you had been in this country, of
this special phenomenon of dust. In a hundred westerns,
filmed on location down here or farther north, you had seen
the dust churning up as the good guys formed a posse and
went larruping after the bad guys, or vice versa. But you did

not think of it as it really was until you had lived in it. It seeped under door-cracks, spread over table tops in slow layers, ground into the leather of your shoes, streaked the body of your car, settled in the porches of your ears, lined your nostrils, crunched between your teeth like infinitesimal raspberry seeds.

Hart appeared in the doorway, jingling silver in his pocket. "Got a nickel says you're dreaming of New England," he said.

"If you mean right now, you lose," Dan said. "Five, ten minutes ago I was thinking of Lenox. This minute I was thinking about the dust."

Hart went to the porch-rail, cleared his throat, and spat. "Gets into everything out here. Out here the old saying about eating a peck of dirt before you die goes double or triple. Nothing like those green-and-white New England villages where we were raised."

He vanished inside again, leaving Dan alone. They *were* green-and-white, Dan thought, even if the white turned rusty-yellow after a run of those northern winters. The aunts did their best with the house at 40 Kossuth Street, hiring the same painter every five years, borrowing from the bank to pay him. It was always a good place to come back to. Just beyond Hagyard's drugstore you followed Franklin to Church, turning left on Tucker until Kossuth branched off and you saw Number 40 on its low knoll, with the two shade-maples and the Norway spruce conically symmetrical on the side lawn. And in summer the two brown rockers and the creaking hammock on the front piazza. Green and white. Not this burning wasteland where the sun beat down.

Hart came out with two more cans of beer. He punctured

one and filled Dan's glass before he settled back with the other into the weathered old morris-chair. Down in the valley, the wagon had stopped beside the decrepit ranch house. The driver had climbed down and was talking to one who had come out to meet him. The two distant tiny figures were distinct against the crumbling adobe wall.

"Thanks," Dan said. "Did you get the brushes clean?"

"No thanks to me," Hart said. "You brought the beer. And the turpentine. Seems as if I get to town less and less. You ought to see that turpentine now. What's that color you mentioned?"

"You mean excremental yellow?"

"Dirty mustard."

"That was Pope's color," Dan said. "Used it on his ene mies."

"All things looked yellow to his jaundiced eye?"

"It was more than jaundice," Dan said. "As a good Catholic he should have taken a sacramental view of the universe. What came out was the other extreme—the excremental view. In one you bless and are blessed. In the other you curse and are cursed."

"Did he ever read the Stoics?" said Hart.

"Maybe. I don't really know. Why?"

"Wait a minute," Hart said. He disappeared inside the cabin and returned with a small volume. His index finger marked the place and he laid the book open on Dan's knees. "Here," he said. "Read that."

It was an old Heinemann *Marcus Aurelius*. The passage was bracketed in blue pencil:

"Say to thyself at daybreak: I shall come across the busybody, the thankless, the overbearing, the treacherous, the envious, the

unneighborly. All this has befallen them because they know not good from evil. But I, in that I have comprehended the nature of the Good that it is beautiful, and the nature of Evil that it is ugly, and the nature of the wrongdoer himself that it is akin to me, can neither be injured by any of them, nor can I be wroth with my kinsman and hate him."

Dan read the passage twice and then looked up from the page. Hart appeared to have forgotten him. Sprawled in the old morris-chair, he was gazing down across the sunsmitten landscape, his crockery-blue eyes like slits under the prominent bony brows.

"It sounds to me as if the emperor had found a program," Dan said slowly. "I doubt if mere stoic resolution can guard us from all injury, though. There is still the dragon in the basement. We come creaking along with our mule-teams, and the noise disturbs his sleep. He comes snuffling up the cellar stairs and you can smell his foul breath under the crack of the door."

"That's a fact," Hart said. "It's also a fact, he says, that the evil-doers do evil because they don't know any better."

"I doubt the assumption," Dan quietly said.

"You'd have to agree they lack something, though. The emperor says they lack a vision of the Good."

"They sure do."

"So in a way you can't blame them for doing evil. They don't have the vision of perfection, or whatever you want to call it."

"It's as good a term as any," Dan said. "I must say that, to me, the emperor sounds a little smug. He's had it. They haven't. So he proposes to face the problem of evil by rising above it. Isn't that what he's proposing?"

Hart did not answer.

"He also says you shouldn't hate evil," Dan said. "Forgive them, for they know not what they do, and all that. I don't know, but it's in my grain to doubt it. I was raised by a couple of maiden aunts—old-fashioned New England Puritans. They would have had a fit if you told them not to hate evil. They thought that kind of hate was a prime moral obligation."

"Well, yes," Hart said, slowly. "I had a Scotch Presbyterian father who felt the same way, and he drummed it into the seats of his three sons. Still, the old emperor had a Puritanical streak. He doesn't say we shouldn't hate the lice that crawl in the underwear of society. He just says we ought to recognize that we are of them. They're our blood-brothers. You can't blame a louse for sucking blood. It's his nature. But the same dirty blood runs through us that runs through them. We just know how to control it."

"How control?"

"We know what's good. They don't. The advantage is ours."

"That's part of it, I guess," Dan said. "But every day we have the problem of recognizing evil, either inside or outside ourselves."

"The vision is supposed to take care of that."

"How do we know the vision isn't an illusion?" said Dan. "All the time we fool ourselves with phoney fantasies. I could be a mystic or a sentimentalist with a vision of Goodness so bright that it would blind me to the presence of darkness."

"That happens. Yes."

"Or I could be what they call a realist," Dan said. "That's one who has looked into the darkness so long that he is able to kid himself into thinking it's daylight. He gets so reconciled, on principle, to the forms of human bastardry that he

takes its milder forms for the Good. We don't have many
genuine mystics, but the sentimentalists and the so-called
realists are all around us. I don't know which is worse."

"You sound as if you'd pick the realist."

"As more dangerous?" said Dan. "I'm not sure. Yeats used
to talk about one kind of sentimentalist. Some kind of moral
Narcissus. He's probably more numerous and so maybe more
dangerous. His vision of the Good is built around his own
self-portrait. He's a genius in the art of self-justification.
There's nothing he does that he can't justify in his own mind.
Narciss—Narcissist—"

"I could never say it either."

"Narcissistic," Dan said in a stuttering burst. "Narcissistic
self-adoration. It's always the others who do the evil, never
old Narcissus. What he does himself he can always find an
excuse for. He was lonesome or he had had a few too many
martinis. He was scared or sick or in love or in heat. The
police-blotters are full of his excuses. A lot of the time he
will tell you that someone or something else was responsible
for what he did. It might be Fate or Destiny, the scapegoat
with the longest and scabbiest beard in the flock. It might
be society, or his stupid parents, or his incompatible wife.
Or the older brother who bullied him or the younger brother
who was preferred over him. After you have used up all the
other excuses, you can always go back to the prenatal con-
ditioning. While your ma was pregnant with you, she went
to the movies and was scared by Rin-Tin-Tin."

"You sound like a moralist," Hart said, laughing.

Dan grinned wryly. "I probably sound like a damned New
England Puritan in a Catholic confession-booth," he said.
"But it's a fact, isn't it? We flip the sacramental universe

upside down and then complain because the blood—the oil of mustard—runs to our heads. The emperor thought he knew how to flip it back, or how never to let it capsize in the first place. I wish I was that certain."

He mopped his forehead and looked over at Hart Mackenzie. Under his heavy brows the old man was gazing into the distant sun-glare. The slow mule and the wagon with the ungreased wheel was turning into the highway in a cloud of desert dust.

"Sometimes it'll flip back by itself," Hart said, slowly. "One thing sure, Dan. You have to give it time."

*   *   *   *   *

He had known Hart Mackenzie for less than three weeks, but they were as friendly already, Dan reflected, as if it had been three years. And it had begun in mid-December with a phone-call from Connie Haybright.

She said she was calling about the interview. It wasn't done yet and now she had no idea when she would get it written.

"It doesn't matter," Dan said. "There are better topics than the Golden West Library."

"That's not it," said Connie quickly. "It's a good interview. I mean it's wonderful material. The problem is that I have to go away and I'm not sure when I'll get back."

"I hope it's nothing serious."

"It is and it isn't," Connie said. "It's my grandmother in Chicago. She's broken her hip. My mother can't leave. So I'm flying east tonight. I tried to call Professor O'Keefe, and I've written Hart Mackenzie."

"O'Keefe's lecturing in California," Dan said. "Who was the other one?"

"Hart Mackenzie. He's the artist. The painter. I thought I told you about him. He lives out of town and he doesn't— he won't have a telephone."

"Out near the canyon?"

"Sabino Canyon," Connie said. "You ought to meet him. You'd like him."

"Maybe I've seen him," Dan said. "What does he look like?"

"He's old. Very white hair. Tall and straight."

"Does he live in that cabin on the left of the road?"

"How did you know?"

"I saw him one day."

"To talk to?"

"No," Dan said. "I was driving past. He was carrying water up the slope to his cabin."

"That's Hart all right," Connie said. "He's got a spring at the bottom of the hill. He keeps saying he'll have it piped into the cabin but he never does. He's too busy painting. Anyway he says he likes the exercise."

"What exercise?"

"Carrying the water," Connie said. "He's a regular Thoreau."

"Then he wouldn't care for visitors."

"I don't know," Connie said. "He's been nice to me."

"Have you known him long?"

"Not long. Less than a year. If you go out there, say I told you to come. And try to get him to show you his pictures."

* * * * *

A few days before Christmas, Dan picked up a bottle of wine and drove out to the canyon. The tires churned and roared on the loose pebbles of the slope. At the top, behind the cabin, the ground leveled off to form a high plateau. It has been neatly raked and he saw, under a rough lean-to, the shape of a jeep, partly covered with a square of tarpaulin.

The man who answered his knock was tall and broad-shouldered. He wore a faded work-shirt, khakis stained with paint, and high-laced brogans whose toes were splattered with a dozen colors. Under the rough white hair, his eyes showed brightly, the color of blue crockery. The leathery creased lines in his face made him look like a mild Indian. As soon as Dan mentioned Connie Haybright's name, Hart Mackenzie stood back from the door and asked him to come in.

After the raw sunlight, the front room of the cabin seemed dark. It was sparsely furnished with cowhide chairs and a few painted chests of Spanish design. Three of the walls were whitewashed and dotted with pictures. The fourth was given over to a partly finished mural in rich browns and tans, a landscape of eroded mountains under a burning sky. Outlines of the unfinished parts were roughly sketched in charcoal on the dry plaster. The air smelled pleasantly of paint.

"Connie talked about your paintings," Dan said, "but she didn't mention the mural. It's like a window looking out."

"I wish it were," said Hart Mackenzie. "The light's bad in here, even with the studio door open. The trouble with a mural is you can't move it. I've thought of putting in a sky-light up there, but right now it's a bigger job than I want to tackle."

"Like the water-pipes?" said Dan, grinning.

"She told you about those, did she?" said Hart. "She thinks

it's my Scotch penuriousness. I told her I'd lived too long in Italy to think improvements matter."

Dan remembered the bottle under his arm. He stood it on the table. "This isn't Italian, but at least it's wine."

"Wine," said Hart, merrily, unwrapping the paper. "Let's break it out. Here. Sit down here somewhere, if you can find a place. I'll see if I can locate a corkscrew."

The old man disappeared into one of the back rooms. Dan looked at the pictures. All but two were clearly the work of one man, bold landscapes in the earthen colors of the desert. The two that were really alien had been set in wall-niches on either side of a large old mission chest. One showed a shadowy gorge where terrified travelers, dwarfed by walls of rock, were rushing their pack mules over a rude bridge. Out of the mist above their heads a huge dragon was descending, craning its neck towards the fear-stricken mountaineers. In the second, two small naked children were at play in a flower-spangled meadow. Nearby, arms filled with blossoms, stood the statuesque figure of a woman, Grecian in profile, auburn-haired, her body half-draped in blue. The foreground was park-like, but the higher ground was overgrown with harsh grass. A red knight in greaves and helmet urged his horse towards an invisible conflict. A bent old man was seated on a boulder, unaware of the skeletal figure behind him whose fingers were locked around a ragged club in the act of bashing in his ancient skull. Between the two groups was a marble fountain, gleaming in sunlight. On its face was the legend:

VITA SOMNIUM BREVE

"What are these?" said Dan, when Hart returned.

"Those?" said Hart, grinning. "They're another Italian

memento. Man named Böcklin—Arnold Böcklin—a Swiss.
We met in Fiesole when I was just getting started. Around
1900 he was famous. Did you ever see one of his called *The
Island of Death?* Rachmaninoff did a piece about it."

Dan took the wine-glass. "Here's to you," he said.

"Here's to old Böcklin," Hart said. "An impossible romantic. He did nymphs and satyrs in flowery forests. There's
another one of the Great God Pan scaring the hell out of a
goatherd in a mountain pass. Nobody likes him any longer.
But he was a good technician and a really brilliant colorist.
We met him one day along the road to Fiesole. My wife was
a great beauty, with masses of sorrel hair. He insisted we
come to his villa to see the fountain-picture. Said my wife
Mary was the spit and image of that lady with the flowers."

"And was she?"

"Not especially. The color of the hair was like, and something in the line of the jaw, and the general build. But Mary
was touched to be a stranger's dream-girl. When prints of
Böcklin's pictures came out, we had to buy a portfolio."

"What about the other one?" asked Dan, slowly.

"The gorge? Oh, Böcklin used to say it was somewhere in
the Alps. He called it *Die Felsenschlucht.* But it's really a
Gothic nightmare, with that fantastic dragon. It might be
one of the doorways to hell, or hell itself."

Dan sat unmoving. The whole business was fantastic. How
many others, in their nightmares or their daydreams, saw
images like these side by side? This park-like lawn with the
half-draped figure and the innocents at play. And in the background, those images of war and death, and the dragon writhing free. The psychologists could explain it. It would not
even make Dr. Jung raise his eyebrows. Maybe Jung even

knew Böcklin. "Life is a dream soon done," said the legend on the fountain. A daydream, sure. Böcklin also knew that it was—could at any rate be—a nightmare, complete with dragons.

In the quiet of the room Dan's voice sounded loud. "What made you pick these two?" he asked. "Out of all the portfolio, what made you settle on that gorge and the field of flowers?"

Hart was holding his glass in a beam of light from the westering sun, turning it in his hands, studying the color of the wine. For a long moment he made no answer. "Oh, sentimental reasons," he said at last. "Poetic reasons. It's an imagination of the way things are, wouldn't you say? Upstairs is where the flowers grow. Down under is the dragon in the basement."

CHAPTER FOURTEEN

In the front lobby of the Pioneer Hotel, Harcomb Wiley was sitting in one of the leather chairs, filing his nails, a loosely folded newspaper neglected in his lap. He closed the penknife blade and lifted a languid hand in greeting.

"Hello, Dan. What brings you here?"

"Nothing but cigarettes," Dan said. "How about you?"

"Nothing but hair," said Harcomb. "Eunice is in the beauty parlor. They just came out to say she'd be there another half-hour. She won't be good for anything the rest of the day. Sit down, Dan. Keep me company. What's new?"

"Let me get the cigarettes," Dan said.

Wiley's high pale forehead shone blandly in the light from the front windows. In his dark clothes he looked more than ever like a Papal legate on leave from the Vatican. "Axel was asking for you," he said, as Dan sank into the deep chair.

"They're back from California?"

"Couple of days ago," Wiley said. "Earlier than expected. They ran into some trouble in the shape of a backbiting female in Berkeley. Moira's a wreck. It was that bitch in Berkeley. Opened up all the old wounds."

"Wounds?"

"You haven't heard that story?" asked Wiley, raising his
pontifical eyebrows. "Well, of course you wouldn't. Not from
Axel, anyway. It's a real piece of demonology. Your friend
Kemp would relish it. By the way, did you ever write that
Cissie Waterhouse?"

"Long ago," Dan said. "I also wrote Kemp's sister Mellissa
and finally Kemp himself. No answers yet."

"It takes time," Wiley said. "Like getting your hair curled.
Did Axel ever tell you why he came out here?"

"Some illness," said Dan. "I gathered it was arthritis. The
first time I met him he talked about Tucson as the—"

"The place of exiles," said Wiley quickly. "The Land of
Nod? I know. That's his usual routine. What happened to
the O'Keefes is a lot worse than arthritis. Or at least as bad.
And now it's opened up again."

In a voice hushed to the confidential level, eyes gleaming, pale hands gesturing, Harcomb Wiley said that Moira
was Axel's third wife. His first had been a German girl from
the Rhineland, who died in a Swiss sanitarium. Axel waited
fifteen years before he married again, this time to an American, daughter of a Stanford professor, a brilliant spinster
nearly Axel's age, a scholar in her own right. After they were
married she taught from time to time, filling in at Vassar
and Connecticut College when people went on sabbatical
leaves. In fact she was driving back from a Vassar seminar
when she was killed in a freak accident, skidding on a rainy
pavement.

"The car ended upside down in a reservoir," Wiley said.
"Just at the end of the last war. You must have seen it in
the papers."

"I don't remember," said Dan.

It was then, said Wiley, that the trouble began. For Axel waited no more than three months before he married Moira. She was one of his students. Somehow it got around that Axel had been having an affair with Moira while the brilliant wife was going around and giving the lectures. It was a damned lie, of course. But the women began to cut Moira dead on the street and there were even some poison pen letters. Axel and Moira ignored it for six or eight months, hoping that the biddies would relent. At last they seemed to, or one of them did. She called up and asked Moira to a tea-party and Moira got dressed up and went. That was the beginning of the end, Wiley said.

More precisely, it was the end. At least it was the end of Axel's career at that college because the next day the hostess noised it around that during the tea Moira had slipped into the bedroom where the women had left their coats and stolen all the money she could find. Axel quit cold. He went to the president and resigned, saying that his health was poor and that his doctors had advised him to look for a warmer climate. He and Moira packed up and came to Arizona.

Wiley told the story with a kind of sotto voce relish. Living in Tucson, he said, was like living in the middle of a race-track. If someone started gossiping, Dan would know the truth. If it happened in California, it could happen here. Moira had taken enough. Dan had probably noticed how nervous she still was.

"What that girl really needs is an outside interest," Wiley said. "She ought to take some courses at the university, or get some lessons in painting, or—"

"If Lee's school ever opens, she could go there," Dan said.

"What I told Eunice," said Harcomb Wiley. "Now where the hell is that woman? Under the dryer, no doubt. Eunice doesn't like this Mandeville Lee, though. Doesn't believe in his what-you-might-call cultural sincerity."

"She may have something there," Dan said. "Still, Moira could learn to weave tapestries, if Lee finds somebody who can teach weaving."

"Oh, I gather he's all set," Wiley said. He fumbled with the newspaper and spread it open across Dan's knees.

It was a full-page advertisement.

GRAND OPENING

THE WESTERN ACADEMY OF ARTS AND CRAFTS
TUCSON'S GREAT NEW ART CENTER
TWELVE FASCINATING NEW COURSES
FOR THE TALENTED AMATEUR

ARCHITECTURAL DESIGN * * *   CERAMICS * * *
CREATIVE WRITING * * *   METALCRAFT * * *
JEWELRY MAKING * * *   PAINTING IN OILS * * *
PUBLIC SPEAKING * * *   RUG WEAVING * * *
SILK SCREEN WORK * * *   WATER COLOR * * *
CLAY MODELING * * *   PIANO AND VIOLIN * * *

A DISTINGUISHED STAFF IS READY TO GUIDE YOU TO CREATIVITY

Visit the beautiful and newly equipped
ACADEMY PLANT
GRAND OPENING, SATURDAY, JANUARY 28, 1950
REGISTRATION DAY
WEDNESDAY, FEBRUARY 1, 1950
TAKE THAT COURSE YOU ALWAYS MEANT TO TAKE

Dan folded the paper and handed it back. "Some spread," he grinned. "Lee's been having some personnel trouble, but he seems to have solved the problem."

"I'll work on Eunice," Wiley said. "She and Moira could take that course in rug-weaving, or the one in ceramics. Dan, excuse me. There's Eunice now. She's wandered out the wrong door as usual. No wonder. They cook your brains under those dryers. So long, Dan. I'll have to put her to bed with an ice-pack."

* * * * *

He was brushing his teeth when the telephone rang. It was Mandeville Lee, asking where the hell he had been lately.

"Come on over and have a drink."

"I'm just going out," Dan said. "How's the Academy?"

"As soon as the paint dries, we're set."

"Have you got your faculty?"

"Come have a drink, Dan. I'll tell you all about it."

"I'm just leaving for a reserve meeting."

"Leaving for a what?"

"Reserve officers' meeting."

"What was your rank coming out of the army?"

"Captain," said Dan.

"Why piddle around that group, boy? You'll never get your majority in a million years."

"Maybe so," Dan said. "In 1946, I missed it by three days. All you had to do was wait around the separation center while they cleared the papers and cut the orders. I didn't wait. I wanted to get married."

"You married?" cried Lee. "I didn't know you were mar ried."

"I was," said Dan, shortly. "How about you?"

Lee laughed gaily. "Not me, Dan. I make them work for free.

"I suppose that goes for your faculty."

Lee chuckled. You could not get under his hide. "Not for you, Dan. You handle the creative writing people and I'll split 60–40. These goddam two-bit Shakespeares going to be buzzing around like flies around a honey-jug. We'll take them in groups of ten. Three hours a week for six weeks. Between now and when it gets hot in the spring we can run a couple of sessions. Three hours a week for six weeks is eighteen hours at three bucks an hour is fifty-four dollars, call it an even fifty, cash on the barrel head. That's five hundred for every batch of ten suckers. With four batches, twelve hours a week, that's two thousand smackers every six weeks on the creative writing alone. I cover my overhead with a forty percent cut, that's eight hundred dollars. You clear twelve-hundred even, right? For a total of seventy-two hours spread out over six weeks, you are getting better than sixteen bucks an hour of the easiest work in the world."

"Who said it was easy?"

"Easy for you, Professor. Ain't you a writer?"

"I'm writing, yes."

"Let it wait," Lee cried. "If it's any good it won't rot on you in six weeks. I'll tell you what will rot, though. A great big juicy pile of lettuce is starting to rot this minute in a thousand pig-skin purses around this damn town. Perishable ain't the word for it, Dan. Harvest time for Arizona lettuce, and I'm letting you in on the ground floor."

"No."

"What more do you want, Dan? Listen, tell you what I'll

do. I'll throw in your house rent on top of that sixty percent."

"I can't take the time."

"Time!" said Lee. "What the hell kind of time is seventy-
two hours spread over six weeks? You waste that much sitting
on the can."

"No."

"Listen," Lee said. "I meant to tell you this before. A
couple of people from Maine are looking for a house out
here. Wealthy lobster people need a place for the winter.
Money is no consideration. Every other day I get an air-mail
letter or a telegram. Friend of theirs tipped them off that
that little place you're in might come on the market. I meant
to mention it to you. The price you're paying,—why, I ain't
even covering taxes on that shack."

"Tell them they can move in tomorrow," Dan said. "You
refund the January rent, pro-rated until they take over, and
I'll get out of the house in two hours flat."

"I don't know," Lee said, musingly. "I'll have to see what
happens. I might have to give them the place. Then again,
maybe not. You think over my little proposition, Dan. Sixty
percent and your rent thrown in. What could be sweeter?"

"I wouldn't touch it with a forty-foot pole."

"You say so now. But wait. Here's another proposition for
you. You recall that little wench Connie? Connie Haybright?
She's away some place now. But when she gets back, how
about you and her taking over the publicity on this school?
With your brains and her build, there's—"

Dan barked the sentence into the phone. "You leave her
alone."

"Hey, wait a minute," Lee said. "Who's running this school, you or me?"

"You make one pass at this girl and—"

"So who's making passes?" Lee interrupted amiably. "Don't get hot, son. How can a man make anything at a distance of a thousand miles? Anyhow, Dan, come see the joint. Come on out and take in the grand opening. Bagpipe music and free beer."

"I hope you enjoy it," Dan said, furiously.

"Now just simmer down with your damned clipped syllables," Lee said. "Just lay down that little old phone that you're gripping so tight and go get suited up in your Boy Scout suit. You don't want to be late for the old military science and tactics. I'll have you on this faculty yet."

"The hell you will."

Lee chuckled. "Take it easy, boy. I sure wish—"

In the middle of his sentence, Dan cradled the receiver with a bang. He was already at the door on the way out before he turned back automatically to wash his teeth again.

CHAPTER FIFTEEN

INTRUSION, he thought now, drinking the coffee at the dusty table. What is human life but a history of intrusions? The telephone, the telegram, the man from Hoboken with the morning mail. The good news and the bad; the welcome and the unwished-for.

Who's not an intruder? Tell me that. Here lie the 5 x 8 cards which show how far you have intruded upon the buried life of Nicholas Kemp, novelist. There is that tall handsome stinker with the taffy-colored hair and the grandiose plan to intrude on the domain of education. Chita intruded to wash your dishes, offer to fix you up with a drink of gin, lean close to give you a whiff of her dime-store perfume. Who escapes? Tell me that. Those biddies in Connecticut invaded the private life of Axel and Moira O'Keefe, driving them into exile in this Land of Nod. And Sachs. Buddy Sachs, invading another man's life, another's plans, edging his noisome bulk through the car-door, settling back into the front seat as if he owned it already. As he did own it for awhile, by what they used to call the right of eminent domain.

Intrusion or invasion runs through a thousand pictures and books. Why not? It is one of the major facts of life.

Actaeon blunders on the bathing Diana; Leda is rudely forced by the great swan Jupiter. King David surprises Bathsheba sun-bathing on her roof; and what about the red-eyed elders and the naked Susanna? The sweating travelers in that rocky gorge of Böcklin's see the invading dragon, writhing its huge bulk down towards them, though they, if you come down to it, are intruders, too. Greek, Hebraic, Gothic: it is re-crudescent. Grendel intrudes on King Hrothgar, stalking through the misty fens, tearing the sleeping warriors to shreds, champing the bones, gulping the blood. Beowulf intrudes on Grendel, sliding down the green walls of water to the cavern where the monster lurks. Satan intrudes on Eden, soaring in for a two-point landing like a bat on leathery wings, or like a horned toad squatting in the dirt of your garden. The gods and the devils. The hunters and the gossips. Sin and death. We build our puny walls against them but they muscle in—they invade.

Still, he thought, it is not all negative. There are also the pleasurable intrusions. Like the girl who stands behind you while you wrestle your luggage into a locker. What was that meeting, no matter how it all ended, but an act of grace? And this other girl, asking for an interview, dressed all in sunny yellow, clean and brisk as a canary, swift as a humming-bird. These are not negatives.

The coffee had grown cold, and he rose from the dusty table to get a second cup. The morning mail still lay where it had fallen—the daily intrusion, he thought—and whether it was positive or negative you could not tell. Coming back from the kitchen with the cup refilled he stooped to gather it up.

The take was slender: two letters and a copy of the *Enfield*

Alumni Recorder. The first letter contained a check from the Englishman who was subletting Dan's rooms at home. The second was so heavy that Dan weighed it in his hand. Covered with French stamps, battered from its long ride in the mailsacks, it came from the office of the Paris edition of the New York *Herald-Tribune.*

It was from Cecilia Waterhouse. Her friends at *Vogue* had forwarded Dan's letter. It was all ancient history, of course, but she was glad to help a fellow-writer. She was on the point of leaving for a holiday in Rome, but she would do what she could. Had Dan seen an old article of hers in the *Literary Digest?* It was the first piece she had sold after she left highschool teaching, and she was still fond of it for that reason. But there was more to it than she had been able to say in that little article.

She had met Nicholas Kemp just twice in her life. The first time was in Fergus Falls, a small town in Minnesota. She had taught English in the high school there and her best friend had been the teacher of French, a girl named Faith Whitaker. Faith was the daughter of a minister; she had lived with relatives in Chicago while she took a degree at the university and graduated in 1916. Then she came home to Fergus Falls, living in the parsonage and trying to teach the local Swedes how to speak French. Impossible, of course.

Cissie said that Mr. Sherwood must be wondering where Kemp came in. She would get to that in a minute, but first there was the story of Faith and a boy named Joe Collier. Faith and Joe had grown up together. Joe's father was the owner-manager of a paper-box factory in Fergus Falls. Joe himself was a tall boy, very thin and angular, not very talkative. He loved guns and hunting and spent his vacations out on the

prairie shooting birds. Summers he worked for his father
in the factory. Faith was a very sweet girl, intelligent and
reserved. She took her French seriously, even romantically.
She was always dreaming of going to France and marrying a
French count, or wearing a Spanish cape and living among
the garrets of the Left Bank. So it was rather ironic, to say
the least, that she should have got engaged to the son of
a paper-box manufacturer in Fergus Falls, Minnesota.

Faith's engagement to Joe was announced in the winter of
1916–1917. They had a little party at the parsonage and
Faith's father gave the news with tears in his eyes because
Faith was his only daughter. Afterwards they had refresh-
ments of grape juice and layer cake. The rest of that winter
Faith slowly assembled a trousseau. There was no hurry because they would not be married until Joe finished his for-
estry degree at the University of Minnesota.

But the war changed all that. The following June, Joe
came back from Minneapolis with one of his fraternity brothers, whose name was Nicholas Kemp. The United States had
entered the war and Joe and his friend Nicholas had enlisted
in the Marine Corps. While the boys were in Fergus Falls
before they left for training in South Carolina, they took
the two young school-teachers out on a double date. Cissie
remembered that the night was very hot and very still. They
went to the picture show and then stopped in for an ice-
cream soda. It was all very sedate, said Cissie, except that
Nicholas had made a pass at her on the way home and she
had to fend him off. She thought at the time that he was
rather crude.

All that summer while Joe and Nicholas were in training,
Faith wrote regularly to Joe, knitting socks and baking nut

cookies, and keeping secret from everyone, including her bosom friend Cissie, what she was planning to do. When Joe's regiment was shipped off to France, Faith withdrew all her savings and followed. Cissie saw her off at the Fergus Falls depot—a serious girl in a dark dress, very anxious to help the French people in their time of trial, and of course intent on seeing Joe if he could ever get leave to visit Paris. After a few weeks' knocking at the door of the Sorbonne, Faith got a job with one of the American Red Cross canteens in Paris. All that winter and summer of 1917–1918 she handed out doughnuts and coffee and whatever else it was that they did. Cissie said her recollections were shadowy. It was about this time that Faith stopped writing to her friends in Fergus Falls.

Cecilia Waterhouse missed Faith so much that winter that she resigned her teaching job in June and went east to New York. She pounded the pavements for some time before she landed a job with Littlefield and Company, and she worked there until 1922, when she went over to Macmillan. She said that Macmillan's was where she had met Eunice Dudley and Harcomb Wiley. She remembered them quite well, and would Dan please give them her very best regards?

It was while she was at Littlefield's that she met Nicholas Kemp for the second—and last—time. One hot day when she was getting a drink at the water-cooler, she felt someone standing close behind her. When she glanced around, she did not at first recognize the man. His left coat-sleeve was pinned up so that it wouldn't flap, and he looked thin and worn. But he recognized her and spoke of the double date in Fergus Falls. She asked him about Joe and he said that Joe had taken a bad dose of mustard gas and was in a veterans' hospital somewhere in New Jersey. Cissie said they ought to go to see him, for auld lang syne, and take him something to read or eat. Nicholas said he didn't know where it was and anyway he understood that no visitors were allowed. Cissie remembered thinking this was an odd answer, since Joe and Nicholas had been good friends and fraternity brothers and had enlisted together and gone through all that business over across. But she had not argued with Nicholas. She pitied those boys who came back with ruined lungs and pinned-up coat-sleeves or trouser-legs. But she did ask Nicholas what ever happened to Faith.

This was another odd thing. Nicholas looked away and murmured that he had not seen Faith for years; he supposed she was still teaching in Fergus Falls. Cissie said, Oh, no. Faith had gone to Paris. She was a Red Cross worker. Nicholas said he hadn't heard about that, and left the water-cooler without taking a drink. After that one talk, he seemed to be trying to avoid Cissie. She saw him only at a distance, thin and yellow-faced, with that shortened coat-sleeve. Then he disappeared.

Faith's father, the minister, suddenly died of flu in the winter of 1920. When she heard about it, Cissie sent off a letter of sympathy, addressed to Faith in care of the parsonage with directions to forward if necessary. In the letter she told Faith of having seen Nicholas in New York. She said she was shocked to hear about Joe's gassing. She was going to say something about Faith's engagement but something held her back. Afterwards she was very glad she hadn't. Because sometime in the next year a girl named Anne Destrow had come back from France to work in Littlefield's. One day in conversation Cissie found that Anne had known Faith Whitaker in Paris. The last time Anne had seen Faith was in one of the small restaurants just off the rue Benoît. She was as certain as she stood there that in the summer of 1919 Faith had been very, very pregnant.

Faith never replied to Cissie's note of condolence, and it was a long time before she heard of Faith again. Then someone sent her a clipping from the Chicago *Daily News*. It said that Faith had married a high-school principal in Chicago. This would have been in 1924. There was one coincidence that made the date memorable: Nicholas Kemp's first novel, *The Hinges of Hell*, came out that same year.

Naturally, said Cissie, she had got it and read it. It was quite an experience. Because if you knew anything about Kemp's background, the autobiographical elements were as plain as the nose on your face. Not only the military events in Belleau Wood, but also—and especially—the love story in the novel. Kemp had disguised it pretty well and changed the circumstances and all that, but it was perfectly clear that Nicholas had met Faith in Paris, seduced her, and then walked out on her.

What happened to the baby was a mystery. It had probably died. If not, to put it crudely, it would not be the first abortion an American girl had had in Europe, nor the last. Of course it was not like Faith to do such a thing, and if you asked Cissie, she would bet that Faith had had the baby. If it lived, it could have been placed in an orphanage. If it died, it could have been buried under some invented name.

So there it was. The whole business stayed in the back of Cissie's mind, even after all these years. Every so often, something would remind her of it, and she would think and wonder about what really had happened. She wished Dan luck with his book. She would be curious to see how he would handle the biographical side. With a mystery man like Nicholas Kemp, he must be at his wit's end trying to run things down.

* * * * *

Dan dropped the letter on the dusty table and took down *The Hinges of Hell* from the bookshelf. Leafing rapidly past the military parts, he reread the final third of the novel. Again he watched with fascination as Kemp's modern version of the David-Bathsheba-Uriah triangle built slowly through betrayal and remorse to a climax of such tragic force that in 1924 the reviewers were beginning to hail Kemp as the Dostoievsky of the nineteen-twenties. One of them had even proposed that the novel should have had a subtitle: *Notes from Underground.* He spoke of that cellar of remorse where, in this novel at least, Kemp seemed to have fenced off his melancholy domain.

Cissie was right, of course. When you knew what she knew about the background of Faith and Joe and Nicholas, the story sprang out of the pages of the novel in shocking bas-relief. The question was not, now, whether the story was in substance as Cissie described it. The question was how you would handle such information in a book about Nicholas Kemp.

There was an intrusion for you. There's where you were sticking your prose into someone else's business. It was all very well to be the dispassionate biographer of the great who had died, poking about in the dusty ruins. But what did you do about the living? Where, now, was that young girl, sedate in the dark dress, who had crossed the Atlantic during that far-off war to help the French while the Boche pounded at the doors of Paris? What became of that very pregnant girl in the restaurant off the rue Benoît? You knew vaguely, of course. She married a Chicago high-school principal in 1924. If she is still alive, Dan thought, she is fifty-four years old, give or take a year or two. She wears pince-nez glasses and goes to meetings of the Delphian Society.

And the child? Assume that it did not die. Somewhere in the rusty purlieus of Paris—or in Lyon or Marseille or Valence—there is a man of thirty or thirty-one. If he survived the fighting in the later war, he is working now as a garage mechanic, a wine salesman, a waiter, a haberdasher, a hairdresser, a clerk in a steamship office, the manager of a provincial hotel. He has a French name, drinks *vin ordinaire* with his meals, has a French wife or a French girl or both. He thinks and speaks in French, yet he is not a Frenchman. If you know the surly face, the round head, the chunky build of Nicholas Kemp, their semblance lives today, if he lives, somewhere in France.

And Joe Collier? The rangy kid who survived the hornet's nest of the Bois de Belleau only to fall gasping and retching into the mud along the Marne, while the gas-cloud rolled on past him and the masked stretcher-bearers, picking their way among the shell-craters, knelt down to see if he were still alive. Last heard of in a New Jersey hospital for veterans. If he is still alive, his chest is sunken. There are grooves in his cheeks and every morning he coughs heavily, reaching for breath in that ruined lung-cavity, his tall frame racked and sweating. Let us say he went home eventually to raise a family of tow-heads; became a pillar of the community. Maybe, maybe not. How would those rugged winters suit a victim of mustard-gas? Say he died of pneumonia long ago, lungless as

John Keats, and never had a family. Or he could have spent thirty years in and out of the veterans' hospitals in New Jersey or Bethesda or one of the others, neither quite alive nor quite dead, hanging to life by a thread that stretched but never finally broke.

Dan sat up suddenly, spilling cold coffee on the table-top. Why New Jersey or Maryland when you had a veterans' hospital in Tucson? Kemp's war-time diary had been picked up, mysteriously, from someone in Tucson. Was it from Joe? What could you reconstruct?

All right, it is June of 1918. Joe leads Nicholas back through the ruined wheat from the edge of the forest, both of them trying to hold onto what is left of Nick's shattered arm. They reach the tents where stretcher-cases are ranged in rows. An orderly makes Nick sit down or lie down. Nick reaches inside his tunic with his good hand. When he withdraws it, it is holding the diary. He hands it to Joe to keep. He is shipped to the rear with his bandaged stump. Joe fights on into July. When they carry him back with the ruined lungs, the diary is inside his tunic.

Joe keeps it for years. In the hospital in New Jersey he reads it over. He wonders what happened to Kemp but there is no word. When he goes home or to another hospital, the diary goes with him. Nick writes *The Hinges of Hell* and *The Kingdoms of the North* and *The Straits of Magellan* and *Pieces of Eight* and *The Sleep of the Fathers*. He is as famous as Joe Collier is obscure. Joe thinks of mailing the diary to him. But he never can part with it. It is a memento of the old war, the former friendship. He keeps it in his desk, or in the bottom drawer of the dresser under the pile of shirts or in the safety deposit vault in the bank. Perhaps he even forgets about it for months or years at a time. It is in that trunk in the attic where he keeps his uniform and the medals and the spiked German helmet brought home as a souvenir.

Years go by and he has a family, perhaps a son to educate. Sitting in a wheelchair or lying in a ward-bed in the Arizona hospital, he reflects that his affairs are at a low point. He tells the man in the next bed about the war-time diary. They speculate about its value. Joe begins to make some inquiries. It is something to do, something to make the time pass. By the winter of 1948 he has found a prospective buyer. His name is William Baxter and everyone says he is one of the best in the business. He flies out and calls on Joe, who tells the story of the diary. Baxter says he will have to authenticate the find and work out a suitable offer. This is done and Joe is paid off handsomely. Baxter telephones a well-heeled New York book-collector named Alexander Stone III. Stone buys the diary and shows it to his brother-in-law, who is working for a doctorate at Enfield.

The rest we know, Dan thought. The brother-in-law from Enfield is now living in a house in Rachel Street, Tucson, and trying to write a book about Kemp. And there is that veterans' hospital out at the edge of town which specializes in lung cases. Over in the corner is the telephone, and all the brother-in-law has to do is to call the number and ask for a man named Joe.

His stomach felt hollow as he crossed to the telephone. A woman's voice answered. Dan explained that he was anxious to locate a veteran named Joseph Collier, formerly of Fergus Falls, Minnesota.

"Do you mean as a patient?" said the woman's voice.

"As a patient, yes."

"I'm sorry, sir. We're not allowed to give out any information about the patients."

"I didn't want any information about him. I mean not necessarily. I only wanted to know if Mr. Collier is there."

"I'm sorry," she repeated. "The rules of the hospital are quite specific. We do not give out such information."

"Could I speak to the director?"

"You can if you like," the woman said icily. "I should warn you that it's the director who makes the rules."

"I see."

There was a click and the circuit was broken. Dan replaced the receiver and sat staring at Cissie's letter while various strategies coursed through his head. You could always call Agnes, he thought. She worked there before she went to Florence Hospital. She could have known Joe Collier. Or stop being stupid. Look at the Tucson phonebook. See what Colliers you can find. He crossed to the table and ran his finger down the column of names. Collender, Colletti, Colligan, Collinski, Colonial Beauty Shoppe. In all Tucson, incredibly, there was no one named Collier. He tried the outlying areas. Colilla, Collura, Comer, Cominski. Coffee, Coleman, Coley, Collis, Colyer, Compton, Cook. Cohen, Colby, Cole, Colt. In Tombstone, of all places, there was a Collier—Maisie P. After a time, a boy's voice answered. He said his mother was out and that he had never heard of any Joseph Collier.

Dan dropped the book to the floor beside his chair. Almost immediately he picked it up again. What about Nagle? Maybe he's back from wherever he went. If you are going to be an intruder, you may as well start intruding. He called Nagle and sat for a long time while the distant signal burred and burred. But there was no answer.

CHAPTER SIXTEEN

FOLDER A: *A SHEAF OF CORRESPONDENCE*

1. *D. J. Sherwood to Alexander Stone, Esq., New York, New York, 2/1/50.*

Dear Sandy:

Belated thanks for the Christmas card. I sent none. It did not seem like Christmas out here. The book on Kemp is coming but still in extremely rough form. It would probably be farther along except for the time it takes to run down various biographical details.

A letter from Paris recently contained one crack in the façade. The lady says Kemp seduced a Minnesota girl named Faith Whitaker. She was Joe Collier's girl, but the business went on while he was fighting on the Marne, or during his hospitalization after having been badly gassed. What has since happened to Faith and Joe is not clear, except that Faith married a high school principal in Chicago in 1924, and Joe was in a veterans' hospital in New Jersey in 1919 (spring). His father is said to have owned a paper-box factory in Fergus Falls, Minnesota, and of course I have written there, though without reply as yet. After 1919 or 1920, Joe disappears.

I have now reached the point at which I would like to study that diary of Kemp's if you are still willing to get photostats made and sent out here by registered mail. If you will, it will be a great favor.

Lately I have been trying to work out a hypothetical sequence of events as to how the diary came to be in Tucson. This is all guesswork, of course, but since there is a veterans' hospital here, and since Joe Collier was a gas case, it's at least possible that Joe sold the diary to Baxter. The hospital won't give out any information. At the moment I am stuck, though with two possibilities for finding out more about it. One is the nurse I had in the Florence Hospital. She once worked for the veterans' hospital here and may know Joe Collier. The other is my Uncle John in Washington. He may be able to get someone to check the records. Sometime today I will wire him and call the nurse.

It is probably an intrusion on Kemp to dig up his past. I wrote him explaining what my pitch is going to be. No reply yet. If there were no autobiographical threads in the books, I would try to keep clear. But then there is the matter of the diary and the missing pages in the diary; and this story of his seduction of Faith Whitaker, his best friend's girl, which is woven in disguised form into *The Hinges of Hell*. So I fly back and forth like a drunken bat between biography and criticism.

Love to you and Jessica,

Dan

2. *Night Letter 2/1/50, D. J. Sherwood to Major General John Sherwood, Washington, D.C.*

CAN YOU GET SOMEONE CHECK OFFICIAL MARINE CORPS SERVICE AND MEDICAL RECORD ON JOSEPH COLLIER, NATIVE FERGUS FALLS MINNESOTA GASSED ON MARNE JULY 1918 HOSPITALIZED NEW JERSEY SAME YEAR OR NEXT MUST LEARN IF COLLIER EVER PATIENT VETERANS HOSPITAL TUCSON IF TOO MUCH TROUBLE PLEASE IGNORE REGARDS

DAN

3. *Winship W. Moore to D. J. Sherwood. Postmarked Salt Lake City, Utah, 1/31/50.*

Dear Sir: This will acknowledge receipt of your recent note. I regret to tell you that my wife, Mellissa Moore, passed away on January 7, 1948. She had not seen or heard from her brother for many years and I know of no correspondence that passed between them. With best wishes,

Yours very sincerely,
Winship W. Moore, D.D.S.

4. *Nicholas Kemp to D. J. Sherwood, 2/4/50.*

Dear Mr. Sherwood:

This is to advise you that I have been in touch with my lawyers, Buckler and Hughes, Ellicott Building, Portland, Oregon, and that I will take any means, including but not limited to the legal, to prevent you from proceeding further with your book. There is no law against your writing whatever you choose. Publication is another matter. Should you persist, I shall do my utmost to block publication of this material in any form. My utmost will be more than enough for the purpose.

My life is my own to live as I see fit. I do not propose to have it guessed at, lied about, cheapened, sentimentalized, or otherwise degraded or misrepresented. Nobody else knows or could possibly know what its actual shape has been. No stranger can either reconstruct it piece by piece or learn the whole truth about it. For twenty-five years I have been making fictional use of the biographical materials in which you profess to be interested. I tell you flatly that you have no more chance of winnowing out the facts from my fiction than you would have of reassembling the oats which fed the horses in the well-known Augean stables.

I have lived too long and seen too much to be impressed by the puny pretensions of biographers. Those I have known or read are either necrophages, battening on the flesh of the dead, or they are charlatans who will not hesitate to falsify what they can never comprehend. The vultures will doubtless gather when I die. While I live, I can still give fair warning. I will tolerate none of this. In my woods the sign means what it says for those who can read: *KEEP OFF*. For the illiterate I have other methods. I assume you are one of the former.

Without knowing in detail what you have set down about the Biblical basis of my books, I cannot tell whether it is true or false. It may interest you to know that within reach of my hand at this moment is a Gideon Society Bible which I stole from a hotel room in Vancouver many years ago. It was with me at Quantico and later in France. I carried it around the Horn and read it ragged while I was working in Los Angeles and Culver City. The early chapters of Genesis and the final pages of Revelation have been torn out. One of my dear friends aboard the *Rameses II* needed some toilet paper and I broke his jaw for him. If you were to examine the book, you would see that the Old Testament is far more worn than the New. If you ever become interested in criticism rather than scandal, you might be interested in the novel I am writing now.

Leave me alone, Mr. Sherwood. If you should be foolish enough to persist, I will have to fight you. I much prefer not to waste the little time I have remaining. I am only sorry that you have already wasted so much of yours.

Sincerely,
Nicholas Kemp

5. *M. W. Petersen to D. J. Sherwood, 2/5/50.*

NORTHWESTERN PULP AND PAPER MFG. CO.

FERGUS FALLS, MINN.

Dear Sir: Yours of Dec. 27 rec'd and contents noted. We regret we are unable to supply information in re Joseph Collier. Possibly you are refering [sic] to the late

Edgar Collier who was in business in this city some years ago. Hoping this will be of some assistance, we remain,

Sincerely yours,
NW Pulp and Paper
Per M. W. Petersen, Treas.

6. *Major General John Sherwood to D. J. Sherwood, 2/3/50.*

Dear Dan:

I have had the devil's own time running down that dope on Joseph Collier as asked for in your telegram of yesterday. But after going through some of the more devious channels, I have at least this much:

JOSEPH DAVID COLLIER, 1ST LIEUTENANT, USMC, RETIRED.

Admitted U.S. Mil. Hospital Tucson: 3/16/35

Released from same: 5/1/39

Readmitted: 12/3/39

Released: 6/6/40

I hope this sparse information will help and that you are in good shape. How are the reserve officers making out these days? Don't work too hard, chum.

In haste,
John

7. *Alexander Stone to D. J. Sherwood, 2/6/50.*

Dear Dan:

Forgive my delay in replying. Jess has not seen your letter. I am taking it with me today to show her. She has been visiting her mother and stepfather for the past two weeks in Rittenhouse Square. She has now had enough. In something like half an hour I am going down there for one of their teas and to bring her back. She will be delighted to know that you are well and working. Since the hitch-hiker episode, she has worried about your welfare.

The photostats of the diary will go forward to you as soon as I can get them made. My new photostat man has been down with the flu lately, but should be up soon. I could use someone else, though I much prefer to work with him, especially with a secret document of such value.

I note that you have been having trouble locating Nagle. The *Times* carried a story last week that Nagle is in Copenhagen. The former sportswriter has now become an international pundit and is reported to be looking into Danish culture. My guess is that his cultural interests are blonde and walk on well-turned legs. The date of his return, with or without culture, was not stated.

This morning I managed to reach Baxter by telephone. He has been on the west coast, and brought back some unpublished MS. material on Joaquin Miller. Would you like to do a book on Miller? No? I thought not. I doubt if I buy it, but I have a date to look it over next week.

In any case, I took the occasion to quiz Baxter about the Kemp diary. I told him about you. I said you were a friend of mine. You had heard the diary existed, and believed that it had been purchased from a war-time friend of Kemp's who was a patient in the Tucson veterans' hospital.

Baxter hemmed and hawed. I then said that the man's name was Joseph Collier and that my friend thinks him to be the same whose J-initial keeps cropping up in the diary. Baxter then said he was not at liberty to make any statement whatsoever. He had promised the person who sold it never to divulge its source. I said that my indefatigable friend was sure to crack the secret sooner or later. All I wanted to do was to save him time. Baxter was adamant. My respect for his integrity rose even as my hopes sank.

I must get up to Penn Station to make that Philadelphia

train. If Kemp replies, I'd of course love to have a photostat of his letter. Look for the diary photostats within the next couple of weeks.

All the best,

Sandy

*   *   *   *   *

All the scattered pieces, Dan thought. Some of them do not want you to finish the puzzle. Some do not give a damn. Some others are sympathetic but powerless. And of the first group, the chief protagonist is Nicholas Kemp. The same who came swinging over the wall of your carefully nurtured garden, shod with hobnails, landing feet first among the nodding blossoms, sweeping his broadsword like a scythe, lopping the blooms with whistling strokes, leaving you aghast at the rubbish in his wake. As was his perfect right.

To placate him, if you could, would require that you go up there, pluck down his *NO TRESPASSING* sign, rap on his door, and talk fast. And where would be the profit in it? Suppose you caught a plane from here to Portland; and from there a train to Yakima; and a bus to Cle Elum; and a packhorse into the northern Cascades? From there you would proceed, no doubt, on snowshoes to the borders of that frozen lake where, across the hip-deep snow, you might catch a glimpse of the home-generated lights in the long, low-built, ground-hugging stone house which, according to the boys with the high-powered binoculars, the literary peeping-Toms, Kemp inhabits with his third wife, who keeps him from being lonesome when he is not busy at the typewriter. And then what?

As for those who do not care? *Mellissa's dead,* says Winship

W. Moore, D.D.S. *Take your problems elsewhere,* says Mr. Petersen of Fergus Falls. *No information given out,* says the woman at the hospital. *Mr. Nagle is abroad,* says the woman at his house.

Sandy is sympathetic. He will send a copy of the diary. But *Baxter won't tell.* Even the dates in John Sherwood's compendium on Joe Collier are enigmatic. They give you both too much about Joe's bad luck and too little about his recent history. 1940 is ten years ago. He could have died in the meantime. Yet, if that were so, the Marine Corps would know about it. The death, the last retching raucous burst of coughing that carried him off, would become, wouldn't it, a word or a line in his official record? No doubt, provided always that they had heard of it, and of that there was no guarantee. Living or dead? You did not know.

Look at the other side. What do these bits of paper tell you that you didn't already know? First, that Kemp refuses to be biographized. That you knew. Second, that he admits to using his life in his works. That you knew also, though Kemp never has admitted it publicly. Third, that Kemp loves his Bible well. Again no surprise, but a welcome admission from the master. Fourth, that he has a new book in process. And this is welcome news indeed.

As to Nagle and Baxter, they can be written off as sources of information. For Nagle is in Copenhagen, date of return unspecified, and who would leave Copenhagen who did not have to? Baxter lives in his professional integrity, and who would ask him to step outside that magic ring even for a moment? Not me, Dan thought. Too many people step out too often.

Finally, the case of Joe Collier once more. He was a patient in the Tucson Veterans' Hospital on two occasions. First, for over four years in the late 1930's; second, for a period of six months well before Pearl Harbor. But he was not there in 1948, when the diary was sold to Baxter, setting up that nice triple play of Collier to Baxter to Stone, with Sherwood left on base and no runs for this inning.

Of course there was the ironic item of Joe Collier's middle name. David. But in *The Hinges of Hell,* Joe played the part of Uriah. Kemp was King David, and Bathsheba was a minister's daughter from Fergus Falls, Minnesota.

* * * * *

When he called the hospital in Florence, an unfamiliar voice answered. He asked for Agnes.

"You mean Agnes Kane?" the woman said.

"Kane? Agnes? Mrs. Alvin Kane?"

"That's who you want?"

"I guess it must be. Is she there?"

"Hold on. I'll see if she's able to come to the phone."

Silence.

"Agnes Kane speaking."

"Agnes, this is Dan Sherwood. Remember me?"

"Dan Sherwood. Where are you?"

"Tucson. I'm calling from Tucson."

"Now that's too bad, Mr. Sherwood. If you was here, you could have a beer with me and Alvin, drink to our success."

"So you *are* married? Why didn't you send me an invitation? I would have sent you a wedding-present. I still will. What would you like?"

"I don't want no more than just your good wishes, Mr. Sherwood. How it was, we didn't have no church wedding.

We went to the Justice of the Peace. My sister and her husband stood up with us. Just small. Just the family."

"When was this?"

"New Year's Day we took the plunge. I tell Alvin it's easy to remember. He can't never pretend he don't recall the day he got spliced."

"Did you take that trip back east?"

"No, west. We went to California. My head is still whirling from that traffic in L.A. Lucky for me Alvin's brother drove us around in the big city. Did you ever drive in California, Dan, Mr. Sherwood?"

"Dan. I call you Agnes. No, I never went to California. How is Alvin's leg?"

"Oh, Alvin is back to work now. Dr. Nash took off the cast. It's all knitted up nice. Course the muscles are still weak but Alvin is glad to be working again. He has worked all his life, Dan, and it don't seem natural to him to just lay around like he had to do."

"Please give him my best, Agnes. I know you're busy and I don't want to keep you. I just had a question. Didn't you tell me you once worked at the veterans' hospital down here?"

"I was there for quite a while, yes."

"Did you ever know a man, a patient, named Joe Collier?"

"Joe Collier? Now let me think a minute. Joe Collier. C–O–L–L–I–E–R?"

"That's right, Agnes. He would have been an older man, a gas case from the first war. I don't know that's he's still alive, but I have to make sure."

"What makes you think he's still alive, Dan? There's mighty few of them gas cases left nowdays."

"Agnes, I'm writing a book about a man named Nicholas

Kemp. He was a Marine in the first war, and kept a diary.
Sometime last year a famous book-dealer was out here in
Tucson and picked up the diary, but it isn't clear where he
got it. I am just checking a hunch. This Joe Collier was a
buddy of Kemp's in France. If Joe inherited the diary and
then sold it to the book-dealer, it would make the pieces
fit together neatly. I called the hospital a while ago but they
wouldn't tell me anything."

"No, they ain't allowed to, Dan. Joe Collier. c–o–l–
l–i–e–r. Dan, that name don't ring a bell with me. I had
some older men, and then towards the end quite a few
younger men just back from the Pacific. I just don't recollect
no Joe Collier, and of course they ain't allowed to tell you
about the patients. Tell you what I'll do, Dan. I'll just give
my friend Bella a tinkle. She works down there now. She
was there before I was and she's been there right along. Joe
Collier."

"I hate to impose on you, Agnes. I really need to know."

"Tell you what, Dan. I'm on duty now but we ain't busy.
I'll call Bella in a few minutes and if I can get hold of
her I'll call you right back. What's your number there,
Dan?"

*   *   *   *   *

"Dan?"

"Yes, Agnes. You must be the fastest operator in Arizona.
I meant to ask you to reverse the charges on this call."

"That's all right, Dan, don't let it worry you. I called my
friend Bella and no luck. She has been at the hospital since
Pearl Harbor and she don't remember any Joe Collier. She
says if she knew him she would tell me, rules or no rules,

but she just don't know him. Are you sure he was in that hospital, Dan?"

"Yes, twice. Once for four years, 1935 to 1939, and again for six months in 1939–40. Could Bella get a look at the records?"

"I din ask her to do that, Dan. They keep the records locked up somewheres and I don't know if they would let a nurse get into them. So I din suggest it. I could call her and ask her again."

"No, Agnes. Never mind. I already feel like a heel to have asked you to call Bella in the first place."

"You ought to not feel that way, Dan. After all, it's something you got to know."

"I'll find out some other way. If I can't, I may just let it go."

"Ain't that too bad you have to go to all this trouble?"

"All my trouble was a phone call to you. *You* took the trouble."

"No trouble, Dan. When you coming up to see your friends in Florence?"

"I may be able to drive up one of these days, Agnes. How is Dr. Nash?"

"Oh, he's good. Works all the time, but then I tell him he don't get a chance to get into mischief working like that."

"Please remember me to him and to Alvin."

"I sure will. I will do that. Changing the subject, Dan, did they ever find that one that hit you?"

"Nothing doing yet, Agnes. There was a story in the paper about that woman he murdered over in New Mexico."

"I seen that, Dan. Awful. Just terrible. Lucky for you you wasn't murdered yourself."

"It's my hard head, Agnes. All you need is a good thick skull."

"You was pretty far gone when they picked you up."

"It came out all right, though, thanks to you."

"Well, Dan, you keep out of hospitals now, unless you was to come see your old pals up here."

"I will," Dan said. "Best to Alvin."

"I will tell him," Agnes said. "Toodle-oo."

CHAPTER SEVENTEEN

WHEN HE came out of the house late that afternoon, the laundry bag over his shoulder, he saw that the whole sky had turned the color of mustard. Far to the west the lowering sun shone faintly with a metallic glare, and he could already feel the knife-edge of the coming desert night, cold at the back of his neck. Along the Speedway the sparse street-lights were already burning and most of the homegoing drivers in the stream of traffic had turned on their dimmers.

He left the laundry at the Chinaman's place and went to peer through the barber shop window. No one was waiting in the row of seats and the barber was lathering the neck of the customer in the chair. Dan opened the door and leaned through it. "Have you got time to do one more?"

"All the time in the world," the barber said. He was a heavy man with an abdominal bulge and thin gray hair. "They keep coming I keep cutting. All the time in the world."

Dan went in and sat down, picking up the ragged newspaper from the battered deal table. He saw that it was dated the day before yesterday and dropped it again.

"Cooling off some, ain't it?" the barber said. "Coming dark early."

Dan nodded. "It feels like winter."

"Ain't that Mr. Sherwood?" said the customer in the chair. "How are you, Mr. Sherwood?" It was Harry Walker, the mailman from Hoboken, his long face yellow in the artificial light, his narrow skull showing whitely through the close-cropped hair.

"Getting cleaned up, are you?" Dan said.

"When it gets so long you trip over it, you come see Joe," the mailman said.

"Don't boast to the man," the barber said. "You got nothing to trip over."

Harry Walker grinned delightedly at his image in the mirror. "It could be you ain't been around at the right time," he said. "Mr. Sherwood, I figure Joe is two parts Indian. You want to get scalped, you come see Joe."

"You want I should stick it back on?" the barber said.

"You hang onto it," the mailman said. "I got no use for it."

The barber stropped the razor and wiped it on his thumb. "Like I said, I could always stick it back on. All you got to do is say the word."

"Leave her lay," the mailman said, happily. "Ain't no use to me. Mr. Sherwood, you watch out this guy don't scalp you."

The barber finished with the neck and began to shave around the mailman's ears in the high looping arcs. Then he evened off the sideburns and folded the razor.

"How many scalps you took in your time?" the mailman said.

"I got so many I lost count," the barber said. "Got 'em all

strung up on a string in the old tee pee. You like to borry some?"

"I'll let you know," the mailman said. "Might have to borrow one back after you get through, keep from catchen cold. Cold out there, now, ain't it, Mr. Sherwood?"

Dan said it was pretty chilly outside. He had picked up the old newspaper again and was turning the pages idly. He said it was probably the worst night since he had come to Arizona.

The barber undraped the cloth from Walker's narrow shoulders, shook it once, and turned to face Dan. "You say it's the worst," he said. "You got to be careful using that word. If you can say it's the worst, it ain't the worst, am I right?"

The mailman finished adjusting his tie at the mirror and jerked his thumb at the barber. "We got a thinker here, Mr. Sherwood, a real thinker."

The barber stood flat-footedly, staring severely at Dan. "If you can say it's the worst, it ain't the worst," he repeated stubbornly. "Like a story in that paper you got. Cowpoke down in Bisbee come home last fall and his wife is in bed with his best friend. Cowpoke gets a pistol, kills them both dead. Now you can say that's the worst. But it ain't the worst if you can say it's the worst."

"Hey, thinker," the mailman said, "I can tell you something worse."

"Sure you can," said the barber. "Like I say—"

The mailman was grinning from ear to ear. "Something worse would be if I was the man in the bed."

"You'd be dead," said the barber cautiously.

"That's the worst," the mailman said. "Ain't that the worst, Mr. Sherwood?"

"You're dead you can't say it's the worst," the barber said. "See what I mean?"

"I ain't dead yet," said the mailman joyously. He sat down beside Dan, still grinning. "Now we know who's the thinker around here. Ain't that right, Mr. Sherwood?"

"You both sound like thinkers to me," Dan said. He sat down heavily in the barber's chair, flinching when the damp cloth was pinned around his neck. "Medium all over," he said.

"Hear what he says, Joe?" the mailman called. His mirrored reflection was still alight with the wide grin. "He says medium. That don't mean take his scalp."

"I cut Mr. Sherwood's hair before," the barber said, with dignity. "I know how he wants it."

The mailman yawned broadly. "I ain't had a good haircut since Hoboken," he said. He had picked up an old copy of *Life* magazine and was beginning to leaf through it. "Boy, the old dogs are sure barking tonight."

"What dogs you referring to?"

"*My* dogs," said the mailman. "I ain't had these kickers off since six ay em. I'm going to get me a few beers, go on home and soak them in salt water."

"Salt your beer is good, make you thirsty for more," the barber said tiredly. "Salt water no good."

"Salt water's best for the feet," the mailman said, absently. "Atherleets uses it. Toughs up the skin." He subsided into the magazine and spoke no more.

The barber worked quickly and quietly. The only sound in the shop was the snick of the scissors and the sonorous labor of his breathing. Dan declined the final razoring and stood up, conscious of both the barber's and his own fatigue. The mailman sat dozing, the magazine in his lap. The barber took Dan's dollar and rang it up on the small cash register. At the sound of the bell Harry Walker sat up, smacking his thin lips.

"Dropped right off," he said. He replaced the magazine and rose to his feet, rubbing his eyes with the knuckles of both hands. He silently handed a dollar bill to the barber and shrugged into a navy blue windbreaker. "Well, Joe, take care," he said.

"I take care, you take care," said the barber. He rang up the second dollar and took off the white jacket. "You take care, Mr. Sherwood." He got a push-broom from the rear of the shop and began to sweep the afternoon's shearing into a pile. He did not say anything more.

The mailman held the door open for Dan and followed him through it. In the cool night air he seemed to revive. His face showed animation in the neon light from the bar two doors away. "Boy," he said, "I got me a real case of dry-mouth. It's haircuts. Haircuts always does that to me. I come out of Joe's, two minutes later I'm standing at the bar. Lemme stand you a beer, Mr. Sherwood, how about it?"

Dan hesitated. The physical lassitude he had felt in the dry air of the barber shop still held him poised between sleep and waking. The mailman stood expectantly, the thin point of his tongue working over the long, uneven teeth. If you waited longer, he might be insulted.

"Sure," Dan said. "Thanks. I'll buy the second beer."

"Fair enough, Mr. Sherwood," the mailman said. "You want to step down here to Ernie's?"

As they came through the door of the bar, a hillbilly voice from the juke-box was wailing *Good-night Irene*. The mail-man led the way to the long counter and held up two fingers to the bar-man, who nodded impassively, drew two beers, skimmed the foam, and slid them across.

"Harya doing, Ernie?"

"Can't complain, Harry. Cold out there they tell me."

"You can say that again."

The mailman winked, raised his beer, tipped back his skull-like face, drained the glass, set it down, and licked his lips. "Hey, Ernie," he called. The bartender brought two more beers.

"Like I told you, Mr. Sherwood, them barbers give me a thirst. I guess you're thinking I got a good name for a mail carrier. Harry Walker."

Dan drank half his beer and said that the name was very appropriate. The juke-box whirred mechanically, a steel guitar swept into a slow waltz rhythm, and the hillbilly voice began again to bid Irene good-night.

"You hear that song?" Harry said. "That was the wife's name. Irene, only she spelled it different. E–I–R–E–E–N. *Eireen,* see? She's Irish parentage, see? E–I–R–E–E–N. Makes a nice spelling, don't it?"

Dan nodded. He finished the first beer and drew the second towards him across the bar. "Did you tell me you lost your wife?"

Harry Walker nodded. "November the twelve, nineteen-forty-eight," he said. "We was on the way back, and the wife is real sick. She's laying in the back. 'I'm gonna die, Harry,' she says. 'You hold on, Eireen,' I says, 'You ain't gonna die.' I got her fixed up good in the back. Mattress, blankets. 'I know I'm gonna die,' she says. 'Now you just hold on,' I says. 'I'm just gonna turn around, get you back there to the hospital.' I pull into a gas station, turn around, go like hell acrost that bridge. Right in the middle of the bridge I hear her gag. I can't stop on the bridge so I keep going. West Memphis, Arkansas." He finished the second beer and signaled for a third. The song ended and the bar was quiet.

"You say you were coming back?"

Harry Walker sipped the third beer and said that they originally came to Arizona in 1947 for his asthma. The wife didn't like it. She was homesick and they picked up and went on back to Hoboken. The weather was terrible. Harry caught cold and had another attack. He laid there on the bed and he told the wife, This is the end. "You wanna stay here, you stay here. Not me. I head back there as soon as I can travel." He laid there a week. Halfway through the week in comes the daughter. She is a junior in high schol. She shows her mother a wedding ring. "What's that?" Eireen says. "It's a wedding ring," the girl says, "and what did you think it was?" She says she is secretly married. Living with her old grandma she sneaks out at night, gets secretly married. She says she is four months along. Eireen cries two days running. Third day she says, "You get ahold of that boy," she says. "We're gonna see Father Foley, get you married right." So they get the boy, he ain't a bad boy, and the priest marries them right. After that is over Eireen has to go to bed. She's got this terrible pain; she was doctoring even before they left for Arizona in 1947; she don't trust them Tucson doctors; she come back to see her own. The doctor says she's bad off; she needs an operation. Eireen is afraid of the knife. She says to Harry, "Look," she says, "you fix me a bed in that car, we'll go on back out there. If I ain't better when we get there, I'll get the operation."

Good-night, Eireen.

"Do you have any other children?" said Dan.

"Just the one," Harry Walker said. "And one grandson I ain't never seen. Eireen couldn't have no more after the first." He drank the third beer and began to twirl the fourth in a sudsy ring on the wood of the bar. "You like hot pastrami?" he said. Before Dan could answer, he had hailed the bartender. "Ernie, set up me and my friend here with hot pastrami sandwiches."

"This is on me," Dan said quickly. He dropped a five-dollar bill on the bar. "Are you ready for another beer?"

Harry Walker emptied his glass and nodded. "Go nice with the pastrami," he said. Tiny flecks of beer-foam stood at the corners of his mouth and he wiped them off with the back of his hand. "I'm buying the beer, like I said." When the sandwiches came he dipped mustard liberally into his own and slid the jar towards Dan. For several minutes he ate hungrily without speaking.

The mustard-pot stared at Dan from the beer-wet bar. He pushed it out of sight behind the napkin dispenser and began to eat his sandwich. The bartender picked up the money from the bar and raised his eyebrows wordlessly. Dan nodded. The bar man rang the cash register and returned with two dollars and some silver.

"Hey," said Harry Walker, his mouth full. "This is my pardy."

"This part is mine," Dan said. "Thanks for the beer. I ought to be going."

"Lemme buy you another beer, Mr. Sherwood. One for the road." In the harsh light of the bar his long face looked tired and a thin stubble showed along the edges of his prominent chin. He spun a silver dollar on the bar and held up two fingers to Ernie, who brought the beers.

Dan looked at the glass sourly. He had had too much too fast. When he sipped it, the beer tasted metallic, like the keg it had come from. The air smelt of mustard oil, and he saw that there was a small smear of the mustard beside Harry Walker's mouth.

"Do you live near here?" he said.

Harry Walker jerked his thumb over his shoulder, chewed rapidly, swallowed, cleared his throat raspingly, and said that he lived only three blocks south. He downed the beer and zipped up the navy blue windbreaker. "Be good, Ernie," he called to the bartender.

"Take it easy, Harry," Ernie said.

Outside, night had fallen and the cold wind was blowing old newspapers down the Speedway. In the unearthly light from the neon sign, Harry's face was the face of a corpse. But the beer and the food had made him happy and he grinned at Dan companionably.

"Glad I run into you, Mr. Sherwood," he said. "I want to thank you for them sandridges."

"You're welcome, Harry," Dan said. "Thank *you* for the beer. I'll see you tomorrow."

Harry Walker grinned. "And tomorrow and tomorrow," he said. "Like in Shakespeare, right?"

"Right," Dan said.

"Tomorrow and tomorrow," Harry Walker repeated. He

shook Dan's hand and departed, a thin figure moving quickly along the gusty sidewalk. At the bleak corner he waved once and disappeared.

"You," Dan said aloud. In the barber shop and the bar and now on the wintry street he knew that the slow wheel had turned again. One more notch, he thought. One notch more.

CHAPTER EIGHTEEN

IN THE night it snowed. When he awoke near dawn he looked with astonishment at the skin-deep layer which covered all the lawns and streets, stretching as far as the eye could see up into the Santa Catalina foothills and over all the gentler slopes of the mountains themselves. *It never lasts,* Hart had said. While it lasted, though, the face of the desert was that of a stranger. The winter-yellowed grass and weeds showed through like an unshaven beard.

At breakfast he found himself thinking again of the old man living alone in the cabin beside the entrance to the canyon.

—You missed him out there last week. He was not around. How do you know he's all right?

—I don't.

—You haven't bothered to check on him since.

—I've been writing.

—He's an old man. He could have broken something, a leg or a hip.

—Old, yes. Not infirm. Not with that barrel chest and the legs like tree trunks.

—Still, you don't know.

—No, I don't know.

—What about your obligation to find out?

—There are many things I have to find out. About Nicholas Kemp, for instance.

—Kemp is far off. The old man is near.

—Going out there will use up a morning.

—It might be a good use for a morning. You are getting stale on the writing.

—Stale is right.

—And there's that business of the dragon that you never checked out with him: how odd you thought it was when he spoke off-handedly about the dragons down under.

—It seemed odd at the time. On reflection not so odd. Everybody has his dragons and his Elysian Fields with the semi-draped female nudes. Old Böcklin was only working in the great tradition. Look at Homer. Look at Beowulf. Look at Milton and Blake.

—No nudes in *Beowulf*.

—But monsters down under, and that dragon at the end.

—You might want to check that sometime with the eminent Dr. Jung. You might even ask him to interpret the private myths of Nicholas Kemp. But here's another old man. He made you jump that time he spoke of the dragons. Finish the coffee and put some stuff in the car and go on out to see him.

—All right.

—One thing more. Wash that damned windshield so you can see where you're going.

—All right, all right. We might as well see things clearly.

*   *   *   *   *

The gravel on Hart's steep driveway was still damp from
the melted snow. The front door of the cabin stood open and
the old man was perched on a high stool, bent forward with
his eyes close to the unfinished mural. He turned to peer
towards Dan in the blinding light of the doorway. When he
saw who it was he beckoned with the brush. Dan slid the box
of supplies onto one of the tables and crossed the room.

"You look busy," he said.

"Passing the time, Dan."

"I came out last week. Sorry I missed you."

"I'm sorry, too. I found your note. I was up the canyon
working—until some lovers busted in."

"In here?"

"No, up there. I had the jeep parked in the gravel pit. I
was part way up the slope across the stream when they drove
up. They couldn't see me. The feller went over and commenced to poke around in the back end of the jeep. I yelled
at him and he drove off with his wench. When I got down
there I found the son of a gun had taken my palette knife
and slashed some canvas."

"Pictures?"

"No, canvas on stretchers. Vengeance on the interloper.
The observer in his love-nest."

"Some love-nest," Dan said. "It looks like a backroom in
hell."

The old man sat on his high stool, holding a paint brush
like a scepter. "Except for the light," he said. "That's what
makes you go back: the quality of light on all that stone. It's
different from any other—drapery, or flesh, or water, or still-
life objects."

Dan pointed at the mural. "That part that's still wet looks like El Greco."

Hart grinned. "Toledo, huh? I wish it was that good. But I'm after light. In the Toledo it's almost dark. You get that ragged sky and all those gray-blacks and violets. Not much stone unless you mean the boulders in the river down under and the buildings up top. The thing I mean is hard to find among the masters, even the Spanish masters who were in love with light."

"What about the French?" said Dan.

"The French are good at buildings. Cézanne loved those stone houses in Provence. Once in a great while he'll give you some light on raw stone, too. Stone that hasn't been smoothed and aligned into buildings. I don't know what he would have thought of all this rock out here, all these ragged skylines and senseless erosions."

"Reckless, heaven-ambitious peaks," Dan said.

"Who said that?"

"Walt Whitman."

"Walt was talking through his hat. They're not reckless or ambitious. Just forms in juxtaposition, moving and changing in the light."

"Like us," Dan said.

"We change and move, yes. But these forms are like nothing else in the world. I wake up before daylight thinking of how to get that light." Hart's voice trailed off. He got down from the stool. He was wearing a canvas carpenter's apron with brushes and paint-tubes in the sack-like pockets. He walked stiffly to the table where Dan had left the box of supplies.

"What's this?" he asked.

"I brought a little food."

"Taking care of the old man, is that it?" Hart said. "Are you hungry?"

"No, that's for you. Look, Hart, I didn't mean to inter-rupt—"

"No interruption," Hart said. "I've done enough for now. What's this? Beer? Is it too early to have a beer?"

"It's around eleven."

"Let's have a beer," Hart said. "Let's open a beer and sit out here on the porch. Are you in a hurry?"

"No," Dan said. "Not if you've got time."

*   *   *   *   *

When, much later, the old man came out again, Dan was reading in one of the cowhide chairs.

"Not too hot?" said Hart.

"There's a breeze. Did you sleep well?"

"The old man's after-lunch nap," Hart said. "Full of odd dreams."

"Vita somnium breve?"

"What?"

"I was quoting Böcklin," Dan said.

"Oh, Böcklin, yes. He had bad dreams when we knew him. Partly from the wine and the cheese, maybe, but he knew he was going to die. He'd had a whole battery of heart at-tacks. Once in a while you could see it in his eyes."

"You mean fear?"

"Not exactly. Just the—consciousness of dying. I saw it once for a split second with my own father. We were out in the back entry at the farm and he was giving me an old shooting-coat, Mackenzie plaid. Said he guessed he wouldn't be using it again and I'd better have it. He knew he was at an age when it could happen any time and he—liked living and he didn't want to die. It was there in his eyes. Sometimes people's eyes are opaque, closed off. But sometimes you can see a reflection of where the eyes have looked."

"Into the cellar?"

"Into the sky, too. But my father had looked down under once in a while. Cellar, pit, bottom of the barrel, whatever you want to call it. It's what sort of opens up under you when there's a gang-up."

"Gang-up?"

"Oh, I don't know. Circumstances. Bad luck coming in a swatch, like Böcklin's heart attacks."

"Maybe it's remorse."

"Maybe sometimes," said Hart. "But it's more than remorse. In remorse you look down and see your own face at the bottom of the barrel, grinning back up at you like a depraved corpse. Dan, forgive me, but it's more than remorse with you. When did you get your first look into the pit—in the war?"

"No. I guess I was mainly lucky in the war. Some of it was bad enough. But the first real gang-up was when I was in college. The gang-up and the remorse were all mixed up together. We were boxing and I hit a kid named Ched Ulman harder than I meant to and knocked him cold against a metal bar. It paralyzed him for months. He had to drop out of school and come back the next year."

"That was an accident."

"I have to think so," Dan said. "But Ched was a big kid with long arms and I was a small one with not much of a reach, and I was—well—bellicose about my size and my height. How do I know I wasn't trying to prove something?"

"What would that prove?"

"Oh, the obvious thing. That I could hit, even if I was small, and hit hard enough to knock down a big, cocky kid."

"Still an accident," Hart said firmly. "The fact that he hit the iron bar when he fell was also an accident."

"That's true. Yes, that was. At the same time of that year one of my aunts was found to have cancer."

"Internal accident. Still no fault of yours."

"True again. Just part of what you call the gang-up. But there was a third thing that was not an accident. I can trace the responsibility in a general way, and in a general way it was mine."

"What was this third thing?"

"Smiley," Dan said. "A kid named Smiley Forward. Ched was still in the hospital in a coma when this kid hung himself. He tied his winter scarf and some neckties together and knotted one end around his neck and stood on a chair beside his closet door and kicked the chair away."

"And was he a friend of yours?"

"Smiley was a friend of everybody," Dan said. "And also of nobody. You'd see him in the hallway or the showers and he was always smiling, as if it made no difference to him that as a junior in college he was as small as a twelve-year-old, and awkward, with big feet and spindle legs and arms, and a plague of pimples even up in his hair. But no one really knew him. He was a loner. Not that he wanted to be, but that was how it was. He roomed alone, studied alone. He'd sit there in his dorm room with the books, or breaking the insurance rules cooking things over Sterno canned heat in test-tubes. He thought he had diabetes, and he'd do these urinalyses, wearing this damn green bathrobe to keep warm, with the black frogs down the front of it. No fraternity would even consider him. Always turned in on the stroke of eleven, kneeling on the floor to say his prayers."

"How do you know that?"

"I barged in once for some reason," Dan said. "Probably to borrow a book. I went in without knocking and there he was on his knees by the bed in the dark. He didn't get up or say anything. I just said *sorry, good night,* and backed out and closed the door."

Hart said nothing.

"He was nineteen years old," Dan said, watching the dustmotes. "At first we didn't miss him. My room was just above his in the dorm and one day inside my closet I began to smell this smell. Hank and I thought it was a rat in the walls. Then it got worse, and after a while it dawned on me that it was some of his chemistry stuff. I went down and knocked on his door and yelled something insulting. The door was locked and he didn't answer. So I climbed up the outside fire-escape and looked through the window and found out. He was nineteen years old and he came from Swampscott, Massachusetts."

"That's too bad," Hart said. "It's bad when they do a thing like that before they ever find out what they stand to lose by doing it. The later ones have lived long enough to find out they don't like it. Mostly they're sick, or living in private hells, or both. But you don't blame yourself for this boy."

"In a way I do," Dan said. "At least I used to. We were about the same height, we lived in the same dorm, and Smiley tried to make friends."

"What did he say?"

"Some simple thing. Asked me to go to the movies with him. He knew I didn't have much money and he offered to pay the way. I said I couldn't go, which was a lie. I could have gone. I was just part of the general rejection of Smiley, and in a way I could guess how he felt. It's the worst kind of exile because you're in it alone—absolutely alone. All around you normal life is going on, and you can see it going on. It's only at arm's length, but even that is too far. They won't let you in, or out, whichever it is. Nobody can be crueler than boys."

"Just say people," Hart said. "The blame lies everywhere and nowhere. You weren't to blame."

"Not entirely," Dan said. "And I don't brood over it. It happened a long time back."

"But you still brood." It was a statement, not a question.

"Some," Dan said. "Hart, this isn't relevant, but I'll tell you a crazy thing. I should have been able to get Sachs with that jack-handle but I held back. I whanged him with it, knocked the gun out of his hand, but it wasn't hard enough."

"So you got whanged instead."

"Yup," Dan said. He was sick of the subject.

Hart was silent, gazing down into the valley where the alfalfa shone like a square of intense green water. "So there's your—excremental universe, wasn't that what you called it?"

"One phase of it," said Dan, uncomfortably. "I mean Smiley must have seen it, looked down into it. It's the state of being damned, feeling that you're damned, and at the same time, all around you, you see the good. But you see it is not for you. Or so you think."

"Satan's trouble," Hart said.

"It's a satanic situation," said Dan. "But Satan was genuinely damned. With this boy it was, apparently anyway, a
conviction that he gradually built up that he was excluded,
alone, unwanted. Some kind of a syndrome. It's as good—or
as bad—as damnation. Or so it seems. And then, in a minute
—I mean, it only takes a minute to kick away the chair and
a few more to strangle in your necktie."

"But behind him he left you, also feeling damned."

"I'll admit the thought crossed my mind. With the other
boy paralyzed in the hospital, and one of the aunts who
raised me far gone with cancer. Then I guess you could
blame adolescence—and even literature. I was reading *King
Lear* and Kemp's *Hinges of Hell* and some Dostoievsky along
about then. Maybe they got mixed up in it, too."

"I never read this Kemp. The others sound dark enough."

"They all knew about the excremental universe. Raskolni-
kov, say. Or Lear. Lear was up to his neck in it, with those
two daughters coming along and pushing him under. And
the good daughter hanged."

"You should have read the happier ones."

"I did," Dan said, grinning. "Or I set out to. But I found
it was like one of those diseases you hear about for the first
time. And then the next week you keep hearing about other
people you know who have it, or have had it. I read Frost,
and there he was talking about his desert places. I read Eliot,
and there he was down under in the twittering dark. And
Robinson. And Jeffers. I read Hemingway and he called it
nada; I read Faulkner and he called it *doom.* Kemp found it
in Belleau Wood and afterwards in other places. The painters, too. Goya for one. Böcklin, though I never heard of him
until I saw your picture."

"Sure," Hart said. "It's their business. They invented Nemesis and the Fates and the Weird Sisters and Satan and the rest. All those wonderful, beautiful, complex, lovingly elaborated imaginations. All those handsomely documented lies."

"But based on truth," Dan said. "Mussolini and his castor-oil torture chambers. Buchenwald. Hells on earth."

"Those are facts, yes. The others are imaginations. Like my stoic emperor, and his imagination of the good. You remember how you demolished him?" The old man was grinning broadly.

Dan grinned back. "Oh, he'll survive my puny picking. I just wasn't certain he was entirely sound about the kind of evil people can perform. He chose to face evil by rising above it—a form of surrender, or so I thought. If the evil takes the form of sudden death, I guess rising above it is about all you can do. Death, be not proud, you won no victory."

"Right," Hart said. "The victory there, if there's going to be one, has to be ours. The victory of the survivors. Accepting the inevitable is a form of victory. The emperor knew about that, too."

"Where does he say that?" said Dan. "Have you got the book?"

"I don't need the book," Hart said. "I know this one by heart. 'Of the life of man,' he says, 'the duration is but a point, its substance streaming away, its perception dim, the fabric of the body prone to decay, and the soul a whirlpool, and fortune incalculable, and fame uncertain. In a word all the things of the body are as a river, and the things of the soul as a dream and a vapor; and life is a warfare and a pilgrim's sojourn, and fame after death is only forgetfulness.' "

"Vita somnium breve," said Dan.

"Sure. Böcklin put it his way. That red knight riding off to the wars is the warfare and the pilgrim's sojourn, and then there's the old man up there about to be brained with the club."

"What about the woman and the children in the garden?"

"They go, too," Hart said. "My wife. Yours. The children in their time. But the emperor forgot that what he had written down would be read, even quoted, by us centuries later. Whenever we can get it down, get it said or painted or hammered out of stone, there's another victory. The rest goes, like last night's snowstorm, into the ground."

"Seems to me your emperor is as gloomy as the others," Dan said. "You've just described, in his own words, a version of the excremental universe."

"Part of the time, yes. Sometimes he can sound gloomy as hell, like the preacher in Ecclesiastes. But other times he convinces you that he's caught the vision of the good—above and beyond the evils that beset the mind, the crazy syndromes you and I devise to torture ourselves and others with. In his own way, and I don't see how, for him, it could be any other way, he recognizes the other side—your sacramental universe. So do the other writers you named. The best of them anyway. They see beyond tragedy."

"Not Kemp," said Dan.

"That's his loss," Hart said.

*   *   *   *   *

Coming down Hart's driveway and heading back to town, Dan still felt the slow burn of elation. They spoke of anger as a slow burn, and it was one of the forms anger could take.

But there were other slow burnings; this curious, newfound elation for one, like the dawn of understanding after an age of darkness. The arrival of love, or whatever it was that you felt whenever you thought of the girl, Connie Haybright, in her dress like sunlight. The strange sense that you were at last rejoining the world after a time of exile.

It was true, as Hart had said, that Kemp had never been able to see beyond tragedy. He had kept his fierce isolation. He would not rejoin the race he had left. Even that island of his in the northern wilderness was the mark and sign of his self-perpetuated exile. And then all those books, the novels you had lived by for years, the dark vision which you had taken as your own. How many times—too many times!— Kemp had heard the rasping screech of the hinges of hell. It was the sound that echoed and re-echoed through all his works. And for a long time, or so it seemed, you had lived within earshot, subconsciously listening for the sound the hinges made. When it came—as at Amherst or at Irsch or in the gray waters of the stormy Sound—you nodded, you nodded almost eagerly, saying, *Yes. I was expecting that. I know that sound. It has rung in my ears. It's the other side of the music of the spheres. It's the cosmic cacophony, the scream of Lucifer going into his power-dive, every nerve alert as a toothache, out of the light and into the dark.*

But now you were done with it. *Retro me, Sathanas.* To hell with Hell. *Vita Somnium Breve,* said Böcklin. Brief certainly. Possibly even a dream. But no longer the nightmare it had so long seemed to be.

At the North Corral Bar and Grill a beer truck was parked, and a man in green coveralls was trundling cases of beer across the yellow gravel. Suddenly Dan caught in the middle of the roadway the high quick bound of a desert jack-rabbit, and behind it the flash of black. He braked and swerved, trying to miss the big dog. But he knew it was too late even before the sickening heavy thump and the lurch of the car told him the body was under the wheels.

Dan pulled to the roadside and wrenched at the door-handle. The dog was screaming in a grisly succession of high-pitched hoots, and leaping, head twisted and jaws bloody, as high as it could go in a crazy travesty of terror, flumping heavily into the roadside dust only to struggle up again and hurl itself, in the senseless and contorted leaps, up and then down. He had begun to move toward the flailing body when he heard a shout and turned to see a thin man running down the walk from one of the small houses.

"Keep away," the man yelled. He wore bedroom slippers. Pink suspenders dangled from the waistband of his pants, and he was buttoning the front of a collarless shirt as he hurried to Dan's side. "You better stay clear, mister. Go where he is he'll chew you, snap at anything comes near. He don't know where he's at."

Dan thrust his shaking hands into the pockets of his jacket. "I guess you're right," he said, miserably. "Both wheels went over him."

"He's a goner," the thin man said. His thin lips were pursed over toothless gums. "He's a goner. I give him a minute more. Mebbe two minutes."

"He was chasing a rabbit," Dan said.

"Happens all the time," said the thin man. "Crazy galoots don't pay no attention to roads or nothing. Just put their goddam heads down and light out."

The high hoots had stopped now and the dog, its coat thick

with dust, lay twitching among the weeds at the roadside.

"I wonder who owns him," Dan said, between his teeth. "I suppose this ought to be reported."

"Like as not he ain't tagged," the thin man said. "After he dies you can go see if you was to want to. If I was you, I'd leave him, go long about your business."

"I'll have to look for the collar," Dan said. Trailed by the thin man he moved toward the dog, which lay still in the dust, its blood bright in the sun. The neck was bare and the eyes were already beginning to glaze over. "Do you have a telephone?" Dan said.

The old man stood stiffly, his mouth compressed, one lock of hair waving in the hot wind. "What you want with a phone?" he asked suspiciously.

"Call the police," said Dan.

"They don't care," the thin man said. "See that bar? Pay phone in there. You could just step over there, call anybody you want."

Dan put the call through to the police. The man who answered asked if the dog was off the street. When Dan said it was, the man said to leave it. He would make a note in case the dog was missed. Someone would get the body later. Dan thanked him and went back to his car. The thin man was still standing on his front walk.

"What they say?" he called.

"They said to leave it."

"They coming to get it?"

"They said they would come."

"Thought that's what they'd say," the thin man said. "You could have saved your nickel."

"Thanks," said Dan, climbing into the car. As he drove off

the thin man still stood gazing toward the black dog by the roadside.

At the house on Rachel Street he parked in the narrow driveway and let himself into the kitchen, looking queasily at the dark coffee-dregs in the cup he had hastily drunk from before he left for Hart's place. The elation was gone. Even in the night when he was awakened by the moonlight he could not bring it back. The black dog flumped deadly in all the corners of his mind.

CHAPTER NINETEEN

EUNICE WILEY had obviously spent days, possibly even weeks, in preparation. Resplendent now in a glittering red gown and a corsage of roses, she moved across the room to where Dan was standing in one corner.

"How do you like my mobile?" she cried, loudly. She pointed to the intricate design of arrows and hearts hung on slender wires, and to the cupid of papier-mâché which slowly revolved at its center, turning the drawn bow with impersonal equity towards each member of the crowd in the dining-room. "Isn't my cupid a dear?" she shouted. "Harcomb made him. Do you know how? He tore up *scads* of old newspapers into shreds and soaked them in flour and water. It took *days*. Then he molded it and wired it and painted it. Wasn't Harcomb clever?"

"You're both clever," Dan said, grinning. "To say nothing of your patience." He waved one hand around the room. "Hearts and flowers everywhere." It was true. Ornate valentines, dripping with paper lace, had been taped to the pictures on the walls. Paper hearts adorned the curtains, hung in festoons from the glass chandelier, and stood out like amatory medals on the white uniforms of the Mexican butler and maid. "It's all highly ingenious, cupid and all."

Eunice flushed with pleasure, gazing intensely down into Dan's face.

"Do you like the punch? It's a tradition at our anniversaries."

"They must all have been gay," Dan said.

"I know what you mean—you mean the punch is too strong. Don't I know it?" She fanned her face vigorously with a lace handkerchief to which red hearts were appliquéd. "I've had I don't know how many glasses now and if you see me with any more I want you to just walk up and *snatch* it out of my hand. Harcomb always makes it too strong. He believes in making it strong. It's his secret formula and he brews it in the pantry. I know there's rum in it. Now, Dan, you need some more. You just came. Manuel, give Mr. Sherwood some more punch. No, no. No more for me. Isn't it stifling in here? Dan, excuse me, I see the O'Keefes coming in. Did you know Moira and I are taking lessons now? I'm working on a heart-shaped watch-fob for Harcomb. It was supposed to be ready for tonight. Have some sandwiches, Dan. Take a handful. Please. Valentina, hold the tray still. Her name is really Emma but her middle name is Valentina, isn't it, dear? So for this party every year I call her Valentina. Isn't that nice? Excuse me, I'll have to show Moira where to put her coat."

Dan ate the sandwiches and sipped the punch. Harcomb Wiley waved to him over some intervening heads and moved across with his prelate's gliding walk. He was carrying a cigarette box and a half-filled punch glass. A large red rose dangled from the lapel of his suit.

"You're losing your rose," Dan said.

"I'm losing patience with that rose," Wiley said. "How's your punch?"

"It's fine," Dan said.

"I hope you're feeling it," said Wiley. "If you don't now, you will. Did you see about the murderer?"

"What murderer?"

"Your friend. The one that killed the girl."

"You mean Sachs?"

"Is that his name?"

"Buddy Sachs. What about him?"

"In the paper last week. Don't you read the papers? It said he robbed a supermarket."

"Where? Here?"

"California," Harcomb said. "They had one of those hidden cameras with a flash-bulb. It went off in his face and they got his picture. Ugly son of a bitch, I must say."

"Anyone hurt?"

"No, this was at night. Late at night."

"What part of California?"

"I think they said Monrovia."

"Where's Monrovia?"

"It's near Los Angeles."

"So that's where he went."

"That's one of the places he went," said Harcomb. "He was seen earlier in Chula Vista. There was a fight in a bar and a Navy gob got beaned with a beer bottle. It said he wasn't expected to live."

"Where's Chula—?"

"Chula Vista. It's way south. Close to Tijuana, down near the border. Chula Vista is a town between Tijuana and San Diego. That bastard gets around. He's ubi—ubiq—"

"Ubiquitous, yes. He sure is. He's a regular Moby-Dick."

Over Wiley's black shoulder Dan could see Moira O'Keefe picking her way nervously through the crowded room. She nodded at one or two people, but came as directly as possible to where Wiley and Dan were standing.

"Hello, Moira," Dan said. "Where's Axel?"

"Hello, Dan. Hello, Harcomb. Oh, Harcomb, you're about to lose your rose."

"That damn rose," Harcomb said. "It needs a woman's touch."

Moira quickly fixed the rose in place. "It's the stem," she said, with a nervous giggle. "The stem's got a hole in it. It probably won't stay."

"Damaged goods," Wiley said benignly. "Thank you, Moira. What happened to your punch?"

Moira poked at her side-hair with both hands. Her eyes looked tired. "We just came," she said. "Axel was the longest time writing something. He just *wouldn't* come out of his study. Now he's in the other room, talking to some university people."

Her voice as she spoke had grown so faint that Dan looked at her sharply to see if her eyes were wet. Harcomb was already moving off towards the punch-bowl. "You need some punch, Moira," he said. "As a reward for the rose."

"Are you well?" asked Dan. "Eunice said you were taking some lessons."

"Oh, yes, we are," Moira said, smiling faintly. "Jewelry lessons. We take them from this nice old Indian."

"This is at the Western Academy?"

"Yes, the converted motel. It's all been changed over."

"Eunice said something about a watch-fob."

"Poor Eunice," Moira said. "She worked so hard to try to finish it for tonight, but she couldn't. Billy offered to help with it. She kept insisting she must do it alone."

"Who's Billy? The Indian?"

"Billy Washagaw. It sounds like Washcloth. He's a Navajo. He smells like leather and smoke and he has long hair. A real Indian. He rolls up this length of red cloth and ties it around his head. He's a very good silversmith."

"Have you seen the boss?"

"The director? He's called the director. Tall and blond. Oh, yes, I've seen him. Do you know him?"

"A little," Dan said. "He's my landlord. I see him now and then."

Moira smiled tiredly. "Now and then meaning rent day?"

"At first I saw him on rent day. He wanted cash. Now I mail him a check. How do you like him?"

"Oh, I don't know. He's certainly very handsome. Eunice doesn't like him. She says when they first came out he tried to sell them a house and she hasn't liked him since."

"I remember. Does he hang around school much?"

"All the time the first week. He was practically a patrolman. He came into our class every day. Lately I've hardly seen him except at a distance."

"Does he talk with the—the clientele?"

"Oh, hardly any. He just seems to be watching."

"What did he watch?"

"You mean that first week? I just meant he was watching to see how things were going. He watched Billy melting silver and pouring it into the moulds. Then he helped me bore a hole in a piece of silver for a buckle."

"Did he help Eunice?"

"No. She turns her back on him. But he's really not so bad. Axel came to pick us up one day and I introduced them. He was very cordial."

"I'm wilting," Eunice said, coming up. "Where's Wiley? Oh, there you are, lover. Wiley, couldn't you open some windows? Isn't it sweltering, Moira?"

Wiley winked. "Calls me by my last name whenever things get warm. Dan, you're out of punch. Moira, toss that down and I'll bring you another."

"Oh, no, Harcomb," Moira said. "It's very strong."

"Harcomb, honey, you'd better start diluting it," his wife said. "Put some more ice in it at least. Just listen to the noise. Everyone's getting squiffy."

"That's the point," said Wiley amiably. "Arrows and hearts. Dan, you'll join me?"

"One more," Dan said.

"That's the way, Dan. Hearts and flowers. Here's Axel. The clan gathers. Axel, how about a spot of punch?"

"Your man has got to me," Axel said, grandly. "Not once but often. But I'll drink your health. Eunice, a libation for your twenty-sixth. Harcomb, I've done some couplets in the manner of the master. Not perfect, mind you, I've had to play hob with the name. Wiley, you see, Dan, is extrasyllabic. I've *chopped* you, Harcomb." He bent the huge, wedge-shaped head to his chest and fumbled nearsightedly in his breast pocket. "Here we are. Now this requires close attention. In O'Keefe as in Pope, every word must count. Are you ready? Moira? Dan?" He adjusted his glasses, bent close to the paper, and in the rich orator's voice read:

> "In brimming glass we toast the tender Wiles
> Who set the best of matrimonial styles:
> Nothing so proves a marriage really sticks
> As having it attain age twenty-six."

"Bravo," cried Harcomb Wiley. "What do you think of that, Eunice? You're immortalized in heroic couplets. You're Poped! I'll drink to that myself. Eunice, where's your glass? Dan? Moira? Axel?" He plunged into the crowd and returned with the Mexican butler, who carried a tray of punch. "Here now, hand them around. A toast to Eunice, the belle of old Tucson."

Picking up his glass and lifting his eyes again to the circle of faces, Dan saw with dismay that Moira's eyes were brimming with tears. Eunice moved quickly, shouldering her way in front of Moira and beginning to lead her towards the hallway, bending to talk continuously into her ear. Harcomb had followed them for only a few steps when he was commandeered by a thin, voluble woman in a burnt-orange dress.

Axel stood holding the punch glass, looking bleak. "Bit under the weather," he said, clearing his throat. "Eunice will bring her round. Dan, how's your book coming?"

"Slowly," Dan said. "I work at it."

"What's your approach?"

"Critical," Dan said. "With biographical interludes."

"Very sound," said Axel, sagely. "I don't know if you've seen my Pope book. My scheme exactly. Set-pieces on the major works. Chunks of biography in between. Very sound principle."

"I blow hot and cold," Dan said, "on keeping or junking the biographical parts."

"Keep them," said Axel. "By all means. The great hungry public eats biography, Dan. They haven't the foggiest interest in criticism. Who cares for a disquisition on the *Ode to a Nightingale* when he can read one of the love letters to Fanny

Brawne? Keep it, Dan. That's my advice. Kemp got around, didn't he? Gallivanted all over? The anecdote is the life of books. Do you remember that young woman who did the interviews? I talked about *The Rape of the Lock*. Thought she'd like Belinda. But what she really wanted was anecdotes. After a half a dozen of those, she went away happy. By the way, whatever happened to those interviews? Are they out?"

"Not that I've seen," Dan said. "She's been away. Had to go to Chicago."

"Too bad," Axel said. "Very pretty girl. Very good leg. Fresh face, dark hair. By the way, your landlord, Mr. Lee, was asking about her the other day."

"What about?"

"Wondered where she had got to, he said. Wants to hire her to write his publicity. I told him I didn't know."

"What do you think of Lee?" said Dan.

"Very cordial, I thought," said Axel. "Insisted we take some tickets for the rodeo. La Fiesta de los Vaqueros, inspired by the Chamber of Commerce. Of course we shan't go. Wouldn't you like to go and see it, Dan? It might amuse you. Moira and I went once." Axel fumbled in his breast pocket and brought out a billfold. "Here, let me give you the tickets. Wouldn't you go?"

"Thank you," Dan said. "Won't you let me pay you for them?"

"Oh, no. He gave them to us, Dan. He tried to give some to Eunice. Eunice dislikes him, you know, because of that business with the house when they first came. A regular Beau Brummel. What's his background, Dan?"

"He was in the war," Dan said. "Wounded in the head

soon after D-Day. He says he has a silver plate in his skull. Now he's out for compensations."

"I daresay he deserves them," Axel said. "What time do you have, Dan? Isn't it late?"

"Around midnight."

"Forgive me, Dan. I must find my wife and drag these old bones to bed. Tomorrow's another day."

"I'm going, too," Dan said. "Thanks for the tickets."

He followed Axel through the crowd towards the front hall. The Mexican butler was adding ice-cubes to the punch bowl. Something struck Dan a light blow on the forehead and he looked up quickly. In the thick haze of cigarette smoke at the top of the room, Harcomb Wiley's armed cupid was blindly revolving. Outside the house the desert air was cool as water. Without surprise, Dan found that he was thinking of Connie Haybright.

CHAPTER TWENTY

THE RODEO was better than halfway gone when Dan saw, or seemed to see, the moose. The yelling Papago squaws had scratched up the dung-speckled dust and departed. The courageous clowns in baggy pants had baited the Brahma bulls, their huge flanks green-stained with alfalfa, and had hidden precariously in the gaudy, red-and-white hogsheads while the animals snorted and lunged, inches away, trying to gore their tormentors inside the splintered wood of the circus barrels. Through Mandeville Lee's binoculars, Dan had watched the bull-dogging of the wild-eyed black heifers. The trained herd-dogs, yapping with pleasure, had efficiently corralled their complement of sheep. Lariat-twirlers had performed and bowed out, and the broncs stood ready in the tall chutes, pawing the dirt while the cowpokes waited.

Now the announcer was droning interminably into the public address system. Dan seized the interval to stretch and beat his arms, peering into the lead-colored sky where a small plane was doing wing-overs and right and left over the wind-bitten fiesta crowd, who were drinking coffee, or often bottled whiskey, and gnawing at the mustard-smeared hot-dogs like a half-time crowd at a football game. Dan lifted the glasses and focused on the chutes across the field. Like railbirds on the fence-tops a dozen cowpokes were perched, ready to open the gates on signal and release the plunging horses.

In the midst of a slow sweep, Dan stopped suddenly. The face, even behind the scraggly dark beard, was unmistakable. So was the hulking figure which sat on the topmost rail beside one of the chutes, still wearing boots and jeans and the dusty green windbreaker. Well back on his greasy curls was a broad-brimmed hat, and the heavy jaws were working rapidly. As Dan watched he leaned forward and spat into the dirt of the arena. Then he turned full profile to speak to the man behind him. It was the moose, all right. Dan lowered the glasses and sat slowly down while the fist knotted and tightened in the muscles of his stomach.

For a minute he sat tensely, his mind racing. So now what? Without rising he glanced toward the nearest exit-ramp. Standing there, chewing slowly and watching the first of the plunging horses in the arena, was a man in policeman's uniform. Dan stood up and began to edge past the blanketed knees along the row of bleacher seats, his eyes on the blue uniform. As he approached, the policeman moved aside to let him pass. Dan saw that he was elderly and unarmed. His false teeth smiled evenly. His voice sounded ancient and companionable. "Lookit that feller go," he said. "Lookit him sticken on."

Dan stood irresolute. What could this old man do, uniform or no? If you looked, you might find a doughtier warrior; at least, say, a man with a gun. Surely they would have to be around. They probably fought for the assignment. I remember one, anyway, he thought. On the way through the gate there was a burly character in an Eisenhower jacket and a bright badge.

"Officer," Dan said, "is there a sheriff around here?"

"What's matter?" the old man twittered. "Get your pocket picked?"

"No, it's something else. Have you seen the sheriff?"

The policeman looked doubtful. Dan saw that he was wearing a gray buttoned sweater under the uniform jacket and that both his eyes and nose were moist with cold. "Might be a deputy around," he said. "What was it you wanted?"

"Where could I find a deputy?"

"Front gate," the old man said. "That's your best bet."

"I'll look," Dan said. "Thank you very much." He glanced over his shoulder across the arena. The moose still sat astride the fence-rail, watching the bronc-busters. Dan half-ran down the ramp to the admission booth. Inside it the ticket-seller sat smoking a home-made cigarette.

"I'm looking for a deputy sheriff," Dan said.

The croupier's eyes in the booth did not waver an instant. "Which one?" the ticket seller said.

"Any one. Have you seen one lately?"

"Seen one a while back," the face said. "Enthing I can do for you?"

"Thanks," Dan said, turning away. He began to walk rapidly around the south end of the arena. The cold air smelt warmly of cattle. Men in well-sweated hats stood peering through the wire fence. In one of the open spaces a mongrel was worrying a dusty gobbet of gristle. Dan was halfway across when he heard the heavy voice behind him. He turned to see a big-bellied man hurrying in his direction. He wore a

Truman hat and a badge was pinned, slightly askew, on the breast of his red-and-black lumber jacket.

"Hey, Mac," he said, breathing hard. "You the one's after a deputy?"

Dan nodded and moved towards him. "Right over here," he said, quietly, "is a man wanted for murder."

The deputy's eyes narrowed. There was no visible gunbelt but the lumber jacket bulged firmly at the left shoulder. "How you know this?" the deputy said.

A few onlookers had gathered. Dan lowered his voice and pointed to the cased binoculars. "I was looking across and I saw him."

"You know him?" the big man said, still breathing hard.

"Sure I know him," Dan said. "His name is Sachs. He's wanted for murder, armed robbery, and some other things. He's over here sitting on the fence."

The deputy turned to the gathering crowd. "Move back, boys," he said. "Get along. This here's private. Watch them broncs like you paid to see." Several men moved off quickly. The others backed away obediently but still stood watching. The deputy seized Dan's right arm above the elbow. "Now you ain't told me how you know him. What's that name?"

"Buddy Sachs," said Dan. "Picture in the paper this fall. They've had his description on teletype for months."

The deputy bent to peer curiously into Dan's face. His breath smelt of beer. "Lots of people looks like other people," he said. "You know them news pictures ain't always clear."

"Listen, sheriff," Dan said. "I know this man close-up. He hitched a ride with me last October and stole my car."

The deputy tightened his grip on Dan's arm. "You that

feller?" he said, his eyes widening. "Now just how did he get the car?"

"We fought for it. He got the jack-handle and hit me and took the car."

"Get away, boys," the deputy said, waving his arms at the bystanders. "You sure you seen him?" he said to Dan. "Man gets a good enough whack on the skull sometimes he sees things that ain't there. This bastard been operating in California. What makes you think he's around here?"

"Maybe California was too hot for him," Dan said. "This was Sachs, all right. I got over the concussion."

The deputy closed one eye shrewdly and fixed the other on Dan's face. "You know what day this is?" he asked.

"Thursday, the twenty-third," Dan shot back. "Do you know a deputy named Notofrancesco?"

"Yup."

"How can I find him?" Dan said. "He knows the case."

"Wouldn't hardly be worthwhile try and find him now," the deputy said. He straightened his shoulders decisively and unbuttoned the top buttons of the lumber jacket. "Now where's this Sachs at?"

"Down this side," Dan said, grinning. "If you're ready." He led the way around the corner of the arena and into a region of sheds and small corrals. Inside the first of the chutes a bronc was kicking vigorously, splintering the dry poles with a sound like gunfire. "I saw him out front," Dan said. "How the hell do you get out front?"

"Got to shinny," the deputy said. "Don't want to get kicked to death you got to clamber over them chutes. About where was it?"

"Halfway down. Near one of the chutes."

The deputy strode ahead purposefully. "Best way's to come up behind him," he said. He reached for one of the horizontal timbers and swung himself aloft with surprising agility. "Now what's this feller get on?"

Dan climbed up beside him to sit on the top rail. He described the moose.

"Lots of them jeans and windbreakers," the deputy said. "Now, boy, you set here and take a good look, see if you spot him anywheres."

A few of the cowpokes watched them idly; others faced the arena. Dan swept his eyes from face to face in the lead-colored light. His mouth was dry. "Not yet," he said. "Not here, anyway. He may be farther down."

Without a word the big man swung to the ground and strode past two more chutes. "Let's try here," he said. With Dan just behind him he began to clamber quickly along the fences, holding the top rail, his head held low. They reached the arena and peered to the right and left. Dan saw that it was almost the spot where Sachs had been sitting fifteen minutes before.

"You see him?" the deputy said.

"He was here, or about here," Dan said. "He must have moved."

"Likely done just that," the deputy said. "Likely seen us coming and ducked back in there some place." He sat morosely on the fence-rail looking from face to face. In the arena a rider was thrown heavily. He scrambled clear of the kicking hooves and limped back to the fence. He wore a green wool shirt.

"Taint that one?" the sheriff said. "Sure taint him?"

Dan shook his head. "Black beard, greasy hair, cowpoke

hat," he repeated, drily. "Heavy-set. Big shoulders. Thick gums. Baby teeth."

The deputy hawked and spat. "Tell you what," he said. "You and me'll just get to a tellerphone. Got to a-lert the office, get some more men out here. What'd you say your name was?"

Dan told him.

"All right, Mr. Sherwood," the deputy said. "Let's get going."

*   *   *   *   *

Mr. Notofrancesco threw back his head, gulped down the rest of the coffee, carefully placed the empty container in the overflowing trashcan, hitched up his belt, and said that there was no reason to hang around any longer. In the dim light under the grandstand his broken nose gleamed dully, and he looked, in spite of all he had done, as eager as a morning hawk.

He had done, thought Dan, all that there was to do. With three other deputies, all of them bigger than he was, he had swept through the main gate in a dust-streaked squad car less than twenty minutes after the phone call to headquarters. In ten minutes more he had posted guards at all the exits and thrown a loose cordon around the far side of the field. He had even set a motorcycle patrol on the jalopy race-track. Then for two hours, with Dan at his elbow, he had stalked through every shed and stable in and near the grounds, shining his flashlight behind the pyramided bales of hay and into obscure corners where the crouching figure of Sachs might have been.

"Might of beens," he told Dan. "Might of beens is what

you got to watch." When the rodeo ended he had stationed Dan beside the main gate to examine the faces of the dispersing crowd. The only man he recognized in the hundreds he looked at was, however, Mandeville Lee. Most of the spectators had departed when Dan saw the red car nosing slowly down the exit-ramp. The passenger seat was occupied by a brown-eyed blonde in a fawn-colored fur coat and a new white ten-gallon hat. Lee pulled over and stopped, leaving the motor bubbling, leaned down to speak to the girl, and then strode across to Dan's station near the ticket booth.

"Any luck yet, Dan?"

"None yet. How about yourself?"

Lee dropped his voice to the confidential level, softly simulating a southern accent. "Ah reckon you might just call it luck," he murmured. "Little old Callie Brown over there is just about to bust onless and ontil she can make me a real old-fashion mint julep just like her daddy done taught her."

"Local girl?" said Dan.

"Montgomery, Alabama," Lee said, running his tongue-tip over his upper lip. "Old daddy just naturally owns all the steel mills in that town. Callie got herself a nice little king-size suite at the Santa Rita. Think you can make it home all right, Dan?"

"Sure thing," Dan said. "I'll ride back with Noto."

"Don't get shot."

"Don't get dizzy on juleps."

"I'm dizzy already," Lee said, grinning. "Take it easy, now."

As the red car moved out, Callie smiled widely at Dan. He returned the smile and turned back once more, without special hope, to scan the stragglers' faces. When the last of them had gone he spent another hour with Mr. Noto checking the bars and restaurants outside the grounds. At the Boot Hill Grill, the last they tried, the lady proprietor refused their pay for the coffee. "On the house," she said, flashing a golden grin. "How about a nice slice cheese-cake? You like cheese-cake?" She wrapped two thick wedges in wax paper, dropped them into the bag with the coffees, and slid the package across the counter towards Noto.

"Don't worry, sheriff," she said. "If I see this lug I call you. Right?"

"Good," Mr. Noto said. "Thanks for the coffee, Maxine."

"Any time you're around," Maxine said. "Nighty-night now."

They ate in the squad-car inside the rodeo grounds. The deputy who had climbed the chutes with Dan emerged from the shadows to lean tiredly against the front fender and roll a cigarette. They got out to join him.

"Looks like the show's over," he said gruffly.

"Over for now," Mr. Noto said. "We'll cover again tomorrow."

The deputy in the red shirt licked the paper liberally and shaped the cigarette, twisting the ends. "If you say so, Note," he said. "But he ain't going to show. If it was me I'd be a hundred miles from here right now." He looked quizzically at Dan.

"Maybe so, maybe not," Mr. Noto said. "Could be he don't scare easy."

"Looky here, Note," the deputy said. "Scuse us, Mr. Sherwood." He led Mr. Noto part way up the shadowy ramp and began to talk rapidly. Neither of them looked in Dan's direction. When they returned, he waved and moved off through the front gate. It was then that Noto dropped his coffee container into the trash can and said that they might as well leave.

On the way into town he drove the squad car with taciturn concentration. For some minutes Dan sat slumped in his corner of the seat, watching the procession of motels and drive-ins. Sachs was gone as if he had never been, like yesterday morning's nightmare. Now in your mind he still squatted on the fence-rail, hiding, if that was the word for it, behind that scraggly beard, yet so sure of himself that he had not even bothered to change his clothes. Or had he? Was it really Sachs, or was it some nameless cowpoke, some anonymous wrangler or hanger-on who went along with the rodeo as a circus-punk follows the greatest show on earth, nomadic, ambitionless, shrewd, and lazy?

Dan turned his head. "What's the name of that deputy?"

"Feller we just left?" Noto said. "That's Tom Dubman."

"He still doesn't believe me, does he?"

"How so?"

"He thinks I'm seeing things after the rap on the head. Wasn't that what he told you just now?"

"Tom's a doubter," said Noto, chuckling.

"And he knows I had the concussion."

"He did mention it."

"But that was in October, months ago."

"Sure thing."

"He also knows that Sachs was seen in California."

"I guess he brought that up, too."

"But Sachs could easily have come down here."

"Sure thing. If you saw him, that proves it."

"You say *if*. Does that mean you doubt it, too?"

"Tom's the doubter," Noto said, with a sidelong grin. "If you saw him, you saw him. Tom never saw him and what a man can't see he ain't very likely to be sure of. Likely this Sachs smelled a rat and took off."

Dan said no more. He sat silently, watching the crowded sidewalks of lower Main Street, looking into the faces. "Lots of people looks like other people," Tom Dubman said again, his big face twisted with nascent skepticism. Of course it was true. In that gabbling crowd twenty feet from the coursing squad-car, Buddy Sachs might have a dozen doubles. The imagination played queer tricks.

Dan sat upright, straightening his shoulders. That was no fantasy, he thought. I saw him as plain as day, as ugly as sin.

But in the next moment he was not so sure.

CHAPTER TWENTY-ONE

WHILE EUNICE gabbled on about the anniversary party, Dan held the receiver some inches away from his ear and gazed idly into the mouthpiece. It was covered with dust. For more than three weeks he had neither called nor been called. The reason was no more than an arm's-length away. Their edges already crinkling in the moistureless air, the yellow and the white sheets, covered with typescript, lay in ordered piles on the dusty table.

"It was a very fine party," he said, when Eunice paused for breath.

"It was fun, wasn't it?" said Eunice, in her big woman's voice. "Except that I didn't finish Harcomb's watch-fob."

"What watch-fob?"

"The silver one I was making at that awful man's school."

"Lee's Academy? How are things at the Academy?"

Eunice paused. He could hear her breathing into the mouthpiece. "Dan, that's what I called you about. I can't say it over the telephone. Are you terribly busy today? Could you come for a drink this afternoon? Harcomb is sitting here shushing me. He says you're doing all that writing and that's why we haven't seen you. But this is terribly important. Could you come?"

"What time?"

"Would five suit you? My cleaning-girl leaves at four-thirty and Harcomb drives her home. He'll be back by five."

"Five will be fine," Dan said.

It was well after five before the all-important topic came up. The Wileys both met him at the door, led him to the study where a ragged heap of mesquite-wood blazed fitfully on the hearth, put a drink into his hand, and for some time chatted amiably about his work. Even in the Land of Nod, they pursue the amenities, he thought. Eunice in the gray dress and Wiley in his usual dark clothes looked like what they were—a pair of expatriated New Yorkers getting slightly and slowly older. In the end Eunice cleared her throat, glanced at her husband, and said that she and Harcomb had decided to call Dan—or at least she had suggested it and Harcomb had finally agreed—because it was such a mess and because they knew that Mandeville Lee was a friend of his.

Dan grinned. "He's my landlord, Eunice. Not a special friend. He's also your school director."

Eunice sat up straight, her bracelets clanking indignantly. "Oh, no, he's not! Not now he's not. We've quit the place. I could just skin that man alive."

Dan glanced at Harcomb, whose monkish dark face was completely expressionless. "Do you mean Lee?"

"You bet I mean Lee. Just when we were learning so much and having so much fun, he had to go and spoil it." Eunice looked towards her husband, her large brow darkening under the reddish hair. "He insulted Moira. Harcomb, you tell Dan."

A faint smile played around Wiley's mouth. He made a roof with his long fingers and peered at Dan over the top of it. "Some women would have been complimented. Eunice never cared for our friend Lee."

"Harcomb, you didn't either," Eunice said. "Now you know you didn't. He's an awful man."

"He's an awful handsome man," Wiley said, smiling.

"You know I can't *stand* him," said Eunice, fiercely. "Tell Dan."

"It's one of those things—" Wiley began.

"But to *Moira!*" cried Eunice. "To Moira of all people. If he'd said it to me, I'd have slapped his smug face for him. Tell him, Harcomb."

Over the roof of his fingers, Wiley was still smiling at Dan. "Eunice is suggesting that Lee—er—propositioned Moira."

"Harcomb! That verb."

"It's what it amounted to," Wiley said, his smile broadening. "Stud horse approaches filly, making suitable noises. Filly runs like hell to the other end of the pasture."

"Harcomb, stop it. Oh, Dan, he refuses to take it seriously, but I say it's just terrible."

"I point out to Eunice," said Harcomb sententiously, "that it's one of the things that happens all the time."

"But to Moira," said Eunice again. "It's especially terrible when you know—I mean, Dan, this awful clothes-horse of a man, with that weak, overpretty face of his, has been making up to Moira ever since that school opened. Leaning over her shoulder—ugh!—Dan, he used to peer down the front of her dress, pretending he was there to help. She's so innocent, so really unsuspecting, and then when that steward or whatever they call him came into our class one afternoon and told Moira she was wanted on the phone at the school office, she just turned all colors of the rainbow because she thought something had happened to Axel, and it *could* happen at his age—he might have been hit by a car or had a heart attack or just dropped dead—and so she dropped her work and hurried out. But all it was was that awful man. You tell Dan, Harcomb."

Wiley still smiled faintly. "He was most courtly, I believe. Nothing crude. He simply offered his services."

"Nothing *crude*," said Eunice, loudly. "What could be cruder? He knew Axel was old. He'd met him out there. Oh, Dan, you're a boxer. Didn't you tell me you boxed? Couldn't you just *punch* him?"

"Eunice," said Wiley, in the apostolic voice. "What could be cruder than that? Of course it's true, Dan, that the O'Keefes are rather exercised about this. Axel deplores the departure of duels."

"Axel could probably beat Lee to a pulp," Dan said.

"Moira wouldn't tell him at first," said Eunice. "The poor little thing. She thought he had taken enough on her account, and then she was afraid of what he might do. But she cried so much—"

"Moira is given to tears," Wiley said. "She even voted for Dewey. What my sainted father used to call the waterworks."

"I don't blame her," cried Eunice. "Exiled out here, with that awful lie about stealing at those teas in Connecticut. Oh. If I was Moira I'd have died of shame."

"If you were Moira you'd have taken a sock at Lee," Wiley said. "You'd have biffed him right there in the office."

"I would, I really would," said Eunice, smiling at the thought, and nestling her large frame more firmly into the chair.

"When was all this?" said Dan.

"It was last week," said Eunice. "It was early last week. We just left the school then and there. I insisted we leave right away. He owes us money, too. Can't Axel sue him?"

"Eunice," said Harcomb, gently. "Sue him for what?"

She sat firmly, Juno-esque, the jeweled hands in her lap. "For the money," she said positively. "For alienation of affections. I've heard of that. Haven't you, Dan?"

"No affections were alienated," Wiley said, "with the possible exception of yours and Moira's against this Lee. And there were no witnesses."

"Moira was certainly a witness."

"Moira was the—er—victim," Wiley said, "unless you want to count Axel. Dan, there's obviously nothing to do, no reason to involve you. Eunice—"

"Eunice insisted, yes," Eunice interrupted. "Eunice hates that big clothes-horse, yes. Eunice knows what it did to Moira and Axel. If neither of you men—"

"I'll talk to Lee," Dan said. "I doubt if it will help anything. This horse is already stolen. But I'll see him tonight or tomorrow."

"Good," said Eunice, triumphantly. "I hope you *punch* him, Dan. Harcomb, dear, Dan's glass is empty. Get him another drink."

*　*　*　*　*

As always, Lee's answering voice was shaded with arrogance. "Mandeville Lee. Who's calling?"

"Dan Sherwood."

The tone warmed. "Dan, how they hanging, boy? Where you been?"

"Mostly here."

"Fill me in on that alley-cat."

"What alley-cat?"

"The killer. Whatsisname? Sachs. The one you saw at the rodeo. Dan, you sure had that place flooded with cops. Did they get him?"

"Not yet. What about your southern peach? Did you get her?"

"Flew back to old daddy," Lee said, complacently. "Writes me postcards twice a week. Views of Montgomery and points nearby. Old daddy owns that town. What's on your mind, son?"

"A few things. What are you doing now?"

"Dinner-date coming up. Right now I'm having a gin. Come on over and join me."

"I'll be there," Dan said. He picked up a pack of cigarettes from the carton in the kitchen and walked acrosslots to Lee's house. When he opened the door and stood aside, Dan saw that he was in clean wool socks, jodhpurs, and a green turtle-neck sweater. He held a half-filled glass. Behind him the room was in dusty disorder.

"How's the boy? Or did I ask?"

"I'm still all right."

"Place is a mess," Lee said. "I fired Chita. Caught her swiping gin. Find yourself a spot and have a drink."

"No thanks."

"You on the wagon?"

"I came to talk."

Lee sat down on the couch. "Talk away. If you change your mind, the gin's there."

"Plenty of gin with Chita gone," Dan said.

"Old Chita," Lee said. "Got to look her up, get her back. She's working down at Pancho's. Old Chita. You seen her lately?"

"No, I've been seeing some other people."

"Such as who?"

"Such as the Wileys. Do you know the Wileys?"

Lee looked blank and shook his head.

"The Wileys are friends of the O'Keefes. Do you know the O'Keefes?"

"What is this, a game? Who the hell are the O'Keefes?"

"O'Keefe is an old man with a young wife," Dan said. "Ash-blonde girl, rather nervous. She was out at the Academy until last week, in the jewelry class."

"Oh, that one, yes."

"The word is you had a little talk with her."

Lee sipped the gin and tonic. "Whose word was that?"

"Never mind," Dan said. "But when it was put into words and the facts were considered, it added up to a dirty trick."

"No tricks in that monkey," Lee said. "She was out of there like a shot. Slight case of misjudgment."

"Do you make them often?"

"Mostly . . . Make what?"

"Misjudgments."

"Rarely," said Lee. "I'll admit this little blonde was one. No harm done."

"Who said so? You don't know. She's worked up about it."

"Then all I can say is she works up easy—and in the wrong way. What the hell, Dan—"

"You don't know the background," Dan said. "You don't have the slightest idea what it means to be a young wife to an older man."

Sprawling on the couch, his legs under the coffee table, Lee finished his drink and poured another. Except for the chink of the ice in the glass, it was silent in the room. Lee was smiling. "No, frankly, I don't, Dan. I never was a young wife or an old man."

"What made you pick on her?"

"Oh, good looking girl, nice build, just loved it when I helped her with the damn jewelry."

"So on that basis you fake a phone call and get her into the lion's den."

Lee set the drink down on the coffee table and spread his hands. "What if I did? No harm done. It happens all the time. Where've you been lately?"

"I've been around enough to know you raised hell in that family."

"She's the one raised hell. She could have kept her sweet pointed little mouth shut."

"She didn't though. You almost had a duel on your hands."

Lee laughed incredulously. "Duel? What kind of talk is that? Listen, Robin Hood, it takes two to make a duel."

"One and one. You and her husband."

"Not me," Lee said. "I had my little duel with a piece of shrapnel. Duel, huh? And you're the messenger, is that it? Or just how do you muscle into the picture?"

"Call me a friend of the family," Dan said. "The harm is done now. Maybe more will be. I wouldn't promise that the husband won't walk over here and take a shot at you."

"Shot for what? I didn't even make a pass at this lovely. Just got her in there and calmed her down and talked to her low and sweet."

"Studfarm special. Why don't you save your sweet-talk for your Alabama peach with the big black eyes?"

Lee was grinning. "I told you. She done flew home to daddy."

"So after she left you were feeling lonesome."

"Not lonesome, just banging around, making a little music."

"It came out discords."

"All right. So whose teeth ache?"

"Mine for one. And several others. If O'Keefe were only a little younger, the teeth might be yours. Maybe they still will be."

"Don't make me laugh, Dan. This guy is old. He's tottering."

"He wasn't tottering the last time I saw him."

"Don't kid me. I've met him, seen him. One leg in the grave."

"Lee, it's none of your business how old he is or how young she is. You just made a hell of a mistake."

"I'll tell you something, Danny boy. The trouble with you is you're a goddam Puritan."

"And the trouble with you is you're a goddam lecher. You had no right to move in on this girl."

Lee picked up his glass and gestered with it crowingly. "Aha! No poaching, is that how it runs? You like 'em young yourself."

Dan took an angry step towards Lee. "Cut it out," he said furiously.

"Aw, sit down, Dan. Stop racing your motor. Cool off, boy. Have a gin and cool off."

"I'm cool enough. You're the hot one. A real hotshot."

"Old furnace roaring," Lee said, comfortably. "Got to keep the ashes hauled. Where the hell are you going, pal?"

"Out of the basement," Dan said.

CHAPTER TWENTY-TWO

DEPUTY SHERIFF NOTOFRANCESCO sat in one of the modern-istic chairs in the living-room, making notes on the back of an envelope with a ball-point pen. He had taken off the sweat-stained Truman hat, which lay on the floor beside him, and his thin black hair, grizzled with gray, stood up in small ringlets all over his bullet-shaped skull. He was not yet shaved for the day; his long jaw showed blue-black against the buff-colored shirt where the badge was pinned. He had drunk the coffee, cooling it carefully in the saucer, and had checked through with Dan what he called the time-table of the stab-bing.

Lee still had not talked. He was unconscious from the anesthetic. He had lost a lot of blood. They called his con-dition serious, possibly critical. The weapon was a small knife of some kind. It had cut deep, though how deep was not yet clear. The blood on the handle had obliterated the fin-gerprints, if any.

"Now, Dan," Noto said, "let's move on a little. You know this guy. Who do you think stuck him?"

"It could have been a burglar."

"That line don't make too much sense, Dan, but let's run

through it. He is found in the right-hand seat of his own car, with a blanket over his head, in the empty lot behind the Chinese grocery on the Speedway, half a block from his house, at around five this morning. In his house there is no blood; there is no evidence the house has been ransacked. So what makes you think it was a burglar?"

"The thought crossed my mind. Maybe he was held up in his car."

"Maybe so. But his billfold had fifty bucks in it. He had not been rolled. What put the idea of robbery in your mind, Dan?"

"Only that Lee is a money-maker. Anyone who knows him knows he makes money. He's always talking about it. The news could get around. Lee thinks it has."

"Did he tell you that?"

"He said it once. He was going away and wanted me to watch his house."

"He must trust you. How well do you know him?"

"The way you know your landlord—"

"I got no landlord," Noto said, grinning.

"I see him off and on."

"You seen him since the rodeo?"

"Once, yes."

"Where was this?"

"I went to his house."

"When, Dan?"

"Couple of weeks ago. Maybe a little less."

"What were you doing, paying the rent?"

"No, I pay by mail. I went to see him about something else."

"Anything special."

Dan looked at the floor. "It was a sort of private thing."

"Sorry, Dan. Private things is what I'm after."

"Sure, I know. This was about a woman at his school. He called her in and made a few suggestions." Dan described the O'Keefe affair.

Mr. Noto held the pen poised over the envelope. "What was that name again?"

"Mrs. O'Keefe. Moira O'Keefe."

"You know this woman?"

"Yes, I know her."

"Is she the one did it, Dan?"

"The stabbing. Oh, no, that's impossible."

"Why impossible, Dan? In my line of work the impossible happens."

"Moira's just not the type."

Mr. Noto shifted in his chair. "You say this woman is married?" he asked, patiently.

"Yes, married to a retired professor."

"So she's old?"

"No," Dan said. "Moira is young. O'Keefe is old, but he married a young wife."

Noto crossed his legs. "You don't think she's the one did it?"

"Not Moira. She couldn't, Note. She's too shy. She weeps."

"What that feller said over there, blood and tears," Mr. Noto said. "You know. Churchill. Tell me, Dan, what does she weep about?"

"Quite a lot. It's a long story."

"I got time," Mr. Noto said.

Dan told him about Axel's late marriage and the social

ostracism and the accusation about purse-robbing at teas. Mr. Noto watched him closely.

"So she helped herself, did she?"

"No," Dan said. "I don't think so. In fact, I would bet on it. It was a lie they used to punish her."

"Punish her for what?"

"For marrying Axel."

"Take another angle," Noto said. "Does she need money now?"

"Very doubtful," Dan said. "They have enough. They own a house."

"Sometimes you get a rich one," Mr. Noto said. "She don't need it but she goes ahead and takes it. Now, Dan, about that school. You say she went there."

"Until Lee got chummy, yes. She was making silver jewelry."

"And they use raw silver, and the lady steals some and Lee catches her at it."

"That's not the way I heard it, Note. Lee admitted that he sent for her, faked a phone call, got her to his office."

"Nothing about silver, then? So how about the professor?"

"You mean O'Keefe stabbing Lee? It's possible. But I'd say it's very unlikely."

"When Lee makes a pass at his wife? Is he jealous? Some of them are."

"I doubt it."

"Have you talked to the professor?"

"Not for a long time. Not since the—er—office visit. I've talked to the Wileys. They're friends of the O'Keefes. Eunice Wiley went to Lee's school with Moira O'Keefe."

"So what do the Wileys say?"

"Eunice—Mrs. Wiley—doesn't like Lee. She was much in-
censed." Dan laughed shortly. "She heard I used to box. She
wanted me to take a sock at Lee."

"Did you?"

"I came close."

"What stopped you?"

"Oh, I don't know. He probably had one coming. But,
Note, it's like war. It never settles anything."

"Sometimes it does."

"Yes, sometimes. It always does in the movies, or in westerns. But it's a childish idea that a punch in the nose reforms
the unreformable."

"Dan, don't get sore, now, but I ask this: "You didn't stick
Lee?"

"No. I thought of hitting him, but never of stabbing him.
In a way I feel sorry for him. He's a veteran. He's on some
kind of disability pension. He's got a silver plate in his skull.
He's got the usual appetites and once or twice he has made me
sore as hell with his arrogance, but none of that adds up to
a knife in the gut."

"Except it has," said Noto. "Who else don't like this guy?
Business associates?"

"The staff at the school might or might not like him. Some
of those he didn't hire might have a grudge. There might be
some bums at the race-track."

"He wasn't there," Noto said. "I checked that. But I'll ask
him when he comes to. Who else don't exactly love the guy?
Any other babes?"

"The last one I saw him with seemed to like him. Or so

Lee said. But she's back in Alabama. She sends him post-cards."

"Name of Collie or Cullie? Montgomery, Alabama?"

"Callie," Dan said. "How'd you know?"

"Postcards lying around his house. Boy, what they won't write on postcards! Why I don't think it was robbery, Dan, is the cashbox was over there, too. Untouched. Right there in the kitchen. So I don't see larceny in this one, Dan. The party that stuck Lee was aiming to rough him up, cut him up, wanted to hurt him some. Any more dames?"

Dan sat staring at the floor. "There's a girl named Chita," he said at last. "I forgot about Chita."

"Who's Chita?"

"She used to clean his house. Lee fired her. I think he said she works in a restaurant downtown. He met her down there the first time—sometime last year."

"What's her last name?"

"I never knew it."

"What about the name of the restaurant?"

"Blank again. Some Mexican name. Wait a minute, Note. It'll be in the phone-book. All I can think of is Bosco."

Noto grinned. "Bosco is what Pruney drinks."

"How is the boy?"

"Oh, the kid is fine," Noto said. "Do me a favor, Dan. Check the book."

Dan turned to the yellow pages and ran his finger down the list of restaurants. "Here it is," he said. "A place called Pancho's."

Noto scribbled it down on the envelope. "Okay, Dan. We'll check it out. And the other leads. Right now, you don't mind,

I'll use your phone. Got to call the hospital. It could be this Lee has woke up."

*   *   *   *   *

The day waned without further word from Notofrancesco. Early in the evening Dan called the hospital for news of Mandeville Lee. "I'll give you his floor," said the girl at the hospital switchboard. But when she had put him through to the nurse in charge, all he found out was that Mr. Lee's condition was still critical and that he was now asleep.

"Will you tell him I called?"

"I'll tell him tomorrow, sir. What was the name?"

"Dan Sherwood."

"I will tell him. Good night."

"Good night," Dan said, but the circuit had already been broken.

There was no answer from either the Wileys or the O'Keefes. He read for two hours and tried them again. Once more the signal burred emptily and far away. Outside, the night wind had risen. He locked the doors and returned to his chair. Who had done the stabbing? Sleepily he tried to reconstruct the scene:

Not traffic, no. At that hour, on the Speedway, all traffic is gone. Buildings stand, stark and ugly, shouldering the wind. Lights show, blue and baleful, in the rear of locked stores. In empty lots the brown reeds tremble. The air from the desert sets asway the looped telephone lines, rustles and stirs in the roadside debris. Now, far off like eyes, the paired headlights appear, come closer, round the corner. The car bumps down from the blacktop into East Rachel Street. Dust rises in the wake of the wheels' passage, is caught in the warm wind, settles invisibly. A block beyond Lee's house the car edges to the weedy roadside and stops. Headlights dim and disappear. The engine dies. A tall figure swings out of the driver's seat, coat-collar up, hat-brim down. In one gloved hand is a flashlight. From the other, as he crosses under the single streetlamp, there is a momentary glint of steel. At Lee's driveway he pauses. The torch-beam winks toward the red low car parked on the coarse desert gravel beside the house. He keeps it burning, sweeping it down from horizontal to vertical, as the feet silently follow the path to the front door. They nearly but never step into the moving golden pool of light. It shines on the welcome mat, climbs the door, stops to encircle the brass button of the bell. The gloved finger flicks out, the bell echoes within the house. Tall in the darkness, the figure waits without a sound.

For a long minute he hears nothing. Then rapid footsteps ring across the inner floor, the door is wrenched open, bright light glares in Lee's astonished eyes as he stands—handsome, tousled, fully dressed, gin-smelling, hand raised like a shield, trying to peer beyond the blinding beam into the identity of this dark, man-shaped segment of the night, scissored from its surface like a silhouette from black paper. He cannot see. "Get that light out of my eyes," he says, "and what the hell do you think you're doing—" But he is not answered. Without words or warning, he is seized, pulled out of the door and into the assailant's embrace. The knife rips twice and again. Lee grunts with the jolt of it, the searing hot pain of it, and bends almost double, clutching his shirt just above the smart striped belt where already the bright stain has leaped to being, begun to sop and spread. But no blood falls. The dark figure steps

forward, closes the door, drags Lee to and into the red car,
covers his head with the car blanket. . . .

—It makes no sense. Where did the attacker get the key to
Lee's car?

—He found it in Lee's pocket.

—Why did he drive the car away from Lee's house? Why
did he leave it, with Lee in it, no more than a block away?

—Something scared him. A police squad car went past on
the Speedway.

—How do you know it was a man who did the stabbing?
Why not a woman?

—Women don't use knives.

—In Altoona, Pennsylvania, a couple of years ago a woman
stabbed her sleeping husband sixty-eight times with an ice-
pick. It may have been another state or another town, but
otherwise the facts are as given.

—Why does it have to be someone you know? Why not any
one of twenty or thirty people you never saw or heard of?

—You start from the known where the visible motives are.
What about Axel? The figure at the door could have been
Axel. Easily.

—Not easily, no. Axel's too old and wise to believe in force
or vengeance.

—That's one of the comforting illusions. Axel was not too
old or too wise to marry a girl half his age. He was not old and
wise enough to wait for what they call a suitable interval.
With the young man's wife he took on the young man's
obligations.

—Non sequitur. The argument is preposterous. Axel is no
duellist.

—In Tennessee a year ago a man of seventy-five married a sixteen-year-old. Two months later he shot and killed the girl's lover with a squirrel rifle.

—That was Tennessee. It's traditional in Tennessee. In April, August, October, the assignation is made in whispers, takes place, is known to one too many. When they meet, clasp, the old man is there. At the edge of the glade, behind the clump of mountain-laurel, the gun-snout swings, oil-dark in the afternoon. It points, holds steady on the mouth of the cave. He tongues the well-chewed cud across the store teeth, from one cheek to the other. The left eye closes. One gnarled finger crooks and waits. The boy finishes, proud and laughing, rises, pulling up his pants, comes to the mouth of the cave already groping in his shirt pocket for the post-operational cigarette. He never lights it. The crash in the vale is louder than the crack of doom. The boy, astonished, falls and kicks. The girl cries and cowers, invisible. Scared birds leap airwards from the trees. You'll find it all in Red Warren and Uncle Billy Faulkner, the Rover Boys on the Old Frontier.

Dan jumped at the phone-bell beside his ear.

"Hello."

"Hello, Dan. You're up late. Noto on."

"You're up late, too."

"Not for long, Dan. Give me ten more minutes I'll be out like a light."

"Note, what time is it? My watch stopped."

"Eleven o'clock news just finished. Eleven-o-five."

"And what's the news?"

"We're coming, Dan."

"How is Lee?"

"He's woke up a couple of times but he don't make sense yet. That boy was lucky."

"How lucky?"

"Three holes in his gut but they missed the jackpot."

"What's the jackpot?"

"I mean the places where they might have killed him. Missed the liver, missed the spleen. Two cuts stuck in the muscle. Just the one went through."

"Through where?"

"Tip of the knife got through to the stomach. They sewed that one up."

"What about infection?"

"No fever yet. Oh, maybe a degree, but that's from shock. They shot him full of penicillin."

"So he'll live?"

"They say he'll live all right. He'll live unless he starts serious bleeding inside."

"But no talk yet?"

"Oh, he's been gabbling. Dan, reason I called so late I thought you'd want to know. It looks like Lee got cut downtown."

"Downtown? How did he get way out here?"

"Somebody drove him and left him in his own car."

"What makes you think he was driven?"

"The blood was all over the right-hand seat. Looks like they wrapped a blanket around his head, drove him out there and left him."

"Who's they?"

"Somebody from way downtown. Likely somebody from Pancho's place. He was seen down there around ten, ten-thirty. One of the cops saw his car at the curb close to midnight."

"What about Chita?"

"Still looking out for Chita. We got her cousin, so he says. Some says it's her brother."

"I've heard there is a brother. What does the brother say?"

"Admits Lee was there. Says he left before one. Says Lee musta stabbed himself by mistake."

"Ha ha on that one."

"Ha ha is right. He also says Lee must have gone someplace else and got himself stuck."

"What do you think?"

"I'll know better when we find this Chita. What kind of a girl is Chita, Dan?"

"Oh, good enough. Not vicious certainly. When I first came out here, I got the idea she was Lee's cleaning-girl, plus."

"That's still the rumor. Especially the plus. So it all multiplies okay. Lee dumps her and tries a few others, like this Collie from Alabama. Then he gets lonesome, or his house gets too dirty, or both. So last night he hoists a few and goes back looking for Chita, right?"

"It sounds plausible."

"Then we get a little scramble, say, a little scrap. Chita or her brother or her cousin gets a little excitable and that's when the cutting starts."

"It's better than anything I've been able to think of," Dan said.

"So I'll let you know when I know. Take it easy, Dan."

"You, too, Note. And thanks for calling."

So, he thought, cradling the phone, you have been romanticizing again—you and your faceless figures looming out of the night, beaming their flashlights, cloak-and-daggering, for all the world like something out of Demarest Palley's Golden

West Library. It's your chronic affliction: recurrent inflammation of the imagination. And the actuality? It is as bald as an egg, dull as a drone. The case of the playboy and the little Mexican floozy. And all that business of the excremental universe is nothing but another inflammation, another hallucination, like that sight of Sachs at the rodeo, like Herr Böcklin's predatory dragon, like the vision of a hell-on-earth in the novels of Nicholas Kemp.

But he knew in his heart that it was not so, could not be so. For if you wrote off all the blackness as mere illusion, diseased imagination, what would you do with that sun-bright vision of the girl in the library, the pensive and beautiful face poised above the notebook, the voice like quiet music?

CHAPTER TWENTY-THREE

Sunday, May 21
1 9 5 0

Dear Mr. Sherwood:

Since your non-committal answer to my former letter, I now write to ask you flatly how you are planning to proceed. As I read over your letters and the carbon of mine, I see that there is room for misunderstanding. You profess to be no stranger to my novels. My point was, and is, that you cannot help being a stranger to my life. Ideally, that is the way it should stay. But in recent weeks certain matters have come up that call for reconsiderations. It is because of these that I now write you.

First, though, let me rehearse the situation. In the past twenty years I have read enough lies about my alleged actions to fill a freight train. Hardly a week goes by in which the mails do not carry some fresh inquiry. The pattern is familiar. Some total stranger has discovered or invented some new biographical tidbit. He arrogantly requires my comment on it. Years ago I was foolish enough to answer a few of them seriously. Then I had the incredible experience of reading what was done with my replies. I say incredible advisedly. My replies were twisted, excerpted, edited, corrupted, and used as clubs to beat me with. Since that time I have adopted a more or less uniform policy, which is to ignore these invaders of my freedom as a writer and my privacy as a man. If I expected the policy to work, I have been disappointed. What they did not know they could always invent. They invented, usually out of the whole cloth, and the barrage of lies has continued unbroken.

During the past month I have been repeatedly written to, telegraphed to, and even telephoned to by a man at Minnesota. Unlike some of his predecessors, he is reasonably polite and at least puts up a good show of having my welfare at heart. But he is also determined. I gather that he is also quite young. It has been a long time since I inhabited academic circles, but I gain the impression that whether or not I agree to help will in some way determine whether he gets his promotion, whether he and his wife can afford to have a baby, and whether they continue to get enough to eat. So I am put in the position of the ogre who denies them a livelihood. This man has prepared what he calls an "annotated bibliography" of the so-called criticism which has been done about my work. Over my protests he sent me a copy of the typescript. If I ever had anything that could be called pride of authorship, I can assure you that this bibliography would quickly dispel it. For here, soon to reach the permanence of print, are all the lies of almost a quarter-century. It makes you wonder why you ever put pen to paper. What morality prevails among American critics, Mr. Sherwood? What perversity makes them invent what they do not know, passing invention off as fact? My Minnesota friend assures me that I should cooperate with the university where I spent two student years. He says he would value my commentary on any of the items in his bibliography, which runs to almost thirty pages. He vows to print exactly what I write, without comment or excerpting.

I don't doubt his honesty, though I should. What I doubt is the wisdom of doing as he asks. For what earthly good would it do? The lies and distortions are now so firmly fixed under the ground, and so interwoven and entangled aboveground that they can never be uprooted or disentangled. Even if I had read all the junk this man lists, it would take a year of work, four or five hours a day, to set the record straight. I neither care—nor dare—to take the time. It would mean pushing aside my new novel, mangling all my days, and to what end? I suppose to the happy end that a whole new generation of so-called critics could get a fresh start. They could read between the lines of what I would write for this man. They could begin the endless process of elaborating, embroidering, and conjecturing until a whole new tissue of falsehood would come to supersede the one that now prevails. I have told this man at Minnesota that I will not help him. To publish a compendium of twenty years of lying can hardly help in the establishment of truth.

At first glance, exacerbated by another less recent experience which I had to take to the courts, I took you for another in my tribe of furies. It is still a fact that I will oppose any attempt you may make to invade my private life. But there was one item in the bibliography mentioned above that caught my eye. It was by you, and it appeared a couple of years ago in the *Sewanee Review*. I sent for a copy and read the piece. Except for one minor factual error, it is sound, interesting, very well written, and exactly on the right track. On the strength of that, I have reread your former letter. Although it may be no more than wishful thinking, I would like to think that your book might turn out to be what I have never had since I began writing, that is, the work of a man who has seen what I have tried to do, and who could be trusted to explore the novels instead of continuing those lies and libels which hang around my neck like a ball and chain.

I do not use the image from self-pity. It is close to literal fact. If you knew that every time you published a new book, with all the toil and sweat that this entails, you could count on its being received not for what it is but for what grist it provides for the manipulators and the counterfeiters, you would perhaps come to feel, as I have, that it is hopeless to look for truth and decency among the tribe of wolves that call themselves critics. Take an instance. I often read, these days, that I have not published a book for a number of years. Don't ever let them tell you writers don't read about themselves, whatever the writers pretend. So the wolves howl with pleasure that the spring has dried up. They gloat over the fact, as they think that another writer has succumbed to the great American malady.

Don't they know, Mr. Sherwood, that they are choking the spring with their garbage? Don't they realize that, even with the best will in the world, a writer can get discouraged when another truckload of junk—and another and another—is dumped in his clean front yard?

The garbage appears to be in infinite supply. Take the case of my parents. At my elbow now, ready to feed the fire in my fireplace, is a current issue of a popular magazine. It contains an article which purports to explain my lifetime of writing as an outgrowth of an alleged Oedipus complex. The author of this piece is supposed to be a reputable critic; in the contributor's notes, he says he is, and the magazine editors believe him. They even use the adjective *great*. He is great all right. He has the currently stylish vocabulary and a whole arsenal of weapons. I know him not as great but as a pusillanimous turd, a fake, and a liar. He does not even know, Mr. Sherwood, where my father was born. He misspells both my mother's and my sister's names. He repeats, licking his lips, the ancient canard that my father used to tie me belly-down to a barrel in the backyard and flog me with a wire carpet-beater until I bled. Where he got the new instrument I do not know. Former liars have mentioned razor-strops and a brass-studded belt. Out of all this he evolves a theory that I hated my father and doted on my mother. When this dawned on me, it is alleged, I could not take it and fled to the forests. Having got there, this ass says, another complication rose up. I discovered in myself a latent strain of homosexuality—an entirely fictitious French-Canadian top-faller is invented for this purpose—and the rest of my life is explained by my having fled from this double realization.

What can a man do in the face of such malicious lying, Mr. Sherwood? Does the American public feed on such garbage as that? This "critic" could have gone to Boise and asked some people. He would have found that my father was a mild and somewhat stupid man who kept a small store, which did not make much money, and who married, as the phrase runs, above his station. My mother was a decent and slightly gifted person who decided that my father needed an infusion of culture. The disparity between them slowly widened. With what I can only suppose to have been the best of genteel intentions, she attempted to force my father to become what he could never possibly have been. On his side, nagged by this gentility to a thick man's despair, and loaded with debt, and always on the verge of failing in his small business, he took to drinking more than was good for him. He had already the ulcer—or ulcers— which eventually killed him, and the liquor made him sick. But he was a mild man. Never once, while I was home, did he ever lift a finger against me, let alone beat me with a brass-studded belt. He did not even own one. My mother was the disciplinarian. Infractions by my sister and me were punished by banishment upstairs, never by beating. My mother would pray over us. She was given to tears and to the writing of sentimental poetry. Except for the books I read while being punished in my room, I found this intolerable. It was that which made me run away from home. I would do it again. Contrary to this lying critic's views, it had nothing to do with Oedipus or any other king. It had to do with a situation, to me unendurable, that had arisen between two very obscure members of the great American demos.

You can believe this or not—I expect nothing—but as a green kid in the first lumber-camp I drank too much Canadian ale one night and puked liberally in the bunk-house woodbox. Except for that and one shot of very foul tequila which some-one gave me when I was wet and half-frozen and seasick on a voyage around Cape Horn, I have never since touched alcohol. That is my legacy from my father, such as it is. The legacy from my mother, who was probably a good woman and certainly a foolish one, is whatever talent I happen to have.

In all the Minnesota man's bibliography, there is no hint of
the foregoing. Nor is there any hint of the fact that my first
wife, who was also a good and talented woman in her way,
began trying with me the kind of thing my mother had tried
with my father. Again I found it intolerable. I was beginning
to write seriously, and I had to be free. She would never let me
alone. I would come back from a job I hated to the place where
we lived and find my manuscripts corrected, whole paragraphs
inked out, material transposed, even new words added. When
I objected, she would refuse to listen. Decent as she was, she
had delusions of grandeur. She would edit me, build me, delete
me into a writer of heroic stature. Together we would win the
Pulitzer, even the Nobel prize. Mr. Sherwood, I had to rewrite,
secretly, almost every paragraph of *The Hinges of Hell* in order
to make it my own and not hers. It is commonly said that she
was responsible for whatever good is in that book. This is
another of the interminable falsehoods. She tried her best to
make it so, but the final version was mine. In the end I had to
pretend to her that I had abandoned the book. I worked on it
secretly in the studio. I smuggled it to the publisher and even
had the proof-sheets sent to the studio to keep them away from
her blue pencil.

You have doubtless read that I used her to get established
and then ran out on her. The truth is otherwise. It was soon
clear enough that I could look forward to a lifetime in which
I would fight her every day for the right to say what I had to
say. So I took a way out. I faked an affair with a girl, whom I
disliked, at the studio, which I hated, and was promptly sued
for divorce after a scene such as you can perhaps imagine. I
threw up the studio job, hired a third-floor room in a small
hotel in Los Gatos, and went on writing. My first wife, who still
keeps the name of Mrs. Kemp, is now (or lately was) teaching
school in Nevada. I think she is happy, but I do not know.
She does not have to work at all unless she wants to. I assigned
her the royalties on *The Hinges of Hell*. They send me dupli-
cate statements and the book earns steadily. I also put the
money from the sale of movie-rights two years ago into a

legacy which will guarantee her an income for life. When the film is released, sometime soon, she will be even better off, for my lawyers fixed the contract in such a way that she will profit whenever the film is shown. For what it is worth, I have tried to repay her.

My second marriage was a different kind of washout. The lady, now dead, thought it would be a great adventure to marry an established novelist, forgetting that established novelists, like any others, must have time to write what they write. As far as I know, she never read any of my work beyond a few of the short stories. Her dreams were of literary cocktail parties in New York, of travel in Europe, of bohemian sun-and-swimming fests in Majorca. My dream was to have a family and freedom to write. The dreams clashed. She would neither consent to child-bearing nor understand that my traveling days were behind me. I should not have married her. She was a good and foolish woman. She went back to Texas and I went back to writing.

Now, Mr. Sherwood, I have a third wife, also good and not foolish. Her wants and her tastes are simple. She knows and respects my need for time. Quite soon, barring accidents, she expects a child. I am fifty-two and she is thirty-seven. Since I married her I have commenced to write again, after some years in the horse-latitudes.

You cannot read any of this in the inventions of Mr. Oedipus Freud, the eminent literary critic with the dripping jaws of a vampire and the moral probity of a hyena. He thinks he has my hide pinned to his study wall just above the typewriter. He reaches out to scratch it whenever his courage gets low. His lies are reproduced and praised in the annotated bibliography of my young friend from Minnesota. Until I die I will continue to assert that they are stinking garbage.

It is very far from my intention to suggest that you, in your own book, should undertake to correct twenty-odd years of this kind of dumping. In fact, I hereby put you on your honor as a gentleman to read and remember what I have told you, and *not to use it in your book in any way, shape, or form.* I have lived too long in this twilit world to imagine that such a book as yours, always assuming you have not abandoned it in discouragement, could ever redress the balance. I have given up hoping that the truth, honestly stated, could ever counteract, now, all the years of lying. But there was never a writer, I don't care who, who did not live in and on hope. He hopes to be read, hopes to be understood, hopes to be taken for what he is, hopes for the eventual triumph of decency even though he knows, in his heart, that the dice are loaded against any of this.

I cannot pretend to have led a blameless life. You, who seem to know my books and to be on the right track about them, must realize that in the struggle to get, and to remain free, it has been necessary to be cruel, if that is the word, to some of those who would have constrained or limited me. They were not always, perhaps they were not ever, consciously evil in the limitations they sought to impose. They could not understand, they could never in the world appreciate, what it takes to be a writer in terms of time and integrity. I once read a statement by a fellow-writer whose work I respect. They asked him how he got his work done, how he found the time. His reply was that some of his time he had stolen like a thief, some he had taken like a man, and some (though very little) had been handed to him on a silver platter. This is my situation exactly, except for the silver platter. I would like to be able to count on you, as a fellow-writer, for some of that understanding. If not, Mr. Sherwood, able and decent critic as you have shown yourself to be, I will have to fight you, as I have to fight all the others, for my right to be a free man.

Yours sincerely,
Nicholas Kemp

*   *   *   *   *

Hart Mackenzie grunted, deep in his throat, and lowered the last of the pages into his lap. The late sunbeams flooded the cabin room with golden light, glinting on the steel frames of the old man's glasses, and gilding the unfinished mural at the other end of the room. "Quite a letter," he said. "When did it come?"

"Last week," Dan said. "I guess you could call it a historic document. In a way it solves my problem."

"How do you mean—solves?"

"It settles the biography question. Now I know the facts and I'm honor bound not to use them."

"Sure it settles that question," Hart said. "The other one is still hanging fire: can you believe all that this Kemp writes? Strikes me he's being a little crafty. It's a good way to head you off in case you need heading off. He suspects you're a man of honor. He's counting on that to keep you shut up."

"Don't you believe what he says?"

"Yes and no. After all, Dan, this man's a novelist. A novelist is a liar by profession."

"Do you spot any lies in his letter?"

"I don't know enough about him to know. Even if there are no outright lies, it stands to reason he hasn't told you the whole truth."

"No, he hasn't. He skates and skims over a good deal. There's nothing on his education, or the Marine Corps, or the loss of his arm. Nothing on the Paris episode, either. It's—"

"What's the Paris episode?" asked Hart.

"It's a long story."

"It's a long afternoon."

"It doesn't take long to summarize it," Dan said. "It's one of those triangles. Kemp had a good friend in college. They were fraternity brothers; they enlisted together, went to

France together. Kemp lost the arm. He met his friend's girl while he was recuperating in Paris. She was a Red Cross worker. Kemp seduced her and then came on home—back to the States, I mean. I assume she had the child. It either died or else was left behind when she came home, though she may have brought it with her. Later she married someone else. That's the word from Cissie Waterhouse."

"Who's this Cissie Waterhouse? Can you trust her?"

Dan sighed. "You never know. I guess so. A lot of it was hearsay, but it made a credible pattern."

Hart folded the letter and handed it across to Dan. "Kemp says here that even garbage can be arranged in credible patterns."

"Right. But at least Cissie's story matches the one in Kemp's first novel."

"Did she ever read the novel?"

"Sure. Long ago. She read it when it first came out."

"And then she wrote you a long time later. Couldn't fact and fiction have fused in her memory?"

Dan grinned. "It's been known to happen."

"It happens to everybody," said Hart. "From this letter I'd gather it happened to Kemp, too. It's a letter of self-justification. You had a good word for the process."

"Word?"

"You lectured me on it like a Dutch uncle. We were talking about the emperor."

"Oh, narcissism? Do you see that in the letter?"

"Some of it, anyway. When a feller wants to justify himself to someone else, especially to a professed admirer, what will he do? Obviously, he'll hide what he thinks is ugly and he'll play up what he thinks you'll like. Suppose Narcissus found

he had a wart on his face that day he looked into the pool of
water."

"He'd cover it up with his hand."

"Or not look at the place where the wart was."

"Kemp has some warts, sure. We all do, and I suppose we
all have a built-in tendency to overlook them, for our own
sakes, and to conceal them from others in order to persuade
them to take us for what we are not. It's all done with mirrors, like Narcissus's forest pool. The mind's mirrors—filled
with delusions."

"It's mind all right," Hart said. "Fancy, Imagination. Emo-
tions of attraction or repulsion. Home-made hells and
heavens, limbos, purgatories. Dante knew all about it. All that
gorgeous structure, all that machinery—they were just ways
of objectifying what he privately knew, what he had felt—
the horror and the beauty, the park-like garden and the
worms down under."

Dan watched the dustmotes in the beam of horizontal light
from the western windows. "And the reverse," he said,
slowly. "Or I guess you'd say the reverse. We get the delusion
from objective experience. I mean objective experience sub-
jectively interpreted. Once in college, I remember, we drove
down to the ocean. It was hot weather and we wanted to swim
in salt water. We went off some rocks up around Cape Ann.
The tide was coming in and the water was cold and the ocean
floor in that channel was covered with this yellowish-brown
kelp. It was very unpleasant. If you went deep enough, you
brushed against it with your arms or your legs. Even on the
surface, which was blue and beautiful, you had this feeling of
something cold and slimy down under you."

"But you still swam."

"We swam. We just stopped diving. We stayed on the surface. It was fine on the surface. Hart, it's curious, but the same thing runs all through Nicholas Kemp. I've been reading his diary—"

"That ought to be useful," Hart said.

"It is and it isn't," said Dan. "There's not much of it. But here—here's a photostat page. This is May, 1918. This is a month before they moved over to Belleau Wood. They're dug in on high ground. He doesn't say where, but I can find it."

Hart waved the page away. "Read it aloud, Dan," he said. "These old eyes are tired."

"All right," Dan said. "It's just a verbal landscape, but look what he says at the end. It's like swimming at Cape Ann, with the handsome surface and the horror down under. *May sunlight all day,* he says, *and the boys basking in it. Better now than all winter. Better than March or April when you couldn't get or stay dry. From this ridge the country looks beautiful. Rolling land, with minor ridges and flanks and spurs. Stone farmhouses, some off alone and some clustered by crossroads. At a distance you have the illusion of plowed fields. When you get down there on patrol, you see it's not from plows but from shelling. The whole place was fought over in the spring of '15. There are shell-craters with puddles and inflated, floating rats. The grass has come back in some places, but a lot of the land is too sour even to grow grass. From up above, though, there's enough roll to the land and patches of woods so that when the grass turns green and the leaves come out, you forget the rats and the craters. In some of the valleys you come on patches of white flowers, very sweet-smelling, maybe lilies of the valley. But anywhere you dig in down there, there are the bones. New bones from 1915,*

*and for all I know some others down under, century-old bones
of the poor bastards who fought for Napoleon...."*

Dan's voice trailed off. "Of course it isn't great prose," he
said. "But you see why I brought it. There's another section I
didn't bring about mustard-gas in shell-holes. It's the way
Kemp's always seen things, Hart. It runs through all his books
in a hundred ways. He can't—or won't—shake loose from it."

"Then it's his loss," said Hart. "As I guess I said before in
some other connection. The power of mind over matter can't
ever be complete if matters like this are allowed to dominate
mind. But you know that, Dan. You've known it all winter."

"Not all winter," Dan said. "Just lately. Or if I knew it, I
didn't really believe it."

"But you believe it now?"

"More and more. Until something happens."

"Like what?" said Hart, quietly.

"Oh, I don't know. Like running over that dog in the
highway. Or like somebody stabbing my landlord and leaving
him to die."

"How is he?"

"He's all right. I guess he's all right. He's recuperating at
Palm Springs. I guess you could say he bounced back."

"We all have to bounce back. Or crawl back. Something
will always happen. You can count on that."

"And when it does, you say: *See! I knew it. The devil's
loose again.*"

"Yes," said Hart. "If you're a New England Puritan that's
exactly what you say. But they were deluded, too. Their
minds were dominated by a Hebraic vision of sin. They committed great crimes in the name of their vision—against themselves and against others. Your man Kemp's a kind of Puritan,

transplanted to Idaho or wherever. Probably took it in with his mother's milk, the way you and I did. He's never cut loose from it, and that's his loss."

"Also his gain," Dan said. "He made great fiction from it."

"I'll have to take your word for that," said Hart. "If you say it's great, I won't doubt it. But not the greatest. He's got all the crucifixions, I'll bet, but not the resurrections. Is that right?"

"It's partly right," Dan said. "I almost said that in my book, in a piece I was working on last week. In the end I scratched it out. I didn't really believe it. But it's probably a fact, and if it's a fact it ought to be said. I'd better go on home and put it down, Hart, before I forget it. All the crucifixions and no resurrections."

"You know his books and I don't," said Hart. "It's just an idea."

"It's a good idea," Dan said. "It's the bridge from hell to heaven."

"Or from hell to reality," Hart said, "according to how you see it."

PART FOUR

THE GARDEN

CHAPTER TWENTY-FOUR

BEHIND the thick glasses, Henry's eyes held the merest polite hint of accusation. "It came a few days ago," he said. "I've been keeping it for you. I ought to have kept calling you, but after the first few times when I got no answer, I thought you must have left town. When the June heat starts, many people do leave."

"You say it's from Chicago?"

"I think so. It's back in my office. Could you wait a minute while I finish this?"

"You bet," Dan said. "I didn't know you worked at night."

"Usually I don't," said Henry, primly. "Students handle the desk at night. I'm pinch-hitting for one of them. He had a date. There. That's that. Now come on back to the office. Where've you been?"

"I just left a meeting and the building was lighted so I came in."

"A meeting tonight?"

"Reserve officers," Dan said. "Do you know Masters?"

"The man in the Economics department?"

"That's the man. He heads up the group. We meet once a week."

Henry snapped on the light in the office. "I suppose you were in the war," he said.

"Yes."

"I missed it," Henry said. "It's one of my great regrets."

"Don't ever regret it," Dan said. "It was a dirty mess."

Henry removed his glasses and held them under the desk lamp. "It was my eyes," he said. He began to polish the lenses with a clean handkerchief. "Now where did I put that letter? I put it somewhere for safe keeping."

He opened the right-hand drawer. Dan saw that it was nearly filled with a neat pile of papers. "Here it is," Henry said. "I hope it's not important."

"Probably not," Dan said. "It's probably just another useless answer to another of my useless queries."

He was so sure of its unimportance that he thrust it unopened into the pocket of his shirt. Undressing at home, he found the letter again and carried it into the living room. Reading it through quickly, he was astonished, and yet not astonished, at the sudden lightness of his heart.

It was from Connie Haybright. She was coming back home. Her grandmother was recovered, even to the point of putting away her crutches. You knew she was better because she had been to the hairdresser's and had rejoined the circle of old ladies in her bridge club. There was a companion now, also, a middle-aged widow who would clean and cook for the household. So Connie was free to come back to her job.

She would arrive, with luck, on the sixteenth, the morning plane. During the winter she had read all of Dan's novels. She thought they were splendid, no matter what Squirrel Burrell might have done to them. Now she would be able to do a decent interview for the Tucson paper. And after all these months there was no time to spare. Could she please come to see him on the seventeenth or the eighteenth? She would telephone. She hoped he had had a good winter. She had missed Tucson and was anxious to be home again.

Three paragraphs, he thought, and each of them as open and candid as those gray-blue eyes. He remembered the dress, yellow like sunlight, and the compact carriage, smooth-shouldered, brown-handed, unaggressively breasted, trim in hips and ankles, and crowned with the dark brown hair, crisp as leaves.

He reread the letter quickly and glanced at the calendar. In ten days she would be coming. He looked up the number and called the airport. The morning plane from Chicago generally arrived at seven. Did he wish to book passage for California? No, he said, he was meeting someone from the East.

By the time he had replaced the telephone in its rack, the resolution was fully formed. "Why not?" he said, half aloud. It's a long time. Too long now. Too long alone now. Neither of you has forgotten the other. Go and meet her.

* * * * *

At the airport ten mornings later he drank a coffee in the canteen and went outside to wait. The wind was still fresh, though warming fast as the sun climbed the sky. The flight, they had said, would be a little late. He had waited half an hour before it appeared, small as an insect above the eastern mountains. It roared closer, dimensions swiftly enlarging, wings glinting silverly in the sunlight, and he watched it circle overhead, find its angle, dip down to the runway, and waddle home across the acres of concrete.

She was a small and brisk fourth in the straggling line of

passengers. She wore a brown suit and a yellow hat and carried an overnight kit in one gloved hand. At the sound of her name she looked up quickly, and he saw with a kind of bemused delight how the expression in her eyes flashed from impersonal coolness to warm recognition.

"You came for me," she said, a simple declarative without interrogative shading. "Oh, nice. That was nice." She surrendered the small bag and began at once, in the crisply pleasant voice, to talk of the flight and the strange marvelous colors of the morning mountains. Yes, she had had breakfast on the plane. She had not slept much, though the flight had been smooth enough except for one rocky stretch somewhere over Texas. Yes, there was a suitcase. She gave him the claim check and walked beside him to where he had left his car in the almost deserted parking lot. "You don't even know where I live, do you?" she said. "It's miles away. It's way over at the other side of the city."

"You direct me," Dan said.

"Straight through the town," said Connie, happily, watching the morning desert. "Isn't it a strange town? After Chicago it looks almost heavenly."

"Axel calls it the Land of Nod," said Dan. "Westward from Eden."

"Mr. O'Keefe?" Connie said. "I hope he's not angry with me about the interview. Shall I tell you a secret?"

"Yes."

"I lost the interview notes. Yours and Hart Mackenzie's and Mr. O'Keefe's. I mean I left them. I took them on the plane to Chicago and I remember reading them over, and then I left them on the plane."

"It's probably just as well. Now we can have more interviews."

"Oh, but not now," she said, laughing the silvery laugh.

"Then at lunch. How about lunch?"

"Lunch today?"

"Today. Whenever you say. It's been a long time between interviews. Will you come?"

"Oh, yes," she said softly. "Yes I will."

"I'll get you at—when? Noon? One?"

"Could it be one?" she said. "But don't come for me. Let's meet where we met before."

"In the library?"

"Yes, in the library," she said. "Once more in the library."

* * * * *

At the other side of the city, she pointed one gloved finger towards the street which slanted northwards toward the Catalina foothills. Dan rounded the curve too quickly and she was thrown towards him across the seat. She braced one hand against his shoulder, and he swallowed the constriction in his throat, conscious of the warm presence of her body and the near odor of her perfume. After a moment she slid back and away and began to talk about her family's house. It struck him that her voice had taken on a different timbre.

The house was high up in the Calle Leone. When they had moved up there ten years ago there were only a few old ranch houses among the saguaros, but now the bulldozers and the builders had come in and many small houses were going up. Luckily, she said, they were still widely scattered. No one had yet built a house that blocked off their view of the sunsets.

"My father loves the sunsets," Connie said. "They're one of his pleasures. And at night from up here the city looks like a necklace of diamonds and rubies. Now, there. There's the house. The pink stucco with the shrubbery. And there's my mother's car in the driveway. Oh, Dan, it's good to be home."

At the door she took the bags firmly from his hands. "They'll be awake but not dressed," she said. "Goodbye until one. You were so nice to meet the plane."

"Until one," he said.

* * * * *

It was just after one when he came into the reading room and saw her at the table in a haze of golden light. She was wearing a pale summer dress. It was the first time he had seen her arms bare. They were the pleasant color of old ivory and her brown hair, drawn back across the perfect ears, shone smooth as silk in the powerful light from the windows. He opened his mouth to speak, but something in his throat held back the words. Her hands lay unmoving on either side of an open magazine and she was looking him full in the eyes.

"Oh, Dan," she said softly. "I thought you'd never come."

His voice sounded foreign in his ears. "It was Axel O'Keefe," he said. "He hailed me across the campus and I couldn't get away."

"Was he angry with me?" she asked. She was smiling and the clear eyes had not wavered from his face.

"I didn't ask him," said Dan. "My interview comes first. Are you hungry?"

"Yes," she said, still so quietly that he heard no more than the soft sibilant. She closed the magazine and pushed back the chair to stand beside him, near, compact, graceful, right-sized, smelling cleanly and faintly of a perfume he did not know.

Outside the sun was blazing from the highest part of the sky. A procession of cream-colored clouds marched out of the west and a warm breeze stirred among the massed leaves of the orange trees. In the shade behind the library Dan took her hand and drew it into the crook of his arm. Through the thin cloth of his sleeve he could feel the light returning pressure of her fingers. The street, under the chiaroscuro of the olive trees, had never looked handsomer. A white-haired woman was sweeping the sidewalk in front of one of the houses.

A few green olives had fallen onto the hood of the car. "I left the windows open," Dan said, "but it'll probably be like a furnace."

"Never mind," she said. "The breeze will cool it."

"Did you say you were hungry?"

"Is it a sign of hunger when you're dizzy?"

"Are you dizzy?"

For an answer she pressed both the slender hands just below her breasts. "In here," she said. "Like a storm."

He looked at her in the dappled shade. A shaft of sunlight was around her head and the breeze moved a wisp of hair against one of her cheeks. He had taken a step toward her before he drew back. He opened the near door. She gathered her skirt and got in. As he slid behind the wheel he saw that she was in the middle of the seat with the slim hands quiet in her lap. While he guided the car downtown through the stream of afternoon traffic she still said nothing. At one of the stoplights he felt her finger-tips, cool and momentary on the back of his hand. But when he glanced quickly toward her profile, he saw that she was looking straight ahead.

In the brown-gold light of the hotel dining room, he watched her face while she gave the simple order.

"How's Hart Mackenzie?" she asked when the waiter had gone.

"What made you think of Hart?"

"You," she said simply. "He's another of my interviews. Did you ever see him again?"

"We're old friends now," Dan said. "We argue about the meaning of sin."

"He's a wonderful old man," Connie said. "He might be you grown old."

"Did he tell you about his life?"

"Not much," she said. "He wouldn't listen when I asked him about it. He kept asking me about mine."

"What *about* yours?"

"About what, Dan?"

"About your life."

"Oh, Dan, *you* know. Where I was born and what—"

"Where were you born, Connie? I don't even know that."

He watched the perfect lips protrude and part over the single word. "Chicago."

"I have to know all about it."

"It's nothing important. I was a May-basket."

"May first?"

"May 1, 1928," she recited, "and I weighed exactly seven pounds. And the next year my father was killed in an accident."

"What kind of accident?"

"In a car. On the lake front near Evanston. He had a new Marmon car. It was the first new one he had owned and my mother said he was very proud of it. This night it was raining and freezing and a tire blew out and the car skidded and the steering wheel crushed his ribs and he died before they could even get him out of the car. I can't remember him at all but in his picture he is a nice-looking medium-sized man with a mustache. His name was George Foster Haybright."

The waiter brought the lunches. Connie stirred her iced tea. "Good," she said to Dan over the rim of the glass. "Aren't you thirsty?"

"Yes, and hungry," Dan said. "I didn't know how hungry. I'm sorry about your father."

"It was too bad for my mother," Connie said, practically. "I was still a wetting baby and at first she couldn't leave me to go back to work. Then the next year my grandmother came to live with us and my mother started teaching again."

"Out here?—"

"At first when we came out here she didn't. All she could get was tutoring and sometimes substituting. Then they found out how good she was and hired her."

"What made you come out here?"

"It was for my stepfather. He was gassed in the war. He had to be in the hospital for a long time."

He felt like one on the edge of a crumbling cliff. "Your stepfather," he said. "What's his name?"

"Joe Collier," she said. "It's sort of romantic, Dan. When they were small, my mother was Joe's best girl."

"What's your mother's name?"

"Faith. What's the matter, Dan?"

"Nothing," he said.

"But you look so pale!"

"It's nothing," he said. He drank water deliberately. "Where were they when they were small?" he asked.

"A little town in Minnesota. Fergus Falls. And then Joe got into the war. He was in the Marines and he was gassed and my mother never saw him again until one night in Chicago. He had read about my father in the papers and he came to our door with a bouquet. Dan, are you really all right?"

"Yes. Fine. When was it that he came to Chicago?"

She looked at him curiously. "You're like Hart," she said. "He came, I mean Joe came, when I was still a baby. He wanted to marry my mother but at first she wouldn't."

"But she did?" he asked foolishly.

"Eventually she did. We had the wedding in our house. I had a new dress with blue-and-gold smocking on the front and a long blue sash, and Joe gave me a bouquet of rosebuds to carry. Then we moved to Minnesota, to Fergus Falls. Joe's father had a factory there. Joe built my mother a house, but he wasn't well from the gassing and the very first winter he had to go to a veterans' hospital. And the third winter they made him come down here. He got another man, a partner, to run the factory and we moved to Tucson. We lived in a little house near the university and we stayed until I was eleven."

The waiter came back to clear the table.

"What will you have now, Connie?"

"Nothing. Thank you."

"Wouldn't you like some coffee?"

"Yes. Please."

"Two coffees," Dan told the waiter. "What happened when you were eleven?"

"We went home," Connie said. "We loaded the car and went back to Minnesota. Joe was fine all summer but the first winter he almost died again. We stayed until the day after

Christmas and then took the train back here. All the way, almost the whole time on the train, my mother had to hold him up so he could breathe. We got him to the hospital and found an apartment. Mother went to see him every day after work. That was when they decided to stay. Joe sold half the factory to the man in Fergus Falls and built our stucco house and when it was finished we moved in. The first year Joe worked inside, upstairs and downstairs, making cabinets and things like that for my mother. He's very good at it, a real carpenter. Then he had to go to bed."

"Shouldn't he have gone back to the hospital?"

"They said he could go but he wouldn't do it. He said he was sick of it. I think he thought then that he was going to die and he wanted to die in a place he had built."

"How did you live?"

"My mother taught school and Joe had the pension from the government, and then every month he got a check for his half of the factory. I wanted to work but they wouldn't let me. So we went through the war and it was all right until two years ago."

"What happened two years ago?"

"There was a fire in the factory and it burned flat. They didn't have enough insurance. It was almost a total loss. And then the checks stopped coming."

"So then you got the job with the paper?"

"Yes. I was through the university and it was what I had been wanting to do. Wasn't it lucky, Dan? It was only the second place I tried."

"The paper was lucky," Dan said. "And after that I was lucky."

The waiter brought the coffee in a glass jug. He poured it,

uncovered the sugar bowl with a flourish, and padded silently away.

"How were you lucky?" she said.

"A pretty girl came to interview me."

He watched the quick blush glow and subside. "And never wrote the interview," she said.

"I said it this morning. Now we can have more interviews."

"We are, right now, aren't we?" she said. "Are you going to make notes and write about it?"

"I'll put it into a book," Dan said. *"The Sleeping Princess of Pima County."*

"Do I look sleepy? This coffee will wake me."

"I'll call it *The Waking Princess of Pima County.*"

"Like Squirrel Burrell," she said. "Don't let him rewrite this one."

"It was one of his favorite stories."

"What?"

"Sleeping Beauty. In his version she wore a ragged sarong on a desert island and the Prince was a shipwrecked sailor. But the Squirrel won't rewrite this. He's dead. You're beautiful alive."

Even as he spoke he saw the shadow cross her face. She did not reply. Don't spoil it again, he thought. You pushed it too far too fast. But he knew that a wall had been built across the table between them.

"What is it?" he said.

He saw that her hands were clenched on the tablecloth. For what seemed a long time she did not answer. "In Chicago," she said at last, "in the winter I met a boy named Mangan. Jerry Mangan. Do you remember him?"

"Yes," Dan said. "At Enfield. We were graduate students at the same time. What's he doing in Chicago?"

"He's an instructor at the university. I went to a party and met him. We talked about you."

"How was he?"

"He was a little drunk," she said. "He told me all about your wife."

"So. What did he say?"

"He said it all. I mean the drowning, and how he knew you and how—" She stopped. She still had not lifted her eyes.

"How what?" said Dan, gently.

She unclenched the slender fists and laid both hands flat on the tablecloth. "—how you were drinking one night and how depressed you were and how—he said you thought—"

"What did I think?"

She spoke in a rush. "He said you thought you were—damned."

"I don't think I said so. We were talking about damnation. I may have said I believed in it. I meant on earth, not afterwards. And anyway, I wasn't talking about myself."

"No," said Connie. "Mangan said you meant on earth. And he didn't say you were talking about yourself. But I think he thought you were."

"If I was," Dan said, "I was drunker than I remember being. It was drunken self-pity."

"Mangan didn't say that or think it. But anyway you had a right to it. He said your room-mate in college committed suicide, too."

"Not my room-mate," Dan said. "There was a boy who hanged himself."

"Mangan said you hated the world."

"I only hated what can happen to people in it. I still do."

"Like what happened to your wife."

"Yes. And some other things. No worse than what happens to a lot of people. But things can change. Out here they have changed."

"How changed?"

"People mostly. A system of guardianship. Through many people who didn't know what they are guarding, people who didn't know what they were changing, or how. Like my brother-in-law, my ex-brother-in-law. He was the one who wanted me to come to Tucson."

"Good," said Connie.

"And Axel O'Keefe and Hart Mackenzie. Even Mandeville Lee."

"How did they change things?"

"Do you remember talking to Mandeville Lee?"

"Yes. Long ago. Out at that school he was starting."

"I was there in his car," Dan said. "That was the first time I saw you. And then I talked to O'Keefe about those stupid novels of mine, and O'Keefe suggested you add my name to your interview list."

"Good," she said again. "And Hart Mackenzie."

"You told me about him and I went to see him."

"And now you're friends," said Connie happily. "And you've stopped hating the world. When did you stop?"

Dan grinned at her. "Don't try to trap me. I didn't say I hated it. But if I did, the change came gradually. Not over-night, but over the winter; and not by any miracle. Just by people, including you."

"How by me?" said Connie. "Oh, how by me?"

"It's one of the things you can't explain," Dan said. "What makes a plant grow?"

For a moment she sat silent. "Guardians," she said. "Gardeners."

"But if it hasn't any guardians?"

Again she hesitated. When she spoke once more, her voice was so soft that he could scarcely hear the words. "Something inside it," she said. "And something outside it."

"Yes, and something from the outside working inside. Like sunlight."

The blue eyes were wide and shadowless.

"Yes," she said. "Oh, yes. Yes. It is. That's what it is."

"Is what?"

"Like light," she said. "Like a storm of light."

CHAPTER TWENTY-FIVE

So, HE THOUGHT, the question you have played with all winter is now suddenly resolved and settled: you do not include Kemp's biography in your book for the simple reason that its publication would hurt too many people. Tell what you know, or think you know, about Kemp's wartime betrayal of Faith in Paris, and you automatically become a betrayer of another kind. By one move you hurt Faith, hit Joe Collier the lowest of blows, kick over the confidences of Nicholas Kemp, and cruelly reveal to Connie Haybright what she never needs to know. It is clear enough, given the sort of girl she is, that Connie could recover from the effects of the revelation. People everywhere are daily recovering from shocks far worse than this would be. But if she ever learns of it, he thought, it is not going to be from anything I say or write.

The rest of the biography of Kemp could conceivably be published. Only the autobiographical origins of *The Hinges of Hell* remained as forbidden ground. In an enterprise replete with small ironies, the final one was perhaps that you could now say nothing about the Paris episode, which was the very sequence you knew most about. You could skirt the peripheries, of course, omitting or disguising names, hinting at the actual circumstances. But such a move would only serve to set others on the trail. In the end they would get through to Cissie Waterhouse or to some other informant. They would develop their clues, make their guesses, print their accounts of the seduction, and then crowingly assert from the dunghill of their labors that we must know the truth, for the truth is what makes us free. But does it? There is a truth which binds men of honor to secrecy. All right, he thought. I'll be bound.

He turned to the table where the pair of cartons lay, gathering dust. In the Ivory Soap carton were the white sheets of the critical part of the book. The Campbell's Soup carton held the yellow pages, nearly two hundred now, on which he had typed and scrawled a rough draft of Kemp's biography. The critical part was done, finished, ready to be sent off to New York and the presumably eager publisher. As for the yellow pages, let them go. Make it a clean sweep. Tear them up and burn them. They were nothing but high-level gossip anyway.

But something in him recoiled at the notion of destruction. Like other bookburnings, it would be an evil and wasteful act, no matter how worthy the motive behind it. There were other methods—like sequestration. Seal them in an envelope, mark it NOT TO BE OPENED UNTIL CHRISTMAS, A.D. 2000. That would put them out of circulation a full fifty years. By then, perhaps, Nicholas Kemp and all his works would be forgotten. If the novels survived, the contents of the envelope could well be a bonanza for some graduate student in the opening year of the new century. By this he could make his reputation, earn his promotion, begin his ascent to the lordly pinnacle of a deanship. And if memorials were what you worked for, it would be as good a memorial as any: a sentence, say, in the introduction. *I owe the preservation of these materials to Dan Sherwood, man of honor.* As good a memorial as any, he thought, and a hell of a lot better than most. He turned his back on the dusty cartons and the winter of his labors to stare moodily through the bright hot oblong of the open door across the sunburnt grass towards the unpaved street beyond.

The strident jangle of the telephone made him jump. It was a woman's voice, nervous and high-keyed.

"This is Faith Collier," she said. "I don't know how to begin. It isn't my line or anything I wanted. I'm calling you about your book."

"Yes," Dan said. "It's about finished."

"Nicholas Kemp is worried about it," Faith said, still in the half-choked voice.

"He needn't worry now," Dan said.

"He thinks you are planning to talk about us in the book. He said I must not see you or speak with you about anything. What he doesn't know is that you've been seeing my daughter."

"Yes. I took her to lunch."

"And had a little talk."

"Yes, we—"

"What did you talk about?"

"Her life. Where she was born. Her father. Joe Collier. You."

"So Nicholas Kemp was not far off in his fears. You didn't need to talk to me. All you really needed was to pump my daughter, and that's done."

"It wasn't pumping at all."

"You seem to have got what you were after."

"Not by—any subterfuge."

"If you keep on with what you are doing, it can only hurt us all."

"I don't intend to hurt anyone—least of all Connie."

"Then it should be easy," Faith said. "Just stop seeing her now. This is the time to stop it—before anyone gets hurt."

"I'm supposed to see her again tomorrow."

"I know. Please don't."

"If it's assurances you want—"

"I don't want your assurances," Faith said. "I think you've been unfair and—surreptitious. Will you call it off or shall I?"

"I'm afraid you're jumping to conclusions."

"I've already jumped," she said. "This is my conclusion, my decision. Connie's out of the house now. When she comes home I'm going to tell her that you called and cancelled the date."

He was on the point of protesting when the metallic monotone told him that Faith had rung off. He put down the instrument, and stood staring out of the window into the garish afternoon. So now they were fighting back. "Keep off," said the sign on Kemp's island fastness. "Stay away," said Faith Collier. It was no more than you might have expected, having selected the role of intruder, the mask of interloper. What you hadn't expected was this sudden disbarment. He thought suddenly of Sandy Stone, long ago in the Wall Street office, displaying the copy of Kemp's diary, setting in motion the train of circumstances which now had reached this curious station. If Sandy had planned it all, it could hardly have worked out more smoothly. Correction, he thought. Roughly.

And where does the fault lie? Not with Sandy, certainly, whose motives could hardly have been more magnanimous. Not even with Kemp, who has a right to his secrets. Not with

Faith, who did what she had to do. How can you blame her for not wanting the old ashes raked up, the new fuel heaped upon a fire which can only burn her husband, Joe Collier, and her daughter, Connie Haybright? Not even with you, the inadvertent intruder, whose part in it began with the decision to write a much-needed book about the novels of Nicholas Kemp.

What matters now? Two matters, he thought. First, to do with the book as you have already decided: sequester the yellow pages, and ship out the white ones. Second, Connie Haybright matters. The old lovers, with what strikes them as good reason, have chosen to attack. For the young lovers—one of them anyhow—there is no choice but counterattack. Again, the method is clear and certain. Kemp has frightened Faith. Now he must be made to reassure her. The countermove must focus on Kemp himself.

In the next half hour Dan devised a day letter to Nicholas Kemp. When he unrolled the final version from the typewriter and took it across to the telephone, he paused only momentarily. It was no masterpiece. There was much more to be said than these forty-odd words could possibly suggest. But now—for now—it would have to do.

ABANDONING ALL BIOGRAPHY WHATSOEVER AND CONCENTRATING SOLELY ON NOVELS FAITH UNDERSTANDABLY UPSET ON TELEPHONE TODAY URGENTLY REQUEST YOU ADVISE HER BY RETURN WIRE THAT I AM NOT USING HER DAUGHTER AS PROBE INTO PAST OF ANYONE CONCERNED CRITICAL BOOK FINISHED AM SENDING IT TO NEW YORK TOMORROW REGARDS

D. J. SHERWOOD

When he had telephoned it in, listening critically while the girl read it back, he locked the front door and went over to one of the stores on the Speedway to buy string and wrapping-paper. Back in the house, he cleared the dusty work-table and began to separate the original pages from the carbon copies. He was halfway done when the telephone jangled harshly once more.

Loud music, heavy with drumbeats, poured from the receiver. From somewhere in its midst he could barely hear a voice calling his name. "Yes," he said. "This is Sherwood. Who's calling?"

"One guess," said the voice loudly. "And who the hell does it sound like?"

Even through the wail-and-rattle he caught the familiar tone. "Lee," he said. "Where are you? How're you feeling?"

"Home on the range," Lee shouted. "Back in business, boy."

"How was Palm Springs?"

Someone turned the music lower and the hillbilly wail sank into the background.

"I didn't get that last question, professor," said Lee.

"I said how was Palm Springs?"

"A rat dance," said Lee, complacently. "A real old desert rat dance. But it did the trick."

"How's the old gut?"

"It don't leak, Danny. It holds liquid. Come on over and hoist a few."

"Aren't you afraid of rotting the stitches?"

"Best thing for 'em," Lee said. "No better disinfectant

known. Listen, Dan, little girl over here dying to meet you. How about dropping over?"

"Girl. What girl?"

"Little girl from the hospital. Old Daddy Lee's favorite nurse. A real little witch with alcohol rubs. Says she's dying to meet a real writer. I told her about your westerns. She's already finished a couple. She says she never did meet a writer and she's downright curious."

"Um. When did you get back?"

"Four or five days. Six I guess. I ain't keeping count, Dan. You know this Noto?"

"What about Noto?"

"Good man is all. Noto's been handling my case."

"I know."

"No, I mean he's the gumshoe on this, Dan. We take long rides and to hell with speed limits. Nogales and back twice lately."

"What's in Nogales?"

"Where you been, Danny? Mexicans in Nogales."

"No, I mean why did you go to Nogales?"

"Once to get Chita."

"So you found her?"

"Sure. Chita's back. Chita's beat but she's back. All she's going to need is some bridgework."

"What do you mean, bridgework?"

"Hermie roughed her up some. You don't know Hermie, but Hermie's the husband. Some operator. Chita just naturally dropped out of Hermie's life, and old Hermie wasn't having it. You know what I mean. Hermie's the jealous type."

"Is he the one that cut you?"

"That's the story, Dan. Cut me, conked Chita, dragged her on home. Real old-style operator, even to the black mustache. Hermie thinks the woman's place is the hacienda. Had Chita shacked up down there on bread and water. Noto pried her loose."

"Down where do you mean?"

"Just down inside Sonora. You been there, Dan? Some shack Hermie maintains. I don't wonder she lit out. Anyway, that's been the problem. Those spics down there are not getting excited about alleged crimes. They figure he's well inside his rights. They figure he's one of the tribe."

"Offended husband rightly offended?"

"So they figure. Little extradition problem. I'm about ready to drop the charges."

"How is Chita?"

"She don't grin so good now, Dan. He puffed up her face for her, knocked out a couple of teeth."

"That's too bad."

"Oh, she's okay. She's happy as a clam. Old Daddy Lee buys the spare parts. Dentist says he can easy fill up the gaps. Say, Dan, where you keep yourself? I call you from the hospital. No answer. I call you from Palm Springs. No answer."

"I've been in and out. Did you get the books?"

"Sure I got the books. While Birdie was off duty I read 'em all. Great stuff, Danny. Birdie thinks so, too. You're quite a writer."

"Well, I'm glad you liked them. Flowers didn't seem like the thing to send."

"Sure, Dan. It was nobody's funeral."

"Almost but not quite."

"Don't scare me, kid. I figure I got seven more lives left.

Come on over and meet Birdie. I'll get her to fix you a drink."

"I might have a phone call. I mean I have to wait for a possible call. How long will you be there?"

"Quién sabe? One hour. Two. As long as it takes. If you get that call pretty soon, trot on over."

"If I can, I will," Dan said. "I'm glad you're better."

"Raring to go," Lee said. "So long, kiddo."

The sunset glowed blood-colored through the western windows. As always at nightfall, after the furnace of the day, the breeze from the mountains was beginning to stir through the house. Dan finished sorting the typescript and sat down to read the book through once more.

The words were familiar—too familiar. He found that he could not concentrate. With luck, now, in the hours just past or in those that lay immediately ahead, Kemp would be reading the afternoon's day letter, or listening to those fifty well-chosen words while the far-off operator phoned them in to his island domain. If he believed them, if he decided to act as urgently requested, he might even already have dictated a reply, reassuring Faith, opening once again the door he had closed.

Suppose he has done it, or will do it, Dan thought. That is only half the battle. The other half is Faith's hypothetical response. What, after all, can Kemp say—in ten or fifty or even a thousand words—that will allay her suspicions, change her mind, soften the note of asperity in her voice, make her turn back to the telephone to say the words, bridge the abyss, raze the wall, reopen the closed door?

He sat down in the chair beside the silent telephone and returned to the final reading of his book. By eleven o'clock he finished the last page and dropped it face down on the pile of typescript beside his chair. Whatever its faults, and there were still some minor ones, it would have to do. Like that day letter to Kemp, he thought, and why the hell is he taking such a long time about it?

It was cool in the room and his joints were stiff from the hours in the chair. He rose yawning, found string and paper, piled the typescript into its box, and wrapped, tied, and addressed the package. Now it was ready. Except for the trip to the post office in the morning, he had done precisely what he had promised to do. The next move—or moves—would have to be theirs. A telegram, a letter, a phone call could settle the matter. And the sooner the better. They would not call him now, close on midnight. Tomorrow, then. Let it come tomorrow. Let it come bright and early tomorrow, and the earlier the brighter. But let it come.

In fact it was not until three afternoons later that he discovered what their next move was going to be.

CHAPTER TWENTY-SIX

IN THE waning sunlight, the woman on the doorstep stood poised and resolute, her brown eyes level and steady. She had already caught both the surprise and the recognition in his face. In her own, he seemed to see fleetingly a glint of what might have been humor, the suggestion of a smile suppressed before it burst, as if she knew and was faintly amused by the fact that the shape of her face, the curves and hollows of cheek and chin, had told him what she did not need to say.

"Yes," said Faith Collier. "He changed his mind. Are you going to let me come in?"

Dan stepped back, pushing the door wide, watching her as she advanced to stand in the middle of the faded brown rug, her eyes now swiftly appraising the room, the table, the hooded typewriter, the manuscript piled in the two cartons, the library copies of Kemp's novels ranged on the dusty shelves beyond. Holding the white purse in both brown hands she turned toward him, nodding sidelong, as her daughter might have done, in the direction of the cartons on the table.

"That's it," he said, swallowing once to wet his throat.

"It looks like a lot." Her voice was low-pitched, calm, natural, perhaps even friendly. All its former sharpness and suspicion had dropped away, and he wondered whether, in forming her resolution to come here in person, to confront him now, she had likewise resolved to soften and subdue the former asperity. She gave the impression of will, not impulse: the suggestion of power held in check by determination. Given what he already knew of her, Faith could not possibly be as simple as she outwardly looked now, in the low-heeled shoes, the white summer handbag, and the neatly unobtrusive dark dress.

The heavy braid of hair that framed her face was shot becomingly with gray, and the faintly Indian look of the cheekbones hinted at what could in no way be true, that some strain of the primitive lay hidden beneath this calm exterior. He thought her very handsome, though she had long since lost, if indeed she had ever had, the April-like beauty of her daughter, with the quick, mobile alternations of shyness and directness which held you lightly, as wire is held against the prongs of a magnet.

Although she was standing beside the table where the cartons lay, she made no move to look at their contents. He came to her side.

"Those white sheets are the carbon copy of the book I sent to New York. The editor sounds enthusiastic. He wired acceptance yesterday. The yellow sheets are a very rough first draft. They're what I know about Kemp himself."

Faith nodded once more, with the characteristic quick bob of her head, towards the ashtray heaped with dead cigarette butts. "I should think," she said practically, "that you'd be afraid of fire."

"It crossed my mind," Dan said. "Last fall I lost a book. By theft, though, not fire."

"Yes," said Faith. "That's when I first knew you had come to Tucson. Why didn't you complete the yellow part?"

"I've been waiting—had been waiting, I mean."

"Waiting for what?"

"To get it all straight. There were too many gaps in what I knew. I was waiting for the truth."

"You would have waited a long time," she said. The tone of the words held neither rancor nor ridicule. They lay flat, a simple declarative, without spine or thorn.

He answered in the same tone. "You mean for ever?"

"For ever is a long time," she said slowly. "If it's truth you wanted, that's how long it might have taken. If it's facts, —of course there are facts—dates, days, arrivals, departures. But truth—" She did not finish, and once more he caught, or seemed to catch, the nascent glint of humor in her eyes.

"I've known from the first it was facts I'd have to settle for."

Easily, without self-consciousness, she turned to one of the chairs and sat down. "I can't tell you the truth," she said. "But I'll tell you any facts you want to know."

"Why did you change your mind?"

"I didn't change it. It was changed for me."

Dan looked at her sharply. "You're quoting Kemp."

She seemed genuinely puzzled. A vertical line had appeared between her eyebrows. "Whatever do you mean?"

"You said you didn't change your mind, it was changed for you. It's what Angie says in *The Hinges of Hell*."

She smiled outrightly. "It's just something he remembered. It's a phrase I've often thought and said. He knew it and remembered it and made her say it."

"But just now, when you said it, you were thinking of something else. Who did change your mind for you?"

"Isn't it enough that it was changed?"

"If you say so."

She opened and closed the zipper on her handbag. "Forgive me," she said, after a moment. "I didn't mean to sound that way. Two people changed my mind for me. One was Nickie, who says he loves me still. The other was my daughter, who says she loves you."

He felt his heart leap and sink. "I thought Connie didn't know."

"She doesn't," Faith said. "That's one reason I'm here now."

"I wasn't planning to tell her."

"If you put it into the book, she would read it and know."

"I thought of not using names, disguising it that way."

"You couldn't disguise it. She would know."

"Yes, that's why I decided not to put it into the book."

"Nickie thought so. He says you are an honorable man."

"I'm glad he thinks so. When did he say that?"

"Today, on the phone. He said if I came and talked to you and told you the story, then you'd—"

"Not use it?" he finished. "Didn't he think it was taking a chance?"

"No, he thought it was the safest thing to do."

"And you agreed?"

"I don't know whether to agree or not. I agreed to come."

"To see if I looked honorable?"

She smiled on him. "I told him if I thought so I would tell you the story. Reluctantly."

"Never mind," he said. "It isn't necessary. I can do without it."

"Can you?" she said softly. "And to be wondering ever after? Wouldn't it be better to get it settled?"

"It's settled as far as I'm concerned," he said. "I'll keep the secret."

The note of asperity flashed and subsided. "How can you possibly keep what you don't even know?"

"I mean the fact that the book's a true story."

"Facts?" she said. "True? But it isn't either of those. It's only Nickie's dream of how it was. It's his illusion."

"The girl Angie isn't you?"

"Do you remember Valloa in the sea-book?"

"The Indian girl, yes."

"Do you think she was a fact?"

"The critics called her a dream-girl."

"Angie is, too. He used some facts. He remembered some things I said and put them into the book—into Angie's conversation. But Angie's not me. She's only what he wanted me to be, wishes I had been. Now go ahead. What do you want to know?"

"But it's a fact that Kemp—seduced you."

"No," she said. She had lowered her head and he saw her brow darken.

"You had his baby."

"Yes."

"And he left you alone and pregnant and came back to New York and —"

Her head came up. "No," she said. "Those are not the facts."

"But he left you?"

"He sailed home, yes. He took a job in New York to earn some money. He wanted to get married before he left Paris, but I refused. I told him we'd get married in New York."

"What changed your mind?"

"It didn't change. I never meant to marry him. I didn't love him."

"But he loved you."

She smiled with a look of distance. "It's one of his illusions," she said. "He's got them by the dozens—the hundreds. They run all through his novels."

"Illusions!"

"Is that so incredible?"

Dan laughed at her tone. "Excuse me. I'm having trouble changing my mind."

"No wonder," said Faith steadily. "You're a man. You were taking Nickie's point of view."

"You mean sharing his illusions?"

"Why not? You had no other point of view to—to correct them by."

"That's true. I thought I had got hold of the truth."

"That's one of the common illusions. That's why I came here."

"To tell me the truth?"

"I didn't say that. Only to give you another point of view."

"What I knew—thought I knew—put Kemp in a bad light."

"I guess he's used to that by now."

"I meant long ago."

"Long ago he was a boy. He was a boy in the war. He was very badly hurt—wounded."

"And you were charitable."

"That's still Kemp's point of view. In fact I pitied him. But there was someone else I pitied more, much more."

"Joe?"

Smiling, she made a gesture of negation. "Not Joe," she said. "He never wanted or needed pity. I was foolish enough to resent it. No. I was the one."

Baffled, he shook his head. "I don't see—"

"Don't you see the plain young girl in the small town, the minister's daughter, the teacher in the high school? She is engaged to her childhood sweetheart. She looks around at the others. She knows exactly the direction her life will take, the grooves like the ruts in a prairie farm road."

"Yes."

"And the war. The feeling of it coming on, even out there. When we still thought wars were noble. When the new world would rescue the old. And the bands playing John Philip Sousa and the boys going over there and the general who looks exactly like a general saying *Lafayette, nous voici....*"

"I used to read about it."

"And all the prairie mice baking cakes and knitting socks and sweaters and rolling bandages in the church basement. When what you really wanted was to go, get out and away, to leave the cakes and the socks and the swaddling bandages, to get free."

"Free from what?"

"Free of the rut, the groove, the life you could see stretching ahead like a gray road—like year after year after year of teaching the same thing in the same school through the same kind of muddy springs and children-smells and wet-wool-smelling winters. They even had a song about it, written by a man. 'Keep the home-fires burning while our hearts are yearning.' All my yearning was in the other direction."

"France?"

"To France. I had the language, even a fine Parisian accent. My old professor drilled us and drilled us. I thought I knew the people. For years I had worshipped Paris. When I got there, after a week, after two days, a day, I would have died to defend it because in Paris was a kind of freedom I had never dreamed was possible."

"Even with the Germans at the door?"

"Especially with the Germans at the door. And with your own true love, who never wanted or needed pity, outside there holding them back. Do you see?"

"Not exactly."

"No. No one can. You have to see all the walking wounded in the streets and the bars. The wounded you pitied until you realized that in pitying them you were really pitying yourself because you knew, every hour of every day, that any one of them might be, might have been, your own true love."

"There I lose you."

"Because you're not a woman."

"Maybe so. But I would think of that as an illusion."

"I don't deny it. Women have them, too. When Nickie came into the Luxembourg that day in the fall with his arm gone and his sleeve pinned up, I wouldn't then have admitted or even thought it. But the fact was that I pitied myself far more than I pitied him."

"In the fall? 1918?"

"Yes, in November."

"Where was Joe Collier?"

"Here. I mean home. The United States. He almost died coming home and they said he couldn't live. I was ready to go where he was, full of self-pity that the war had wrecked our plans. But by the time I found out that he was going to live and where he was, it was too late. I couldn't go. I was going to have the baby."

"Did you?"

"Did I what?"

"Have the baby?"

Her black brows lifted. "Of course. In the summer I went to Aix and worked in the vineyards. I bought a wedding-ring and told them I was Madame Whitaker."

"Them? Who were they?"

"The Thibodeaus. They had a *bistro,* and outside the city they had a little farm. They were very practical. They understood that my poor husband, Monsieur Weetacaire, had died of influenza. They loved the baby; they made me hurry to get it christened. And when my father really did die of influenza and I had to go back to Minnesota, Madame insisted it was too young to be taken, that she would keep the baby. I gave them the money Nickie sent and took the diary and went back to Minnesota."

"The diary?"

"Nickie's diary. The reason we own our house. The reason you are here in Tucson. The reason I saw Nickie when it was sold."

"I've lost you again."

"I don't wonder. Am I going too fast? What do you want to know?"

"How do you know it was the diary made me come here?"

"Mr. Baxter said so. He warned me about you—after I knew you had come to town. He wanted me to know he had kept his word."

"His word not to say who had sold him the diary?"

"Yes. Do you know a man named Stone?"

"Yes, very well. It was Stone who bought the diary from

Baxter. Stone wanted me to do a book on Kemp. All he knew from Baxter was that the diary had been sold in Tucson. After the—accident, when I was in the hospital in Florence, he called me up. He said I must come to Tucson. He advised me to look up Nagle. What did you mean about owning your house?"

"Just that I paid off the mortgage with some of the money from the diary. We were all right at first. Then there was a fire, the fire—"

"The factory burned."

"Yes. How did you know?"

"Connie told me. She didn't mention the diary."

"She didn't—doesn't—know about it. Neither does Joe."

"How did you keep it from Joe?"

"At the bank. I kept the diary in the bank. It had Nicole's name in it like a family Bible. It had the date of her birth and her baptism certificate pasted in. And a lock of her hair in an envelope."

"Nicole? The baby?"

"Yes. And some writing of Nickie's in the back, too, very sentimental and addressed to me."

"I meant how did you explain the money to Joe?"

"I lied," Faith said simply. "I lied when I left Fergus Falls, I lied to the Red Cross, I lied to Nickie in France, I lied to the Thibodeaus, I lied to my mother, I lied to George Haybright and Connie, and I lied to Joe."

"I mean how did you lie about the money?"

"I told him it was left me by my uncle in Chicago. When the check from Baxter came I endorsed it and sent it to the bank in Fergus Falls. I knew the cashier. I knew him as a little boy. Syvertsen. I taught him French in high school. I told him my uncle had left it. I asked him to acknowledge

it by letter. I even told him what to say. He was so pleased
to have the money in his bank that he did exactly as I said.
Joe believed it. He grinned and pinched my behind and said
I was Mrs. Ford."

"Mrs. Ford?"

"It's a joke, a Marine joke. They had an old car in France,
a tin lizzie. They used it to haul ammunition. They called
it Elizabeth Ford. Elizabeth Ford got them out of a tight
spot."

"I remember. I read about the car. It's in Catlin's book."

"Joe has the book. His name is in it, and Catlin signed it
for him."

"Did you tell Kemp what you had done?"

"That was the tightest spot. I told him before I did it. After
the factory burned, I wrote him at his publisher's. It was his
diary, his property. I owed him the right—"

"To refuse?"

"Yes, but he didn't refuse. He was all business. He wrote
Mr. Baxter. He made an affidavit that it was—authentic. He
set the price, made all the arrangements. He seemed to be
relieved. He *looked* relieved."

"You saw him?"

"Secretly. He loves secrecy. He pretended to be on a hunt-
ing-trip. There was really a mountain-lion. It had been attack-
ing cattle up in the hills. Someone recognized him and a
reporter from Tucson heard about it and drove up there.
Nickie was furious. He would have liked to kill the poor reporter. It almost spoiled his plans."

"What did he do?"

"He got rid of the reporter. He wouldn't come to the city.
He bribed a driver and sent a car for me."

"Where did you meet?"

"In the back room of a roadhouse. It was at night. We borrowed a razor-blade from the man who ran the roadhouse and cut out the pages about Nicole. Then we wrapped it, wrapped the diary in brown paper, and Nickie paid the man, the driver, to take it to Mr. Nagle's house."

"Why Nagle?"

"That was Mr. Baxter's idea. He knew Nagle. Nagle's a collector."

"So Baxter picked it up there?"

"Yes. He flew in and flew out the next day. I never saw him. The check came to me at the school."

"How—"

"How much was it? You needn't have stopped. It was twenty thousand dollars."

"What happened to the pages you cut out?"

"Nickie took them. He wanted them. Nicole was the only child he ever had. So I gave him the pages and the lock of hair and the certificate of baptism and lied to him one last time."

"Lied?"

"I told him Nicole was dead."

"And she isn't?"

"She may be now. She wasn't in 1945. In 1945 she was in Nice and they had shaved her head because she had lived with a German officer. At the end of the war, this war, I wrote to the Thibodeaus. Both of them were dead, but their daughter was there on the farm. Nicole had taken the name of Thibodeau. Marie, the real Thibodeau daughter, was very bitter about what the Germans had done to Nicole. She sent me the clipping. Would you like to see it? I brought it."

She began to unzip the white handbag.

"No," said Dan. "No."

"You don't sound very happy," Faith said. "Does this spoil things for you?"

"No."

"It limits your freedom. It tangles you in all my lies."

"No," he said, firmly. "It's better to know the truth."

"Truth," she said. "I never—"

"All right, then, facts. Like the facts about Nicole. What the boys wouldn't give to know Kemp's child—"

"You promised," she blurted. Tears were running down her cheeks.

"Please," he said, touched. "I didn't mean it that way."

"I know you didn't," Faith said. "It's not your fault anyway. All your work gone."

"Not all," he said. "I still have the white book. It's what I really wanted to say. I backed into the biography. Now I back away."

"And Nickie was right."

"About what?"

"About your being an honorable man."

"Maybe that's another of his illusions."

"No," she said. "It's tr—It's a fact. And all winter I thought of you as Nemesis."

"That was no illusion. All winter I was trying to track you down."

"I knew it. That's why I leaped at the chance to send Connie to Chicago. She came home from that library interview half in love with you already. What I didn't know was what would happen when you found me—found us. Now I know and all I can do is thank you."

"Thank me? For what?"

"For—setting me free."

"Free? I don't—"

"Yes, free. Don't you see I've told it out, told it all out? After thirty years I found someone to tell it to."

"Couldn't you have told Kemp?"

"Not what I've told you. He—it was clear that he would have to go on keeping his illusions. After all I stole from him, it's the one thing I really gave him."

"Stole?" Dan cried. "What did you steal?"

She spread her hands over the white purse in her lap. "Too much," she said. "His best friend, Joe Collier. His only daughter, Nicole. Possession of the—a woman he loved. Maybe even peace."

"And what did you give him back?"

"It was little enough," Faith said. "But call it the illusions he lives by. His dreams of the heaven on earth that he thinks he missed when I refused to marry him. And his vision of the hell on earth where he thinks he is. They're the two subjects he's always written about. They're the real, whatever you call it—the theme of all his novels."

Dan could feel her direct eyes upon him. It was a fact. Also, she had contrived to speak the truth.

"He should be grateful to you," he said, slowly. "Those are the illusions that made him a great writer instead of a small one."

"I'm sure he's grateful," said Faith, smiling. "Only he' grateful for the wrong reasons."

"They ought to be good enough for any man," Dan said.

"Facts are better," said Faith.

CHAPTER TWENTY-SEVEN

THE ROOM where Joe Collier lay, propped with pillows in the large bed, was full of cool air from the conditioner in the window. Outside, the July sun blanketed the dry land in heavy light. Coming into the shadowy green of this room was like entering an oasis at nightfall. Flowering plants lined the windowsills. In one of the farther corners stood an open cage where two parakeets sidled companionably, ignoring a third which sat preening its feathers on the cage roof above their heads. A fourth roosted sleepily on the back of a wheelchair. When Dan and Faith appeared, a small black dog leaped down from his station on the foot of the bed and came to sniff and prance at Dan's ankles. He leaned in passing to scratch its velvet ears.

"Down, Fergus," Faith said. "Joe, here's Dan Sherwood."

The tall man in the bed lifted one thin arm in greeting. His long face, tobacco-colored under its frame of closely-cut white hair, looked as worn as an eroded boulder. The light blanket showed that his legs and torso were almost incredibly emaciated.

"Down, Fergus," said Joe hoarsely. He held out his hand and Dan shook it. His eyes were the shade of corn-flowers. Looking into them, Dan saw that they were curiously, almost fiercely, opaque. It must be from the pain, he thought. He won't let you see into it. It's the way he's developed of hiding the pain.

The dog was still leaping excitedly against Dan's legs. "Down, Fergus," said Joe, again. "Push him down, Dan. He's too damned affectionate. I can see you're accepted, though. If old Fergus likes you, you're practically a member of the family."

"He'd better like me," Dan said, smiling. "It took me twenty years to get here."

Joe did not understand. "Twenty years is a long time," he said politely.

"He means he read about you in Catlin's book," said Faith quickly from across the bed. "He's been writing about the Marines in Belleau Wood."

"Oh, Catlin," Joe said. "Good old Catlin. The ramrod. He made us sound like a bunch of damn heroes."

"I don't wonder," said Dan. "I was over there looking around four or five years ago. I saw the woods and the monument and the cemetery. It looked like a rough situation. A downhill attack without cover."

"No damned cover at all," said Joe in the hoarse voice. "Some of the boys did a pretty fair job. Most of us were scared p—scared to death. But after a while we cleaned them out of the woods."

Dan cleared his throat. "Somebody said you brought Kemp back after he was hit."

Joe's legs stirred under the blanket. "Something like that. I walked him back. He could still walk." The hoarse voice trailed off to silence. "It was a long time ago," Joe said. "Faith, what happened to that book?"

"Over here," Faith said. As she crossed to one of the book-cases, the parakeet on the wheelchair flew around her in a wide arc and alighted on the telephone beside the bed. Joe held out one long finger and the bird immediately perched on it.

"This one is Sammy," Joe said. "Sammy has an idea he owns me. The one on the cage there is Myrtle. If she starts to come over, Sammy always drives her back."

He took the book from Faith and opened it to the fly-leaf. Dan read Catlin's angular inscription.

"He signed his book for some of the boys," Joe said. "He's dead now. Most of them have died." The opaque eyes flashed darkly, once, in Dan's face before they dropped back as suddenly to the pages of the book.

"How did you like it?" said Dan. "I was in high school when my uncle gave me a copy. I've still got it back home."

"Pretty good for a soldier," Joe said. "He's good on the battle, the general strategy. Some of it's corny, but what the hell. How's your own book coming?"

"It's done," said Dan. "They've got it in New York. I wish I'd known you were here, but I couldn't find you. There's no Collier in the phone-book."

"What they call an unlisted number," said Joe. "Didn't anybody tell you? Faith got it to cut down on useless calls. What made you do Kemp, Dan?"

"It's a long story," Dan said uncomfortably. Faith's eyes were on him from across the bed, but he did not look in her direction.

"I meant did you ever see him?"

"Never met him," said Dan. "In a way I didn't want to. My

book's not about Kemp. Only the novels and stories—the way
he used the Bible."

"Is that so?" said Joe. "I'll have to read your book. Maybe
I'll get around to reading Kemp. One time, years ago, I
picked up the short stories—what did he call them?"

"Pieces of Eight."

"Yes. I read three or four. I thought they were good but
goddam gloomy. When I knew him I never thought he was
gloomy. I'd have called him reserved but not gloomy. He
could be snotty with people he didn't like. Maybe the gloom
started with the arm. You know he lost the arm?"

"Yes," said Dan. He could feel the cold sweat-drops inside
his shirt. He glanced over at Faith. She was sitting impassively in one of the armchairs. "Some people say his first
wife got him started."

"I've heard that, too," said Joe. "I also read somewhere he
got to be a lush."

"It's one of the rumors," said Dan. "I doubt if a lush could
write that well."

"They'll say any damn thing to make a good story," Joe
said. "When I knew him he wouldn't even touch wine. We
never had him tagged as a writer, Dan. But then, you can't
tell. I wouldn't take you for a writer. Connie says you're good.
Hey, Faith, where is that girl?"

"She's still upstairs," Faith said. "She had to make the
sandwiches first. Dan, did you remember to buy a swimming
suit?"

"I got a pair of trunks. I'm wearing them now."

"It's a good day for a swim," Joe said. "Where do you
swim?"

"Connie's keeping it a secret," said Dan.

Now that they had finished with the talk of Kemp, relief had come in like a warm and welcome flood. The dog had retreated to a square of sunlight on the rug and lay with its head on his paws. Under the scruff of black hair, its brown eyes still peered watchfully at Dan. Except for the faint whirr of the air-conditioner, the room was quiet. Dan mopped his forehead with a handkerchief and sat down.

It had been both easier and harder than he had expected. Kemp's bitter ghost faded into the background. The tall man on the bed neither looked nor sounded tragic. You could imagine the opaque blue eyes stabbed with pain, the bony frame racked with desperate coughing. There would have to have been ten thousand times when the bed and the wheelchair—even this pleasant room itself—must have felt like straitjackets, when Joe would gladly have settled for the freedom and relief of death. Yet he never, said Faith, wanted or asked for pity. His indomitability was a presence in the room. Beside it, Kemp's whole dark choir of fables had begun to take on a tone of querulous complaint. Was Faith's own resolute manner formed and fixed by having loved and lived with Joe Collier? Was it this quality which had caused her at last—after the madness of the war, the bearing of two daughters, the sudden widowhood—to agree to marriage with a potential invalid? Now, in Joe's company, it was more than conceivable. Perhaps, in coming here, you had reached the real hub of the wheel. From this center of courage the influence might for years have been flowing, as along radial spokes, to those on the slowly turning rim—to Faith, to Connie Haybright, and now, he thought, through them to you.

Suddenly the parakeet called Sammy spread his wings and

flew towards the doorway. The dog stretched and rose expectantly. Dan twisted in the chair in time to see the bird alight on Connie's outstretched finger.

"It's about time," said Joe, with gruff gaiety. "Where's your swim-suit, girl?"

"Under my dress," said Connie. She came to stand beside Dan's chair as he rose from it, the dog capering at her feet, the bird rocking excitedly along her slender wrist, and smiled across at Joe Collier. "And the picnic's waiting in the front hall. Any more questions, pappy?"

"One more," said Joe, his dark face alight. "Where do you plan to take this man?"

"Over the hills and far away," she said, laughing. "Where the water is."

"I see," said Joe. "Very informative. You're going for a swim in the Pacific."

She went to the bed and leaned to kiss Joe's forehead. "Wrong again, pappy," she said. "You can't pry it out of me. I'll tell you when we come back. Here, take Sammy before he scratches my arm to pieces. Get down, Fergus." She turned back to Dan, her face glowing. "Are you ready, Mr. Sherwood?"

"All ready," Dan said, his eyes on her face.

Outside, in the immensity of day, she still refused to say where they were going.

"But I'll give you the direction," she said. "Go east."

"So it's the Atlantic you want to swim in."

"I'd like that. I've never even seen the Atlantic. But not today. Today the Speedway."

"Today the Speedway, tomorrow the world. There's a good mercantile slogan."

But Connie made no answer. As he guided the car into and along with the perpetual stream of traffic, she sat watching the cluttered landscape, her hands at rest in her lap. At the crossroads near the North Corral Bar she pointed down the fork that led to the mountains.

"That's the way to Hart's place," Dan said.

"I know."

"Do you want to stop and see him?"

"Not today," she said. "I saw him last week. Do you remember when you called and cancelled our date?"

"Yes." It was better to lie. From his memory Faith looked at him.

"And you still haven't told me why."

He kept his eyes on the black ribbon of the road. "I was writing," he said. "I had to finish the book. To get free to go swimming with you. So how was Hart? Did you interview him again?"

"We just talked."

"About you?"

"About his work. He was trying to finish his mural and I knew it. I told him he must go on painting while we talked. I stayed an hour. It was as if—he seemed to be hurrying, but sort of calmly. I had the feeling he thought he had to get it done. Either then or the next day or the next."

"He's always seemed to have plenty of time."

"Yes, it seemed so before. Now—I mean that day—I thought he knew something he—wouldn't say."

"What about?"

"I think about himself," said Connie. "I thought that day that there was something wrong with his eyes."

"Isn't it just that he's old? His eyes are old."

"It's more than age. It's something coming on him. He bumps into furniture. Twice. He did it twice while I was there."

"There's his cabin," said Dan. They had come into view of the crumbling adobe ranch house in the flat valley. The alfalfa field had been harvested, and the incredible green was gone. Only yellow-brown stubble showed where it had been. On the rocky height beyond it, Hart's cabin loomed against the eastern sky. They both peered upwards, but the old man's white head was nowhere in sight. Then the car swept around the final curve and into the mouth of the canyon.

"So this is where we're going?"

"Why do you sound so disappointed?"

"Did I? Yes, I must have. Once in the winter I came out here."

"And didn't like it."

"Maybe I wasn't in the mood to like it."

"What was wrong with it?" asked Connie, defensively.

"Have you ever been up to that gravel pit at the far end?"

"Oh, *that!*" cried Connie, laughing. "They used to call it the Passion Pit. Was it messy?"

"Fairly."

"Aren't people awful?" she said. "They'll clutter up anything—their own houses, their towns, their parks—"

"It's no park up there," said Dan.

"No, it's not. But there's another place that is. It's down in the valley away from the road. You can't even see it from the road, even in winter. It's a wonderful clean pool—"

"Even in July?"

"Even in July the water's still there. All around it is a screen of trees and there's grass and great flat rocks like tables.

That's where I thought we'd go, if you still want to, and if nobody's beaten us to it."

"Let's go there," Dan said. He pressed the accelerator. Dust boiled up in thin clouds behind the laboring wheels. The green prongs of the saguaros stood like sentinels along the rocky slopes.

Connie was staring into the valley. Soon she touched his hand. "Here," she said. "Good. No one's here. You can park on the shoulder. Oh, Dan, let's hurry. Give me your hand."

They had come nearly to the base of the rock-strewn trail when they heard suddenly the welcome sound of water. Between its grass-covered banks, the brook ran foaming over a series of stony ledges. Green plants flourished all along the borders of the stream and flowers of a kind he did not know nodded here and there in the delicate lush grass. Under the rustling shade of the tall screen of cottonwoods and aspens, Connie kicked off her shoes and stepped free of the white dress like a naiad from a cluster of foam. Dan whistled softly. Her brief suit was the color of roses and all her dark beauty leaped to startling life. Under the cloth, independently of it, the firm soft lines of her body rose and fell as she ran to stand ankle-deep in the lucid water, already lifting the brown arms to gather her hair at her neck and tie it with a strand of ribbon.

"Hurry, Dan," she said, over one perfect shoulder. She waded knee-deep, plunged suddenly halfway across the small pool, and swam three or four strokes to the lowest of the ledges. He watched her as she turned, mounted, and settled on the rock-shelf, the water foaming around her waist, before he bent to untie his shoes and drop them with his shirt and slacks beside her folded white dress.

The grass was moist underfoot. The movement of the water stirred the air to coolness and he felt it flow around him as he stood, poised to dive, on one of the bankside boulders.

"Don't dive," she called. "It's much too shallow."

"I'll dive shallow," he said, and did, feeling like a benison the cool shock of the water over his head and body as he surfaced, kicked twice, and came up beside her moving legs at the far end of the pool. "Come on down," he said, tossing water from his eyes. "Come swim with me and be my love."

Smiling, without the words that might have spoiled it, she slid down from her ledge into his waiting arms, and then warmly in the cool rush of the water to the first of his kisses.

"You're strong," she said breathlessly, her hands lightly on his shoulders.

He kissed her again. "That's what you're supposed to say, even if the man's muscles are like marshmallows."

"Yours aren't," she said, laughing. "They're like—"

"Like steel," he said. "Like iron bands. Isn't that it? And as for you, you're as light as a feather."

"That's what you're supposed to say, even if your girl weighs a ton. Now swim, Dan. You said we were going to swim."

He let her go and plunged backwards, his head under, laved in the wealth of water. When he came up for breath she had gone back to the ledge and he pulled himself up beside her. She glistened with drops of water, like one arrayed in pearls. There were diamond-drops on some of the tendrils of her hair. She ran one finger lightly down his breastbone.

"And hairy," she said.

"Do you mind?"

"No. I'm glad."

"That's what you were supposed to say."

She began to kiss his face. "Oh, Dan," she said softly. "And you're supposed to say I'm smooth."

"You're smooth and lovely. All over."

"That's right. You said it right."

"And this place is like a park," he said, his head up, looking past the trees to the saw-toothed peaks and the enormous sky.

"Like Eden," she said inscrutably. "Before the Fall."

"Let's not think of the fall. It's summer, high summer."

"Let's not think of anything," she said, her hands locked behind his head.

"I'm thinking of plenty."

"There was plenty in the Garden, and then they had to lose it."

He looked at her curiously. "In that story they lost it. But there were always other gardens. And parks and fortunate islands."

"And other people to lose them."

"And others to rebuild them," he said, astonished at the sudden note of harshness in his own voice.

She took away her hands. "You're shivering. Are you cold?"

"Not consciously," he said. "Do you want to go over and dry out?"

"Yes," she said. "On that flat rock where our clothes are. In this air you'll be warm in five minutes. Won't you, Dan?"

"Three minutes," he said. But he knew it would take longer. Somewhere at the bottom of his mind a door had swung silently ajar, and the air that came through it was dank with the dankness of a cave.

CHAPTER TWENTY-EIGHT

BAREHEADED, his uniform cap riding comfortably in the nearly empty mail-pouch, Harry Walker stood mopping his skull-like forehead. "Another scorcher awready," he was saying. "Now you got that book done, Mr. Sherwood, it's time you and me took off. Time we had us a little trip up there where this one come from."

"Up where do you mean, Harry?"

Harry laid a yellow finger-nail on the postmark of the top-most piece of mail. "Wawshnun," he said, succinctly. "Up there amongst them tall trees. Seen a movie about up around there couple nights back. Real colored movie make your mouth water." He handed over, and Dan took, the heavy manila envelope. It was ornamented with a multicolored mosaic of stamps, and addressed in the familiar rounded script of Nicholas Kemp.

Dan weighed it in his hand, tempted to rip it open at once. But he waited politely for the close of the colloquy.

"I was never up there," he said.

"Me neither," said Harry, winking. "Vacation time get me a car, drive on up there, cool off under them high pines with Maureen O'Hara. Just wanna see is it like the movies say."

"Nothing's ever like the movies. That's why we have movies."

"You can say that again," Harry said. He stuffed the experienced handkerchief into his hip pocket, resumed his uniform cap, shouldered the sack, and began to move off. *Now,* thought Dan. But he saw that Harry was pausing, struck by one final thought.

"That goes for them red-heads," he said, grinning and winking. "Take it easy, Mr. Sherwood."

"You, too, Harry. So long."

Inside the house, Dan slit the envelope carefully and riffled through the pages. It was a typescript called *The Sullen Company: A Novel by Nicholas Kemp.* Under the title was an epigraph in Italian. Clipped to the topmost sheet was a note from Kemp.

Dear Sherwood:

I think you said your book's about done. Here is the evidence that I've beaten you to the tape. Attached herewith is the second carbon of my first book in ten years. In fact much has been happening here. My wife recently had a son. This book is for him.

Except for the stories, this is my first shot at a novella. You know the rest of what I've done well enough so that I need not bore you with explanations, boasting, or other comment. Every writer thinks his latest is his best. I thought you might like to see it, perhaps even make use of it in your own book. This copy, signed by me at the end, is for you to keep. If you ever get fired, or fall on evil times, I suggest you sell it for what it will bring. You are the only one besides my wife who has seen it. Later on, I plan to send it to Littlefield's. My plan is to have it out in time for my son's first birthday.

I called Faith and told her you were an honest man. You

and she can take it from there. Renewed thanks for staying off the biography. It is of no importance whatsoever. I will look forward to your book, though not wholeheartedly. Good luck to you and pray for all writers.

Sincerely,
Nicholas Kemp

Dan kicked off his shoes and read the pages slowly. It was a kind of naturalistic fable about a boy and his elders, and the first paragraph set the tone for the rest:

"At the farthest edge of the lichened rock, the boy squatted on brown haunches and gazed down into the gulf where the dying stream meandered yellowly among the heaps of fallen stone. Behind him in the shallow caves, quiet voices were babbling and he could smell the acrid smoke of the fires where the women and the older girls were preparing the evening meal. Across the gulf were the earthen-ware jugs, ranged in orderly rows, each encased in a web of leather lanyards by which they could be lowered down the cliff to the stream by the three old crones who tended the gardens. Soon the narrow bridge would groan and sway under their weight as they came, one by one, back to the place of the caves."

For an hour he read on slowly before he reached the final page. Except for an occasional echo of Biblical prose, it was nothing like anything else of Kemp's. Yet still, mysteriously, it bore his special imprimatur, the inimitable merger of voice and vision that made Kemp Kemp.

The whole tale read like a parable. Slowly, year by year, the water of the stream at the base of the cliff was lessening. Soon the tribe would have to move, as the ancient Indians of Walnut Canyon had been driven out by the drying up of their life-giving stream. The elders in Kemp's fiction took the drought as a sign of supernal disapprobation. They were the sullen company, hunched morosely in the smoke-filled caves. Around them in the arid land, hostile tribes kept watch.

But the boy on the cliff would not accept defeat. The book told the story of his lone rebellion, his emergence into manhood, his rise to leadership. Kemp's note had not hinted, unless you read closely between the lines, at the startling novelty of what he had done. After all the years of big novels filled with hell-fire, this small one led you forth to air and light. You laid it down with a sense of gain. Obviously— though perhaps not so obviously—the book embodied in some strange way Kemp's future hopes for his son, as if this new child might follow the example of the boy in the story, might turn his back on the wide and sullen company which filled his father's fiction, all those spiritually scarified and tormented characters who reflected and incarnated Nicholas Kemp's fiery vision.

In any serious study of Kemp this new book clamored for a place. It would fit like a crown or a capstone. Yet it had arrived too late. There was the critique, already in New York, already accepted, finished, rounded off, a *fait accompli.* Here suddenly came the new confrontation, Kemp's epochal about-face, his seeming farewell to all he had done before. Sooner or later you would have to handle it, if only in an epilogue. Without it, your own book would be ridiculously incomplete. There was really no choice, and all the steps were clear. Write the editor, tell him you would have to add one final chapter, reread the new novel four or five times, take your notes, decide what must be said, and begin.

Dan sat staring at the sheaf of pages in his lap. On the topmost leaf the Italian epigraph stared back. *"Tristi fummo,"* it said, *"nell' aer dolce che dal sol s'allegra, portando dentro accidioso fummo; or ci attristiam nella belletta negra...."*

Except for the prose form, it could have been something out of Dante. *Fummo,* he thought. What the hell is *fummo?* All right, linguist. Figure it out. You should have studied Italian instead of German. *Tristi* must be *sad. Sol* is *sun, negra* is *black. Aer dolce* is *soft air.* And *allegra,* courtesy of Milton and Longfellow, means *laughter* or *joy.* The syntax is what licks you, as when the Army hurled you headlong among the umlauts and the ablauts. Again the choice is plain. Find yourself a grammar and a dictionary and get to work.

Or better, he thought, go on out to the canyon and see Hart Mackenzie. It's time you saw him, anyhow. And he should know Italian from living there, painting there, talking to the people. If there had been anything in Connie's guess about his eyesight, you more than obviously owed him a visit.

Half an hour later he stopped his car behind the cabin and walked rapidly around to the weathered and sun-dried door. It opened immediately at his knock.

"Dan, come in," cried Hart with evident pleasure. He was wearing the paint-splashed khakis and brogans. The room smelled of turpentine. "I'm just cleaning up."

"I can smell it," said Dan, shaking his hand. "Go right ahead. I only came to talk. How's that mural?"

Hart gestured sweepingly with the brush. "Done," he said happily. "Come over and have a look. Better leave that door open for the light."

Dan stood astonished. The old man's landscape of mountains and sky glowed out of the shadows down the length of the room. Whatever it was he had done to it in the past month had given the picture a new depth, an awesome and lofty grandeur that stirred the heart, but also a strange internal luminosity beyond anything Dan had seen before.

"The light's in the picture," he said.

Hart only nodded, but he was plainly pleased.

"It's better than words," said Dan.

"Oh, I don't know," said Hart. "Genesis does it pretty well. Four words only. But they're what the whole Bible's about."

"You mean the Old Testament."

"Old and new both," Hart said, grinning. "It's my contribution to the higher criticism. *Let there be light.* That's the whole history of Jesus and Paul and John. Light. The Creator commanded it; the Redeemer embodied it; and the Apostles acted to spread it around."

"I didn't think you believed in mythology," Dan said.

"I don't," Hart said. "Dan, I defy you to find a smidgen of it in that mural. None of Whitman's—wasn't it Whitman's? —reckless, heaven-ambitious peaks—wasn't that how it went? No, Dan. I believe in what my eyes can see, and what they see is darkness and light. I'll go along with the Book: *Let there be light.* That's where it all began."

"You're forgetting," Dan said. "All Christendom has it that Light is Love."

"Sure. And Love is Light. The absolute equation, the one we're always looking for. In what I do, it's what I try for. And always fall short."

Dan was gazing at the mural. "Not here," he said.

"I'm glad you think so," said Hart, quietly. "The hell of it is it's part of the wall. I can't move the damn thing when I move."

"Move? Are you going to move?"

"Just closing up shop for a while," Hart said, briskly. "I expect to be back."

"Where are you going—back home?"

"First to Phoenix. Then maybe back east. It all depends on what they say in Phoenix."

"Who's they?"

"The eye-men. Got a little eye-trouble, Dan. It's been coming on. Lately it's worse. I even had to quit driving the jeep. Feller down here at the ranch helps me out now. Nice feller, name of Fletcher. We were downtown last week checking on it."

"What's wrong? Do they know?"

"Yup," said Hart hurriedly. "Case of cataracts. They want to try to get them fixed up right away. I'm waiting to hear. They'll telephone Fletcher when they want me to go. He's going to drive me to Phoenix. Then he'll kind of keep an eye on things here while I'm gone. Never mind, Dan. They sound cheerful."

"So do you."

"It'll be something to look back on. I don't say I look forward to it."

"Neither would I."

"I tell 'em it's a family affair," Hart said. "We're all in the same business, the power and light business. You, too, with words. The Sherwood Power and Light Company." The old man chuckled. "Pretty good, Dan? I'll tell 'em that. Tell 'em I'll appoint 'em Vice Presidents in charge of production. We'll steal the motto out of Genesis."

"When will you go?"

"Couple of days. Maybe a week. What's that you got, Dan, your book?"

Dan glanced down at the forgotten envelope in his lap. "No. Not mine. This is Kemp's. It came today. Now Kemp's in the Power and Light business, too. He's got sick of the dark. How's your Italian, Hart?"

The old man dropped the clean brushes into a tin container under the mural. "Italian?" he echoed. "I'd call it rusty. I could order a room, vino, pasta. I still read it some. I doubt if I could carry on an abstract conversation. Why?"

"Kemp quotes some Italian on his title page. It might be Dante but I can't tell. Are your eyes good enough—"

"Wait a minute," Hart said. "Let me get the high-powered specs." He disappeared into the bedroom and immediately returned with the glasses and a worn green volume. "Where is it?" he said, briskly. "Have you got it there? Read it out, Dan."

"I'll mangle it."

"Never mind," Hart said. "Just take it slowly."

Dan read the lines aloud.

Hart nodded. "It's Dante all right. The *fummo* tips you off. That's the old infernal smoke. Some people are speaking, some of the damned. *Tristi fummo nell'aer dolce:* We were sullen in the sweet air. Here, Dan, let me have the paper. I'll get up to the lamp. Um. They say they were sullen in the sweet air that the sun makes glad. Had this sullen thing inside them. *Accidioso fummo.* That's something like

dirty smoke, dark smoke. *Portando dentro accidioso fummo.*
We held the dark smoke in our hearts. That's it, roughly.
Now they're in hell. *Belletta negra.* Now, they say, still sullen, we lie here in the black mud. While they were alive,
they were the sullen ones. Now this is their punishment."

"The Sullen Company."

"Company. Group. Corporation."

"I meant that's Kemp's own title for his book. *The Sullen
Company.*"

"I see," said Hart. He settled back into the horsehide
chair and opened the green book. "Maybe we can spot the
place."

"What's the book?"

"It's Mary's old copy of Dante. Here, Dan, look along the
margin, see where the fourth circle begins."

Dan saw that the book had been published in Milano in
1895. *"Cerchio III.* Is that *circle?"*

"Try Canto Seven, Dan."

"Canto Seven. Cerchio IV. It starts out, *Pape Satan! Pape
Satan!"*

"It's past there. Try the fifth circle."

"Cerchio V. Stige," Dan read. "What's *Stige?"*

"Styx," said Hart. "It should be around in there. This
Styx is a bog, a marsh. See if you can see *belletta negra.* The
black mud's in the Stygian bog."

"Here it is," said Dan, after a minute. *"Fitti nel limo dic-
con: tristi fummo* and so on. Shall I read on?"

Hart nodded, listening with his eyes closed.

"Well, roughly it says something like this," he said when
Dan had finished the page. "As usual the kind master, that's
Vergil, is showing this to Dante. *Figlio,* he says, now take a

gander at this. And Dante does. Under the water are all these damned souls. When they sob it comes bubbling up to the surface. They're down under, stuck in the mud. Quite a conception. Dante says that this is the hymn that comes gurgling up out of their throats. Some word there: *gorgoglian*."

"Gorgon," said Dan. "Sounds like the name of Böcklin's dragon. Gorgoglian, the sullen dragon."

"Pure mythologizing," said Hart, laughing. "All it means is *gurgle* or *gargle,* what you do with Listerine."

"Never mind," Dan said delightedly. "Mythology or not, it's Dante's version of the excremental universe. These damned ones were too sullen to see the sacramental universe. Now they're dead and up to their chins in the other one."

"Up to their chins, hell," said Hart. "It's over their heads. Does that do it? I mean does it fit Kemp's book?"

"Fits fine," Dan said. "Kemp's been knocking around down there in the basement for twenty-five years. Now he's decided to come upstairs."

"You can't blame a man," Hart said. His old eyes twinkled. "Up here it smells better. I don't mean we don't have our stinks, but after a while the *aer dolce* blows them away. Light and air, Dan. The Sherwood Power, Light, and Fresh Air Corporation, We'll sign up Kemp, too. Second Vice President in charge of—you pick the title. He's your man."

"Nicholas, Lord Kemp," Dan said. "In charge of the Light Brigade. I'm sorry as hell, Hart, about your eyes."

"Never mind," Hart said. "You never know what's around the next corner."

"Or down in the basement," said Dan.

CHAPTER TWENTY-NINE

WHEN HART'S summons came, Dan insisted, over the old man's protestations, on driving him to the hospital in Phoenix. After the dry heat and dust of the afternoon, the lobby seemed cool and the tile floor shone cleanly in the light that came through the glass doors.

The receptionist was a small woman with pale red hair. She took Hart's bag efficiently. "They want you put right to bed, Mr. Mackenzie," she said.

The old man stood solidly, unhurrying, his hand on Dan's right arm. "Looks as if I'm under orders, Dan," he said. "Thanks for the ride."

"You're more than welcome," Dan said. "If you need anything, have them call me. Have them call me anyway. I'll be anxious to hear how it goes."

"Sure thing," Hart said. "It might take a while."

"Whenever it is," said Dan. "And good luck. And when they let you go home, I'll be back to get you."

The red-headed receptionist had taken Hart's arm. Dan shook hands quickly and went out through the glass doors without looking back.

Night had fallen before he reached home. He parked in

the car-port, pocketed the keys, glanced once at the distant stars, and went inside to telephone Connie.

"I wish it were over now," she said.

"So do I."

"Do you think it's risky?"

"It's always risky," Dan said. "He knows it's risky, but he's still cheerful. Finishing the mural was the great thing. All the way to Phoenix he kept coming back to it, kept saying it was the best thing he'd ever done. And he kept saying, too, that it might never have been finished without this business of his eyes. Kept talking about the big push. Said human beings are always reluctant to finish anything, but that when they have to, when they finally resolve on the big push, they can call on reserves they didn't know were there."

"Did he talk about you?"

"Not directly, Connie. But always by implication."

"About your book?"

"Obliquely about it. By indirection, the way he always works. The hovering idea was that I'd better finish it."

"Why don't you, Dan?"

"I've been thinking about it. All the way home."

"How long would it take?"

"Not long. If I could stop day-dreaming—"

"What do you dream about?"

"None of your business."

"I know. It's a girl, isn't it?"

"Still none of your business."

"You haven't answered my question, Dan. Could you do it in a week?"

"I don't know. I could try it."

"I mean if I don't interrupt you."

"I guess so."

"I'll interrupt you at night," she said. "Every day you can go into hiding and then every evening you can come out."

"Like a bat out of hell."

"Like a mountain lion," she said. "An old, sleek, handsome, hungry catamount."

"Well, some kind of nocturnal predator, anyway."

"And I'll be your prey."

"Some morsel," he said. "A tender dish."

"Oh, I'm tough," she said. "All bone and gristle. And after you've finished, I'll type it for you."

"If there's anything to type."

"Oh, there will be," she said confidently. "How many days, darling? Three? Four?"

"Better call it five," he said. "That'll allow for the day-dreaming."

*   *   *   *   *

By the afternoon of the seventh day the new final chapter was two-thirds done. He clipped the yellow pages together, laid them carefully beside the typewriter, and stood restively by the window, gazing out. After the quick small rain of four o'clock, the air had turned humid and the car, parked in the narrow driveway, was streaked with a mixture of mud and dust. A week of work, he thought sourly, and still the damned thing isn't done. And no word from Hart, either. Why the hell don't they get it over with? Too much is hanging fire. Too much is always hanging fire, and procrastination is the thief of time. But at least you can wash the car. You can at least pick up your girl tonight in a clean car. If you can't finish the chapter or hurry them through the operation on Hart's eyes, that is at least one thing you can do.

Half angrily, he attached the hose to the faucet in the car-port, rinsed the dirt-streaked body, filled a pail, and set to work. Faint whorls of steam rose from all the surfaces and in five minutes his shirt was soaked through. He had finished the body and the wheels and was drying the glass when he heard a shout behind him and turned to see Mandeville Lee clambering out of the red car.

"What's the use, boy?" said Lee, angling across the lawn. He was wearing a spotless white suit and a pale green shirt with a black knitted tie and he stopped well short of the fresh yellow mud near the Ford. "In fifteen minutes the damn thing will be dirty again."

"Drive yours in here and I'll wash it for you," said Dan.

"Too late in the day," Lee said. "My date won't wait. You look like you could stand a wash yourself, Danny. And a shave. Don't you scholars ever shave?"

"Shaving is next," Dan said, running a finger over his chin. "After that a drink. Or let's reverse the order. How about a drink now?"

Lee waved one hand grandly. "Not today, pal," he said. "Some other day but not today. Where I'm going there's plenty drinks. Also caviar. Also a swimming pool. Also dinner for two and a disappearing butler. Vanishes for the night at the stroke of ten."

Dan grinned across the space of grass between them. "Sounds nifty," he said.

Lee threw back his head. "Why, Dan," he said, "the word

nifty don't even come close. This doll just don't care how she spends it. Before the divorce she was worth close to a million bong, and now on top of that she comes into a juicy slice of alimony. Only thing is, she'd better spend it while she's got it because Old Harry's moving in."

"Old Manny Lee, you mean?"

"No, I don't," Lee said. "I mean Old Harry. Potomac Pete. Lives down there in that big white house in that big white city, pushing the congressmen around and acting like God Almighty."

"Oh, *that* Harry," said Dan, laughing. "What's he got to do with your grass widow?"

"Wait till he starts jacking up the income tax."

"I thought they were talking about cutting taxes."

"Like hell they will. Not the Democrats. Not with a war on."

"War? What war?"

"What war he says! Don't you read the papers?"

"Hardly ever. Not lately. What's up?"

Lee thrust his hands into the pockets of the white suit. His tone was sarcastic. "What's up he says! Nothing but a bunch of little yellow chinks raising hell with some more little yellow chinks in a lousy country nobody ever heard of. So what makes sense? I'll tell you what makes sense. You keep to hell out of it and let the little bastards slug each other until they get sick of it. But not noble Old Harry. Commie aggression, he says. Defense of freedom, he says. So what? I'll tell you what. Here we go again."

"What country is it now?"

Lee spat carefully on the sun-burned grass. "Korea," he

said, with scorn. "Rhymes with *diarrhea*, Dan. And from what I hear, that's about the size of it."

* * * * *

For two days he would not face it. Korea, wherever it was, seemed as far off as the moon. Each morning, absorbed while the hours raced past, he worked on *The Sullen Company*. Each afternoon he revised and tightened the morning's desperate scrawlings. Each evening he spent with Connie Haybright. He told himself repeatedly that it was none of his affair. Once when she mentioned the war, he quickly changed the subject. If it comes, he thought, it will come. If not, not. Until it does, the hell with it. There is the book and there is Connie.

But on the third morning it came. He signed the form, closed the door, ripped open the envelope, and ran his eye down the mimeographed page. It was from the HQ in New Jersey; Captain Howard M. Palmer had certified it as a true exact copy; and it seemed to say in plain words that Captain Daniel J. Sherwood would not be in this war.

He allowed his heart a single leap before he picked up the telephone to call Bill Masters.

"What's up?" said Bill.

"It's a set of orders, Bill. Mind if I read them out?"

"Let's hear what the man says."

"It says, quote, the fol-named officers, USAR, for failure to obtain the minimum retirement point credits within the past retirement year, are transferred from Active to Inactive Reserve, close quote. Which sounds very fishy to me. They should know I've been doing the weekly sessions out here. Or do they?"

"Dan, I just don't know. What else does it say?"

"Well, there's a clause that says I'm released for assignment to the New Jersey ORC Central Gp Inactive Reserve. Whatever the hell that might mean."

"Dan, as I say, I just don't know for certain, but I must say that to me it sounds like the business. What they're doing here is probably the same thing they're doing now in a lot of the reserve units. They need junior officers for this show."

"Lieutenants?"

"Lieutenants and captains are the group they're working on. It's a huge job, Dan, and I must say I'm surprised they're this far along. I think what you've got there in your hands would be the first step, say. First they transfer you from Active to Inactive, then the reverse. Don't ask me why they do it this way. It's some legal business. When did you get this?"

"Airmail special today. My chairman sent it out."

"Do you plan on going back east?"

"Not till I have to. If I have to."

"Tell you what I'd do," Bill Masters said crisply. "Wire your chairman and get him to phone you the next set of orders."

"You think there'll be another set?"

"My guess is they'll be cutting them shortly."

"What's your idea of shortly?"

"Anything up to a month. Give or take a week. I'd also guess you're in for another stretch."

"How long this time?"

"Twenty-one months is what I hear."

"Um."

"Um is right," Bill said. "Didn't you tell me you could have been a major?"

"If I'd wanted to wait around the center, yes."

"I'm sorry, Dan. It kind of interrupts a career. And of course I could be way wrong. But, Dan, I don't think so. If it's any consolation, there are a lot of others in the same spot."

"It's a consolation of sorts."

"Let me know if I can help, Dan."

"All right, Bill, and thanks."

In the car that night he told Connie. For half an hour he had driven silently south through the starlit desert, turning over in his mind the ways it might be said. Now he slowed, edging the car onto the shoulder of the road, the tires crunching hollowly on the yellow gravel, and switched off the motor. In the first of the brooding quiet, the words sounded crude and loud. "It could be a false alarm," he added, lamely.

"It's certainly alarming," she said in a stiff small voice. "I knew something was wrong. I thought—it might be Hart, something gone wrong with the operation."

"No, they're still waiting."

"Waiting," she said. "Oh, waiting. If it's true, if it's not a false alarm, when will you have to go?"

"Masters said anything up to a month."

"How does he know?" she said fiercely. In the dim light from the dashboard her eyes were glistening and the slender fingers were twisting the handkerchief in her lap. "How *does* he know, Dan?"

"There are others. It's happening to a lot of others."

"I'm not in love with the others," she said. "Will they send you over there?"

"Nothing's settled yet. They might. Or it might be a desk job or a teaching job in a training area."

She had turned her head away to face the black aperture of the open window. A strand of her hair moved in the night wind from the desert. For a long moment she said nothing. Then, slowly, spacing the words: "It's a good thing your book's done."

"Almost," he said, uncomfortably. "The end's in sight. The thing is to get there."

She was still gazing into the darkness. "Do you think Kemp will like it?"

"He'd better like it."

"When do you want me to type it?"

"I'd better finish it first."

She glanced once, quickly, into his face, before she lowered her eyes to her lap. "Everything's unfinished," she said in a voice dry with pain. "Your book. Hart's eyes. This war—this damned war."

He took her cold hand. "They'll get done," he said. "One by one they'll be finished."

A car rushed by, heading south along the road. He watched the small receding light in the enormous brooding dark. He could not think of anything else to say.

Her hand was growing warm in his. He felt her thumb caressing the backs of his fingers. "Do you remember that day in the canyon?" she said.

"Of course."

"All at once you were so cold. Your teeth even chattered. Did you know then about Hart's eyes or about the war?"

"No, Connie. How could I?"

"I meant inside?"

"No."

"I said it was like Eden—our place, our waterfall. And that they lost Eden. And you said there were other gardens, and I said there were always people to lose them. And you said—what did you say?"

"That there were always others to rebuild them."

"Yes," she said quickly. "And then you began to shiver. Why?"

"I'm not prescient," he said. "It was just the cold water."

But she had turned her head away once more. The night wind moaned around the body of the car and a gust swept through the open windows. "Dan," she said, "let's go. It's too dark here. Oh, Dan, let's go home. Let's go where it's light," she said, her voice rising. "Let's go back to your house and turn on every last light. I want to start on what you've written. At least we can finish that. If we can't finish anything else, at least we can do that."

"Don't cry," he said.

*   *   *   *   *

When the telephone rang, she was typing at the table by the window, the light around her head like an aureole. She stopped, her fingers on the keys, as Dan picked up the receiver. "Speaking," he said. There was a metallic click and a babble far away. Webb's voice sounded distant as a voice in a dream.

"Hello, Webb," Dan said. "Can you hear me?"

"I can hear you, but it's a poor connection."

"It sure is. What's the news, Webb?"

"Dan, I feel like a heel, but I'm just following your instructions."

"Sure. Go ahead."

"It came this morning," Webb said. "Half an hour ago. Date of eighteen July. It says you are ordered to active duty effective twenty-eight July. On that date you will proceed from your present location—I'm reading this from the orders, Dan—from your present location to Dispensary U, Pennsylvania Avenue and Air Field Road, Fort Dix, reporting not earlier than 1300 hours nor later than 1330 hours for the purpose of undergoing final type physical examination. That's the substance, Dan. How will you get here?"

"I'll have to fly."

"What about your car?"

"I'm leaving it here. Connie—"

"If you're planning to fly, you'd better book it fast. They say it's getting tougher now. Air's all full of generals and admirals."

"I'll book today. What was that date?"

"Check-in at 1300 hours on the twenty-eighth."

"What day of the week would that be?"

"Hold on, I'll look. Just a second...Twenty-eighth is a Friday."

"I'll try to get back the first of that week. I'm finishing the Kemp book now."

"Kemp? I thought you had him wrapped up."

"Windfall from Kemp. He's done a new one. A short one. I'm making a new final chapter. When do you go to Vermont?"

"Not till early August," Webb said. "Shall I meet the plane?"

"Oh, no. No. Thanks. I'll call you when I get back in town."

"Anything I can do on this end?"

"If you could take care of the university part of it."

"I already have, Dan. The dean knows. We keep your place. This counts as a military leave."

"Thanks, Webb. I'll see you shortly."

"Sorry about this, Dan."

"Never mind. It's all right."

He turned from the telephone to see her sitting before the silent typewriter, her hands in her lap. "That was John Webb," he said.

"Yes, I heard."

"I'll have to call the airport."

"Yes, you surely will."

"There's still a week, anyway."

"Not if you leave Monday. That's only five days."

"I'll wait till Wednesday or Thursday. That's a week."

"Will that give you time?"

"The only time I need or want is here."

She lifted her fingers to the keys. "It won't take long to finish this," she said.

He felt the rage stirring in him. "I don't mean that. To hell with that. Come on, Connie. Let's get out of here."

"I'd better finish, Dan. It's only a few more pages."

"No, not now. Leave it. Skip it. Have you got to the part about *belletta negra?*"

She was looking at him curiously. "I'm way past that," she said. "You've got him out of the mud. He's up in the *aer dolce.*"

"It's a good place for him. Let him float blissfully."

Dan crossed the room and put his arms around her shoulders.

"You ought to call the airport," she said softly.

"Tomorrow," he said. "Let's get out there."

She rose and turned in his arms, her eyes searching his. "Out where do you mean?"

"Our place," he said. "The garden. The waterfall."

"Someone else might be there."

"We'll drive them away. It's our place."

"Let's hurry, then," she said. "Let's not waste another minute."

*   *   *   *   *

The Catalinas loomed dirt-colored against the northern sky. Already he could feel the immense weight of the sun. As he came rapidly up the walk with the package in one hand, the door swung magically wide and he saw her standing in the gloom of the hallway. She was wearing the pale green sleeveless dress and the ring he had given her shone in the light from the open door. With her arms around his neck he kissed her so long and hard that they were both breathless when she stepped back to close the door behind him and to smooth her brown hair with the palms of both her hands.

"Do that again," he said.

"Wasn't that one enough?"

"No. Yes. I meant smooth your hair."

"This way?"

"That's the way. I wish I had your picture."

"I'll send you one."

"A picture of a picture."

"Won't that be better than nothing?"

"Much better. Not as good as now."

"Now is late, Dan. We'll have to hurry. Did you call Hart?"

"Just now. He was cheerful. They'll operate next week. He'll have them call you."

"Good. I'll get him when he's ready. Did you say the other goodbyes?"

"I guess all. Agnes and Alvin. The Notos. The Wileys. Axel and his wife. She was almost gay. Maybe Mandeville Lee was good for her."

"He's not so bad," said Connie. "Did you see him?"

"Last night," said Dan. "He brought over some bourbon." He set the package on the hall table. "Could you give it to Joe after I've gone?"

"Yes, Dan. Do we have time to see them? Just for a minute?"

"Sure," he said.

The room at the end of the hall was yellow with the risen sun. Faith sat in a deep chair by the window. Joe lay as before, propped high with pillows. They were drinking coffee. Dan glanced once around the pleasant room. The parakeets' cage was hooded and the black dog was not in evidence.

Faith put down her cup and came quickly to his side. "Good morning," she said. "Would you like some coffee? Is there time?"

"Another time, I guess," said Dan.

She leaned forward to brush his cheek with her lips. "It's a beautiful ring," she said. "Connie's so happy."

"She's a beautiful girl," said Dan. "I'm lucky."

"You can say that again," said Joe, from the bed.

Dan crossed to his side. "I'll say it all the time I'm gone."

"Hurry back, boy," said Joe hoarsely.

"It won't be long."

"Not as the crow flies," said Joe. "And give 'em hell, Dan."

"They can have it," said Dan, firmly. "They're welcome to it. I'm through with it."

Joe's eyes were steady upon his own. For a fleeting second a shadow crossed them and was gone, as if a curtain had been twitched aside and as quickly dropped by someone inside a dark house.

"That's it, Dan," Joe said. "That's what we got to believe. Whether it's so or not."

"Yes," Dan said.

EPILOGUE

FROM WHERE he lay prone in the saucer-like depression on
the low butte, he could see the ruin of the filling-station like
a black smear on the yellow-green dirt of the desert. The useless fire-engine had come to pour on the useless foam, and
later the sleek fast ambulance had come and gone. From
parts of the wreckage sluggish columns of smoke still rose,
thinning now in the bright and burning air. But the troopers
were still around. Their cream-colored squad car was parked
along the shoulder of the highway, and they were still poking
and prying in the smouldering debris.

Get goen, you bastards, he thought. If they quit that poking around and jumped in the car and got to hell back where
they belonged, he could move off this lousy rock-pile, get
down to the highway, hop some dope's car, be a couple
hundred miles away by dark. Maybe more. But no. By God
no. They are standing around, kicking them timber-chunks,
going over to the car to chew the fat on that goddam two-way
radio, and coming on back to kick the wreck some more. Get
goen, he said, half aloud. You think you gonna find clues
you ain't gonna find no clues because clues all blown to hell
anyhow when them tanks went. Clues still droppen halfway

to Texas. Them tanks sure went, though, he thought. Some fireworks and it ain't even the Fourth of July.

He ran the tip of his tongue over his dry lips and then turned his head slowly, keeping below the screening boulder, to spit on the hot rock beside him. Even as he watched he could see it drying. In a minute it had vanished without a trace. You can still spit, he thought. But you better not spit no more, you better hang onto your spit. Not a goddam drop since sunrise except that half a bottle of coke you was drinking when you seen the kid at the phone trying to call the cops.

Stupid fool kid, he thought. He's seen my picture some place, gonna be a goddam hero, get his picture in the papers, grab himself a big reward. So he found out what the reward was, except he never knew. Here he is in full view with the receiver down and that pump gun in his hand and the gas-hose still stuck in the back of the car. And where the hell does he think I am? Stupid lousy little jerk. I am sitting in the front seat watching him tryna call them cops.

So what would you do? Right. You would snake across the seat and start firing through the car window. Which is exactly what I done. I see him drop the phone and I think I got him and I am reaching for the door-handle to get out and go in there and finish off the little jerk when the first round out of that goddam pump gun caroms off the roof of the car and I duck and raise up again and shoot again and I know this time I got him because the next one he throws is way off, you can hear it sing to hellandgone, and he throws one more and it hits the gaspump hose and that is when the fire starts.

So he sure started that one but he was not around to see no finish. I doubt if he seen when that tank blew and sprayed the whole front of his crummy little station. He sure never seen that ambulance come roaring in, doing seventy or eighty, slewing to a stop in the gravel and the cops right ahead of it and they all pile out and poke through the timbers until they find the kid and roll him in that canvas and drive off screaming to beat hell like they had some place to go besides the county morgue.

The station had this coke machine and it is nothing now but melted metal and the melted glass of the bottles. By the time I get out the far side, side away from the kid, the whole rear end of the car is on fire and the hose still pumping gas on the ground, hot as hell already, and I duck away and get around the back side of the building and it is just then the gas-tank on the car blows and I am running back over the gravel and through the sage-brush when the big storage tank goes and the whole front of the station starts to burn and you can hear all the windows bust and tinkle when the concussion wave hits and I never got a goddam thing for breakfast but half that bottle of coke.

The plane was suddenly loud in the windless sky. He froze and held the freeze. They could see you from the air. But he slowly relaxed as the ugly drone held steady, neither louder nor lessening, and he lifted himself on one elbow inch by inch to scan the morning sky under the shadow of his hand. After a minute he spotted it, like a silver bug far away to the south, high over the low mountains, ten thousand feet or better, heading east for Dallas or San Antone or Corpus or wherever.

All right, he thought. No problem there. Now we get rid of them goddam coppers we are set. He peered cautiously around the edge of the boulder. They were still there. They were still there an hour later when he awoke from a hot drowse to hear the sound of a motor starting. One of them was in the car and the other was walking towards it. The car backed around, the other cop got in, the door slammed, and he watched them move off, the dust-cloud moiling up as they left the roadside, the car gliding smoothly onto the blacktop, gathering speed quickly and glinting in the light as they headed west.

Before it was out of sight he was slithering down the far side of the butte, slipping and cursing over the loose stones, angling towards the highway east of the smear where the filling-station had been. Looking back over his shoulder in the heavy glare he could see the burned out hulk of the car he had come in, lying on its side in the blackened gravel. He reached and crossed the highway to squat like a toad in the farther ditch.

The first one was a sixteen-wheeler doing seventy and even if he seen you and slapped on the brakes he'd been halfway to Texas before he could stop that one. The second was a dirt-streaked sedan heading the other way, going ninety or better, and how the hell do you know it ain't a deputy sheriff sitting there with your picture pasted on his windshield? He ducked back and sat still and waited until the sedan was out of sight. He had sat for ten more minutes when he heard the jalopy coming.

The engine was laboring and clanking and in the silence you could hear it from a long way off. He waited until it was a hundred yards from his place in the ditch before he rose to stand in the middle of the road and lift his hand in brotherly greeting. He planted himself where they would have to stop or else hit him and he grinned as the old brakes squealed and he knew that the boy in the driver's seat had seen him.

The boy was scowling and the girl beside him was hastily buttoning the front of her dress. Only when they had pulled over and stopped and he had gone up to lean companionably on the side where the girl was sitting did he see the nursing baby in her lap.

He grinned widely across at the boy. "Nice little family you got," he said. "Mind given a man a lift? Up ahead there you can turn around easy. I know you ain't gonna mind just taken me back a few miles east—"

The boy's face was white under the thin stubble. His Adam's apple slid up and down as he swallowed. "East?" he said. "Sorry, Mac. I'm going west."

But he had already got the door open and was hulking in beside the girl and the baby. The baby began to howl. "Right up there you can turn around," he said. "Up where you see the fire was."